Other Books Written By The Author
In The RUSTY CHARM Series

WITH WINGS OF AN EAGLE

ASHES TO HONOR

WHEN THE ANGELS SLEEP

The
RUSTY CHARM

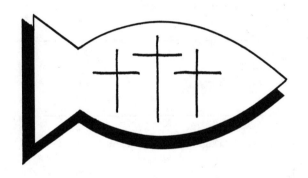

JAMES H. GOODMAN

LARKSDALE

First Printing—September 1986

The Rusty Charm

Senior Editor — Fred Zuber
Cover Design — D'Anne Luetge

Library of Congress Cataloging-in-Publication Data

Goodman, James H.
    The rusty charm.

    1. United States—History—Revolution, 1775-1783—
Fiction. 2. South Carolina—History—Revolution,
1775-1783—Fiction. 3. Dick family—Fiction. I. Title.
PS3557.05837R8   1986   813'.54   85-82055
ISBN 0-89896-270-6

LARKSDALE
HOUSTON

Printed in the United States of America

To Emily
My Darling Wife

CONTENTS

1. **From Ashes and Dust**
    1733-1740   *11*

2. **The Beginning of a Tradition**
    1740-1741   *37*

3. **The Long Search**
    1741-1779   *57*

4. **Among the Swamp Foxes**
    1779-1781   *105*

5. **Trouble at Home**
    1780-1781   *137*

6. **The Foxes Finish the Chase**
    1781-1783   *165*

7. **Building a Dream**
    1783-1800   *211*

8. **End of the Dream**
    1800   *253*

THE RUSTY CHARM

One man's trash is another man's treasure
    It depends on how he sees his part.
The widow's mite is abundant measure,
    For him who understands the heart.

The poor is rich and the rich is poor
    And only wise men understand.
The skillful man must be a doer,
    Knowledge alone can't heal the land.

The strong is weak and the weak is strong.
    And who can ever really know
Who is right and who is wrong?
    Since value from the heart must grow.

Moth and rust cannot erase
    Treasure that was meant to last.
Golden charms cannot replace
    Greater wealth from treasured past.

Little is much when God is in it.
    And wealth is safe from spoiler's harm.
Worthless, as a term, may fit.
    But priceless is the rusty charm.

The
RUSTY CHARM

JAMES H. GOODMAN

1

From Ashes and Dust

1733-1740

"Fetch all those buckets, Josh! Enoch, you run about town and gather up all the good hands you can find! I believe that's Josephus Dicks' house ablaze! For God's sake, hurry! Somebody may be in that house!" yelled Zeke Dunbar.

A red-faced, rotund merchant, Dunbar had just closed his general store. He unlocked it again, however, when he saw the rolling black smoke rising wildly above leaping red and yellow flames down the street near the edge of town. He grabbed all the buckets he could carry and proceeded to wobble as fast as he could down the dusty main street of Charles Town.

Responding to his shouts were Dunbar's two sons, who had just left the store and were about a hundred feet ahead of him. Josh was fifteen years old and, although about fifty pounds overweight, was known all over town for his brute strength. Enoch was as different from his brother as a giraffe is from an elephant. He was tall, thin and appeared as delicate as one who had been sick for a long time. In fact, he had spent most of his eighteen years in bed with one ailment or another. They were both good boys, however, who brought pride to their immigrant father.

The men of the town responded to Enoch's call as fast as a rabbit moves when the hunter's musket sounds. In a matter of minutes the bucket brigade was in position, and water was moving from the town well, which was about a hundred yards from the flaming inferno. Unfortunately, the flames had completely engulfed the house by then, and the men could do little more than prevent the fire from spreading to neighboring buildings.

Zeke wobbled back and forth, waving his hands, instructing and encouraging the men of the town in his usual frantic way. He had become the natural leader of the unofficial bucket brigade.

"I'm afraid it's too late!" he bellowed. "It's gone! But keep tryin'. This time of evenin' Josephus and Darlin' may be in there!"

"Papa! Papa! Over here!" shouted Enoch, as he headed toward the hedgerow that bordered the backyard of the little log house.

Zeke ran over to where his oldest son was bending over what appeared to be a little Negro boy in his early teens. "Lad, what are you doin' here? Were you in that fire?" he asked as he reached in his rear pocket for his bandana. "Hush now! Quit cryin' that way and answer me!"

"Mamma and Papa are in the house! Mr. Zeke, Mamma and Papa are in there! They were in bed, and I was on the back porch! I had been swimming! When I saw the fire I tried to get back in the house, but I couldn't. I tried, Mr. Zeke! But I couldn't."

"Oh God, is that you, John? Enoch, fetch me a bucket of water!" Zeke yelled as he picked up little John Dicks and headed for a cooler spot farther away from the flames.

"Give me that bucket, Enoch. Run tell Josh to let someone else take his place on the line, and clear all that crowd away from here. The dust is about to choke the men. The smoke and heat are bad enough without the dust."

Zeke took his bandana and soaked it in the water. He wiped little John's face and excitedly whispered, "Thank God, son, you're not burned as bad as it looked."

Little John had appeared to be burned almost black. His ragged shirt and knickers were almost burned off his skinny frame. After a good washing it was apparent that while he was burned over much of his body, he had a chance to live.

"Enoch, run fetch Doc Smith. This child needs a doctor real bad. I must help the boys finish this job." Turning to John, he continued, "Son, you lie here and don't move. The doctor will be here in a minute. Everything's going to be all right."

When he returned to supervising the bucket brigade, Dunbar found that little remained for him to do. The house was burned completely. There was nothing left but ashes, a few pieces of twisted metal that once had been bed frames, several metal pots over in the corner near the fire place, the old stone chimney, and the large stones that had served as foundation pillars, outlining the area of the log house. It appeared even smaller now than it had been before. All was lost. Everything was ashes.

The weather had been hot and dry for almost two months, and fighting the fire had been an impossible task for the untrained firemen. The men of the town had fought the blaze for almost an hour and had been soundly defeated. They stood there almost motionless, as if in shock, staring at the ashes as though they were staring at death itself.

Josephus and Darling Dicks were among those ashes. They had no family. They had come over from the old country about fifteen years before, and had only one son, John, who was about twelve years old. They had been good, decent, God-fearing people who had come to the new land looking for an opportunity at a fresh start, which somehow never came.

Darling had been a frail woman, but always had a pleasant smile for everyone. Josephus had been a big, robust man who had earned the respect of the town, honorably serving as the only blacksmith within forty miles. Both had been well thought of though very few people knew very much about them or their background. This was probably a result of their being dirt poor, and being devout Quakers. And now they were ashes. Their son would be all alone in the world . . . if he survived.

"Thank you, men! There's no need for you to do anythin' more. When the ashes cool off, we'll get Doc Smith to sift through 'em for any remains," announced Zeke. "Go on home, now. You did the best you could."

The men moved wearily down the dusty street. One by one, they stacked Zeke's leather buckets in front of his general store as they passed by on their way home. It had been one of the worst fires since the winter of 1729 when Will Smith, his wife, and five children were burned to death in their home during the Indian uprising. Zeke vowed he would organize a more effective fire brigade, as he, Josh, and Enoch slowly walked toward home.

It was July 13, 1733, and as he fell wearily into bed, Zeke promised his wife that not another day would pass without his starting a drive to organize a modern fire brigade for Charles Town, South Carolina.

Dr. Smith was tired and weary, but he would not sleep for several hours yet. For a man of sixty, he had never-ending energy. He was the only doctor in the small seaport village. His frame was tall and thin, and his gray hair covered only about half of his head, ringing around a bald spot which showed his shiny crown. His white beard was well-groomed and came to a point about an inch below his chin. His dark brown eyes still gleamed behind the round gold-framed spectacles that sat atop his long, thin nose. There was something about his hands and feet that caused people to take notice. Maybe they were a little larger than usual. But then his heart was a little larger than usual, too. He was a man dedicated to his work and to serving others.

He had been up since four o'clock that morning, delivering a baby for Ginny Lagree. Now he could not rest until he had done all he could do for young John Dicks. He had placed the boy on the single bed which he always used for his patients, and had washed him carefully and thoroughly, amid groans and cries. The only assistance he had was that of his faithful wife of thirty-five years.

Catherine Smith was several years younger than her husband. In her mid-fifties, she had become a round, pleasant, and loving woman. Her hair was long and dark and was always wound into a neat ball which sat on the top of her head near the back of her crown. Done up that way, it looked very much like a hat without a brim. Her eyes were a piercing gray, slightly crossed, and seemed to be peeping around her dainty little turned up nose. She seldom wore a bonnet, even when working in her garden, but her skin was fair and free from wrinkles. She almost never took off her big homespun apron which covered her dress all the way to the floor. She had never had children, and had totally dedicated herself to making her husband happy.

"Catherine, dear, please hand me another bucket of salve and that box of sulphur. And I'm about to run out of bandages. Please hurry and tear a few more so I can finish taking care of this child." Turning to the boy, he went on, "John, I'm sorry I can't give you something for the pain, but this salve and sulphur mixture will cause your burns to heal quickly."

After another hour, Dr. Smith had done all he could. "Well, that's it, John," he said, as he stretched and yawned. "You just lie still until morning, and we'll talk then about what to do with you."

"If you need anything during the night, just call me and I'll come running," Catherine whispered as she blew out the lantern and followed the doctor out of the room.

They paused a few minutes and sat down in the drawing room. Dr. Smith finished drying his hands and lit up his old favorite pipe for a moment of relaxation.

"Catherine, even though we've never had any children of our own, I'll never become accustomed to seeing a child in pain," the doctor said with a serious look on his face. "And the worst is yet to come," he continued thoughtfully, "when the loss of his parents really hits him."

"It breaks my heart too, dear, but come, now, you must get your rest," she replied. "You never know when someone might need you during the night."

"I suppose you're right. I'll be right along after I rest for a while."

John awoke early the next morning and looked at the bandages which almost covered his body. When he tried to move, he realized it was not just a nightmare or a horrible dream. There had been a terrible fire, and his Papa and Mamma were gone forever. He had always tried to be a little man like his Papa wanted, but he could not keep back the tears. He collapsed into heavy sobbing.

His crying awoke both the doctor and his wife. She came running into the little anteroom and whispered, "John, what's wrong? Can I get you something?"

"No, ma'am," he sobbed. "I'm all right. I was just thinking about Mamma and Papa."

"All right, John, don't be ashamed to cry. Get it all out," she stammered as tears began running down her cheeks. "Don't you worry now. We'll take care of you. Daniel, come see if John needs anything," she called as she stared at what looked like a wrapped mummy lying on the bed.

John was a skinny little boy with black hair. His hair had been singed and almost looked like wool from the black sheep. He was small for his age; not more than four feet tall. One of his legs was about half an inch shorter than the other, just enough to be noticeable and to indicate that he had suffered some mild crippling disease at an early age. His complexion was extremely fair. The tips of his little fingers, which protruded from under all the bandages, showed little nails which had been bitten down to the quick. He was the picture of a serious-minded little lad of whom much had been expected, and from whom much had been attempted. His little hazel eyes looked pitifully up at Catherine.

Dr. Smith came into the room and began lifting the bandages in several places so as to get a better look at the burns in the bright morning light. "They're not quite as bad as I had thought. But they're bad enough, so you just stay in bed today. In a few days you'll be good as new," assured the doctor as his mind moved to the unpleasant task he had before him this morning. "I'll be back in a little while," he said to his wife as he turned and started for the door.

In the barn, the doctor hitched old Dolly to the buggy and started on his dreaded journey to the ashes of the Dicks' house. He had seen the horrors of death many times during his thirty-five years of practicing medicine, but still he just could not get used to this kind of thing.

Arriving at the fire scene, he dismounted from the buggy. Several children and old ladies stood in front of their houses and shaded their eyes as they watched, from afar, the curious lone figure methodically walk through the ghastly death scene. Dr. Smith poked and scratched around in the ashes, and little by little placed the remains of Josephus and Darling Dicks onto a sheet he had neatly spread just outside the area of the house. A few bones, several teeth, and a large metal belt buckle were all he could find.

"I'll wrap these remains and carry them to the coffin maker. They must be given a proper Christian funeral," he thought aloud as he folded the sheet over the skimpy remains and placed them in the back of his buggy.

There were not many townspeople present as the kindly old Huguenot minister quoted from the Twenty-Third Psalm and a few other scriptures over the single coffin which contained the remains of both Josephus and Darling Dicks. Dr. Smith had made the arrangements, and had also brought John to the funeral. His kind wife, Catherine, sobbed as if she had lost a member of her own family. She had not known the Dicks family very well, but her heart went out to John, who now had no family and no place to go.

As the little group slowly left the graveyard, Catherine helped John into the back of the wagon. They had placed several quilts in the wagon, making a soft bed for his trip to the funeral.

After they had ridden for a few minutes, John called out to Dr. Smith, "Sir, could we stop by the house? It's on our way."

"Are you sure you want to do this, John?"

"Yes, sir. I want to get one last look at it," he stammered between sobs.

Dr. Smith looked at his wife, and somehow neither could speak. The guarded silence was broken only by the sobs of the small lad and the squeaking of the buggy wheels, as Dolly slowly plodded toward the dreaded ash heap.

Dr. Smith stopped the wagon and helped John out. There was almost no place on his body for the Doctor to take hold. He was wrapped from head to toe, and the thick bandages were noticeable, even though the doctor had put his own shirt and pants on the boy, and had let him wear a long coat to the funeral. After setting the boy down, the doctor climbed back onto the seat of the wagon beside Catherine where they both waited in silence.

John carefully made his way into the heap of ashes which had once

been the place where he played around his mother's knees. He had
spent many hours here, watching and listening to his Papa read from
the large family Bible, every morning and every evening. It was
about the only thing his parents had been able to keep when they had
left the old country.

As the doctor and his wife looked on, John scratched around in the
ashes as if looking for something. After a few minutes, he carefully
stooped and picked up the only thing in the world that belonged to
him. It was the little iron fish that his father had made for him in the
blacksmith shop. It was small enough to hold in the palm of his hand,
and had three crosses clearly cut into its side. He had watched his
father make it. He had helped by pumping the bellows to keep the
fire hot. Now it was bent from the intense heat of the fire. The three
crosses could still be clearly seen, however, and his own initials
"J.D." were also recognizable on the back.

John clutched the little iron fish in the palm of his hand as he cried
out in confusion and sorrow, "Mamma, Papa. I love you. I need you.
Why did you leave me? Why?"

His confusion and sorrow turned to anger, and in a burst of rage,
he threw the little charm as far as he could. As it fell in the briar patch
near the hedgerow, he fell to his knees and began hitting the ground
with his bandaged fists.

"I don't want it. I don't need it. I don't need anything. I don't need
anybody!" he cried as the ashes scattered before his raging blows.

Daniel and Catherine had sat for several minutes in silence as they
watched John among the ashes. Now they became concerned.
Catherine started to jump from the wagon, but her husband took her
by the arm and quietly said, "Just wait. Let him get all the anger out.
It'll help."

"But Daniel, he's all alone in the world. He has no one!"

"I know, dear. Maybe we can take him as our own child. He has no
family and no place to go. I've always wanted a son. What do you
think, dear?" the doctor said with a tremble in his voice as he looked
into her crying eyes.

"Oh, Daniel, I think that is a splendid idea," she answered quickly
as she wiped another tear from her eye. "You could train him in
medicine. He could travel with you when you make calls. He's a

bright boy. He could pick it up fast."

"Hold on now, Catherine. Let's don't move too fast. We'll take one thing at a time. We'd better wait a while before talking to him about it," he cautioned with a weak smile.

John returned to the wagon, wiping his tears with his bandaged hands which were now almost black from pounding the ashes. Dr. Smith helped him into the wagon and made him comfortable before starting for home.

"John, it's been two weeks now, and you've not eaten enough to keep a bird alive. You've not spoken ten words. You can't go on this way, son," Catherine said as she took his untouched bowl of soup from the table. "I know it's difficult to accept what has happened, but you must not become bitter. I haven't seen you shed a tear since you returned from the funeral. I see only anger and bitterness in your eyes."

"You don't know how I feel. You're not my Mamma. I don't have a Mamma or Papa. I don't have anybody. I don't need anybody."

"I'm sure I don't know how you feel, John," she replied with hurt in her eyes. "I'm sorry you've got to go through all this. I know you feel like you don't have anybody to love you, but I do love you, and Daniel loves you too."

"How could you love me? You're not my Mamma."

"I could be your Mamma, John. How'd you like that?"

"I don't know," he answered, as his countenance fell and a tear slipped from his angry little eyes. "I don't know how you could do that."

"Well, your Mamma's gone, and I can't take her place. I don't have a son to love, except you. Maybe if we love each other enough, I can be your Mamma, and you can be my son. I'm willing to try if you are," she said as she placed her arm around his shoulders. "Come on, son, let's give it a chance."

"I'm scared," he stammered, as his anger melted with his tears. "Mamma and Papa are gone, and I'm all alone. I'm scared. What am I going to do? I don't have anything or anybody. The only thing left was my fish charm, and I throwed it away."

"You have us, John. We love you. We'll take care of you. You don't need anything but us."

"I need my fish charm. I don't know why I throwed it away. It's the only thing I've got left. I must've been crazy to throw it away," he cried as panic began to grip him and tears began flowing.

"Now don't worry, son. We'll find the fish. We'll look for it just as soon as you're better."

"No. No. I must look for it now. I know I'll never find it. What would Papa think if he knew I throwed it away? He made me promise I'd always keep it. He said it was a secret code of honor just between me and him. Why did I throw it away? I've got to find it now!"

"All right, John. Calm down. I'll take you to find it. Daniel is gone with Dolly and the buggy. Do you think you can walk all the way there?"

"Yes ma'am, I think so."

Catherine felt a little embarrassed as she and John walked down the long dusty street. She felt she and John appeared bizarre to all the neighbors as they stared and smiled politely. After all, he was still wrapped from head to toe and should have been in bed. Daniel would not approve, but little John was stubborn and overly upset. Besides, how else could she prove her love for him?

"I think it went into the briar patch," he said as he quickened his pace, leaving the street and darting through the tobacco field which lay to the south of the hedgerow. "I just know I'll never find it."

"Now, John," she said as she tried desperately to catch up, "you're not going to quit before you start, are you? We'll find it if it takes all day and all night."

For what seemed like several hours they searched in and around the briar patch, sometimes crawling under the briars and sometimes stepping on the thorny bushes to push them down. Several times, John ran to the remains of the burned house and stood in the exact spot among the ashes where he had stood on the day he threw the little charm away in anger and tried to sight where it would have landed. Then he rushed back to the briar patch and scratched around desperately for it. Catherine watched him intently and tried to look in the area where he thought it had fallen. Finally, exhausted and tired, they sat down on the ground to rest, with little hope of finding the small piece of worthless iron which had become so important and valuable in the mind of the frail, injured orphan.

"I should have known I couldn't find it," he said, as he tried to get up. The bandages on his right leg would not allow him to bend the knee, and he fell backward into the edge of the prickly thicket. Before Catherine could get to him, he began screaming hysterically.

"I found it! I found it! We've looked all around it! My hand fell right on it! I can't believe it!"

The little charm was covered with rust from lying in the cool morning dew and hot summer sun. He rubbed it feverishly on the bandages, inspected it, and wiped it again and again as if it were vitally important that it be perfectly clean.

"Can you believe it? We've really found it," he exclaimed with a broad grin, as his eyes lit up with joy. He proudly showed her his little rusty fish charm as if it were made of gold. "Thank you for helping me find it. I'm so happy. I'll never throw it away again!"

"It's good to see you so happy, son. Now let's hurry home. Daniel may be at home wondering where we are."

Doctor Smith listened with great interest as both John and Catherine tried to talk at the same time to relate what had happened at the briar patch. He stopped puffing on his strong pipe long enough to say with a wise and pleasant smile, "Always remember, John, you can find what you're looking for if you look long enough. Now, let's get some clean bandages on those hands. We wouldn't want you to have a setback with infection."

Six weeks later only about half of the bandages remained on John. The burns had been covered with sulphur and salve many times by the doctor, but Catherine had re-wrapped them and had spent many hours rubbing the mixture of ointments on the sores as the burns started to heal. She was determined that the boy would not have ugly scars, especially on his face.

The six weeks seemed like an eternity to John. He felt like a prisoner who was gradually becoming free of his bonds, one bandage at a time. His young mind had busily sorted out the hurt, anger, bitterness, and confusion. Daniel and Catherine Smith had quickly begun to fill the tragic void in his life. Their genuine love and concern had almost compelled him to look upon them as a real

Mamma and Papa. He was uneasy about those feelings. It just did not seem right to let anyone take the place of his parents. Even though he was appreciative and mannerly to them, he vowed to never let them take the place of his real Mamma and Papa.

"Well, son, it's been six weeks now. I believe we can leave off the bandages," observed the doctor as he unwrapped the last of the bandages. "It looks a lot better than I ever expected. As long as you have your clothes on, it'll be hard for anyone to know you were ever burned. You can thank Catherine for that."

John knew he was almost well. He had imposed enough on the doctor and his wife. They had taken care of him night and day for over six weeks. He did not have one single penny, much less the many pounds which it had cost the doctor to take care of him.

"Doctor Smith," he said hesitatingly, "I don't have any money to pay you, but I'll work it out if you let me. I'll be your servant or your slave. I'll do anything you want me to do until the debt is paid."

"John, I don't want you to be my servant or my slave," replied the doctor, who was greatly moved by the boy's sincerity and integrity. "I want you to be my son. Catherine and I decided several weeks ago that we would talk to you when the time came, and you became strong enough. We want you to live with us, as our very own son. We'll love you and help you to find a good life."

"You need us, John, and we need you," Catherine added pleadingly. "So please say yes!"

"I guess so," he said tearfully, as he hugged them both tightly. "But I must work to pay you back for taking care of me and arranging a funeral for Mamma and Papa."

"We'll see. We'll talk about that later," whispered the doctor, as the lump in his throat swelled so that he could hardly talk. "We just want you to be like our own son."

Over the next few years, the lives of Daniel and Catherine Smith were filled with new meaning and purpose as they shared their lives with the son they thought they would never have. Catherine made clothes for John and sang as she prepared his meals. Daniel was proud to have John sitting on the seat beside him when he made his calls throughout the surrounding countryside. He felt mighty proud, knowing he had a son who might be able to take over for him someday.

"Wake up, son," yawned Dr. Smith. "It's four o'clock in the morning, and Simon LeGrow's little Negro slave just brought word that one of his children is sick. I want you to ride along with me. I'll look at his horses and cows while I'm there."

John jumped out of bed like he was expecting to see the queen. The doctor knew how to arouse his excitement. Just to mention doctoring on horses, cows or any other animals caused John to jump to attention. He had shown a special interest in caring for animals, and in one short year had become quite good at it.

John ran out the back door, thinking he would beat Dr. Smith to the barn and surprise him by having the horse and buggy ready when he came out. Sitting on the door step was a little Negro boy, shivering in the cool morning air. His face was so black it appeared almost like a featureless blur until he opened his eyes or mouth, revealing dark brown eyes and big white teeth. He was thin and dressed skimpily but had a warm smile.

John almost stumbled over the boy, caught himself, and came back. He stuck out his hand and said, "I'm John Dicks. What's your name?"

"I'ze Isaiah," answered the little Negro boy, who was about the same age as John. "I'ze belong to Massa Simon LeGrow, and I be fourteen years old come September."

"I'm glad to meet you, Isaiah. I'm fourteen now," John quickly replied with a smile, "You want to help me hitch up the buggy?"

Isaiah's white teeth made his face look even more black as he grinned broadly and answered excitedly, as if he were not accustomed to such warm treatment. "Sho' 'nuff, boss. I sho' do!" They went into the barn and had the buggy waiting when the doctor came bounding out the back door.

All along the way, John and Isaiah chatted about every subject, from raising tobacco on Mr. LeGrow's plantation to watching the hogs drop their litter of piglets. John was all ears while Isaiah told about how Mr. Simon LeGrow used his whip on the horses and the slaves if they did not please him.

Mr. LeGrow's plantation looked like a town. There were rows of small, run-down frame houses where the slaves lived, and dozens of little buildings with smoke circling out of their chimneys. The big plantation house looked like it was rising out of the ground among the large moss-filled oak trees. John had never visited any place so magnificent.

"What are the buildings with the smoke coming out?" he asked Isaiah as they rode by close to one of them.

"Dat's de 'bacco barns. Massa LeGrow got 'em all full, dryin' out. De boats'll be comin' soon to fetch it," Isaiah proudly answered, as if he were happy to know something the white boy did not know.

"I never saw a tobacco barn before. I wonder if Mr. LeGrow would let me see inside one of them?"

"I'll ask him to let you look at them, John," interrupted Dr. Smith, as he pulled the buggy to a stop in front of the plantation house, "that is . . . after we finish our work."

When the buggy came to a stop, Mr. LeGrow greeted the doctor and said, "Doc, I just don't know what's wrong with Henry. He's had a fever for two days." He turned and bellowed, "Isaiah, take the doctor's horse around back. Get him plenty of water and feed."

Simon LeGrow was a man of average height but had broad shoulders and large rough hands. His face was about as rough as his hands, with skin that looked like an elephant's hide. He wore a long brown beard which hung about three inches below his chin. He had a full head of unruly hair and a big red nose which looked like a large strawberry sitting on his face. His dark beady eyes peered out from under bushy brown eyebrows and reminded John of a nightmare he once had. His voice was hoarse and coarse.

John followed Isaiah to the back of the big house and helped him draw water from the well. As they went into the barn to get some feed grain for Dolly, Isaiah said, "Massa Dicks, how come your name is Dicks and de docta name Smith, if you his child?"

"That's a long story, Isaiah," John answered defensively. "I don't like to talk about it . . . well, I guess I can tell you. My Mamma and Papa were killed in a fire. I was burned pretty bad myself. Dr. Smith saved my life and said I could live with him and be like his son." He raised his shirt and continued, "See these scars? They were caused by fire."

"Dem mighty bad scars, Massa John. Dey's worse dan mine!"

"You've been in a fire?"

"No suh! Dese scars are from Massa LeGrow's bull whip!" Isaiah answered, as he lifted his shirt for John to see. "Mamma died, and Pappa got sickly, so Massa LeGrow say I must do as much work as dem both if I want to eat."

John had to turn his head. Isaiah's back was covered with stripes. It looked like someone had taken a red hot fire poker and branded him with it again and again. "Let's get the feed and get out of here," John blurted out. He shivered at the thought of Mr. LeGrow using his whip on Isaiah.

Mr. LeGrow and Dr. Smith walked around the corner of the house as John and Isaiah finished feeding Dolly. "Doc, I want you to look at one of my mares before you leave. She's ready to drop a colt, but it looks to me like she may need help," he said impatiently as they all walked toward the stables.

John suddenly felt like he didn't like this man very much. All he could think about were the stripes on Isaiah's back.

Dr. Smith examined the mare, pushing on her belly in several places. "Looks to me like it'll come feet first. What do you think about it, John?"

Now it was John's turn to feel proud. He had helped care for many animals with his adopted father, and had an unusual knack for it.

He pushed and felt several places on the mare's belly and said, "I'm sure you're right. This mare's in for a hard night."

Dr. Smith turned to Mr. LeGrow and said, "Si, I can't stay here tonight. I've got two patients who may get down any time. Mrs. Lockley is already overdue. I'll be glad to leave John here with you if you like. He's about as good as I am with these animals. He'll need some help." John did not like the idea but was willing to do anything Dr. Smith agreed upon. He felt better when Mr. LeGrow replied, "Isaiah can stay with him. He's pretty strong and has helped with the horses and cows many times. I'll be busy with Henry and his fever, but I'll send George to look in on them during the night. He's my oldest boy and is real smart about these things."

"Si, can you have Isaiah bring John home in the morning, or whenever the job is done?" the doctor asked, as he closed his medicine bags.

"I'll be glad to, Doc. Thanks for everything," he answered as he walked the doctor to his buggy.

John thought to himself as he and Isaiah stood watching the buggy move out of sight, "LeGrow seems to be nice enough. Maybe my feelings about him are wrong."

"Let's go, Isaiah," John mumbled. "We've got a lot of work to do before that mare is ready to drop that new colt."

About sundown John and Isaiah finished all their preparations and sat down together on the hay to relax and wait. The silence of the night made the breathing of the mare sound like the blowing wind of a storm. The lowing of the cows and grunting of the pigs nearby sounded like music compared to the uncomfortable, labored breathing of the mare.

The quiet was suddenly broken, however, by a shrill cry of anguish. The sound of a whip pierced the night air like the cracking of a giant tree which had been cut almost through and had surrendered with one final crack. Again and again the whip sounded its sharp, crisp crack, among loud wails of pain and anguish.

"What on earth is that?" John nervously asked as he looked at Isaiah.

"Massa John, dat sounds like Massa George. He likes to use dat whip on every nigger dat quits work 'fore dark. Massa LeGrow is bad, but he's kindly as a saint 'side Massa George. He 'as born mean, and he's still da meanest thing on dis place."

John shuddered at the thought, but Isaiah appeared to be used to it.

"This kind of thing ought not to be allowed anywhere in the world!" John exclaimed, as he started pushing on the belly of the mare.

"Yessuh, Massa John . . . nowhere."

John and Isaiah worked with the mare most of the night. When the colt started coming, the feet appeared first as had been predicted. No matter how hard they pushed, it was impossible to turn the colt and change its position. They rubbed down the mare as best they could, and helped her deliver the colt in its breech position.

After about five hours of pushing and pulling, the mare expelled a fine colt. Isaiah washed it and pushed it into a standing position while John washed and doctored the relieved mare with his salve mixture.

When the mare and colt were standing together like a beautiful picture of new life, John and Isaiah lay down on the stable floor and stretched out for a few moments of rest.

As the rays of the rising sun peeped through the cracks in the stable door and across John's face, he awoke and stretched himself. Isaiah was lying over in the corner of the stable, still asleep. John looked at the mare and her colt. He had a sense of accomplishment as he saw the mare nursing its colt. He knew that without help, both would have been lost. Noting that the mare was without fodder, he got up and walked to the hayloft ladder. As he climbed to the hayloft to get an armload of hay, the front door burst open and in walked George LeGrow. He had failed to show up when they needed him most. He saw Isaiah over in the corner and yelled in his gruff voice, "Hey boy! What you doin' sleepin' on the job?"

George was an arrogant and nasty character. It was hard to understand how a person could get so mean in so few years. He was about the same height as John, but was muscular and proud of it. He looked a lot like his father with unruly brown hair, rough skin, beady brown eyes, and a ragged beard without a mustache. From his manner, it also appeared that he got his enjoyment by exercising his authority with the whip. Just as he raised his bullwhip to teach Isaiah a lesson, John slid a batch of hay out of the loft, letting it fall between the two boys.

"I'm sorry! My foot slipped, George. Come and see what a beautiful colt your mare has! We had a hard time of it, but both are fine," John called as he hustled down the ladder.

George gave John a long icy stare as if he knew the batch of hay had been dropped on purpose. "You better be more careful, Dicks. That's a good way for somebody to get hurt."

John took the hay and carried it to the stall where the mare was more than ready for her breakfast. George looked pleased and exclaimed, "I'll be damned! You did a good job, Dicks!"

John took little note of this compliment, however. George's generally domineering attitude greatly bothered him and made him anxious to leave. His earlier desire to see the tobacco barns and smell the fragrance of the curing leaves was dampened by the events of the night and the early morning. He decided he had better leave while everything was in good order, and they were all on good terms.

"Isaiah, I'm ready to go. Hitch the wagon and let's go. Mr. LeGrow can settle with Dr. Smith later," he called as he picked up his coat.

Isaiah had the wagon ready faster than he could have if he had been a runaway slave. He was anxious to get out of the sight of Master George.

When they were about halfway back to Charles Town, Isaiah pulled the wagon to a halt on the country road and leaped from it. John was not sure what was wrong, but when he saw Isaiah trying to unfasten his suspenders as he ran, he had a pretty good idea. Only a moment after Isaiah disappeared into the woods, however, there was a loud scream of a girl and the bellow of a man, "What you doing here, nigger? Git outa here! Give me that gun! I'll git rid of you!"

Two musket shots sang out through the woods. Isaiah came running from the underbrush, pulling on his pants and trying to fasten his suspenders. His feet barely touched the ground, and he was almost white with fright. He leaped into the wagon, frantically grabbing the reins.

"Let's git outta here!" he nervously whispered in panic. "Lawd God, dat man'll kill us both iffen he gits a chance. I done seed what no nigger should see."

The horse galloped away as Isaiah frantically whipped him with the reins and constantly looked back toward the woods. The man came running from the woods, pulling up his pants as he ran. He had loaded his musket again and raised it to shoot. Another shot echoed again through the woods as Isaiah and John almost jumped out of their skins.

The distance was too great. The musket ball fell short, but Isaiah and John still wanted to put more distance between them and the gunman. Isaiah did not stop pushing the horse until they were safely in the most populated part of Charles Town.

"What was that all about?" John breathlessly asked Isaiah when he had regained his senses.

"Lawd God, Massa John, dat old man was doin' things wit dat gal my eyes couldn't b'lieve. I jes know he'll kill me iffen he ever sees me again."

When Isaiah pulled the old wagon in front of Dr. Smith's house, he paused for a long time and said, "I 'preciate what you done for me, Massa John! You're a good white man."

"Listen, Isaiah, if you ever need anything, you can come to me. I want to be your friend." He smiled warmly and stretched out his hand.

Isaiah haltingly extended his hand as if he were afraid to touch a white man, and responded, "Yessuh! I'd like dat!"

Dr. Smith was getting ready to leave on one of his house calls as John walked in the back door. "Well how did it go, son?" the doctor asked, as he placed his hat on his head and picked up his bag.

"It was a hard night, but Mr. LeGrow ought to be happy. He has a fine new colt and a healthy mare. I met George, by the way. He's a mean sort. I heard the sound of his whip several times during the evening."

"He's a good one to stay away from, John. Just remember, there are good people and there are bad people of every size, shape and color," said the doctor. "By the way, I spoke to Zeke Dunbar about the old blacksmith shop your father was using. He said you could use it, free of charge, if you want to combine blacksmithing with your animal doctoring. You go on and take a good nap, and we'll talk some more about it when I return."

John could hardly sleep even though he had slept only about thirty minutes during the hard night. He had thought many times about doing the work his father had done, but knew he had no money. He also knew he had promised the doctor to work for him until his bill was paid in full. Nevertheless, he was thrilled at the thought of having his own business. "If only I could . . . ." he thought, as he dozed off into a deep sleep, fully clothed, and lying on top of the covers.

He twisted and turned as he dreamed about George LeGrow, the white stranger in the woods, the musket, and the bullwhip. He relaxed as his dreams moved to his new friend Isaiah, the idea of opening his very own business in the blacksmith shop, and his playing around his mother's knees. He dreamed he was pumping the bellows again to keep the fire hot while his Papa made the little iron fish charm for him.

Catherine came in from the garden with an apron full of corn and squash. As she placed the vegetables on the table, she saw John lying on the bed. She went into his room and gently took off his boots. She spread a sheet over him and kissed his forehead as if he were a small boy. She thought to herself as she paused a moment to stare at the boy who had become a strong, muscular, and handsome young man, "Thank you John for being such a fine son. Daniel and I are very proud of you. You will always be our son."

Catherine turned back to the task of preparing the evening meal. An hour or so passed, and just as the doctor returned from his house call, everything was ready.

"Daniel, please wake John. Supper is about ready," Catherine said in soft tones as she took the cake of cornbread out of the Dutch oven in the fireplace. She had made a good supper of succotash, squash, cornbread and salt-cured ham especially for John. She and Daniel had had a long talk about John's future the night before, and she was sure Daniel would talk with him after supper.

After the meal, John and the doctor went to the front porch to sit in the cool night air. Dr. Smith leaned his straight chair against the wall of the house as he puffed on his pipe. Everything was silent except for the crickets and katydids, and an occasional barking of a dog in the distance.

Dr. Smith broke the silence. He pointed his finger at John and said, "Now look here, John, you don't owe me anything. I just want you to know that you've more than paid me back for everything I've ever done for you. In fact, I owe you about fifty pounds, and I intend to give it to you to open that old blacksmith shop if you want to. Zeke Dunbar said you could use it free. Now I'll miss you on my rounds. You've been a big help. You've made my work enjoyable, and I hate to change all that. But it's time for us to think about your future. So, what do you think, son?"

John was flabbergasted. He believed Dr. Smith could read his mind. "I'd be mighty pleased to be able to open the blacksmith shop. Are you sure my bill is paid? I know I can never repay you for taking me in and teaching me like you have, sir, but I'll always love you and Mrs. Smith for making me your son," he stammered with a large lump in his throat.

"Now John, you are not leaving us. You just won't be working directly with me. You're as good at doctoring animals as anyone I've ever seen. You'll be fifteen in a few days. If you start now, within a few years, by the time you're ready to start a family of your own, you can have a good business established—enough to support a family," suggested the doctor. "Catherine and I have talked about this, and we wouldn't feel any different about you if you were our own flesh and blood. We want to see you develop into a leader of this community. We want you to be happy. You're a bright young man, and we both are proud of you."

There was a long silence. Both men appeared to be in deep thought. John was the first to speak. "Sir, I don't know how to thank you, but I'll go to see Zeke in the morning and tell him I want to use the building."

The doctor puffed on his strong pipe and replied, "Son, you don't have to thank us. Just keep on making us proud of you. That's all we want. I must go to bed now, John. Good night."

The doctor somehow looked a little older and more stooped as he knocked the ashes out of his pipe on the door post and closed the door behind him. John sat for a long time on the porch that night, fingering the little rusty charm in his pocket, looking at the moon, listening to the sounds of nature, and thinking excitedly about the morrow.

The doctor and his wife were still in bed when John slipped out the back door the next morning. He walked down the dusty street, almost unaware of the cool morning vapor which was rising from the trees and grass. He was also unaware that Wilma Dunbar was starting a fire under the wash pot in her back yard for the day's washing.

Wilma was a pretty, golden-haired young girl with a bright smile and fair complexion. Her long hair fell in natural waves down her long, thin neck and on down her back. She had a lively personality which was enhanced by her dancing bright blue eyes. Under several layers of undergarments, petticoats, and a thick homespun dress, was a shapely body with a tiny waist, broad hips and abundant breasts. As the only daughter of Zeke Dunbar, she had been pampered but not spoiled. She had stayed at home near her mother, who had never been very strong. She was a loving person who adored her mother and admired her father and brothers.

John had become a healthy, energetic, and happy young man. His hair was still shiny black but his little skinny body had developed into a strong and muscular one which was almost six feet tall. If one of his legs was still shorter than the other, it was difficult to detect. He walked straight and proud. A smart, well-trimmed black mustache was over his thin upper lip, and his face had a healthy ruddy complexion. He was the picture of a confident young man. At only fifteen he had learned a lot from the Smiths. He was quite a different person from the little sickly, burned boy who had been brought to them only three years earlier.

Wilma turned and stretched her long, shapely neck to get a look at the handsome young man who was walking down the road. She had stared at him for several minutes before brazenly waving. "Hey, John! Where are you going so early in the morning?"

John was shocked out of his daydreaming and replied cheerfully, "I'm going to look at the old blacksmith shop. I'll be by the store to talk with your Papa later in the day. Good day to you now, Miss Wilma."

"Good day to you, John," she replied as she flung back her long golden hair and continued her chores.

John stood in front of the blacksmith shop for a long time, staring at the door. He could almost see his Papa emptying the used coals on the ash pile. He shook his head as he opened the door and found himself once again in the place where he had spent many pleasant hours with his father. He picked up the sledge hammer as his eyes moved from the billows, to the anvil, to the water tub, to the fire box: all familiar things and still in good working condition. It appeared that the building had not been entered since his father closed the doors on that fateful evening over three years before.

"It's been so long since I used any of these things. Maybe I'd better practice some before I open for business," he thought as he unconsciously rubbed the little fish charm. "I guess I'd better go on over to see Mr. Dunbar. The sooner I get started, the sooner I can open for business. Maybe I can get in a little practice today."

Zeke Dunbar was sweeping off the porch of his little store. He stopped, leaned on his broom and said, "Mornin', John. I hope you've come to talk about the blacksmith shop."

"Yes sir, I sure did," John answered with a broad smile.

"It's yours, if you want it, lad. No charge," Zeke said as he smiled and resumed his sweeping.

"Thank you very much, Mr. Dunbar. I don't know how to thank you, but I'll owe you something," John responded, as he moved out of the way of Zeke's broom.

"You don't owe me anything, son. You're welcome to the building."

Wilma came up carrying a covered basket, and Zeke smiled broadly as he said, "Child, what you doin' here in the middle of the day?"

She nodded shyly to John as she said, "Mamma baked a cake and wanted me to bring you and the boys some of it. John, come on in. There's enough for you too, if you want a piece."

John followed them through the door and warmly greeted Josh and Enoch who came from the back of the store. John ate the cake, thanked Zeke and Wilma, and hurried away, toward the blacksmith shop.

"I believe you got an eye for John, Wilma. How did you know he would be here? Did a little bird tell you?" Enoch teased good-naturedly.

"Shut your mouth, Enoch Dunbar. You are just plain mean," she rebounded in a playful manner.

"I like John. I never will forget the night I found him lying in the yard of his burning house. I thought he was a little Negro boy. He was in a sad shape. To look at him now, you wouldn't know he had been burned so badly. Doctor Smith sure did a good job on him," Enoch continued in a more serious manner. "I must admit he has made a fine young man. Don't you think so, Sis?"

"I wouldn't know. I haven't noticed," Wilma answered in a casual and disinterested manner as she flipped her long golden hair.

"That was one of the worst fires I've ever seen," Josh interrupted as he wiped his hands on his apron. "We just weren't prepared to deal with it. I'm sure glad Papa has organized a real volunteer fire brigade. The people of this town should really appreciate what he's done for them."

"Now, Josh, I've done nothing more than any other man would've done. I just want to make sure my family is safe. And how can you be safe if there is no fire-fightin' men who know what they're doin'?" the jolly red-face merchant acknowledged with a twinkle in his eye and a modestly bowed head. "We never know when the Injuns will start actin' up and burnin' houses again."

"I'll always believe it was renegade Indians who set the Dicks' house on fire," Josh responded as he reached for another piece of cake. "You can't blame them for being mad. We keep taking their land and pushing them farther into the country. I understand the Crown is going to make them move completely out of the area."

"Well, they've done enough damage to the white man over the past few years," Enoch added as he brushed the last few cake crumbs from the rough wooden counter. "Just ask old William Badger how he feels. Nothing will bring back his wife and three children."

"Well, I'm going home if all you men want to do is talk about such dreadful things," Wilma said childishly as she reached for the empty cake plate. "I've got more important things to be doing."

"Back to work, boys. Wilma, tell your Mamma to check on the sow that's down with piglets. Now run along home, and be careful." Zeke had a satisfied look on his face. It was always there when all his children were together.

John had noticed how Wilma smiled at him. She was a very nice and attractive young lady. He was aware that his heart had almost pounded out of his chest when she offered him a piece of cake, and believed she felt the same way. He smiled to himself as he opened the door of the blacksmith's shop. He had other things to think about today.

There were several small pieces of metal lying near the firebox. A neatly stacked pile of hardwood gave the impression that someone had just brought it in from the woods. John decided he would try to start a fire. After working with the flint and tender for some time he was successful in getting a blaze going. He pumped the billows; slowly at first, then speeding up gradually, just like his Papa had taught him.

Unexpectedly, there was a knock on the door. "Come on in. It's open," John called as he continued to pump the billows to bring the fire to a red hot blaze.

"Massa John, I done been ta Massa Smith's house lookin' fa ya. Missy Cat'rin done told me you be here," Isaiah said as he entered the shop. Somehow he had a sad look on his face, and John stopped his work to give his full attention to his friend. "Has old man

LeGrow been using that whip on you again?"

"No suh, Massa John," he quickly answered as he wiped the tears from his face. "Papa done pass, and Massa LeGrow say I may come ta let ya know. You da only friend I'ze got an' I jes wanted ya ta know 'bout his dyin'."

"I'm sorry to hear it, Isaiah. Is there anything I can do?" John asked with genuine sympathy. It had not been too many years since his own father had experienced a horrible death, and he found it easy to understand what Isaiah was going through.

"Well, Massa John, would it be askin' too much fa ya ta come an' wake wid us when Papa is laid out?" he asked sheepishly.

"Sure I will, Isaiah. What are friends for?" He put his hand on Isaiah's shoulder and asked, "When will he be ready?"

"I b'lieve dey say tomorrow night, Massa John," he answered with a more relaxed look in his eye. "De wake starts at sundown."

"You can count on me, Isaiah," John said with a sincere voice. "I'll be there with you all night. I know what it's like to lose a father."

"I be goin' now," Isaiah replied as he turned to leave. "I'ze gonna be lookin' fa ya, Massa John."

The fire had almost gone out. John rushed back to the firebox and began pumping the bellows vigorously. The flame began to burn hot again, and pretty soon it was ready for working metal.

"What can I do for practice?" he thought aloud as he looked around for tools and materials. "I believe I'll see how good I am with the small hammer. I know. I'll try my hand at making a few of the little fishes like Papa gave me. Papa would like that. This little charm is special to me."

John hammered and heated and hammered again, as the ring of the anvil floated across the streets and paths of the little settlement. It was welcome music which had been silent for too many years, and he worked like a beaver until the evening sun hid behind the huge moss-laden oak trees. He continued for several hours into the night, working by the light of his white hot fire. He hated the thought of quitting this work even though he had been at it for over ten hours without taking a break. He had made a dozen little fish charms, and every one was as good or better than the one his father had made. He slipped one into his pocket and buried the others by the water trough. He was not sure why he did this. Maybe he thought the symbol was too personal, or too valuable for anyone else to know about. They were more than lucky charms to him. They served as his only link to his heritage, and as a symbol of honor.

As he walked toward home in the darkness, he thought how appropriate it was to practice his skills by making the fish charms, especially on his first day of preparation. He hoped that Dr. Smith would be pleased with the one he planned to give him and that he would appreciate the magnitude of his sentiments.

Dr. Smith and his wife were sitting on the front porch when John reached home. The doctor was puffing on his pipe as Catherine exclaimed, "Oh John, did Isaiah find you?"

"Yes, ma'am," he replied respectfully. "His Papa died. I've been at the blacksmith shop all day." Turning to Dr. Smith, he continued, "I made something for you today. I want you to have this little iron fish."

He handed the fish charm to the doctor and continued, "It's just like the one Papa made for me. It's the first one I made in the shop today. Look, I cut your initials, 'D.S.' on the back. I'm not sure what this thing is supposed to symbolize, but to me it represents my heritage and is a symbol of honor. I've never been able to tell anyone that before, but I just wanted you to know."

The doctor appeared to appreciate the gravity of John's sentiments. He held the little fish in his hand for a moment and slowly said, "Well, son, I really appreciate this. I'll always carry it for good luck. Anytime you see me alive it'll be in my pocket. I assure you of that. I'll consider it my most prized possession."

He reached out and pulled John near. He tightly hugged him as the tears came to Catherine's eyes. It was good to have a son of their very own, and they could have asked for no better one.

2
Beginning of a Tradition
1740-1741

There was a sign hanging over the door, "John Dicks, Blacksmith and Animal Doctor." John was nineteen years old. He had been married to Wilma Dunbar for almost a year. His blacksmith shop was very much the same as it had been for the past five years, except for the sign. He had built a very prosperous business with his integrity, energy, and willingness to accommodate anyone, anytime. John had changed very little except for his neatly trimmed black beard. He was busy from morning till night, working with a dedication that was rare.

The year was 1740. Charles Town, South Carolina had continued to grow in importance as a seaport village. Slaves were brought in by the large wooden ships and auctioned off to the big plantation owners, who brought their abundant crops of rice and tobacco for shipment to England, France and Spain.

"Wilma, dear, I must go down to the docks today to deliver some iron hinges to Captain Jones. Would you please stay around the shop this morning to take any messages which might be delivered there? Also, please tell everyone I'll be back by early afternoon." He yawned and pulled on his boots as he sat on the side of the bed.

"Yes, dear," she replied as she turned over under the covers.

He gently kissed his newly pregnant wife on the forehead and left in the darkness of the morning, with a wide smile on his face. As he walked toward the blacksmith shop he thought how fortunate he had been and how happy he was. The void which had been created by the loss of his parents had been more than filled by Dr. Daniel Smith and his loving wife Catherine, and the many friends he had come to love, like Zeke, Josh, Enoch, and Wilma Dunbar, most of all Wilma. She had made life a wonderful adventure for him. She had taught him that there were important things in life besides work.

John hitched Ginger to the wagon which had been loaded with the iron hinges the night before. He turned into the lane and began whistling a tune as the morning sun came streaming through the trees, and a cool fog began rising from the ground. "This is a good job," he said to himself. "I hope Captain Jones will be pleased enough to recommend me to the other sea Captains."

The sun was high and hot in the sky when he arrived at the dock. There were several ships sitting motionless, like bits of bark in a watering trough. He wondered which one belonged to Captain Jones. He had little time to wonder because as he approached the first ship, he heard a loud bellow that sounded like a fog horn.

"Ahoy! Ahoy there, matey!" yelled a big grisly character with hair and beard that were as red as a Christmas flame. "I'm Captain Jones. Bring the hinges on board. My men'll help you. Just back the wagon out on the dock. It'll be just fine."

John followed his instructions, and with the help of several of the captain's men, the hinges were unloaded within a few minutes and placed on board the ship.

When John started for the captain's cabin, he saw a sight which would live with him the rest of his life. In the open hold of the ship were hundreds of Negro slaves. They were packed into the hold like wild animals. They were crying, groaning, and squirming around in their own waste. Some were naked, while others were only partially clothed. It was apparent that some were dead. John ran to the side of the ship and vomited into the tossing water.

Captain Jones came out of his quarters and heaved a loud laugh, "I say there, Matey, ye can't go very far on a ship if ye get seasick from walkin' on it."

John mumbled as he walked into the Captain's quarters, "If I live to be a hundred, I'll never believe what I just saw."

The captain did not hear his comment. He was too busy thinking how best he could haggle down the price of the hinges.

John pulled his wagon away from the dock and tied it up in the shade of a large oak tree. He felt too sick to begin his trip back home. He was curious also about the crowd which was beginning to gather near the docks. He saw Captain Jones and several of his men leading several slaves off the ship, naked and bound with ropes and chains. Each one was made to wash himself in a large wooden water trough and then was led to a clearing among the large moss-laden trees that formed a hedgerow about a hundred yards from the water's edge.

As the auction began, John remained where he was. He did not want to get any closer. He could see too much already, and he was sickened by what he saw. The men were mostly young and middle aged. The girls were young; some were pregnant. Many of them were almost naked, and acted like animals washing themselves in the water trough. Some of the girls held the hands of small children and led them toward the clearing. At least one had a small child in her arms which appeared to be dead.

John was almost thrown into a state of shock when he turned away from this pitiful scene and looked in the opposite direction to get it out of his mind. He saw several of the Captain's men throwing the dead bodies of those who had perished on the trip into a large open hole which had been dug for a common grave.

"My God! How can this be? Are these slaves not human? Do they not have souls?" he asked himself aloud as he untied his horse quickly and proceeded to mount the seat of the wagon. Somehow the sun did not look quite as bright as it had in the early morning. He had never seen so clearly just how inhumane one person could be to another. He was sure he would never see anything else quite so horrible.

John wanted to get away from the scene as fast as he could. The thought of the little children being torn from their mothers was too much for him to comprehend. And the pregnant girls, almost naked and exposing their big bellies, made him think of his own sweet wife who was several months pregnant. He hit Ginger with the reins and gritted his teeth as his wagon rolled toward home.

"John, Mr. Thomas Player came by here yesterday while you were gone. He said he had several horses on his rice plantation that needed shoeing and would appreciate it if you could come as soon as possible," Wilma called as she prepared breakfast over the open fire.

"Well, I might go today," he responded as he stretched and yawned, pulling on his boots while his sleepy eyes remained partially closed. "I'm in no mood to stay around the shop today."

After breakfast, John went on down to the blacksmith shop, hitched up the wagon, and started out for the Player plantation, which lay about six miles outside of the town. The weather was agreeable, making the trip very pleasant. As he arrived at the Player rice plantation, he pulled his wagon over to the side of the road. He wanted to watch the slaves working in the marshes.

There were dozens of slaves of all ages in the rice fields, male and female, trudging through the swampy, infested marshes. They appeared to be harvesting the rice. Each would fill his bag with what looked like straw, then wade to the edge of the field and dump it on a large sheet. The white foreman would then empty the sheet in the wagon which was standing on high ground.

Suddenly there was a loud commotion in the field. One of the slaves appeared to be slinging a water moccasin around over his head. The slave with the snake ran toward John's wagon, still holding the snake by its head.

John jumped out of the wagon, grabbed his large vine-cutting knife and motioned for the slave to bring the snake to him. He told him to hold the snake carefully on the ground while he cut it in half with one heavy swing of the blade. It was a white-mouth water moccasin, one of the deadliest kind.

"Ize bit, suh," cried the slave in a pitiful tone, thinking he was doomed.

"Where did he bite you?" John quickly asked. "I'm a doctor. I'll try to help you."

He had no time to explain that he was an animal doctor, as he reached for his razor-sharp pig castration knife. The slave pointed to the nasty teeth marks on the calf of his right leg. His eyes were filled with fear as he looked into the eyes of the 'doctor' for a sign of hope. John ordered him to lie down in the road as the dozens of slaves stood in a ring around the wagon.

John made two deep gashes across the wound and began massaging downward on the leg with both hands. When it looked like he had drained almost all the lad's blood, he grabbed his harvesting bag and tied it tightly around his leg, above the wound. He then coated the wound with a strong mixture of pine tar and salve which he kept handy for use on wounded animals. Tearing the sleeves off his own shirt, he tied them securely as bandages over the wounds. He then instructed several of the others to help him put the injured boy into the wagon.

John drove the young slave on to the plantation house where he was greeted by Mr. Player. He explained that the boy had been bitten by a white-mouth water moccasin and that he should be kept in bed for several weeks. If he had gotten all the poison out of the boy's system, he should live and, after several weeks of care and good food, should regain his strength.

"By God, Dicks," the surprised master said, "I've lost several slaves this year to those snakes. If this works, I'll be indebted to you."

He called to two of his house slaves who were peeping out of the window, "Ruth, you and Tom come out here and tote David to his bed."

John followed Mr. Player to the horse stables. He spent the rest of the evening shoeing the plantation owner's horses.

Mr. Player expressed his pleasure with John's skillful work over and over again as he was leaving, but John barely heard what he was saying. He was thinking about David, the slave who had been bitten by the snake, and how much he reminded him of Isaiah.

As he moved slowly down the road, watching Ginger lazily swat away the flying insects with her long black tail, he thought back on David and the snake, and on the other slaves who had to go back to the dangerous swampy field. "I sure hope he'll recover," he said to himself as he hit Ginger again with the reins. "I'll have to check back on him when I get a chance."

The rhythmical sound of Ginger's hoofbeats had almost put John to sleep as the wagon rounded the bend in the road which always reminded him that he was only about a mile from home. Ginger let out one of her usual whinnies as she saw Dolly up ahead. Dr. Smith's buggy was parked by the side of the road. John sat up straight and wondered to himself, "What in the world is Dr. Smith doing? He's not in his buggy?"

Pulling up beside the buggy, he paused for a moment and looked around. He did not want to surprise the doctor if he were in the underbrush relieving himself. After a few more minutes of waiting he called, "Dr. Smith! Dr. Smith! Can I help you?"

Somehow John had an uneasy feeling when, after several more minutes, no reply was given. He climbed down from the wagon and cautiously looked over the buggy and around in the setback of the road. He followed what looked like a trail of crumpled and crushed leaves, leading down the embankment and into the underbrush. As he pushed back the limbs of a small tree, he saw in a small clearing, right before him, two bodies. One was a woman who was only partially clothed. The other was Dr. Smith.

John rushed over to Dr. Smith and turned sick at what he saw. His head was bloody and battered. This kind man who had spent his life helping others had been beaten so badly he was hardly recognizable. John felt his neck for a pulse and put his face to his nose and mouth, hoping to feel any little amount of breath. He was dead. John could not recognize the woman. She had been beaten about the head with some kind of large club also.

He brought the bodies up out of the ditch and placed them in the back of his wagon. After covering them with the blankets taken from the back of Dr. Smith's buggy, he tied Dolly to the rear of his wagon, and started quickly on to Charles Town. It felt like it was the longest mile he had ever driven.

It was almost sundown when John pulled to a stop in front of Mr. Dunbar's store. Zeke came running out, and in his usual frantic way he began asking questions as he lifted the blankets to look at the bodies.

"What in God's name has happened? What in tarnation is the

matter with the doctor? Who is this girl?"

"I found them in the ditch by the road about a mile north, where the road bends around the big old sweet gum tree. I don't know what happened. It appears the doctor might have heard the woman crying for help and tried to help her. I just don't know, Zeke. How about taking my wagon and carrying them to the coffin maker? I'll take the buggy. I want to be the one to tell Catherine. Please have Josh or Enoch run over to my house and let Wilma know," John said with a struggle as he untied the buggy. He knew this would be a long journey, even though Catherine was less than a mile away.

Almost the whole village turned out for the funeral of Dr. Smith. He had no family except Catherine and John, but the whole community felt like he was "family." The little St. Phillips Church was overflowing as the minister began with a reading from the large, leather-bound Bible:

> A good name is rather to be chosen than great riches, and loving favor rather than silver and gold.
>
> The rich and poor meet together; the Lord is maker of them all.
>
> A prudent man forseeth the evil, and hideth himself; but the simple pass on, and are punished.
>
> By humility and the fear of the Lord are riches, and honor, and life.
>
> Thorns and snares are in the way of the forward; he that doth keep his soul shall be far from them.
>
> Train up a child in the way he should go: and when he is old, he will not depart from it.
>
> The rich ruleth over the poor, and the borrower is servant to the lender.
>
> He that soweth iniquity shall reap vanity; and the rod of his anger shall fall.
>
> He that hath a bountiful eye shall be blessed: for he giveth of his bread to the poor.

"Beloved, we gather here to pay tribute to our fallen brother, Daniel Alexander Smith. He was a good man. He was an humble man. He gave of his bread, and he gave of his time. He gave of his talents and of his life in service to us all. He was a man of love and peace. His entire adult life was dedicated to bringing comfort and to saving life," the minister projected in his usual eloquent manner.

To the surprise of everyone, he continued in earnest, "The dastardly coward that robbed him of his life in such a cruel and heartless manner will not go unpunished. He robbed this entire community of its very heart. He has cut it out and trod upon it. May the wrath of Almighty God be on his head, as it was upon Sodom and Gomorrah."

The refined minister had departed from his usual sophisticated manner, to the astonishment of everyone. But his display of emotion was a small token of how the community felt. The congregation murmured lightly and from several areas a clear "Amen" was offered. Suddenly every voice resounded together, "Amen, amen!"

As the mournful group walked slowly away from the church cemetery, there was a pervading feeling that the whole town had lost a father. What would they do without the doctor?

John and Wilma helped Catherine into her buggy, and he kissed her hand as he said, "Mamma, I intend to find out who did this terrible thing."

Catherine heard only one thing. This was the first time John had ever called her "Mamma." A different kind of tear came to her eye as she motioned for Dolly to start the trip back to her empty home.

Wilma turned to her father and brothers and said, "You all come home with us. I'm sorry Mamma isn't feeling well."

Zeke responded in a somber manner. "No, Wilma, you come on to the house. You need to visit with Mamma. I'm 'fraid she's not going to be here long."

Zeke had a serious look on his face. Wilma and John could not help but notice it. John shook Zeke's hand and said respectfully, "We'll be there directly. I want to go by the constable's house to see if he has learned who the dead girl is. Maybe if we know who she is, we'll have a clue as to who did this horrible thing."

The constable came to the door and invited John and Wilma in. His wife's eyes gleamed when she noticed that Wilma was expecting. She took her into another room to make female conversation while John and her husband talked serious business.

"Have you been able to find out who the dead girl is, Will?" John asked with a serious expression.

"Yes. Her name is Naomi Richburg. She lived on that little tenant farm out near Simon LeGrow's plantation. Whoever did that to her should be lynched. What a horrible way for a pretty young girl to die," he said, and shuddered as he motioned for John to have a seat. "I sure hope we find whoever did it. If old man Richburg finds out first, there'll surely be a lynching on the hangman's tree without the benefit of the law."

Several weeks later John was in the blacksmith shop making horseshoes. The familiar sound of his hammer and anvil permeated the settlement like church bells ringing. With every stroke of the hammer, his suspicions became stronger and stronger. He just had a gut feeling that George LeGrow was the one who killed the doctor and the Richburg girl. He was the only person John knew who was mean enough to do such a thing.

"I'll find some reason to make a trip out there," he said to himself, as he paused from his work. "Maybe I'll get a chance to talk with Isaiah while I'm there."

He finished the last horseshoe and dropped it into the water. It sizzled like fat meat over a fire while his mind turned to the little fish charm in his pocket. Somehow it represented security to him as nothing else did. Getting down on his knees, he dug up the eleven little iron fishes he had buried. They were covered with rust. After brushing them off repeatedly, he laid three aside and put the other eight in his medicine bag. He beat the initials "W.D." on the first one. It was for Wilma, the most important person in his life. He cut the initial "I" on the next one. It was for Isaiah. He did not know if his friend had a last name, and he certainly did not want to give him an "L" for LeGrow. On the third one he carved "C.S." He knew Catherine must feel insecure and lonely. She had said the coffin maker had not found the charm on Dr. Smith.

"I think I'll search around the murder spot when I get a chance," he thought aloud. "I'm sure the doctor had his charm on him. He always did."

His thoughts were interrupted by a knock on the side door. Isaiah walked in with a big smile as he exclaimed, "Good mornin', Massa John. You sho is lookin' good!"

"Isaiah, you old possum. I was just thinking about you. Here, I've got something for you. This is a symbol of our friendship. Promise me you'll always carry it with you, all the time."

"I will, I will! I sho 'nuff will, Massa John," he blurted out, putting his hand over his heart.

"What are you doing here this time of the day?" John reached into the water trough to take out the horseshoes he had made.

"Massa LeGrow sent me to fetch ya. De hogs a'dyin' like flies. He say come quick as you can," Isaiah answered excitedly.

"I'll be ready in a few minutes," John replied as he looked out of the corner of his eye at Isaiah. "By the way, did you know that Dr. Smith had been killed?"

"Yessuh, I heered 'bout it. I sho is sorry. He 'as a sho nuff good man." Isaiah suddenly became nervous. "I heered Massa George tellin' one dem slave gals he'd do dem de same way he did de Richburg gal if dey didn't please him."

"Are you sure, Isaiah?"

"I heared it with ma own ears, Massa John," he replied with a nervous twitch of his lip.

"Listen, Isaiah, I'm not going to the LeGrow plantation. You go back and tell Mr. LeGrow I can't come. And when you get a chance, tell George I've been accusing him all over town of killing Dr. Smith and the Richburg girl," John said with an intriguing look on his face.

"Is you sho, Massa John?" Isaiah asked in confusion.

"Yes, I'm sure. I know George well enough to know he'll come looking for me. And when he does, maybe I can get him to confess. Now you run along and do as I say," he replied as he motioned him toward the door. Isaiah left as quickly as he had come, feeling uneasy about the instructions, but more than willing to do what John had asked.

That night John gave the little iron fish charm to Wilma. She was overcome with emotion because she and John had talked about the meaning of the little charm many times. His respect for his heritage and his noble ideals had caused her love for him to grow deeper than she had ever expected. Somehow she had not expected him to give her one of the charms.

"I'll always cherish this little piece of rusty iron, my love. I'd rather have it than a golden charm," she whispered in his ear as she embraced him tightly. "I'll always carry it proudly. To me it represents not only a symbol of love, but a symbol of your dedication and hard work in an honest business. You're the best husband a woman could have, and I hope we'll have a hundred years together."

"Sweetheart, you're the most important person in my life, and I'm so proud of you. You always know just the right thing to say," he responded in a whisper because the lump in his throat kept him from speaking any louder. "I love you. Marrying you was the best thing I ever did."

It was about a month later that John had his chance to talk with George LeGrow. He was riding north, on his way to the docks. Ginger was walking with brisk strides as if she looked forward to seeing the ocean. He saw someone coming down the road, with dust flying, as if he were going to a fire. As the wagon came closer John recognized that it was George. When George saw John, he pulled his horse around and blocked the road with his wagon.

"I hear you've been accusing me of killing somebody," George yelled in a belligerent manner, as he drew back his bullwhip in a threatening motion.

"Well, George, what do you know about the death of Dr. Smith and the Richburg girl?" John asked in as calm a voice as he could manage.

"I don't know nothin!" bellowed George. "You must be crazy. I'm gonna teach you to go all over town accusing me of something."

He lifted his whip again and brought the blood from John's face with a sharp crack. The next swing, the whip was stopped short when John grabbed it and pulled George from his wagon to the ground. He jumped off his wagon and on top of George. As the scuffle continued something fell from George's pocket. It was a little iron fish charm. John quickly grabbed it and saw the initials "D.S." which had been cut on the back side of it.

"I knew it! I knew it! You did kill Dr. Smith!"

George lunged at John, with his hunting knife poised to kill him.

John rolled out of the way, and George fell on his face. He just lay there. John gazed at him for several minutes, thinking it was a trick. When he reached to turn him over, he could see that the knife had slipped between George's ribs, probably piercing his heart. He checked for a pulse, but there was none. George was dead.

John placed George in the latter's wagon, without removing the knife, turned it around, and briskly hit the horse with a limb he broke off a small tree nearby. He watched for several minutes in disbelief as the horse and wagon headed toward the LeGrow plantation, carrying the body of Simon LeGrow's oldest son. Then he turned his own around and headed Ginger for home.

On the way home, he was troubled by George's death and how it would be viewed by others. "What should I do? What if Simon LeGrow believes I killed George?" The thoughts raced through his mind as he turned Ginger onto the lane leading to his house.

"What on earth is wrong, dear?" Wilma asked as he walked into the house. "You look like you've seen a ghost."

John waited several minutes before he could bring himself to explain what had happened. After several hours, they decided that they must leave Charles Town. Wilma had an uncle who lived at Silver Bluff, in Granville County, South Carolina, in the western interior of the state. From all the letters she had received from her cousin, Mary Gascoigne, the area was still a wilderness inhabited by large landowners and planters who desperately needed help to clear the new fertile land. It was a land of great risk and greater promise.

The Indians still inhabited several reservations and moved freely about the area. There were certain dangers in the new land, but maybe they could find a new life there, out of the reach of Simon LeGrow. Silver Bluff and the New Windsor Township were over a hundred miles away. It would be at least a three days' journey.

"Dear, you look so big," John said as he tenderly hugged her. "Are you sure you're up to the trip?"

"I'll be all right, John," she whispered softly in his ear. "I love you more than life, and I don't want to lose you. We have no choice. I'll start getting things ready."

"I'd better tell Catherine. I'll stop by and tell Zeke and the others while I'm at it. Dry those tears, sweetheart; everything will work out for the best," he whispered as he kissed her gently and turned to leave.

Wilma dried her eyes and pondered, as the words of her wedding vows kept ringing in her mind, "Wither thou goest, I will go . . ." They took on added meaning under these new circumstances. She shrugged her shoulders as if trying to be brave, and proceeded to make things ready to leave.

Catherine greeted John with a big hug as he walked into the house, but sensed something was amiss. "What's wrong, dear?" she asked as she stood back and looked into his eyes. "You look worried, son. Is there anything I can do to help?"

"Mamma, I have some bad news. I know who killed the doctor. It was George LeGrow. He and I had a fight today, and he's dead. He fell on his own knife, but I'm sure Mr. LeGrow and the rest of his sons will come looking for me. Wilma and I have decided we'd better leave Charles Town," John explained rapidly, dreading to see her reaction. "We're going to Silver Bluff where Wilma's kin folk live. We'll send for you when we get settled, if you want to come live with us."

"Son, is there nothing else you can do?" Catherine pleaded in earnest. "Surely you can prove your innocence."

John held his head in his hands and replied, "I'm afraid Simon LeGrow won't give me a chance to do that. Wilma and I have talked about it for several hours, and we feel it's the only thing to do."

"Well, if you're sure, John," she responded with sad eyes. "But it's such a drastic thing to do. Your whole life will be changed."

"I know, Mamma," he answered slowly. "But it's something we must do."

Catherine walked over to the fireplace, and after several moments was able to pull out a loose stone. She reached into the hollow spot and brought out a little brown bag. Turning to John she said, as she offered him the bag, "Here, son, I've been saving this for a long time. There are about fifty pounds here. Take it. You may need it to get a new start."

"I can't do that, Mamma," he insisted. "I can't take your money."

Catherine placed the bag in his hand and firmly replied, "John, I insist. I'm an old woman, but I've got plenty to wear and plenty to eat, and a good roof over my head. Now take it. Don't argue. Just do it."

John put the money in his pocket as they both fought back tears. They embraced for a long time as if it might be their last. Catherine stood at the door and watched him as his wagon rolled out of sight, among the dark shades of evening. He was the only son she had ever known, and now he, too would be gone out of her life. She had never felt so alone.

Wilma had most of the smaller items ready to go by the time her husband returned. John loaded the pots, kettles, quilts, tools, and as much of the other larger pieces of furniture as the wagon would hold. They decided to rest a while and leave just before daybreak so they would not have to say any more goodbyes. Leaving before daylight might be safer also, they agreed.

Both went to bed, fully clothed, and tried to rest. But sleep came to neither as they thought about how their lives would be changed and what lay ahead of them in a new and strange land. They lay motionless all night, holding hands, awake but deep in thought and not speaking a word. Just before daybreak, they arose, had a hurried breakfast, loaded a few final items onto the wagon, and departed.

On a rise just outside of the town, John pulled Ginger to a halt. He and Wilma turned and looked back a last time at the sleepy little settlement of Charles Town. Smoke was rising from a number of the chimneys on this chilly Indian Summer morning. The large full moon gave its bright light freely. The stagecoach trail was clearly visible, as were the houses and the shops they were leaving behind.

In the distance an owl struggled out its familiar sound, and a dog barked wildly somewhere on the other side of town. Another dog answered from some distant spot, overpowering the smaller sounds of nature.

"Let's go, Ginger," he commanded as he pulled on the reins. "We've got a long way to go before sundown."

Wilma pulled the quilt tighter around her and leaned closer to him as if to say, "We're on our own now."

John knew he had to go through St. Georges and Saltketchers before he could reach the main road to the New Windsor Township where Silver Bluff was located. He hoped they might be able to reach St. Georges by sundown if they did not take the wrong trail. He stopped many times during the morning to ask directions. Every time they came near a spring or creek he helped Wilma down to the water so she could wash away the dust and cool her swollen feet. As the afternoon wore on and the road seemed to become more and more bumpy, he noticed that behind her quiet smile were weary eyes.

They stopped at a public well about five o'clock in the evening. It was an artesian well, flowing with crystal clear water. Wilma drank until she could drink no more. She soaked her feet in the watering trough as Ginger filled herself. John had almost made up his mind to find a place near this well to spend the night when a farmer leading his horse came to the well for water. He was a ragged and sickly-looking skeleton of a man. A big frayed straw hat covered his thin gray hair, and his eyes were so crossed John wondered how he could see. He looked like he had the mind of a child.

"Good evening neighbor, I'm John Dicks and this is my wife, Wilma. We're headed to the New Windsor Township, and I understand we'll have to go through St. Georges. Do you happen to know how far it is to St. Georges?"

"Yep. I sho do. I'm Miles Brewton. Dis is my hoss, Red. It's 'bout five more miles. Jes keep on dis same trail," he said with a grin.

"Do you think we can make it, dear?" John asked with concern in his voice. "I don't want to push you too hard."

Wilma took her feet out of the water and smiled as she said, "Sure, sweetheart. This big belly won't stop me. Let's get going."

She was tougher than he had thought. He smiled to himself as he climbed into the seat beside her, and said, "You're just as tough and stubborn as your Papa. And I love it. I bet you'll have a fat little boy with red hair just like Zeke."

She smiled as she slid nearer to him and placed her hand on his knee.

As the sun slowly set behind the tree line up ahead, they saw a clearing in the road. As they drew nearer, John realized it was St. Georges. Wilma asked him to stop at the first house and ask if they could tie up the wagon in their yard. She wanted to be near someone's home when she slept in the wagon. The first family he met was large and had no extra room, but invited them to sleep in their barn. They were thrilled at having fresh hay as a soft bed. It was better than sleeping in the wagon.

The following day appeared to be harder on Wilma. She acted brave and tried not to let John know just how uncomfortable she was. She looked weaker to him, and he decided as the evening shadows began to fall that he would stop at the first place which looked comfortable enough for her. They were only a few miles from Saltketcher when he noticed an old frame church on the left of the trail. It had a well and a watering trough.

"Would you like to sleep in that church tonight, dear?" he asked as he pointed toward it.

"Whatever you think best, sweetheart," she weakly responded.

John took the blankets into the church, made a bed for her on the last pew, and returned to the wagon where she was waiting. He picked her up and carried her in his arms, gently laying her on the bench. "I'll be back in a minute, just as soon as I water and feed Ginger," he whispered as he gently kissed her on the forehead.

After feeding and caring for Ginger, John returned to the church. He and Wilma had a quiet meal together. Afterward, exhausted from the day's travels, they both went to sleep on some blankets in the center aisle of the church.

About two hours later, John was awakened by a loud noise. The light of the bright moon streamed through the cracks in the window shutters of the little church building. At first he could not make out what it was. He listened carefully and decided it had to be the voices of several people. They talked low and loud alternately, and laughed wildly like drunk men. After a moment he heard Ginger whinny and stamp her feet restlessly. Whoever it was meant no good, he thought.

He slipped on his boots and quickly ran out the door, yelling as he went, "What's going on here? What are you men . . . ?" He was hit on the head with a large club.

"I believe you done killed him, Morgan," one of the men said slowly and fearfully. "Drag him under the church."

As daybreak began penetrating the surrounding woods with its rays, John was awakened by a big friendly dog. The animal had crawled under the church and was licking the blood from his face.

John quickly remembered where he was, rolled out from under the building, and ran up the steps to the door. He stopped short, as if afraid to open it.

"My God, my God, please don't let her be hurt!" he groaned as he leaned against the door.

Glancing around, he quickly realized that Ginger and the wagon with all his possessions were gone. He turned again and burst through the door. There Wilma was, laying half clothed, in the aisle of the church, on the blankets. Her swollen abdomen was showing, and her face was covered with blood.

John rushed in and fell upon her, sobbing uncontrollably for the first time since the morning after the fire that had killed his Mamma and Papa. After a while he sat up and looked at her face. It was beaten and bloody. It was too late. She had been raped by the drunken men, and he had not been able to protect her. There was blood under her fingernails. Apparently she had resisted and, as weak as she was, had fought to the very last. As he pitifully stroked her hair he noticed stab marks on her neck. He was in such a daze he could not think clearly. Covering her with the blankets, he stumbled outside the church to sit on the front steps. There he threw up, as he had done on the slave ship. It was so horrible he could not feel anything, not even anger.

He sat on the church steps for a long time, before he finally accepted the reality of the nightmare. Taking a shovel from under the church, he dug a grave in the little cemetery. He then brought Wilma's body and gently lowered it into the ground. His whole world had disappeared into a haze, blurred by the overwhelming tragedy and the tears he could not restrain.

Giving her a simple funeral, he quoted from the Bible, just like the minister had done over the grave of his Mamma and Papa. He gathered several stones and placed them upon her grave in the shape of a cross. He had no other way of marking the grave, but the sight and the date would be burned forever into his memory. September 15th, 1741, was the day he lost his wife, his unborn child, and possibly his will to live.

John sat in the edge of the woods for what seemed like hours. He could not bear the thought of leaving his sweet, warm Wilma all alone in that cold ground. He was crushed. He had lost everything. He had the same feeling again as he had on the day he sifted through the ashes of his Papa's house. He was once again reduced to ashes. Finally, he decided he must continue on his journey to the New Windsor Township. As he stood at the entrance of the church yard, he looked back at the fresh grave once more and then slowly turned toward the main trail.

As John entered the main road from the church lane, he saw Ginger coming toward him. She had no bridle, no reins, and no yoke. The thieves had taken everything. She must have walked off during the night. John ran toward her, overjoyed to see his faithful horse. He rubbed and patted her neck as he turned her around and started walking together toward Saltketcher.

About a mile up the road John saw his medicine bag lying in the ditch. He went over and quickly picked it up, clutching it tightly to his chest, as proudly as if it were his newborn child. All his medicines appeared to be in good order, and the eight fish charms were untouched. He clutched the bag tightly as he walked on down the road, still in a daze. The events of the night before were a real shock for John. He was so crushed, he could not muster enough energy to be angry. He felt only overwhelming sorrow and loneliness. In his current state of mind, he was just too numb to think of anything, even of revenge. Revenge, for the moment at least, would have to be left to a higher power.

After a while he reached into his pocket and felt the money bag that Catherine had given him. It was the first time he had thought of it. He also felt the little fish his father had made for him. Somehow, it made him feel better. As he fingered the charm in his pocket, he thought out loud, "It has withstood the raging fire. Somehow I'll do the same." He gritted his teeth with new determination as he and Ginger walked toward the unknown.

3
The Long Search
1741-1779

"Mamma, look over there!" Mary shouted excitedly as she continued stirring the clothes in the boiling wash pot. "The rider of that horse looks sick. He's about to fall off his horse. Do you suppose he's coming here?"

Mary and Catherine Gascoigne stopped their work and watched the horse and the strange rider turn down the lane which led to their house at Silver Bluff. The horse came to a stop at the edge of their yard, and the rider fell to the ground in complete exhaustion.

Mary's long black hair hung down her back in one large braid. Her light blue eyes were about the same color as the sky on a bright summer morning.

For a young girl of fourteen she had a well-developed and attractive figure. Her face was fair and quick to show a pleasant smile. As the only daughter of Catherine and William Gascoigne, she had learned to be helpful around the house and in the field. She had been sheltered from the unpleasant things which went on in the frontier area, but had been kept from the pleasant things as well. She felt alone and isolated and nervous when strangers were present.

Catherine was the sister of Zeke Dunbar. Her uncommon accent was very much like his. They had come to the new world from

Ireland when they were children. Her flaming red hair gave the appearance of a woman full of life, and her bright green eyes were not dimmed by the hardships of the frontier life. She was still tall and thin, with a frame much thinner than Mary's. Her complexion was ruddy, and her well-preserved teeth had a wide space in the front. For a woman of thirty-five, she was well-preserved and appeared much younger. To an unsuspecting stranger, she and Mary might pass as sisters.

"Come help me with him, Mary!" Catherine yelled back to her daughter, who had stayed back near the washpot because of fear.

"What's your name?" she asked as she bent over the young man.

"I'm John Dicks," he answered with a struggle as he tried to get up. "I'm Wilma Dunbar's husband. Could I have some water? I've had none all day."

Catherine led John to the big bench by the well and began drawing up a bucket of water. She handed him a big dipper full.   "Mary, run get your Papa," she called. Then, turning to John, she asked curiously, "Wilma didn't come with you? It's been so long since I've seen her. I'm not sure I would know her."

Catherine fell silent. She could tell by the look in his eyes something dreadful had happened. She was shocked into disbelief as John related how Wilma had been killed on the way to Silver Bluff.

As John was relating this story to Catherine, William and Mary came riding around the corner of the hedgerow. They were both on the horse which he had been riding as he supervised his slaves in the field. William was a rotund but hardy man, who was ambitious and had dreams of building a fortune from trading with the Indians. His dark brown beady eyes gave the impression that he could be devious when necessary or when advantageous. He had a red face and a long forehead which stretched about halfway back on his crown. His ruddy face was well-shaven except for a neatly trimmed mustache above his upper lip and a small brown goatee on his chin which matched his slicked-back hair.

"What's wrong, Catherine?" he called as he dismounted and helped Mary down. He turned and yelled to several of his slaves who were peeping around the corner of the house, "You all get back to work, or I'll use my whip!"

After Catherine told him John's story he turned to her and said, "Let's take him in and let him take a nap while you fix supper. We'll talk some more after he's rested. I'll try to think of some way to help," he continued as he took John's arm and led him into the house.

It was the following morning before John opened his eyes again. He was awakened by the smell of ham cooking over the open fire in the chimney. As he opened his eyes he saw Mary again. She was bending over him, shaking his arm, and coaxing softly, "Breakfast is ready. Are you able to get up?"

She looked a lot like Wilma, except for the shiny black hair. Her beautiful, warm face caused the pain of the nightmare to return. He turned his face to the wall to hide the tears and pain. She patiently waited until he could get control of himself, and led him by the arm to the kitchen.

After a hearty breakfast of ham, bread cakes, and corn mush, John and William sat and talked for several hours. William tried to change the conversation away from the tragedy. He began talking about the differences between Charles Town and Silver Bluff. He had obtained his six hundred and fifty acres of land at Silver Bluff in 1738, and had cleared little.

"John," he said, as he rose to his feet. "As you can see, my Indian trading business is very small. I've turned to stock farming and planting. I just don't have a place for you here. I've got to check on my slaves in the field. I'll be back in about an hour. I'll take you over to George Galphin's trading post. He's been in the business several years longer than me. He has a large store with a blacksmith shop attached. It has been vacant since old Joe Zuebly died last year. I expect he'll be glad to have someone like you take over that shop. He trades with almost all the Indians—the Creeks, the Cherokees, and Euchees. He has learned to speak the language of almost all of them. I suppose that's why they flock to him. He also trades with most of the white settlers and planters on both sides of the river. It'll be good for you if you can make a deal with him."

"Thank you, Mr. Gascoigne," John responded. "I really appreciate your help. You've been more than kind to me, and I hope to repay you."

A little more than an hour later, William returned from the fields.

He and John then hitched up a wagon for the trip into Silver Bluff. The countryside they traveled through was very pleasant. The moss-filled trees looked very much like Charles Town. The sandy trails reminded John of the low-country roads he had traveled with Dr. Smith so many days and nights.

"We're almost there. Galphin's trading post will surprise you. That clearing is the Silver Bluff landing," William explained as he pointed with one hand and shook the reins with the other. "George Galphin's trading post is almost in sight."

As the wagon neared the landing, John noticed that the sand appeared to be mixed with silver. "I see where this place got its name," he said with a grin. "I'll bet many a man thought he had discovered silver when he first saw this sand."

"That's true," William responded. "I've heard the old Indian tales about DeSoto landing here in 1540 and thinking he had found unlimited wealth. He let one of the Indian girls outsmart him. Don't let that happen to you, John."

George Galphin was not quite as old as John had pictured him. He was a red-haired, red-faced Irishman with a big belly and a big laugh. He grabbed John's hand, shook it strongly, and with his big red nose glowing, thanked William for bringing him to see his competitor's trading post.

"I sure can use a good smithy," he said as he pointed to several horses waiting outside the main building. "There's not one on this side of the river. Old Joe Zuebly always stayed busy when he was alive."

The trading post was stacked full of thousands of items, some of which John had never seen, not even in Charles Town. There were food stuffs like dried beans, corn, salt pork, dried venison, salt mackeral, apples, Irish potatoes, molasses, barley corn, vinegar, grits, brown sugar, best sugar, wines, pepper, tea and coffee. The walls were covered with animal furs and skins, leather goods, as well as white ruffled shirts, gilt belts, handkerchiefs, yellow, blue and scarlet ribbon, felt hats, thread, cotton stockings, and other assorted items of clothing. Every corner was filled with falling axes, grubbing hoes, crosscut saws and files, beaver traps, hatchets, augers, and assorted housewares. John was particularly interested in the pipes and tobacco as well as the sheet iron, flint, smith's hammer, smith's anvil, bar iron, and chisels. Near the front of the building were wooden boxes full of bright beads, feathers, and bracelets of silver or pewter. These were popular with the Indians. In the back of the store, Mr. Galphin kept several large wooden boxes out of the sight of everyone except those whom he permitted to look. Several of the boxes contained large earthenware pots filled with homemade liquors and beer. Others contained French wines, Scotch whiskey, brandy, and rum. This department was also popular with the Indians as well as the planters. In a controlled area there were trader's guns, read lead, mohawks, square-eyed hatchets, gunflints, guns, French knives, razors, riding saddles, shrouds, scalping knives, ammunition, hook knives, and muskets. The store was so full of merchandise there was hardly enough walking space left for traders. There were several white settlers in the building and at least a dozen Indians waiting to see Mr. Galphin.

John and William walked over to the old unused blacksmith shop while Mr. Galphin waited on his customers. The building was pretty much ready for use. John was pleased with the room across the back of it. He decided immediately that he would live in that room until he could do better.

"Well, Dicks," bellowed Mr. Galphin as he came over from the trading post, "do you want it or not? It's yours if you'll make good use of it." He lowered his head and looked out of the corner of his eye as he continued, "All I expect is half of what you take in."

"That's a little steep," John complained as he looked with distress toward Mr. Gascoigne. "I don't know if I can get by on half."

"Awright, I get one quarter of all you take in," Galphin said with an air of finality. "Take it or leave it."

"I'll take it!" John quickly responded. "I'll move in today, just as soon as I can get back from Mr. Gascoigne's with my horse, Ginger."

John had been operating the blacksmith shop for about a month when he noticed that Galphin had not been riding his large white stallion, which was his most prized possession, and which he proudly referred to as General. "What's wrong with General, George?" he asked when Galphin came to bring by a customer for the blacksmith shop.

"I don't know. He won't eat, and he's too weak to stand alone. I love that horse. It's like a member of the family."

"I'll be glad to take a look at him, George, if you want me to," John said with confidence. "I've had some good experience with doctoring on animals."

The clever Indian trader appeared a bit surprised and answered, "If you can do somethin' to help General, I'll forever be in your debt." He called one of his Indian servants and instructed her to take John to see the horse.

"Follow me," the beautiful Indian girl said with a broad smile as she motioned to John. She was tall and thin and appeared to be more than a servant. Her beautiful white teeth showed frequently as she looked back and smiled with almost every step. She led him to the rear of the stockade where Mr. Galphin's beautiful white stallion was kept in a well-built stable. The sturdy building, the clean hay and well-stocked feed troughs gave an indication of how much the horse was treasured.

"I Captain Galphin's woman," the attractive Indian girl said as she gracefully fell to the floor on a pile of clean hay and stretched out in an alluring pose. "I wait on you."

John felt a little uneasy and tried to make small talk as he examined the horse. He could not help noticing how the beautiful Indian girl looked at him. "What's your name?" he asked.

"Captain Galphin calls me Angel. My real name is Tender Leaf. He bought me when small. I been his woman ever since. He got five women. He don't need me much now," she answered as she twisted and turned on the hay.

"Where do you live?" he asked as he felt his face begin to flush warm.

"I live in house behind trading post. I alone most of time. Maybe you come see me some night."

"I couldn't do that, Angel. My wife was killed just a few weeks ago. I couldn't look at another woman. Not now. I'm not sure if I'll ever be able to love anyone again," he answered as he nervously tried to feed the horse some of the medicine he had mixed with feed.

"Will horse live?" she asked, sensing that she should change the subject.

"I hope so. I've done about all I can do now. I'll come back later and check on him."

John turned to leave, and Angel reached out her hands toward him, indicating she wanted him to help her up. He nervously took her by the hands and helped her up. She held on to his hands after standing, drew him near and whispered, "Remember what I say. I make you happy."

For the next two weeks John stopped by almost daily to check on General and to feed him the mixture of medicines. Each time he entered the stable, Angel was either already there or came in shortly after he arrived. Fortunately, General was completely well by the end of the second week. John's nerves could not have stood much more of Angel's advances.

Because of the spectacular recovery of the beautiful white stallion, the reputation of John Dicks spread throughout the entire New Windsor Township and for many miles around, on both sides of the river. Before long, everyone called upon him when they needed help or advice about their animals. He was anxious to serve everyone: Negroes, Indians, Swiss, Germans, Irish, French, or English. They were all friends to him.

By late May, 1742, John Dicks had been in the Silver Bluff area for nearly nine months. He had made a number of friends and earned the respect of a fair portion of the local residents. It also gave him a good deal of satisfaction to be of assistance to so many people.

One morning while he was working in his little shop, John was struck by spring fever. The sun's rays were streaming through the cracks in the shop roof and the birds were chirping in the walnut tree outside. With every ring of his hammer, John grew more and more restless. Finally he could stand it no longer. He dropped the hammer and threw the last horseshoe into the water. There were no customers waiting, so he decided to slip out while he could.

"I don't have anyone to feed except myself," he thought. So why am I keeping my nose to the grindstone like this? I'm going fishing."

He took off his heavy leather apron and ceremoniously threw it to the ground. Grabbing the old pole and line that had been left across the rafters of the shop by Joe Zuebly, he darted out the door, and headed toward the high bluff just below Silver Bluff landing. He fished a while in that spot and then moved a little farther south. After many moves he was several miles downstream.

Just as he was becoming disgusted with his luck and was about to pull his hook out of the water for the last time, John heard a spine-chilling scream. It sounded like a girl. He threw down his fishing pole and ran toward the sound. As he approached a clearing among the tall virgin trees, he saw two white men struggling with an Indian girl. They were trying to tear off her clothes. He yelled as he continued running toward them with his hunting knife in hand. The men turned the girl loose and ran off into the woods.

John had just put away his knife and was bending over her, looking at her cuts and bruises when nine young Indian men came toward him from all directions, with their spears outstretched and knives in their other hands. The Indian girl motioned to them not to harm him, but they bound him anyway and marched him and her on to the Indian village.

John's knees were about to buckle on him when he was brought before the Chief of the tribe. The young braves all shouted excitedly to the Chief in a language John could not understand, and several of them poked him with the ends of their spears. From the general excitement and the way the Chief treated her, John surmised that this girl was the Chief's daughter. The Chief gave her a fatherly look and lovingly drew her to himself, much like any father who had a hurt child. She pulled his head down to her and whispered something into his ear. The Chief smiled broadly, raised his arms, said several Indian words, and motioned the young men away. Then he stretched out his hand toward John and began speaking in broken English. "Daughter say it not you who hurt her. She say you save life. Thank you much. Come sit in my tent. I think of way to repay. I know, I give five best horses."

John thanked the Chief and told him he was honored by his friendship. He said, "I also have a gift of friendship I want to give to you. I'll bring it back to you tomorrow if you'll allow me to."

The Chief stood, folded his arms, and declared, "I, Brown Eagle, Chief of the Euchees and counselor of the Creek nation, I make you blood son. You not be harmed by my people . . . never! You welcome here forever."

John left, riding on a fine black horse with a white star on its forehead. He was escorted by four of the young men of the Cofitachequi village, who were riding the other four horses which the Chief had given to him.

The next day John returned to the village and was graciously escorted to the Chief's tent by two young men who apparently were serving as guards for the village. After the formal greeting, he reached into his pocket and handed the Chief one of his treasured fish charms with the three crosses. He had stamped "B.E." on the back and punched a hole in it near the sharp point of the head. He had threaded a leather cord through it so the Chief could wear it around his neck. He explained what the charm meant to him all his life and how his father had given him one before his death. He stood and helped the Chief put it around his neck, as he explained, "I'm a poor man. When I arrived here, I had nothing left. This is the most valuable thing I can give to you, but I give it with respect and honor. I hope you'll receive it as a symbol of our friendship and trust. You and your people are also welcome at my place anytime."

The Chief thanked John and assured him he would wear the symbol always. They would be friends always. John returned to Silver Bluff landing and his blacksmith shop, not realizing just how important this new friendship would eventually become.

Later in the week, William Gascoigne visited the trading post and stopped by to admire John's new horses, which were being kept behind the shop in the horse pen. "Those are the finest horses I've ever seen," he said as he saw John coming out the back door of the shop. "I don't know how you do it, John." He turned from the horses and continued, "Catherine has been asking about you. She wants you to come to dinner on Sunday."

John shook his hand as he warmly responded, "It'll be a pleasure. I'll surely be there."

The Sunday sun was uncommonly bright and welcome on the crisp June morning as John headed Ginger in the direction of the Gascoigne house and trading post. He was happy to be visiting with the people who were the nearest thing to family he had.

Mrs. Gascoigne busied herself with the cooking, while William showed John around his trading post and farm. Mary helped her mother in the kitchen, even though she was not needed. The kitchen slave was apparently doing most of the work. William tried to convince John to set up his blacksmith shop at his trading post. He realized now that it would bring many customers his way. John felt sure it was too soon to make a move. He had just established a fairly good business at Galphin's trading post and did not want to leave yet.

After a hearty and delicious dinner, John, Mary, William, and Catherine walked the little path down to the River and watched several canoes of Indians headed north to Silver Bluff Landing. The trees were green, the grass was lush and thick, and the sweet smell of honeysuckles was in the air. John felt relaxed for the first time since the day he arrived at Silver Bluff. Somehow that dark day did not seem real. It was more like a nightmare that had never happened. Mary walked along near John. She was fair and beautiful with long shiny black hair. He should certainly have fallen head-over-heels in love with her, but it had been only nine months since Wilma had been killed. He would need more time before he could take a genuine interest in another woman.

John stayed in constant touch with the Gascoignes and visited them for Sunday dinner several times over the next few months. Each time he came, Mary's heart would throb at the sight of him. Catherine also had a warm feeling for him. To her he was like a son she had never been able to have. William had business in mind. He continued to pressure John into leaving the Galphin trading post. His trading business was declining fast, especially with the Indians, and he was sure that John could draw many of the customers from Galphin.

After about a year at Silver Bluff, John started taking a special interest in Mary, who was about five years younger than him. They took long walks in the woods and along the river on the Sunday afternoons when he came to have dinner with them. Pretty soon he started coming to visit upon Mary's invitation.

Catherine seemed pleased enough, but William was a little

apprehensive about the developing relationship. Mary was too young for marriage, and furthermore he had looked forward to her marrying a wealthy planter or merchant. In fact, he had thought about sending her to Charles Town to stay with the Dunbars for a while. Surely she could meet the right people there. However, if John became a part of the family, he would certainly be obligated to move his blacksmith trade away from Galphin's trading post.

"I would certainly have him obligated to me and my business," he told Catherine one day in September of 1742, as they were watching John and Mary walk toward the sheep pasture. "He'll never be a rich man, I'm afraid. He's a smart and hardworking man, but we know he was cut from Quaker cloth. He's just not in the mainstream of the area. I doubt if he'll ever be willing to own slaves. I just can't see a long term future with him," he continued as Catherine started back into the house. "Wait a minute, Catherine. What do you think about the situation?"

"Well, I like him. He's an honorable young man," she replied with a satisfied look. "There's a lot of things worse than not being rich."

"That's just like a woman," William complained as he followed her into the house. "They never think about where the money comes from."

Later in the evening, John and Mary came into the house holding hands. They had a nervous look on their faces. John addressed William in serious tones, "Mr. Gascoigne, I would like to ask your permission for Mary's hand in marriage. I'm not a wealthy man, as you know, but I'm sure I can provide for her in the manner she's accustomed to. We would both appreciate your blessings."

William thought for a while and responded, "I don't know, John. She's so young. Catherine and I will talk about it and let you know tomorrow."

John left the Gascoigne home and rode back to the room behind his blacksmith shop, his mind both exhilarated by the prospect of marrying Mary and concerned at the thought that her father might not approve. Such thoughts caused him a restless sleep that night and the following day. As he worked in the blacksmith shop, his mind kept turning to Mary. Try as he could, he could not put her or her parents' possible disapproval of their marriage out of his mind.

As the day drew to a close and Mr. Gascoigne still had not come by, John grew more concerned. He felt sure that some excuse would be made for rejecting his request. He thought that Mrs. Gascoigne would approve but that the final decision would be made by Mr. Gascoigne.

"I don't believe he's coming," John said to himself impatiently, as his hammer rang out like the trading post dinner bell. "Maybe I should have been more considerate of him. Maybe I should have accepted his offer to open a blacksmith shop at his trading post," he continued, deep in thought, eagerly glancing at the door.

Suddenly, warm and tender hands were quietly placed over his eyes from behind. The surprise made his heart leap. It was Angel.

"Angel, what do you mean, slipping up on me like that?"

"I surprise you. I get lonely. I need somebody to talk," she answered with pouting lips as she moved around to the front of him and pulled on his apron.

"You're going to get us both killed one of these days. If Mr. Galphin catches you here, we'll both be in trouble. Now move and let me finish my work. I've got a lot to do."

"I wait," she said as she put her arms around his neck.

"Now, Angel," he said in frustration. "I'm expecting company any minute. Now do me a favor and go home."

"Is company woman?"

"Yes. I'm expecting Mary Gascoigne and her parents. I've asked her to marry me," he answered nervously. "Her father is supposed to give me an answer tonight."

"Don't do it. Don't marry. I make you happy," Angel said passionately, as she kissed him fiercely on the mouth.

About that time the shop door suddenly opened, and Mary stood frozen, staring in shock and disbelief, while her parents stopped dead in their tracks. For a moment John could not move or speak. Angel still hung around him, even more deliberate now, and flashed a satisfied smile at the visitors.

"Let's go!" William said as he reached forward and took Mary by the arm. A burst of tears flooded Mary's eyes as she turned and looked back at John's embarrassed expression and red face.

"Now look what you've done! Go on home, or I'll tell Mr. Galphin you've been hanging around here. He'll probably give you what you deserve," John said in frustration as he pushed her away from him and rushed toward the door.

The wagon was gone. It had already rolled several hundred feet down the road as John began running after it, yelling, "Wait up! Please stop! Let me explain! It's not what you think!"

The wagon stopped without a word being spoken. John caught up with it and stood speechless, looking into Mary's watery eyes.

"How could you, John?" Catherine asked with a hurt tone in her voice. "I had complete confidence in you."

"I'm sorry this happened, but you must let me explain," he stammered nervously. "I've never laid a hand on that Indian girl. She belongs to Mr. Galphin. Ever since I doctored his white stallion, she has slipped in and out of the blacksmith shop several times, and always at the wrong moment. I've asked her every time not to come back, but I've been afraid to talk to Galphin about it. I had just asked her to leave. She knew you were coming, and that's why she tried to make a scene. Please believe me. It's not what it looked like."

"I believe you, John," Mary said as she reached toward him with both arms. "I guess we shouldn't have left without giving you a chance to explain."

The anger in William's eyes slowly melted as he and his family climbed from the wagon. He turned and said, "We'll give you the benefit of the doubt, son. I guess we owe you that."

After shaking hands, William announced in a very formal manner, "John, Mary's mother and I have spent most of the night and day discussing the good and bad aspects of a marriage between you and Mary."

John's heart sank in his chest. Mr. Gascoigne was again looking too serious to suit him.

"We've agreed," he continued. "We'll be pleased with the marriage and will give you our blessings."

The shadow of a smile came across John's face, while Mary and Catherine appeared overjoyed. He could not believe what he had heard. He had been prepared for the worst.

William continued as he looked John in the eye, "There is one condition. I expect you to move your blacksmith trade over to my trading post, just as soon as you can."

"It's agreed, Mr. Gascoigne," he eagerly responded. "I'll tell Mr. Galphin tomorrow, and see you early in the day so we can start making plans for the building."

"We must go now," William announced. "I'll be looking for you tomorrow. We can make plans for the new blacksmith shop while they make wedding plans."

John thanked William and Catherine as they mounted the seats of their wagon again. Mary grabbed his hand and kissed it before quickly turning and climbing into the wagon by herself, before he had a chance to help her. The following morning, John rode to the Gascoigne farm and discussed plans for the new blacksmith shop. He and William decided to locate it beside the trading post which was set about two hundred yards from the Gascoigne house, near the bank of the river. With the help of several slaves, the shop was completed in two weeks.

John's shop proved to be good for Mr. Gascoigne's business. There was a steady stream of settlers as well as Indians coming, to either have their horses shod or requesting John to come doctor their animals. They usually traded with William at his trading post since they had already made the trip and it was so near the blacksmith shop.

The Indians did not particularly like Gascoigne because of the bad treatment they had received in the past, but they traded with him anyway when they needed John's help. William was very satisfied with the new arrangement. It appeared his business might recover and become prosperous like George Galphin's.

It was a cold and windy January day in 1743. William was in a particularly good mood, especially for a Saturday morning. He took John and Mary in his wagon for a tour of his property on the Town Creek side. He proudly showed them the virgin timber which consisted of oak, pine, cypress, walnut, and cedar. Some of the land was low and flooded when the river rose, but much of it was high on a bluff. "This is the land I'm going to give you and Mary when you are married," he said in a pompous manner. "There's at least two hundred acres in this tract. There's plenty of good wood to build a house. Most of this land can be cleared to raise indigo and other money crops as well as table vegetables. You can have hog lots, cowpens, sheep pastures, and horse stables. There's plenty of land in this tract for the support of a big family." He paused a few seconds. "In fact, John, you may start building a house now, if you like. Maybe you can have it well under way by the time the license arrives from Charles Town."

John was excited about the property. It had a very good potential. It was rich with deer, wild boars, rabbits, squirrels, wild turkeys, and game of every sort. The woods were full of black walnut, hickory, and black cherry trees. In the summer he had seen blackberries and plums.

"I believe we could live off the natural food of the land," he said as he smiled at Mary. "We appreciate this gesture, Mr. Gascoigne."

Mary's excitement was showing plainly as she added, "We'll try to give you many fine grandchildren, Papa." It was a day Mary and John would never forget, and they looked forward to the time they would be married and settled on this new land of their own.

Now it was Mary's turn to keep slipping into the blacksmith shop. Her warm embraces and passionate kisses were always welcomed and desired. John had no intention of asking her to leave. As they lay beside each other on the fresh hay and talked about the future, the incident with Angel seemed unimportant. Mary did not feel insecure in any way. Her faith and trust in John was unshakable, but her patience was not. In fact, both were growing restless and impatient. It seemed the marriage license would never arrive from Charles Town.

For the next several weeks their impatience was only satisfied by the many times of intimate sharing on the soft fresh hay of the blacksmith shop. All the world was bright and promising, as they were oblivious to everyone and everything else around them. Nothing could darken their beautiful, small, personal world. They knew love as neither had known it before. Together they could conquer this new land and overcome all hardships.

John had forgotten how sad he had been. He had forgotten the pain of tragedy. All he could see was a happy and contented life with Mary. Nothing else was very important to him anymore.

On April 2 the stagecoach stopped at Gascoigne's trading post on its way to Galphin's trading post, Fort Moore, and Fort Augusta. The driver had a letter from Zeke Dunbar, addressed to John. He gave it to Mary, and she immediately took it over to the blacksmith shop.

John had no apparent excitement nor apprehension as he opened it because he had written many letters to Zeke since the first one telling of Wilma's tragic death. He had also received many from Zeke. As he read the letter, however, his countenance fell.

"What's wrong, John? You look sick. Is anything wrong with Uncle Zeke?"

"No, Mary," he answered as his eyes became moist. "Zeke says that Catherine Smith is dead. She was a mother to me after Mamma and Papa were killed in the fire. I must go to Charles Town. He also said old Simon LeGrow is dead."

On April 5th, Mary, John, William and Catherine set out for Charles Town in their heavily laden wagon. It was decided that John could take care of the unfinished business Catherine Smith had left behind. They would visit Catherine's brother, Zeke Dunbar, and the marriage could take place in the St. Phillips Church while they were there.

Catherine Smith, having no other children, left all her estate to John. He paid the funeral expenses, sold the property to Zeke, and tied up all loose ends that came to his attention. Zeke had also tried to be helpful with the estate until John could make the trip. He had gladly bought all the household furniture and other goods, except Dolly and the buggy. Zeke had told him that Catherine's last request was for him to keep the little cedar chest and the doctor's black medicine bag—something by which he could remember each of them.

John made his last trip to the house that once had been so familiar to him. He felt the emptiness of the house, which was not home without Catherine and Daniel Smith. He found the little cedar chest, opened it, and fumbled through the numerous contents. The little fish charm he had given her had been carefully preserved in this box, along with her gold wedding band and several other pieces of jewelry.

"I'll give Mary this wedding band," he said to himself as he closed the chest. "Money can't buy anything so precious as this."

He found the black medicine bag in the pantry where it had been since the death of Dr. Smith. "I'll use his bag in my animal doctoring business," he thought. "I'm sure he would like that." He took one last and final look at the house, then turned and slowly walked out.

John Dicks was married to Mary Gascoigne in the St. Phillips Church in Charles Town on April 14th, 1743. It was properly recorded on page 178 of the St. Phillips Parish Register in Charles Town.

The day after the wedding, the family started on their long journey back to the New Windsor Township and Silver Bluff. John and Mary were riding behind Dolly in the buggy. William and Catherine Gascoigne were in their wagon which had been filled with goods which William believed would bring a good profit at the Gascoigne trading post. The journey took three days because they all agreed they would not push too hard, but would enjoy the sights and sounds of spring along the way.

With their return from Charles Town, John resumed work on the cabin that was to be his and Mary's home. He had been working on it since the weather had become warm enough. Following the wedding, however, the cabin's completion became all the more important. He and Mary stayed with the Gascoignes for about two weeks, while he and several of William's slaves completed the cabin and made it ready to live in. John even traded William two of his best horses, which had been given to him by Chief Brown Eagle, for furniture and household goods.

John and Mary felt very prosperous as they moved into their new home. They had about five hundred pounds sterling, which he had received from the sale of Catherine Smith's estate. They still had three of the gift horses, Dolly, Ginger, the buggy, a wagon, and the blacksmith tools. John had no doubt that he could provide for his new bride and for as many children as they were blessed to have.

The following year their first child, John, Jr. was born, and in 1745 William came. Thomas was born in 1746 and Catherine followed in 1748.

A couple of months after the cabin was completed, John moved his blacksmith shop to his own property. He was one of the hardest working men in the New Windsor Township, which boasted at least three hundred and fifty white settlers, plus Indians and slaves. Beech Island, which was located several miles north had about a hundred Swiss settlers, and Augusta, which was on the Georgia side of the river, had a population of a hundred and twenty.

John felt that he was growing with the developing frontier. He had a fine herd of cattle, a large flock of sheep, a pen full of hogs, and a pasture full of fine horses. He worked from sunrise to sunset almost every day of his life, except Sundays. He had cleared more than a hundred acres of land and cultivated indigo, corn, and many vegetables for his own use and for sale. He also continued serving everyone who needed his blacksmith and animal doctoring talents.

The year 1749 brought an interruption to the peaceful development of the frontier which threatened the security of all those living in the area. In the spring of the year, the Creek Indians became hostile. The younger generation wanted to burn out the new white settlers who were becoming too numerous and too oppressive. The settlers had raped the young Indian women and killed several young Indian men. The Indians had had enough. The Euchees had not yet joined the rest of the Creek nation in a declaration of hostility, but anti-white sentiment ran deep in the Cofitachequi village.

In Beech Island, Fort Moore was being rebuilt with six-inch planks nailed to pine posts. It had four corner towers for small field pieces. Barracks for a hundred soldiers of the Crown were being built, even though there had been only about twenty-five stationed there over the past several years. There were signs of danger everywhere, and John feared for the safety of his wife and four small children. He decided he would visit his friend Chief Brown Eagle.

John punched a hole in his little fish charm. He threaded it with a piece of leather cord and placed it around his neck. He saddled the black horse with the white star on its forehead; the animal had been given him by the Chief. He emptied the doctor's black medicine bag and filled it with tobacco he had ordered from Charles Town, as well as two of his finest pipes. Mary reminded him to be careful as he hugged all four children and kissed her goodbye. He mounted his horse and headed for the Cofitachequi village.

About a thousand yards before he reached the clearing of the village, six young Indian men jumped out from behind the large cypress trees. They looked different, with bright colored paint on their face and arms. They also had a hostile look in their eyes. John raised the fish charm as a symbol or sign to them. They must have recognized it as one like the Chief wore. They immediately led him to Chief Brown Eagle who warmly greeted him by raising the iron fish he wore.

The Chief called for his daughter, whom John had saved from attackers. She came immediately, with her husband who was one of the respected leaders of the tribe. John greeted them by raising his fish charm. They all followed the Chief into his tent where John opened his bag and filled a pipe with tobacco.

The Chief, his son-in-law, and John sat for several minutes, passing the pipe around while the Indian princess waited patiently. John waited for the Chief to speak first.

"Now what can I do for blood son?" the Chief asked. "I not forget my word."

John slowly and carefully responded, "Honorable Chief, I have a wife and four children, and I've been working very hard to make a good life for them in this land. I know there is a threat of danger brewing in the whole area. I want peace and safety and honor, for your people and mine. Is there some way we can avoid the spilling of innocent blood by both our peoples?"

The Chief interrupted, "My people try to live in peace. Your people take our land. They fleece us in trading and now kill and rape our young. I too old for trouble, but young men restless and want to fight."

"I don't want your children to be in danger any more than mine," declared John. "There must be some way we can live together in peace. Please don't do anything until I have had a chance to have a meeting with our leaders."

"I, Chief Brown Eagle, will not let my people do anything. I not join Creek nation treaty for two days. You return in two days with plan," the Chief said in a deliberate and firm tone as if to impress his young son-in-law.

John was escorted from the village and lost no time in carrying the message to Mr. Gascoigne, George Galphin, John Tebler, the leader of the Swiss settlers in the highland section of New Windsor, and several of the other large planters. They agreed to have a meeting that very night at George Galphin's trading post.

There were at least fifty people at the meeting. All were either the head of a big family, a large landowner, or a leader in their particular section of the township. John told of his visit with the Chief, and the grave concerns of the Indians. After a meeting of about six hours, with the lanterns dimly burning, and with the arrogant pride of many having been partially melted, a plan was finalized. John acted as mediator in hammering out a plan which was acceptable to them all.

The following day he returned to the village. After all the formalities were observed, he outlined the plan for the Chief which he had written and which included the signatures of all those present at the meeting. He addressed the Chief and several of his tribe leaders in careful and deliberate tones, "Honorable Chief and brave men. I would like to read what we have all agreed upon." He unfolded the paper and began:

"We, the people of the New Windsor Township, realizing that the Indians have legitimate complaints, do order and will enforce the following: (1) No settler will set foot on the Indian property without invitation. (2) Any person causing harm to any Cofitachequi Indian will be brought to justice by whipping, imprisonment, or hanging, depending upon the severity of the harm. (3) Cofitachequi Indians will have full right to hunt and fish on any land in the township so long as they bring no harm to settlers' persons, family, or property. (4) Indians will have freedom to trade with any trader without fear of reprisals. (5) Indians will retain right to execute justice on anyone who invades village and property and harms its people. (6) Any Indian suffering harm at the hands of the white man or harmed on property of settlers will be avenged by local court of settlers in a speedy and severe manner. (7) Settlers will petition the Crown for an annual grant of foodstuffs and other supplies to ratify this agreement each year and to compensate for any inequities which may have occurred during the preceding year.

"As a consideration of this agreement, the Indians will bear no arms against the settlers. They will bring no harm to the settlers, their families, or their property. Dated and signed on this second day of May, 1749 by all the following . . . "

John folded the agreement and handed it to the Chief. He sat down and waited for the Chief to speak. He observed the pleased look on the faces of the young men, but the Chief gave no sign of his emotion.

"Blood-son will keep word. Will other white men do same?" asked Brown Eagle as he rose from his seat.

"I'll do all within my power to see that they do," reassured John. "We've set up a local court to deal with any violators. I've been chosen as the judge. I promise your people justice and honor, to the best of my ability."

"If blood-son be judge, we be satisfied," the Chief stated in an official manner and tone, as he read the eyes of his tribe leaders. "Bring eagle quill. Chief will sign."

The settlers kept and honored the agreement under the leadership of John Dicks. The Cofitachequi Indians honored the agreement under the leadership of Chief Brown Eagle. The Silver Bluff Indians were the most peaceful of all the Creek nation. There was never another threat of an uprising. John was thanked and honored by the Indians and by the settlers of the township for many years. He was given the title "Esquire" by the local settlers first, and later by the Crown. He took great satisfaction in signing his name, "John Dicks, Esquire."

On March 15th, 1750 another child was born to the Dicks family. She was named Sarah.

John took his duties as judge of the local court very seriously. He read every magazine and any other book or publication which he could order through the trading post of his father-in-law. When the publications were limited in Charles Town, he ordered others from England. Within about another year he had become the most well-informed person in the township on the law. Perhaps it was because of his study of the law, or perhaps because William Gascoigne's trading business was again on the decline. For whatever reason, in 1751 John and Mary became concerned about their land.

"Mary, your father has never given us the deed to this property," John said to Mary one night as they were discussing the events of the day. "Did you know that if he died, or anything happened to him, our seven years of hard work would be down the river? We would be without a home. Where could we start looking to find our children another place? We would have to start all over, developing and clearing the land, building a house and out-buildings. I think I'll ask him for the deed."

"I'm sure you're right, John," responded Mary. "I'm sure Papa will give you the deed. There's no need to worry."

The next day John made a special trip to see William Gascoigne. He was at the trading post. The building was almost empty, and there was not a single customer in sight.

"Good morning, Mr. Gascoigne," John said in pleasant tones. "How's business these days?"

"Bad, John. Very slow. Looks like I might as well close the trading post and start planting," William responded with a sick and old look on his face. "What brings you here this time of the day?"

"We would like to get a deed to our property. You know we have never asked for it, but if anything happened to you we would be left out in the cold."

William dropped his head and said, "I can't give it to you, John. I'm almost broke. This land is about all I have left. Catherine and I are getting old, and we have to look out for ourselves. My business has been declining since you moved the blacksmith shop away. Besides, I'll need the property as security if the time comes when I need to borrow on it."

"I'll buy the land, Mr. Gascoigne," John pleaded. "How much do you want for it? If I can't pay all in cash, I'll trade it out, or pay you in several payments."

"I can't give it to you, John. I can't sell it to you. I've already let George Galphin slick me into signing an agreement giving him the first right of refusal on the property. If I ever sell it, Galphin has the first right of refusal. I'm sorry," he said as he walked toward the back of the store, as if to say he didn't want to talk anymore about it.

By the time John returned home he had already made up his mind about what to do. "Mary," he called as he opened the door. "We might as well get ready to move away from this house. Your father refuses to give us the deed. He says he's broke and has agreed to give George Galphin first right of refusal if he ever sells the property.

"But he gave us the land," cried Mary. "I don't understand why we have to move. There must be some mistake."

"I tried to reason with him, Mary. I even offered to buy the land. He said he couldn't even sell it to me!" John explained with pain in his voice. "There must be something more to it than meets the eye. He must be secretly mad about my moving the blacksmith shop up here. He said his business has been declining since I moved it. I just believe he doesn't want us to have it, now that we've built the house and all the other outbuildings and barns. I guess I'd better start looking for another place. It'll sure be tough to start all over again."

For the next several weeks, John spent a good deal of time searching for a place to buy. He found a 200 acre tract of land several miles north of Gascoigne's property, on Town Creek. It was too good to be true, he thought. Every acre of it was useable land; no swamps at all. He visited Charles Town and searched the records. No owner could be found. It must still be public land, he thought as he left the Surveyor General's office.

On November 16, 1752 John presented the following petition to the Lords Proprietor:

To Lords Proprietor of the Province of South Carolina, send greetings.

Read the petition of John Dicks humbly showing that the petitioner hath been a long settler in this province and lived at New Windsor Township about 10 years, on land his father-in-law promised to give him, but now refuses and has put your petitioner and family in great distress. The petitioner has found a plat of land on Town Creek which he has begun to improve and there also to settle his family, and it is convenient for his trade of farming. But he apprehends it might some years ago have been owned, but whether by purchase or a grant, the petitioner can not tell. He having searched the Surveyor General's office but neither a warrant or any plat appears returned for same. The petitioner John Dicks humbly prays his excellency and honors to order the Surveyor General to lay out to the petitioner 200 acres of land on Town Creek as aforesaid and that he may have a grant for the same, and the petitioner as is duty bound, shall also stay. Charles Town the 16 Nov. 1752. John Dicks.*

*Copy on file in S.C. Archives, Vol. 21, Part 1, p. 105

John returned to Silver Bluff and started immediately to move his family and all his goods to their new home, which he had built during the summer and fall. He had assurances from the Surveyor General in Charles Town that the granting of the land would be a mere formality.

For the next two years John and Mary continued improving the new property and enlarging the little log house which he had originally built. He executed his duties as Judge of the local New Windsor Township court with dispatch and wisdom, attending to many small and insignificant claims. He had a good reputation among the settlers and the Indians as a just and fair judge and mediator.

The peace of the area, and John Dicks' abilities as judge and mediator were put to a severe test in late August, 1753. In that month, a German immigrant named Morgan Sweitzer passed through Silver Bluff on his way to Augusta. He had stopped at Galphin's trading post and was intrigued by the beautiful Indian maiden who had ridden her horse alone to purchase provisions for her father. As she left the trading post he followed her and overtook her about a quarter of a mile outside the Cofitachequi village. He raped and killed her but was captured by several young braves of the village.

When they brought Sweitzer before the Chief the latter decided that he must send him to Judge Dicks for judgment since the crime occurred outside the village. He took the fish charm from around his neck and placed it upon his son-in-law and sent him, with five additional escorts, to carry the violator, bound, to appear before John. A date was set for Sweitzer's trial, and he was kept bound in the stockade at Galphin's trading post. The trial was scheduled to be held there also, since it was an event of major importance.

On the day of the trial there were about twenty-five Indians present, including Chief Brown Eagle. About fifty white settlers were also present—with settlers coming from the Swiss, German, English, French and Irish communities. Several British soldiers were on hand to observe and keep order. John knew his career as judge was at stake in the case, as well as many friendships. His Quaker heritage had instilled in him a loathing for violence and a high value for human life; yet the crime was heinous and deserving of the most severe penalty. He did not want to offend any of his white settler friends either, and he knew that some of them would be sympathetic to the prisoner, especially the Germans. If he did not make the sentence severe enough, the Indians would lose confidence in him and the treaty and probably would not honor it in the future. He wanted to maintain their friendship and confidence.

The trial lasted all day and most of the night. George Galphin was called upon to testify concerning his seeing the immigrant in the trading post and seeing him follow the girl outside. The Indian braves testified as to catching him in the act of trying to hide the body.

John listened to all the proceedings with great concern, asking questions of each witness. He wanted to feel sure—beyond a shadow of a doubt—as to whether the accused was innocent or guilty as charged. After all the testimony was finished, he had a private meeting with George Galphin, John Tobler and Chief Brown Eagle, one at a time.

About four o'clock in the morning John said he was ready to render his judgment. The prisoner was guilty as charged. The penalty would fit the crime. He would be hanged by the neck until dead, at sunrise on the third day after the trial.

The prisoner fell back in his seat as if he would faint. The Indians smiled as they filed out of the building. The white settlers sat motionless and expressionless. John felt about as sick as the condemned man. This was the first time he had felt compelled to take the life of another person. He felt the weight and responsibility was squarely on his shoulders.

It was almost daylight when John reached home. He took off his boots and started to get into bed, but could not get his mind off the burly-looking German prisoner named Morgan Sweitzer. He was satisfied the man was guilty, and felt sure the sentence was the only one he could have passed upon the brutal crime. Still, something bothered him about the man. Maybe it was because this was his first serious case, or maybe it was because he had never been responsible for the taking of another human life. After sitting on the side of the bed for a while, and looking at Mary and the children who were sleeping peacefully, he pulled his boots on and started back to

Galphin's trading post.

When John arrived again in Silver Bluff, George Galphin was already up and open for business. "Mornin', John," he called as he opened the gate to the compound. "What're you doing back here so soon?"

"I just wanted to talk with the prisoner one more time, George," he replied in sober tones. "Where is he?"

"He's back in the stockade being guarded by two British soldiers," Galphin answered with a questioning look. "You can go on back."

The prisoner was in a large cage behind the main building. It had been constructed to imprison wildcats or other wild animals. The guards stood in front of its door, but moved out of hearing distance when John indicated he wanted to talk privately with the prisoner.

"I just wanted to talk to you one more time before your sentence is carried out," John said with a long face. "I'd like to know if you have any family."

The prisoner was silent for a while. He appeared to have no interest in talking to the man who had placed the death sentence upon his head. He looked at his hands and rubbed them for a moment and hesitatingly began to speak in broken English. "No, I got no family. I had family in Saltketcher: three cousins, uncle and aunt. I lived with them ten years. They all burned up in house, except aunt. It bad, bad death. Cousins burned black, and suffered three weeks 'fore death. They scream, cry and pray, but nothing help but whiskey."

"What were you doing in Silver Bluff?" John interrupted. He did not want to hear any more of the horrible story.

"I on way to Augusta. Aunt say it good place to find work."

"Do you have anything you want to send to your aunt?" John asked, still feeling a burden of guilt.

Morgan felt around in his pocket and answered, "Yes, dis is all I own. Give to my aunt. Her name Birdie Sweitzer." He stuck his hand through the bars and placed all the contents into John's hand.

John's heart skipped a beat as he looked at his hand. In his own palm he held several coins, a piece of flint, and a little rusty iron fish charm with three crosses on its side. He quickly flipped it over and was almost paralyzed when he saw "W.D." cut into the metal.

"Where did you get this fish?" he asked quickly, with his eyes searching those of Morgan.

The prisoner became highly nervous and answered in almost inaudible words. "I had that several years. I got it at Saltketcher."

"Who did you get it from in Saltketcher?" John persisted, now realizing he might be talking to Wilma's killer.

"I not remember," the scared prisoner answered with an evasive air.

"Morgan, you might as well clear your conscience," John continued as he stared him straight in the eyes. "Did this fish come from a woman. In a church. Late at night?"

Morgan turned pale and shook, as if standing before an omniscient God, turned his head from John, and waited a few minutes. Apparently he was nervously wrestling with himself over something that had been bothering him for a long time. He wheeled around and with wild eyes, blurted out, "Yes, yes, it did. I was drunk. Cousins were drunk. But I never been able to get that woman out of mind. I done lots of bad things that not bother me, but I see that woman face every night!"

John did not want to hear any more. He turned and walked away leaving the prisoner screaming. "Help me! God help me! Somebody help me!"

John stumbled around to the front of the building again and leaned up against the log wall. His guilt turned to bitterness.

"Oh God, I'm glad I didn't know this before the trial and the sentencing. There's no way I could have been unbiased!" he thought aloud as he held his head in his hands.

August 24, 1753 came and went without the world taking notice of the happenings in the new and primitive settlement of the New Windsor Township, located along the Savannah River in Granville County, South Carolina. As the first rays of sunlight streamed through the trees near the Silver Bluff landing, the men who had been appointed for the unpleasant task held the prisoner on his horse, placed a bag over his head, as well as the hangman's noose. A third man swatted the horse gingerly with a switch, and the body swang free as the horse ran out from under it. It swang high and long without so much as a grunt or a groan.

Almost every Indian in the area had gathered to watch. Many

stood in the clearing, but more stood behind trees. There were only about ten white settlers there to observe the execution. John was among them. He believed that since he had been responsible for passing the severe, savage, and fatal sentence, he should feel the total impact of his decision. After about five minues, all the observers streamed silently away, leaving the body still swinging from the big old oak tree, and John lingering, lonely, and deep in thought.

Chief Brown Eagle caught his eye, lifted his fish charm as a symbol of satisfaction and continued friendship, and led his people away. John Tobler, the good-hearted leader of the Swiss settlers, placed his hand on John's shoulder and said, "Stop worrying, John. It sickens me too, but you did what you had to do. It was the right thing."

Tobler walked away with a serious look on his face. Only John and the three persons who had been appointed to carry out the execution remained. He knew it was the only judgment he could have rendered, but that knowledge did not make his burden any lighter. He turned and started for home. He would always remember this occasion. It had a sobering and maturing effect on his life. This had been a weighty responsibility for a young man who was only thirty-two years old.

The winter winds and frost had just about passed. The bright March morning made John and Mary feel that spring was not far away. He was down at the horse stables and she was sweeping the yard. William, Thomas, and Catherine were playing hopscotch beside the house in the bright sun, while John, Jr. sat against the house with Sarah in his arms. The stagecoach from Charles Town came by on the trail and stopped. The driver began waving something, so Mary ran down to the road to meet him.

"Good morning, Mrs. Dicks," the driver said as he tipped his hat. "I have a pretty thick letter here for John. It's from Charles Town."

"Thank you, Mr. O'Brian," Mary replied as she reached for the letter. "I'll take it immediately to him. He's been expecting a letter from the Surveyor General's office for several weeks. I surely do hope it's the grant to our land."

"I truly hope it is," Mr. O'Brian responded as he turned to mount the stagecoach again. "You have a nice day now, and tell John hello for me."

Mary ran back to the house, calling John all the way.

"What on earth is it, Mary?" he asked as he came around the corner of the house. "I thought one of the children was hurt, the way you were yelling."

"It's the letter you've been looking for," she exclaimed as she handed it to him.

He quickly opened it, and a broad smile covered his face. "It is indeed the grant. We don't have to worry about anyone taking the land from us now. It's ours, now and forever!" he exclaimed as he unfolded the grant and began to read:

"South Carolina,

"George the Second, by the Grace of God, of Great Britain, France and Ireland, King, Defender of the Faith, and so forth, To all to whom these presents shall come, Greetings: Know ye, that we of our special Grace, certain knowledge and mere motion, have given and granted, and by these presents, for us our heirs and successors, do give and grant unto John Dicks, his heirs and assigns, a plantation or tract of land containing two hundred acres, situated in Granville County and being bounded on a branch of Savannah River named Town Creek and all the other sides on vacant land.

And hath such shape, form and marks, as appears by a plat thereof, hereunto annexed: together with all woods, timber and timber trees, lakes, ponds, fishings, waters, water courses, profits, commodities, appurtenances and hereditaments, whatsoever, thereunto belonging or in any wise appertaining; Together with privilege of hunting, hawking, and fowling in and upon the same, and all mines and with minerals whatsoever; saving and reserving nevertheless to us, our heirs and successors, all white pine trees, if there should be found growing thereon; And also saving and reserving to us, our heirs and successors, one tenth part of mines of silver and gold only; TO HAVE AND TO HOLD, the said tract of two hundred acres of land and all singular other the premises hereby granted, with appurtenances, unto the said John Dicks, his heirs and assigns forever, in free and common foccage, he the said John Dicks, his heirs or assigns yielding and paying therefor; unto us our heirs and successors, or to our Receiver-General for the time being, or to his

Deputy or Deputies for the time being, yearly, that is to say, on every Twenty fifth day of March, at the rate of three Shillings sterling, or four Shillings proclamation money. For every hundred acres, and so in proportion according to the quantity of acres, contained herein; the same to grow due and be accounted for from the date hereof. Provided always, and this present Grant is upon condition, nevertheless, that he the said John Dicks, his heirs and assigns shall and do within three years next after the date of these presents, clear and cultivate at the rate of one acre for every five hundred acres of land, and so in proportion according to the quantity of acres herein contained, or build a dwelling house thereon, and keep a flock of five head of cattle for every five hundred acres, upon the same, and in proportion for a greater or lesser quantity; and upon condition, that if the said rent, hereby reserved, shall happen to be in arrear and unpaid for the space of three years from the time it became due, and no distress can be found on the said lands, tenements and hereditaments hereby granted, that then and in such case, the said lands, tenements and hereditaments hereby granted, and every part and parcel thereof, shall revert to us, our heirs and successors, as fully and absolutely, as if the lands had never been granted. Provided also, if the said lands hereby mentioned to be granted, shall happen to be within the bounds or limits of any of the townships, or of the lands reserved for the use of the township now laid out in our said Province, in pursuance of our Royal Instructions then this Grant shall be void, any thing herein to the contrary contained notwithstanding.

"Given under the Great Seal of our said Province. Witness his excellency James Glen, Esq. Captain General, Governor and Commander in Chief in and over our said Province of South Carolina this 2nd day of January Anno Dom. 1754, in the Twenty Seventh year of our Reign.

"Signed by his excellency the Governor in Council. Alex Gordon, G.C.

"And hath hereunto a plat therof annexed, representing the same, certified by George Hunter, Esq., Surveyor General, the 18th day of January 1754.

"Alex Gordon, G.C."*

"We must put this in a safe place," John announced with an air of excitement. "Now is a time for celebration. After all those years of scratching and trying to build a home, and of thinking we owned our land, we're now, finally, land owners. We must do all we can to preserve it and keep it for our children. With God's help, I'll never mortgage this property."

The years following John's receipt of his land grant marked a period of prosperity and stability for the Dicks family. On January 26, 1755, John and Mary had their last son. They named him Joseph, after John's father Josephus.

John continued to clear his land and experiment in farming. He did very well with indigo and corn but never could make a real successful crop of tobacco. His herds of cattle, sheep, goats and horses continued to grow and expand. He had over two hundred hogs. He had no slaves. He did most of the work by himself, though John, Jr. and William were growing up to be strong boys. They were a great help in feeding and caring for the animals.

On a regular basis the Indians as well as the settlers still sent for John to come doctor their livestock. He was still the only blacksmith in the New Windsor Township. Between working his own land, working in the blacksmith shop, and tending to livestock, John had little time to call his own.

In 1756 Wilma was born. Martha came in 1757, and Elizabeth was the last Dicks child, born in 1760.

One day in 1762 when John came in from a hearing at the local court, Mary met him with a grim face. "Mamma and papa are leaving," she said. "They're moving back to Charles Town. They have sold their land to George Galphin." With tears in her voice, she continued, "I know we haven't been very close over the past ten years, but they are my parents, and they're getting old. Let's go visit with them. Maybe we should stay for a while. It may be the last time

*Copy in S.C. Archives under Royal Grants, Vol. 15, p. 331
Copy of plat is listed on p. 381, Part 2, Vol. 5

we'll ever see them. It may be the last time they ever see their grand-children.''

John could understand her feelings for her parents. He had strong feelings for his parents, and for Daniel and Catherine Smith, who had been like parents to him. He was also the kind of man who could not carry a grudge. "All right, Mary, call in all the children and have them get ready. I'll hitch the wagon and get it ready. It's the least we can do.''

They visited the Gascoignes at Silver Bluff and spent the night. The children enjoyed sleeping on pallets and playing with the pet deer that Catherine had tamed. John and Mary could see that William and Catherine looked old and tired. It was apparent that he had fallen upon bad times. "When are you leaving?" John asked as he lit his pipe.

"We hope to be ready in about two days," William replied soberly. "We surely dread the trip, but we'll feel better I'm sure when we're back with our relatives in Charles Town.''

"You don't have to leave, Mr. Gascoigne," John said, with an air of sincerity. "You and Catherine can come and stay with us.''

"Thank you, John," Mr. Gascoigne replied with a tear in his eye. "I'm a failure here. By the time I paid George Galphin what I owed him, there was nothing left from the sale of this land. I think I might do better in Charles Town.''

John and his large family started home early the following morning. As they rode along, they talked about how bleak the Gascoigne household looked.

"Wonder where their slaves were?" Mary asked with concern. "I didn't see a one the whole time we were there.''

"I noticed the house was almost bare. The food looked mighty scarce to me," John added with concern in his voice.

The following morning William and Catherine were packing their wagon with what few belongings they had. They were getting things ready to leave. As they were loading some cooking utensils onto the wagon, Catherine exclaimed, "There's Mary, John, and the children! I'm so glad they came to see us off!''

John helped Mary out of the wagon as the children jumped out into the sandy yard. While Mary hugged Catherine, John started unloading the provisions.

"William, I have a cured ham, some dried venison and dried beans I want you to take with you. Here's a bag of grits and a bag of corn. Here, help me with this side of bacon. And here's a case of my homemade berry wine," John said with a pleasant smile, not wanting to embarrass a proud man. "I know you don't need it, but we just wanted to give this to you as a going away present."

"Thank you, John and Mary," William said with a sad face. "I know I don't deserve this. But God bless you anyway."

"Oh, I almost forgot," John added as he took a small brown bag from his pocket. "I want to give you this. It's the same little bag Catherine Smith gave me when I left Charles Town. It's about fifty pounds sterling, the same amount she gave me. I couldn't have made it here without that money."

It was a touching scene. John was forty-one years old, a respected and successful man. His shiny black hair and beard showed many strands of gray, but he still stood tall and straight. His ruddy complexion still maintained a healthy appearance, indicating that hard times and hard work had not been unkind.

Mary was a wholesome pleasant-looking woman at thirty-six. Her long black hair was still free from gray, and her bright blue eyes had a gleam of contentment and hope. Her fair, smooth face was free from wrinkles and was the semblance of kindness. For a woman who had given birth to nine children, she appeared strong, healthy, and happy. Her figure was still shapely and was no more fleshy than it had been as a young girl.

Catherine, on the other hand, had aged drastically since the first time John had met her. Her frame was still thin, but now appeared weak. The red flaming hair, which had once made her appear so full of life, was entirely gray. Her bright green eyes were darkly sad, and her ruddy complexion had become pale. Her beautiful teeth still had a wide space in the front, but appeared loose and twisted.

Time had been equally unkind to William. He was only sixty-six but looked more like eighty. His dark beady eyes looked defeated. His once red face looked a sickly pink, and his head was totally bald except for a few strands of gray hair which ringed the back of his neck. He still had a thin gray goatee and mustache, but they too appeared sickly and dreary. The hard times had turned his rotund and hardy frame into a much thinner and fragile body.

It was a traumatic time, a time when the older generation would be separated from its younger, more vibrant, and promising future. A time when both needed each other the most.

"I can't take that, John" William Gascoigne responded, referring to the leather bag.

"Yes, you can. Go on. Take it," he insisted. "We want you to have it. If we never see you again, we want you to know that we love and respect both of you and pray that you will be happy and secure in Charles Town."

John shook William's hand and hugged Catherine tightly. Mary hugged and kissed them both as if it might be the last time. All of the nine children hugged and kissed their grandparents before they left in the wagon, looking back and waving as they went.

In 1768 John purchased another 150 acre farm in July. As she had done often before, Mary once again raised the question of buying some slaves. "John, you must buy a few slaves," she insisted. "Trying to work all this land without slaves is like digging with a rusty hoe. You'll die young and leave me a widow if you don't stop working so hard."

"I know you're right, but I just haven't been able to bring myself to own slaves yet. Maybe I should. I'll think about it," John responded with a serious look on his face. "John, Jr., William, Thomas, and Joseph have been a great help to me, but I know they won't always be around. In fact I don't think it'll be much longer before one of them gets married and wants to leave home.

John's prophetic statement came true much sooner than expected. In 1769, John, Jr. married the daughter of a wealthy Beech Island landowner and moved away to become foreman of his father-in-law's farm. In 1770, William married into a family of wealthy planters, and he too left his father to become the master of a plantation with many slaves. And in 1773, Thomas moved to Augusta to become an Indian trader like his grandfather. Joseph was the only boy remaining home. He worked as hard as any slave, but he and John could not get all the work done on both farms.

In outward appearance Joseph was almost a duplicate of his father. His hair was black and wavy, and his skin was clear and well tanned. He was already a tall young man of almost six feet in height. Inwardly, however, he was quite different from his mild mannered, peace loving father. He was more aggressive, and less inclined to be a pacifist. Nonetheless, he loved farming and delighted in learning the blacksmith trade. He also became good at doctoring animals, and gave his father great pride and satisfaction.

At twenty-five, Catherine was the oldest of the girls. She was plump and homely looking. She wore her dark brown hair in a bun, on the top of her head, and looked older than she was. Her face was round and dimpled when she smiled. She was short and stocky of build. Her mind was filled with good thoughts but was not as keen as that of any of the other children. It took her longer to learn and understand most things. She was always so bright and cheerful, however, that no one gave a second thought to her handicap. Her chores were always in the house, near her mother.

Sarah, the second of the Dicks girls, was twenty-three years old. She was always getting involved in things which complicated her life, except relationships with young men. She was a shy girl with a sharp mind and a big heart. Her long golden hair was never in need of brushing, and her light blue eyes were almost never blurred by tears. She was tall and thin but had a fully developed figure. Her pretty teeth gleamed through shapely lips which had never been kissed. Outwardly she had a happy personality and was usually singing or humming a tune while she worked. Inwardly she was a very private person. She had stories to tell which her lips could never utter and secrets which only she knew. One such secret was her brief romance with an Indian boy.

One morning while she was milking the cows, Sarah had heard a groan. Following the sound into the woods, she discovered a wounded Indian boy near death. He had been attacked by a wild animal. After frantically running for help, she, Joseph and Catherine dragged the boy to the house and attended to his wounds.

When John came home, he decided he would go to the Cofitachequi village to notify Chief Brown Eagle and to find out who the boy was. The Chief's daughter quickly recognized the string

of beads which John had taken from around the boy's neck. It was her
son; the Chief's grandson. The Indian Princess returned to the Dicks'
home with John and stayed several days until the boy was well
enough to travel. Sarah sat up late with her every night and
developed a strong feeling for her and her dark handsome son.

The family thought this was the end of the episode. Only Sarah
knew differently. Several weeks later, the well and strong Indian
brave waited until he saw Sarah heading for the cow barn. He
whistled, and Sarah met him at the edge of the woods. He was tall,
muscular, and handsome, wearing his animal skin breeches, leather
moccasins, and a colorfully painted leather band around his head. His
strong bare chest showed the scars of the wild animal attack.

Sarah dreamed about Running Deer almost every night. Her
dreams were always of passionate lovemaking between the dark
bronze Indian brave and his white princess. She felt guilty about her
feelings when she awoke, but was too happy to give them up.

For several months the couple met in the woods near the cow barn
when he gave the familiar whistle. Many times they walked down by
the creek, sat on a log or an old tree stump, and had long talks about
how they felt about many different things. Their conversations came
easy.

Sarah knew she was in love with Running Deer and believed he
was in love with her, but she was too respectful of her parents'
feelings to let it be known. She knew in her mind she and Running
Deer could never have a relationship together, but always tried to
put the thought out of her head. She loved being with him too much.
Her heart burned and longed for him, and she continued dreaming
about him at night. Yet her feelings had to be kept secret. The only
relationship between an Indian and a white person that she had ever
heard of was that of George Galphin and his common-law Indian
wife. People could accept the relationship of someone like old
George Galphin, but if a young white girl fell in love with an Indian
brave, she would be an outcast.

Running Deer was a clever young man as well as the grandson of
the Cofitachequi Chief. Apparently he knew the ramifications of an
affair with a white girl. After several months of regular visits, he
suddenly stopped. Sarah looked, listened, and hoped every day that

she would hear his familiar whistle. It never came. He never returned again.

Sarah found it hard to appear normal and happy after Running Deer had failed to show up for several weeks. Her heart yearned for a glimpse of him. What made her burden so heavy was the fact that she had to feel the heartache alone. She could never tell anyone, not her mamma or papa, nor even her sisters. She could not get him out of her mind or out of her dreams. It was a secret with which she and she alone had to struggle. Her life would never be the same again.

In early 1774, word came to John that the Crown was pleased with his execution of his duties in the local court system for the township, and that they wanted him to become one of the Judges of the Quorum for the Orangeburg District. John wrote the Governor in Council and advised him that he would be willing to accept the position and would do his best to be of service to the district and the Crown. He received his appointment, which he first accepted as a great honor. As time passed, however, he found that the demands of the new position and certain new acts passed by the Crown were at odds with his Quaker heritage. Though he decided to remain a judge and do the best he could for as long as he could, the clash of principles became increasingly difficult to reconcile.

One day in 1775, John came in from the field with a tired look in his eyes. After sitting at the table for several minutes with his mind apparently a hundred miles away, he called Mary to his side.

"I've decided to go to Charles Town and look for a few slaves," he said. "I'm tired of digging with a rusty hoe. I just don't have any choice. Either I buy some slaves, or we'll have to sell most of our property." He turned to Joseph who had come in and had also seated himself at the table. "Joe, I'm going to Charles Town tomorrow. I'm depending on you to take care of everything here while I'm gone."

"Sure, Papa," he said as he handed him a little bag of money. "Here's what I collected today. I've got to go back to John Tobler's house tomorrow to check his milk cow, but it shouldn't take but a few hours."

"I'm sure glad you finally decided to buy a few slaves, dear," Mary interrupted as she took the cornbread from over the fire. "I've been worried about the way you've been working so hard. I don't want to be left a young widow."

"Now, Mary," he responded in jest, "if anything happened to me, you'd have every man in New Windsor wanting to come calling on you. You'd forget me within a month."

"Stop talking like that, John Dicks," she replied with a worried expression on her face. "That kind of talk might bring us bad luck."

Mary finished cooking supper and placed the food on the table. Fresh milk, cornbread, fried rabbits, beans, and potatoes were plentiful, and made the meal look as rich as the table of the most wealthy family of the area.

Catherine, Sarah, Wilma, Martha and Elizabeth had also seated themselves around the table, and Catherine leaned over to John and said, "Papa, can I go with you to Charles Town?"

Sarah also leaned forward on her bench and cried, "Can I go too, Papa? I'm twenty-five now, and I can take care of myself!"

"Sarah, Catherine, you are both old enough to take care of yourselves, but I'd better go alone this time. I can make better time, and also I hear the British soldiers have been exerting unnecessary harassment on the colonists since the 'Boston Tea Party' last year." He paused a minute, and continued with a serious look on his face, "In fact the Second Continental Congress just met on May 10 to unite the colonies and prepare for war with England. You girls better stay home with your mother. Anything could happen these days."

Joseph, looking angry and with fire in his voice said, "Papa, I heard yesterday that some of the British soldiers from Fort Augusta made George Galphin give them horses, beer, and food the other day. Can they do that?"

"I'm afraid they can, son," John replied. "When the Crown passed the Quartering Act in 1765, it gave them that right. They've passed so many other oppressive acts I have great difficulty sitting with the Judges of the Quorum. I would resign, but if I did so now, it would be taken as a sign that I'm a revolutionist. I must stay neutral for the time being. I promise, I'll take all of you to Charles Town someday."

John left the following morning for Charles Town as the sun was beginning to light up the trail. Mary had gotten up early and had told him to be careful as she kissed him goodbye. Joseph had been up and was getting ready to start his chores by feeding the hogs. He knew he had to get an early start since he would not have any help.

As the horse and wagon slowly moved down the road, John's mind ran back to the day he had left Charles Town before sunrise on his long journey to Silver Bluff. He had never talked about it, but many times the tragic scene of Wilma lying on the church floor had flashed into his mind and into his troubled dreams. He quickly put the dreaded memories out of his mind as he hit the horse with the reins and turned his mind to the unpleasant task which lay before him.

On the second day of his trip, he was about a mile from Charles Town and stopped in an old church yard to water his horse at the well. As he was attending to the horse he heard a groan over in the bushes. Just for a moment the memory of his awakening under the church with a groan overcame him. When he had regained his senses, he walked over to the edge of the woods and pulled back the underbrush. There in front of him was a British soldier. In fact, he was an officer. He was groaning but had not regained consciousness.

John dragged him out of the bushes, placed him on blankets in his wagon, and began examining him. He had been severely beaten with some sort of club and had been stabbed several times.

"From the looks of the blood on the ground back there, he must not have much left in him," he thought as he opened his bag and began administering first aid. He drew up another bucket of water from the well and washed the wounds with a cloth torn from the officer's white breeches.

When John put sulphur and turpentine on the wounds, the young man woke up and struggled as if he thought his attackers were still at work. He was too weak, however, to put up a good fight. In fact, he could hardly lift his hand. He was very near death from loss of blood.

"I'm your friend," John explained as he held him down in the wagon. "I found you in the bushes, and I'm trying to stop your bleeding. Just relax. I'm trying to help, if you'll let me." The officer relaxed and acted as if he had resigned himself to being conquered.

"Just as soon as I can bandage all your wounds, I'll take you to the infirmary in Charles Town, as fast as my horse can carry us."

"I'm Bob Hunter," the redcoat whispered with a struggle. "I was ambushed from behind and never did see who beat me. I appreciate what you're doing, and I'm sure my father, the Surveyor General, does also."

John knew the lad's father very well. He finished the last bandage and placed other blankets over him as he mounted the wagon. When they arrived at the Charles Town infirmary, John pulled the wagon by the side door so the officer could be taken in and treated without attracting a lot of attention. He followed the doctors and nurses into the infirmary and explained how he had found him.

John was about to leave when the officer weakly called him back to the room. He motioned for John to come close so he could speak to him.

"I want you to have my sword," he whispered with a struggle. "Please pull it out of its case on my side. It has a silver handle. It was given to me by my father. I'll get a regulation sword when I'm well enough to be up again."

"I hope you'll be alright," said John as he took the sword from its case. "You don't have to do this."

The grateful patient nodded his appreciation and made a weak motion for him to keep it. John left, after smiling again at the young lad, and shaking hands with the doctor. He dreaded to face the main purpose of his trip.

He visited Zeke Dunbar and spent the afternoon talking with him, Enoch and Josh. It was too late to visit the slave market so he stopped by to see William and Catherine Gascoigne. They looked a little better than the last time he had seen them. Spending the night with them, he arose early the next morning for the unpleasant task.

John spent almost half a day watching the auction and somehow could not bring himself to make a purchase. He just could not see himself buying another human being. The whole auction scene was repugnant.

Around noon he walked about a hundred yards away from the auction block, sat down, and leaned his back against a tree. He was about to fall asleep when someone nudged him on the arm.

It was a Negro slave who appeared to recognize him. The slave reached in the pocket of his breeches and stretched out his hand. In the palm of his hand was a little iron fish. He turned it over and John could plainly see an "I," even though the little charm was worn thin.

"Isaiah, you old possum," he shouted. "What are you doing here?"

"I'ze to be sold today, Massa John," he said with a sad expression. "Massa Henry LaGrow done fell on hard times an' must sell most us slaves. Dat's him over yonder. An' dat's my family. I don't mind bein' sold, but I hates to haf de family split up."

"Maybe your family won't have to be split up, Isaiah," John said with determination in his voice. "I'll talk to Master LeGrow and see if I can buy all of you."

He followed Isaiah over to where Henry LeGrow was waiting with his slaves for his turn at the auction.

"LeGrow," John began, after he had greeted him. "Do you want to sell any of these slaves?"

"Yes, I do. I want to sell all of them," he answered. "And they're a mighty fine bunch of workers. The men are strong, and the women are smart around the house, as well as in the field. They're worth a lot more than the average slaves. This is Isaiah and his wife Phoebe, Sam, Isaiah's son, and his wife Augustine, and their children, Princess, Lunnon, Sylvia, Sarah and Rose."

LeGrow did not recognize the interested inquirer. He began pointing to the muscles and other attributes, as he continued. "Now Isaiah is still strong as a young man, and smart too. Sam is as strong as any two men around here, and he's as prolific a stud as you'll find. This wench, Phoebe, is as good as any for house work, and the other girls are strong and healthy. They'll work hard for you and produce many more fine slaves to boot."

"All right, you've convinced me. Now, how much do you want for all of them?" John asked impatiently.

"One thousand pounds sterling," Henry replied, without even a flinch in his voice.

"That's a little steep," John protested. "What about the auctioneer's cut? How much can you knock off the price by selling them to me before the auction? I can't pay a thousand pounds. I guess I'll have to look elsewhere."

"Alright, I'll take nine hundred pounds sterling, in cash," Henry quickly responded.

"I don't know," John replied, knowing full well that Henry LeGrow was in a tight spot. "I guess I'll just wait and look somewhere else."

"Wait a minute, I'll take eight hundred pounds sterling. That's my rock bottom price. Take it or leave it," he demanded.

"I'll take it," John answered with a satisfied smile. "I'll take them all."

Isaiah had told his son and grandchildren about John for many years, explaining how they had been good friends. They all jumped up and down wildly and shouted, "Praise de Lawd! Praise de Lawd fa Massa Dicks!"

While John settled with Henry LeGrow, Isaiah loaded all his family in the wagon. He pulled it around and waited.

"Massa, I drive de wagon for ya," Isaiah said proudly as he sat erect on the wagon seat, while John climbed aboard.

Isaiah and all his family were very happy as they huddled in the wagon, not fearing the long trip ahead. They knew their prayers had been answered. They would get to stay together. John was happy too. He had been able to compromise on owning slaves, but he had not compromised his principles about slavery. He had done just what Mary had said, "You may be keeping them from someone who would abuse them."

Since it was late evening, John and his slaves stayed with the Gascoigne's that night and left the next morning just before dawn. The trip was uneventful and John was home in just three days.

Back in the New Windsor Township, John, his family, and slaves worked the farm and raised cattle, sheep, goats and hogs. He was becoming one of the most respected men of the community. He was not a wealthy man but he was one who believed in integrity and peace. Anyone who dealt with him knew that they could trust him and call on him when they were in need. He was respected also by the way he interpreted the law and executed it in his court.

Times were very difficult, however. The Crown had passed new acts as reprisals against the rebellion of the New England colonies. The British increased their troops at Fort Augusta. Fort Moore had been abandoned several years before, but there had been talk of reactivating it. In the past, there had been only about twenty-five troops at Fort Galphin in Silver Bluff, but the Crown now transferred more than one hundred men from Fort Augusta, not only to keep an eye on the Indians, but especially to keep the settlers in line. The soldiers were roaming the New Windsor Township, taking horses, food, beer, cider, tobacco, and anything else they wanted under the provisions of the new Quartering Act. John found it almost impossible to stay neutral. On March 3rd, 1776, he wrote a letter to the Governor in Council resigning as a Judge of the Quorum.

On April 20, 1776, John drew up his will. He was concerned that his life might be in danger if, in light of his resignation, the Crown decided he was taking sides with the revolutionists. He made Joseph and Mary, his wife, executors, and left the homeplace to Mary as long as she lived. Upon her death it would go to Joseph. He drew the will in such as way that the slaves would be given to his wife and children, with the intention that they not be separated.

"John Dicks," yelled old Daniel Dues as he and two of his sons sat defiantly on their horses in front of the Dicks' home, late one evening. "Come out here and fight like a man!"

Joseph heard the belligerent yelling and grabbed his musket from behind the door.

"What do they want, Papa? They sound awfully mad!"

"I don't know, son, but put away the gun. We don't want any trouble," John answered as he got out of bed and quickly slipped on his clothes and boots.

"What's the trouble, Dues?" he asked in a calm manner as he stepped out the front door.

"You know what the trouble is, you yellow-bellied coward!" Dues bellowed as he aimed his musket at John. "Duncan Morgan refuses to pay me, and he said you told him, in court, he couldn't be made to pay. I think I'll take it out of your hide."

"Now calm down, Dues. I'm no longer judge. I resigned several weeks ago. Morgan did come by my house and asked me about your complaint against him. I told him he couldn't be made to pay until the Crown appointed a new judge. I didn't question the merits of the case, I only looked at the legal standing in the absence of a judge. Now go on home and cool off. Neither you nor I need any extra trouble at a time like this."

"Come on, boys, let's get outta here. He ain't nothing anyway but a goat lover and a hog farmer," bellowed the arrogant leader of the Dues clan. "Don't you ever cross me, Dicks. I'll send you back down in the swamp where you belong; with your toes sticking up."

Joseph was scared and embarrassed, but mostly angry, as he watched his father stand like an humble servant and absorb the abuse of the notorious Daniel Dues. "The troublemaker needs someone to put him in his place," he thought, as he walked back in the door, leaving John in the yard. "Someday I'll show him who he can boss around."

"Papa, why did you let that low down rascal treat you like that?" Joseph asked angrily. "If you had let me keep my musket, I'd have put a stop to it," he continued loudly as John came in and sat down on the side of the bed. "He insulted you over and over, and you didn't even try to fight back. Where is your pride?"

"Joseph, there are a few things more important than pride," he answered with a serious look in his eye. "It's better to be a peacemaker than to be proud. It's better to have a clear conscience than to have power over others. Always remember that. I don't believe in fighting."

"I can't see it that way, Papa. There's a time when a man must fight for what he believes in."

"Maybe you're right, son. But be sure you believe in what you are willing to fight for. The old prophet in the Bible said it's better to be a living dog than a dead lion. There's no need to throw your life away foolishly."

Joseph accepted his father's advice about being sure of the cause for which he was willing to fight. As time went on, however, he became increasingly emotionally committed to the cause of the new revolution that was spreading throughout the colonies. One day in 1777 he came home from Galphin's trading post with a copy of Thomas Paine's pamphlet entitled "The Crisis." As the family gathered around the table that night, Joseph said, "I want all of you to listen to this."

He began reading: "These are the times that try men's souls. The summer soldier and the sunshine patriot will, in this crisis, shrink from the service of their country, but he that stands it now deserves the love and thanks of man and woman. Tyranny, like hell, is not easily conquered; yet we have this consolation with us that, the harder the conflict, the more glorious the triumph."

He read on for what seemed like an hour, becoming more excited all the while until he finally read the last sentence with a resounding crescendo, "Look on this picture and weep over it! And if there yet remains one thoughtless wretch who believes it not, let him suffer it unlamented. December 23, 1776."

"Papa, if this thing gets any worse, I might volunteer to fight with the colonists," Joseph said with a glow in his eye. "I hear the British plan an assault on Charles Town, since it's the state capital. They think they must bring it back under British control."

"Don't act too hastily, son," John said with conviction. "You're the only son I have at home. I need you. At least wait a while to see what happens. Your volunteering might not even be necessary."

During the remainder of 1777 and 1778, John read everything he could get from the trading post, to keep up with what was happening in the conflict. He was not the only one interested. Joseph was as much or more interested, and from time to time he talked about volunteering.

One Saturday morning in early 1779, Joseph came home from Galphin's trading post with a nervous look on his face. He went out back to the blacksmith shop to find his father. John continued hammering while Joseph came in and sat down, as if waiting for a chance to talk.

"What's wrong, Joe?" John asked as he continued his work.

"Papa, I'm going to volunteer to help defend Charles Town," he nervously blurted out. "I'll have to supply my own horse and provisions. I just got back from the trading post, and a man was there trying to recruit men for the Charles Town Militia. He said Charles Town is in great danger of attack. The British soldiers were run out in 1776, but they're planning to invade again. He said General Moultrie and General Benjamin Lincoln are recruiting volunteers to defend the town. They hope to defeat them once and for all. Papa, if we don't stop them there, pretty soon they'll be taking everything we own. You know how they've been acting lately."

"I've always tried to be a man of peace," John said as he put down his hammer. "But it seems the time has come for somebody to fight. You're twenty-four years old. I can't tell you what to do. You'll have to make your own decision." He paused for a moment so the lump in his throat could go down. "If I were your age, I might even consider doing the same thing."

"He's waiting at the trading post, Papa. I told him I'd rush back by sunrise. He said several other men from the area were supposed to meet him in the morning so they could leave by ten o'clock."

"Alright, son," he said. "If you go, I'll be proud of you. Just remember what I've always tried to teach you. It's better to have a good conscience than to be rich and powerful."

"I know, Papa."

"Here, Joe, I want you to have one of my fish charms," John continued. "I've told you many times what it means to me. I want you to take it with you so you'll never forget the things I've tried to teach you. I've already put your initials on it. I was waiting for a good time to give it to you. I guess there's no better time than now. I know it's just a little rusty iron fish, but every time you feel it or look at it, you'll know my thoughts and prayers are with you."

"I'll always carry it for good luck, Papa," Joseph responded as he hugged his father and immediately left the shop before his eyes had time to fill with tears.

The next morning Isaiah saddled Joseph's horse. John packed his two large saddle bags full of food and other provisions. Mary mended his coat as she fought back the tears. Catherine, Sarah, Wilma, Martha, and Elizabeth all sat at the table like speechless dolls. Even Sam, Augustine, and their children had a hard time fighting back the tears.

They all gathered around as Joseph started to leave. He hugged Mary and John and the girls. He started to shake Isaiah's hand, but then reached out and gave him a big hug. He did the same to the rest of the slaves, mounted his horse, and rode off.

When he reached the end of the lane, where it turned into the main trail to the trading post, he paused, turned around and waved. The entire Dicks clan waved with their hands, but remained frozen as if their hearts were too heavy to move. Joseph turned again and rode away to join the Charles Town Militia.

4

Among the Swamp Foxes

1779-1781

The early morning sun was glistening on the white silvery sand, and Joseph's horse was snorting hot breath which left vapor trails extending to the man's cold face. Joseph was full of excitement, and the cold wind had lost its bite by the time he reached the trading post.

Captain Moody was waiting in front of the post with two other men from the area who had volunteered to go to Charles Town. As Joseph dismounted, the recruiter said with satisfaction, "This is Joe Dicks. He's coming with us." He stretched out his hand toward Joseph and continued, "This is Malcolm Davies and Pat McElmurray. They're the only other volunteers from this area. If you're ready, we'll leave immediately."

George Galphin was standing in his trading post doorway. He nodded to Joseph and the others. He disappeared and, in a moment, reappeared, his red face shining and hot steam flowing from his big red nose. His arms were full as he looked around to make sure no redcoats were near. He rushed out the door as the three recruits mounted their horses and were about to follow their new leader. As he approached the men, he excitedly yelled, "Wait a minute boys. I might as well give you something to take with you. If I don't, the British soldiers might get it anyway. They've been taking what they want, lately."

He handed each of the three local men a new pistol, a box of gun powder, a box of round lead, and said in a fatherly voice, "Now you boys make good use of these. And most of all, try to be careful. I want to see you back here before long."

The young volunteers put their gifts in their saddle bags, thanked Mr. Galphin, and left in a gallup. They were all dressed in their everyday work clothes, like the Captain, in accordance with his previous instructions. As they caught up and came along beside him, the captain motioned for them to stop. "Now fellas," he began, "we'll ride alone and stay about a thousand yards apart. If we run into British soldiers they'll think we're just farmers on our way to the field. If we all ride close together they may become suspicious."

He paused for a minute to see if everyone understood. "Now we want to keep each other in sight at all times. All right, let's go," he continued as he pulled his horse out ahead to take the lead position. "We need to be in Charles Town this time tomorrow."

After a day's hard riding and an overnight camp in the woods, the little band arrived in Charles Town on time and was led to the headquarters at Fort Moultrie. There were several hundred other new recruits milling around the area, waiting by their horses. They had come from almost every part of South Carolina.

General Moultrie had sent about a hundred and thirty of his men to recruit volunteers from all over the state. About half of them had returned and brought two, three, or more volunteers with them. As the day wore on, more of his men came in, one by one, with additional volunteers. By late evening all recruiters were accounted for, and almost five hundred new men were ready to be inducted into the Charles Town Militia.

Joseph was in the group which was led to the area where Lt. Colonel Francis Marion would be in charge, in the absence of Gen. Moultrie. Pat McElmurray and Malcolm Davies had been placed in another group. They waved goodbye to Joseph, little realizing that it would be the last time they would see each other during the next few years.

Excitement mounted as the troops waited for induction. The smell of a hundred horses mixed with the fragrance of meat cooking over open camp fires served to heighten the excitement. After a few moments, Lt. Colonel Francis Marion walked out of one of the little log buildings, and a hush fell over the crowd. He saluted the new men and yelled, "At ease men, you may be seated on the ground.

"Now men, I want you to know that I appreciate your volunteering for the militia. I must tell you also that your job is not going to be easy. In 1776, we defeated the British on land and at sea, here at the capital. We have information in hand verifying that once again British troops are marching toward us from Savannah. We'll join General Moultrie's other forces and the forces of General Benjamin Lincoln to repel the attackers. Now is the time to show what mettle you're made of. This could be our finest hour, but don't expect thanks or glory. We're soldiers, and we'll do our job." His voice steadily rose to a climatic crescendo as he ended his speech and in a different tone continued, "Now, men, we have a lot of hard work ahead of us, so stand to attention and prepare to be inducted into the Charles Town Militia."

The induction ceremony was very brief. The new men were divided into groups of ten and put under the command of a seasoned veteran for immediate training. During the month of rigorous training that followed, the new recruits became respectable troops. They were as ready as they could be, with only a month's training, to meet the British attackers.

"What's your name, soldier?" the cook asked as Joseph handed him his empty bowl for his ration of soup.

"I'm Joseph Dicks. I've been here about a month. I haven't seen you around. You're not in our unit, are you?"

"No, sir! I'm in Colonel Francis Marion's Second Regiment of the Continental Army. Your cook came down with chills and fever, so Colonel Marion loaned me to General Moultrie until he can find a replacement."

"What's your name?"

"I'm Will James. I've been with Marion for almost a year. He's the best commander in the whole army. If he ordered us to storm Hell, we'd jump to it."

"I saw him the first day I arrived here," Joseph said as he stood near the serving line to eat his soup. "In fact, he inducted my unit into the militia for General Moultrie, since he was away. I'd heard a lot about him, and was surprised to learn how short he is."

"Don't let the small size fool you. He's the biggest man in Charles

Town. He doesn't say much, but when he speaks, you'd better listen. He really cares for his men, and they would die for him. He'll be a general some day. I'd bet on it."

"What's the difference between the Continental Army and the Militia?" Joseph asked with increasing interest.

"The Continental Army is controlled by the Continental Congress. Our regiment is only one of the many that are under the command of General George Washington. The militia is just a local group, put together to protect the local people. The Continental Army pays more, if you can call the little we get, pay."

"Do you suppose I could transfer to Colonel Marion's unit?" Joseph anxiously asked as he put down his bowl.

"Sure. It's done all the time. All you need to do is to talk to your quartermaster. He can tell you what to do. I've never seen Colonel Marion turn down a good man yet."

The idea of transferring to the Continental Army really struck Joseph favorably. He had been very impressed by Colonel Marion. He, therefore, decided to follow Will James' advice and talked to his unit's quartermaster. Two days later he had become a paid soldier in the Second Regiment, under the command of Colonel Marion.

One morning in early May news spread like wildfire throughout the camp that the British troops had been seen crossing the Savannah river and were on the road to Charles Town. Coming from his unsuccessful attempt to take Savannah, General Moultrie crossed the Ashley River near Dorchester and entered the state capital on May 9th, 1779. He immediately strung all available troops, militia and continental, across the Charles Town neck. To form his anchors he sent Colonel McIntosh and the Fifth Regiment into the redoubt on the right flank. Into the redoubt on the left flank, he sent Colonel Marion and one hundred forty men from the Second Regiment.

The British General Provost set up his position in front of the colonial line. All day the light troops skirmished. Rifles and muskets cracked, echoing across the marshes and swamps. Joseph was among those skirmishing troops. He had never been in an actual battle. He ran from tree to tree, scared as a cornered rabbit, and hid behind anything that offered protection, trying to stay out of the line of fire. His ammunition was running low, so he had to make the best use of it.

"Hey Dicks, help me with James, here!" called one of the medics who appeared to be a middle-aged doctor. "The bleeding must be stopped, or he's in real trouble."

Joseph crawled over to where young William James had fallen to the ground. It was obvious he had only a leg wound. The medic moved on to another wounded boy who had been shot in the chest, leaving Joseph in charge of young James. Joseph pulled him out of the line of fire, behind a tobacco barn which was nearby. "How does it feel?" he asked in a voice which he purposely tried to keep calm. "Let's take a good look at it."

He ripped the pants leg and examined the wound. The lead ball had entered the side of James' leg, had missed the bones, and had passed out the other side.

"You're a lucky man," Joseph whispered. "The bullet is not lodged. All we have to do is wrap up the wound to keep it from bleeding."

"Is it serious?" the obviously scared young boy asked as he groaned, and looked up at Joseph with fearful green eyes. The sweat popped out on his smooth forehead as he wiped it back into his loosely hanging black hair. He looked quite different from the confident young man who had influenced Joseph to sign on with Colonel Marion.

"You'll be good as new in a few days," reassured a scared Joseph. "But this leg is going to be sore for a while. You'll need to stay off of it. Here, I'll help you over to the wagon." Joseph got William over to a nearby wagon, and from there, he was taken to the rear for medical attention.

The sight and feel of battle had been a new experience for Joseph. He had not been wounded in the light skirmishes but was deeply shaken. He had killed a British soldier. It was his first experience in real battle, and he was sure he would never adjust to the killing.

During the battle, Joseph had watched Colonel Marion with great admiration. It was hard to believe that he was such a man of a few words since he yelled and rallied his troups with such great effectiveness. Also surprising was the fact that Marion was a Bible-reading man of Huguenot stock. This soon became evident to Joseph, however, by the way in which the colonel showed great compassion for the enemy as well as for his own men.

"I see why all the men respect Colonel Marion," Joseph said to Will

James, when he visited him that evening in the fort. "I'm sure glad I transferred."

"If we beat the redcoats it'll be because of men like him. Would you believe he came by the wagon before we reached the fort and asked me how I was doing?"

During the night Joseph could hear a very heated discussion, but could not make out what was being said. The next day he learned that Governor John Rutledge had rushed to the headquarters of General Moultrie and had asked him to open a parley with the enemy. The General had reluctantly obeyed, but when he received the terms which would have made prisoners of war of his men and the governor as well, he decided to fight to the end.

Early the next morning, before the sun rose, General Prevost mysteriously retreated. He had learned tht General Lincoln had rushed up from Augusta, Georgia, and was almost in a position to seal his escape route. To avoid encirclement, Prevost had moved quickly and recrossed the Ashley during the night, heading again toward Savannah.

After the apparent victory, Colonel Marion told his troops to remain on guard and to stay ready. "They'll be back. You can count on it," he said with an air of certainty.

Joseph had applied for a transfer from the militia to the Continental Army so he could serve under Colonel Marion, yet he had never spoken to him directly. About a week after the small victory, he was admiring the horses when Marion came up and said, "Dicks, we accepted you in this unit because we need men with blacksmithing experience."

"Yes, sir!" Joseph answered eagerly as he snapped to attention, proud to have been accepted and thrilled to be talking directly to the Colonel.

"At ease, Dicks, I want you to spend the next few days checking every horse in the brigade. Every horse must be ready and in good shape, with good shoes. We've received orders to move out in a few days for Savannah. We're to join French troops for a joint attack on General Provost," he said confidently as he patted Joseph on the back. During the next couple of days, Joseph worked hard at tending to the blacksmithing needs of the brigade. Every horse in the unit was checked; those needing attention were given it. Thus, when Colonel Marion and his troops rode out toward Savannah at the end of the week, Joseph could take satisfaction in the fact that every mount was ready for the move. The fighting around Savannah had been in progress for several days by the time Marion's troops arrived. Before they and the forces under General Lincoln could reach the area, Count D'Estaing, the leader of the French forces, had moved upon the city and demanded the British surrender. General Prevost had asked for twenty-four hours in which to give his answer. His request was magnanimously granted.

General Prevost had taken good advantage of the time granted. He sent for Colonel John Harris Cruger, from Sanbury, and Lieutenant Colonel Maitland, from Beaufort, who brought several hundred slaves from surrounding plantations. They dug trenches and erected fortifications. By the end of the truce, Prevost's position was too formidable for D'Estaing to risk, so he waited for the American troops.

With the arrival of the American forces, hostilities resumed. After unsuccessfully bombarding the fort for four days, the French Commander decided to storm the compound. He led his units up Spring Hill redoubt, the anchor of the British line. The American column, led by Colonel John Laurens with the light infantry and supported by Colonel Marion's Second Regiment and Captain Shepperd with the Charles Town Militia, followed D'Estaing and his legion. In a rain of musket shot, they reached the trenches. Joseph plunged into the ditch where Colonel Marion had already taken refuge.

"Have you ever heard of such a thing? Giving the enemy two days to fortify their positions," Marion angrily shouted. "I tell you, Dicks, the blood of our brave young men will be on his hands. Sometimes I wonder about those Frenchmen." Joseph nodded his agreement as the Colonel shouted and waved his sword. Marion urged his men into battle while the enemy riflemen wreaked death on many of them.

Joseph started to grab the blue flag of the Second Regiment, but Lieutenant John Bush beat him to it and carried it over the wall. He was wounded and handed it to Sergeant Jasper. As Jasper carried the flag uphill, he was hit by a sharpshooter and handed it back to Bush before he died. Bush charged back into the ditch after being shot again. He fell upon the crumpled blue flag, right beside Joseph and Colonel Marion. Lieutenant James Gray moved out and placed the blue flag of the Second Regiment on Spring Hill redoubt. He too was downed by the sharpshooters.

By this time, Joseph had climbed over the wall and was on his knees, taking aim at one of the redcoats when he was hit by a musket shot. He fell to the ground and rolled back into the ditch.

"Oh God! I'm shot!" he thought in a state of panic.

After a moment his thoughts became organized and he felt, with his right hand, where he thought he had been shot. There was no blood. He felt the little iron fish charm in his left pocket over his heart. He quickly took the little iron charm from his pocket and almost fainted. It had a deep dent squarely in the middle of it. He had been shot alright, but the musket ball had hit the iron fish charm. All he had was a bad bruise on his chest over his heart.

"My God!" he cried out loud, not caring who heard him. "This fish charm saved my life!"

Colonel Marion was still in the ditch along with several of his dead men. He was a Bible-reading man, so it did not surprise Joseph when he gave him a penetrating look and said, "Son, looks like you had a little extra help from a power higher than the fish charm."

Moments later, Marion caught the signal from General Lincoln, ordering a retreat. So he motioned to his men and yelled, "Retreat!" Passing the order on down the ranks, he turned to Joseph and said in a disgusted tone of voice, "Here, Joe, help me carry Lieutenant Bush. Take the blue flag. I want to keep it to remind me of this battle and the stupidity of the French Commander."

The defeated and demoralized men of the Continental Army and the Militia retreated back down the hill, which was cluttered with over two hundred and fifty bloody and mangled bodies of Carolinians. General Prevost subsequently gave permission to gather the dead, and Joseph volunteered to help bring in the bodies. He was almost in a daze as he helped to pick up bodies which had, only hours before, been warm, alive, and energetic young men. After the bodies were brought back behind the lines, they were stripped and placed in large pits which held about a hundred. They were buried without regard to rank, and covered with the dark Savannah sand.

Joseph had not, even in his wildest dreams, thought that battle could be such hell. His stomach churned as he looked at the blood stains which had been left on the field. He grimaced as he turned his back from the graves and tried to get the images of the mangled dead bodies out of his mind. He could barely mount his horse when the order was given.

After the defeat, Admiral D'Estaing led his French troops aboard his ships and sailed back to the West Indies. General Lincoln, who had been placed in charge of the Southern forces, left for Charles Town, leaving Colonel Marion in charge of the survivors of the three regiments. At this early stage in the struggle, this was the only field army in South Carolina. It was bruised and whipped. Joseph gained a new respect for Colonel Marion as he observed how compassionate the man was to the wounded and as he demonstrated his ability to shape up the beaten men.

On January 20, 1780, Governor Rutledge received orders from the Continental Congress to reduce the number of regiments of the Continental Army to three. He and Lincoln decided that Francis Marion, William Scott, and William Henderson would be the commanders. Not long after this action by Rutledge, Sir Henry Clinton, at the head of a large British force, began his push toward the South Carolina capital.

By this time, Joseph had become a loyal aide to Marion and had received permission to stay with him and several of the other veterans who had the responsibility for training new recruits. William James, who was little more than sixteen years old, had recovered and had matured into a man much older than his actual years. He and Joseph had become good friends, and swapped numerous stories about their homes and families.

On February 1, 1780, Joseph was standing around a campfire with several of the new recruits, warming his hands, when Will James came running up, almost out of breath, and blurted out, "Joe, I just heard that Clinton landed his troops on John's Island. They moved to James Island, and are now waiting on the bloody Colonel Banastre Tarleton."

"Who told you this, Will?" Joseph asked, with an air of urgency.

"One of the Whigs from there sent his slave to the fort to bring the news. I was helping with the cooking at the General's quarters and overheard him telling Moultrie. In fact, he said they were expecting a General Patterson from Savannah, and Tarleton was already rustling horses from the planters around Beaufort so he could remount all his men."

For the next month, every available person worked tirelessly to prepare the defenses of the city. Joseph was put into the blacksmith shop and worked about eighteen hours every day shoeing the horses and making musket balls from square bars of lead. After a few days, William James was sent to help.

About a month later, just when an attack on Charles Town was imminent, Captain Alexander McQueen, adjutant to General Moultrie, gave a dinner party at his home. Colonel Marion was invited but did not like the idea of partying while under threat of an invasion. He called Joseph to his quarters and explained the situation to him.

"I want you to go along with me, but stay in the woods outside the house. I may have to leave in a hurry," he smiled as he continued. "McQueen is a partying soldier who likes to play, and I may need to sneak out before it's over."

After waiting about an hour, Joseph saw the Colonel jump from a second story window, and immediately brought his horse around and helped him upon it. "What in the name of heaven made you do that, sir?" Joseph questioned. "That's a hard way to leave a party, if I may say so, sir," he added with a smile.

"Those stupid Whigs are too drunk to miss me," he answered with obvious pain in his voice. "After dinner, McQueen locked the door and began offering great toasts to liberty and victory, with sparkling wine. I immediately started looking for a way to leave. Finding no better way I jumped from the window. I think I've broken my ankle. I refuse to become drunk when we're in danger of serious attack!"

On April 1, Clinton began a vigorous siege. General Lincoln issued an order that all supernumerary officers, and all officers who were unfit for duty, must leave the city and flee to the country. Joseph and young Will James carried Colonel Marion on a stretcher from Charles Town, and crossed the Cooper River, disappearing among friends and kindred among the Santee River. They would remain with Marion until victory was ultimately won in South Carolina. On May 12, 1780 General Lincoln surrendered Charles Town to Sir Henry Clinton, while General Sir Charles Cornwallis was over-running the state.

Following the fall of Charles Town, Marion and his followers moved about a good bit, seeking to reorganize their forces and to avoid capture by the British. One night while camped deep in the woods, Marion told his few followers that Congress had appointed

Major General Horatio Gates to be the commander of the southern army and that he had issued a proclamation for all continental officers still at liberty in the south to join him at Hillsboro, North Carolina. He paused a few moments and asked, "How many of you men want to go with me?"

They all agreed to follow Marion, so he and Peter Horry, with the little rag-tag band of about twenty officers, ten men, and two servants, came out of hiding and rode to Hillsboro. They found Baron de Kalb at Wilcox's Mill on Deep River and were with him when Gates reached camp and took command.

After the formal meeting, Gates headed his men toward Camden to launch an attack on Lord Cornwallis. Marion received permission to swing far south of Camden and take charge of the Williamsburg Militia. As he and a few followers continued on their way to Williamsburg, they could hear Gates' guns in the distance firing on Camden.

"Do you think he can take Camden, Sir?" Joseph asked as he rode near the Colonel.

"I hope so," Marion answered with a hint of doubt in his voice. "But he's not used to the area and appears to be moving too fast."

After several hours of riding they reached the camp of the Williamsburg Militia at Witherspoon's Ferry. Major John James gladly turned over his command to Marion. Marion then ordered Colonel Horry to ride on and take command of the Lower Santee Militia. Joseph remained with Marion and his ragged group. He saw many faces in the group that were familiar to him. Many of them had fought with the Second Regiment during the early days of the war.

Joseph was destroying boats and canoes on the Santee when a planter rode up and surprised him. He was about to draw his sidearm in defense when the planter raised his hands and said, "I'm looking for Colonel Marion. I've got some bad news for him."

"I'm Private Joseph Dicks, under Colonel Marion's command, sir," Joseph answered. "I'll be glad to take the news to him."

"I must see Marion," the planter responded. "I can't trust this news to anyone except him."

"Follow me," Joseph replied as he led him to the edge of the woods where Colonel Marion was instructing a group of his men.

The Whig planter shook Marion's hand and blurted out," Camden has been occupied by Cornwallis. Gates has fled into North Carolina, and Baron DeKalb has been killed. The battle on August 16th was a fiasco for us!"

Before Joseph could return to his duties, another stranger rode up to the group like a ball of fire. He was one of Colonel Sumter's men who had escaped after the battle. With a pale face and fear in his eyes, he nervously said, "We had captured Fort Carey, which guarded the ferry behind Camden. Instead of moving down the Wateree to meet you, sir, we began retreating slowly. We couldn't move very fast, because of the prisoners and captured supplies. At Fishing Creek, about forty miles above Camden, Tarleton and his men overtook us."

He paused for a breath and continued, "In a fierce charge they caught us by surprise. We were cut to pieces. Survivors were captured, and the Tory prisoners rescued. Sometime during the melee, Colonel Sumter sprang onto a horse without saddle and disappeared. He headed North. I don't think Tarleton caught him, sir!"

Later that day as the men gathered in the deep woods, Colonel Marion asked with a serious look on his face, "What shall we do? South Carolina is lost. The British occupy the capital, and there's no civil government in the state. Cornwallis has shattered any hope of military rescue."

Fear and desperation slipped into Joseph's mind. He had never seen this fearless little Huguenot in such a state of mind. He had seen him fling himself into battle without fear of the consequences. With an admiring eye, he had watched him lead his men into battle, and had seen him shed tears when his men were hurt or killed. He had never seen him defeated. With a forced confidence he said, "Sir, I say let's fight on. What else can we do?"

Marion nodded an approving smile and responded, "If you're with me, we'll continue carrying out our orders."

The summer of 1780 had not been a good time for the American cause in the South. The fall of Charles Town and the other British victories in the region gave Lord Cornwallis a definite advantage.

Despite this, however, he was not able to capture Marion or free himself from harassment by the Swamp Fox's forces. British supply lines were disrupted and American prisoners were freed despite Cornwallis' efforts to minimize such attacks.

One such incident occurred in August, 1780. Joseph and Will James were scouting the countryside when they came upon a wounded man who was lying at the edge of a small creek, cooling himself from the hot sun. They stopped to offer their assistance and soon found that he was a member of the Loyalist militia. From him they learned that a British escort under Captain Johnathan Roberts and a group of a hundred and fifty American prisoners had camped for the night at Colonel Thomas Sumter's house at the Great Savannah. They returned with the news, and Marion ordered all his men to ride quickly as possible to rescue the American prisoners.

Before midnight, Marion's band circled Sumter's house which sat on a hill above the Santee swamp. They sneaked up to it unobserved, behind the cover of live oak and cedar trees. Joseph slipped quickly and quietly up to the unguarded front door. The enemy had stacked their muskets carelessly outside by the front door. He gathered them up in his arms, and for some reason, scrawled a rough semblance of a fish with three crosses on the door with a piece of charcoal from the blacksmith shop. He was not quite sure why he did this. Maybe it was because the charm had saved his life, and he wanted the enemy to know it. Or maybe he just wanted them to know he had been there and had made a valuable contribution to the cause. Whatever the reasons, he had no more time to think about it. With arms full he ran as fast as his feet could carry him back to the cover of the trees.

One of the men stumbled over a British sentinel who fired at him. The Redcoats came running out the front door, half naked, looking for their muskets. Joseph and the men in his area cut loose with fire as the dark sky lit up like a thunder storm. Marion and another group of men rushed the back door. The engagement was one-sided and brief. They killed or captured twenty-two of the escorting troops and two Tory guides. The hundred and fifty prisoners were Continentals of the Maryland line. Many of them hugged their rescuers with great joy and relief.

Joseph felt this act of rescuing the Americans made all the misery worthwhile. To his utter amazement, however, eighty-five of them refused to follow the Colonel and wanted to be carried to Charles Town as prisoners of war. After acquainting them with the reality of the situation, they marched rapidly toward Kingstree.

Marion's band returned to Britton's Neck with only a few of the most faithful followers. By the time they had crossed the Lynches River, most of the Williamsburg militia had returned home. The group that crossed the Pee Dee River consisted of only Joseph, Major John James, William James, and several of the most steadfast men remained. They were in staunch Whig territory, however, and when the news was spread that Marion's men were in the area, many visited the camp and joined up. This trickle of recruits grew even more rapidly after Marion was able to score some small victories over the local loyalist militia units.

Thus, by late August, with his command now over 120 men, Marion began to make plans to disrupt the supply trains from Boston to Savannah. He set up a small redoubt of logs and clay on the eastern bank of the Pee Dee. Behind the hastily-improvised fortification he stationed several guards to watch twenty-four hours a day. He mounted two cannons, brought to him by the militia, and there they stood guard against any British supply wagons.

Lord Cornwallis acted swiftly. He knew that a victory for the guerillas on the supply line between Camden and Charles Town would be fatal. He devised a plan to destroy Marion's men once and for all. He sent the ruthless Major Wemyss and his 63rd regiment, Major John Harrison's Provincials, Colonel Samuel Bryan's North Carolinians, Colonel John Hamilton and a hundred of his troops, as well as all loyalist forces available to put a final stop to these troublemakers.

Cornwallis' actions did not go unnoticed in the Swamp Fox camp. After sending out intelligence-gathering scouts and discovering that the British had marshalled over eight hundred men against his one hundred, Marion dismissed all his men except the most ardent of his followers. Leaving Joseph, William James, Captain John James, and ten chosen men to gather intelligence, the discouraged little band of heavy-hearted fighters recrossed the Pee Dee. They spent the rest of the day resting.

All afternoon scouts rode in with bad news. Joseph discovered that Wemyss' troops had crossed the Pee Dee River at Yauhannah, and were trying to get behind Marion's redoubt. William learned that Moncrief had dispatched Ball and Wigfall north of the Black River. He had ordered them to cross the Pee Dee at Britton's Ferry and march up through Britton's Neck. Captain James found that Ganey and Barefield had also begun mobilizing their militia for action. Marion's choice was to fight or run. He had only sixty men, and they faced more than fifteen hundred men from nine militia, provincials, and regular British regiments. The odds were too great. He chose to run.

As soon as he had crossed the Little Pee Dee, however, Marion stopped and began thinking about the innocent and unarmed people he had left behind. He sent Major James, Colonel Horry, and Joseph, back to survey the situation. When they silently returned under the cover of night, they found a good hiding place deep in the woods, about a quarter of a mile from James' house. Joseph talked Major James into staying out of sight while he and Colonel Horry went on to spy out the house.

The two slipped in through the woods and saw several British troops surrounding the house. They had their muskets raised and appeared to mean serious business. Arrogant Major Wemyss was standing at the door talking to James' wife, Jean. He was trying to find Major James. Wemyss had orders to hang him because he had violated his parole to the British Crown. In talking to Jean, however, he was polite and conciliatory. "If Major James will come in and lay down his arms," he said courteously, "he shall have a free pardon."

Major James' wife may have been naive, but she was too smart to believe his sweet words. She replied, "I have no influence over my husband. In times like these, his conscience compels him to take a part, and he has taken the part of his country." The Major and Mrs. James argued, and she baffled him. In disgust he ordered his men to lock her and her children in one room of their home.

Joseph was tempted to try to rescue them but decided it would be a foolish attempt. He returned to the hiding place, while Colonel Horry remained on watch. He reported the serious episode to Major James but did not tell him all of the story for fear he would lose his head in more ways than one. He then returned to observe the house again.

For two days Wemyss lay in wait, hoping that Major James would come to his family. The lure failed because of Joseph's brilliant tactics. Had Major James known the full story of the treatment of his wife and children, he would have gladly given his life to defend them.

Later, Wemyss held a court martial for Captain John James, Major James' son, who was still at home. He had been paroled after his capture at Charles Town and had violated his parole by firing upon Tories who were raiding McGill's Plantation. The loyal Negroes and the family members refused to incriminate him, however, so the court, with great reluctance, acquitted him and released the James family. But like a bloody barbarian, Wemyss burned their home before their eyes.

Joseph returned again and made his final report. "The bloody Redcoats are gone. It's safe now to visit your family," he said bitterly.

Wemyss believed the way to suppress rebellion was to hang the leaders and destroy the resources of the rebels. Under the guidance of Harrison's Tories, he and his men burned a swath fifteen miles wide along the seventy mile route from Kingstree to Cheraw. He ordered his men to break up the looms, fire the grist mills, and destroy the blacksmith shops. To deprive the Whigs of even the means of existence, his troops shot their milk cows and randomly bayonetted their sheep.

Marion established a simple camp in the Great White Marsh. His troops, all very experienced woodsmen and skilled hunters who had slept outdoors many nights while fishing and hunting, merely turned from the road into the woods, hitched their horses to trees and bedded down. The men cooked their meals in small groups to keep the camp fires small. The camp was concealed as much as possible.

The summer had been rainy and the creeks and marshes had often been flooded. Mosquitoes infested the woods. They swarmed into the camp, stinging and biting, while the farmer soldiers tossed, scratched, and swore. Without warning there was an outbreak of malaria. Young William James came down first, trembling, sweating, vomiting, with teeth chattering. Captain George Logan came down next, and soon many were flat on their backs.

After an absence of about ten days, Joseph, Major James and Peter Horry found the hiding place in the Great White Marsh. They brought bad news. The British had devastated Williamsburg. Wemyss and Harrison had plundered and burned everything in sight. Like savages they had spread destruction and death from Georgetown to Cheraw. Colonel James Cassels, the noted Tory, had told Major Moncrief of the strategic importance of Britton's Neck, and so Moncrief sent him there to take control of the area, and to crush Marion's men. About this time, Major Moncrief sent Colonel Wigfall and fifty men to take a position near Black River Church. He also sent Colonel Ball, with only forty-six men, to take a position on Black Mingo Creek, where he could hit the Whigs around Indiantown or Kingstree. Ball made camp around the Red House, a tavern run by Patrick Dollard.

On the afternoon of September 24th, Colonel Marion limped to his horse, climbed into the saddle, and gave his signal. Quickly the horsemen followed him, like soldiers going home on furlough. The next evening they reached Kingston and rested under the giant live oak trees along the Waccamaw. As the sun set the following evening, they crossed Lynches River. There Captain John James and a squad of ten men waited. With him were Captain Henry Morgan, Lieutenant John Scott, and a few volunteers from their company of militia.

The local militiamen greeted Colonel Marion in the usual way, and James excitedly said, when he found a chance, "Colonel, sir! Colonel Ball is still at Shepherd's Ferry. His troops are encamped in a vulnerable position."

The men were ready. This was the kind of news they had long been hoping for. They jumped back into the saddle and spurred their horses in the direction of Black Mingo. The men seemed so excited and hopeful. Joseph had the feeling that something was about to happen which would make a difference in the outcome of the struggle.

Just before midnight Marion's band reached Willtown bridge, an old structure about a mile above Shepherd's. It was rickety, the planks loose and rattling. As man and horse ran over the bridge, the boards began to rumble. The clatter echoed through the swamp and into the Tory camp. A sentinel fired an alarm gun. John Ball was a skillful soldier, and at the sound of the alarm he aroused his men and rushed them out into the old field west of the tavern.

When Hugh Horry's infantry came charging through the broom sedge and dog fennels, Ball ambushed them. Muskets flashed and thundered, shattering the night like flashes of lightning. Buckshot whistled, then splattered on trees and buildings. Captain Logan was killed, while Captain Mouzon and Lieutenant Scott were badly wounded.

Terrified by the flashing and roaring, Major Horry's men began retreating in disorder. But Captain James, a seasoned veteran, calmed his own men, rallied those of Mouzon, and halted the retreat. Carefully and cautiously, he led them as they began easing forward, firing, loading, and firing again at every moving thing.

By that time, Captain Waties and his men had passed by the Red House and began advancing against the enemy's right flank. Caught between the troops of James and Waties, Ball's men delivered a scattered volly. As they saw the blazing guns of the advancing Americans, and heard the cries of the wounded, they retreated into the swamp.

The battle lasted only fifteen minutes. Joseph was among Captain James' men and once again escaped unharmed. Of the forty-six men, Ball had three killed and thirteen wounded or taken prisoner. Several others died of their wounds before reaching home. Marion left two dead, Captain Logan and a private, but they captured the enemy's guns, ammunition, and baggage.

The rebels' greatest achievement, however, was the capture of the good blooded horses of the Tories. Among these was the spirited horse that had been Colonel Ball's charger. Marion claimed the horse and renamed it "Ball." He always rode him thereafter, as a terrifying symbol to the enemy.

The fall of 1780 saw a marked increase in activity among the rebel forces under Colonel Francis Marion's command. On October 25, Marion swiftly led his troops toward Salem, on guard against surprise or ambush. He rode during the afternoon, forded the Black

River, and approached the Tearcoat Swamp. He halted his advance and sent Joseph and William James to spy out the Tory camp. They rode with haste and spied out the enemy location. Quickly they returned and reported that Colonel Tynes had camped in an overgrown field with his rear against the swamp, thereby leaving his defenses vulnerable. The Tories also had appeared very relaxed and unprepared for battle. Some of them had already fallen asleep on their blankets, which they had spread on the ground. Others, like playing children at a picnic, were merry, their voices ringing with song and laughter. Others were talking and playing cards around the campfires.

At midnight Marion's men attacked. They charged, whooping and yelling and firing as they attacked. Completely surprised, the Tories jumped up in fear and confusion. They leaped from their blankets and dashed for the swamp. The fighting was savage. Marion's men killed three, wounded fourteen, and captured twenty-three men and boys. They also captured eighty prime horses, with bridles, blankets, and saddles, and eighty muskets. The baggage, food, and ammunition of the enemy was also taken.

Marion's men had now become the scourge of the British. Their striking ability impressed Tory and British alike. They seemed to be lurking everywhere; hiding in an unknown camp, striking fiercely on a raid, or making a midnight attack. To further alarm the enemy, Marion kept his men constantly patrolling up and down the Santee Road. British wagoners would not cross at Nelson's Ferry, but took the longer, more tedious route to Camden by way of Friday's Ferry on the Congaree River.

General Cornwallis ordered the bloody Banastre Tarleton to catch Marion. Tarleton chased the Americans to Singleton's Mill, but missed them. Following Marion to Jack's Creek, he arrived again too late. On November 7th Tarleton arrived at the house of Widow Richardson, the wife of the deceased General Richardson. He installed his two cannons and waited with his legion and Harrison's provincials.

Joseph had become a seasoned soldier and moved ahead with the advance guard. The Americans saw the enemy campfires, and the Widow Richardson also sent her son to warn them of the great numbers. They moved back to inform Marion. When Joseph reported to the Colonel that a legion of the British army and the provincials were waiting, Marion turned and called for a retreat. The numbers were too great. He was a brave warrior but a realistic man.

In the moonless dark the Americans felt their way among the trees and underbrush. Every now and then being slapped by a limb, they circled around Woodyard Swamp and never slowed until they had crossed Jack's Creek. During the confusion of their retreat, they let a Tory prisoner escape. He ran to inform the British and was brought before Tarleton just before dawn. Within minutes, Tarleton galloped off toward the Richbourg Mill Dam on Jack's Creek.

Marion was as keen as Tarleton for battle. Before daylight he also called in the men most familiar with the area of the Santee and Black Rivers and placed them in the lead of his horsemen. For several hours Tarleton trailed Marion's men. At Ox Swamp, about twenty-three miles above Kingstree, Tarleton stopped. Ahead was a roadless swamp. His men and horses were tired and hungry. Slowly he turned his horse around. In his thick British accent, he said in disgust, "The Devil himself could not catch that damned old Fox."

Harrison's Tories chuckled at the "damned old fox," and from Ox Swamp to Camden they spread the story. The Whigs along the Santee were also amused. Before long, everyone began calling Marion the "Swamp Fox."

Shortly after his failed attempt to chase Marion through the swamps, Tarleton retreated back to the Santee and began punishing rebellion with the torch. A friendly Whig rode into the camp and reported with bitterness that Tarleton had burned thirty houses between Jack's Creek and High Hills. His punishment of Widow Richardson had been particularly ghoulish. He had ordered his troops to dig up General Richardson, who had been buried for six weeks. As the Richardsons wept at the sight, the men had plundered their home. Then, like a conqueror, Tarleton had called for dinner. After he had dined, with a spirit of vengeance, he had ordered his troops to drive all the cattle, hogs, and poultry into the barn. Then he had burned it, together with all the livestock and corn.

"Can you believe that?" the Whig cried out in anger. "He's a bloody scoundrel. He'll do the same thing to me if he gets a chance."

Joseph shuddered at the thought of making a widow look at her husband who had been buried six weeks. He thought of his mother and sisters and wondered if they were alright. Somehow he felt he needed to go home and check on his father and family. He fingered the little fish charm in his pocket as if it had some mystic spell over him. He felt safe so long as it was in his pocket.

As the British continued to control South Carolina with the help of the Loyalist Tory militia, Marion found himself without an army again. The British desperately wanted to crush the Swamp Foxes, who were still a great threat to them. The sons of Widow Jenkins said they knew of a hiding place which was high, dry, and inaccessible. They led the Swamp Foxes through Britton's Neck to Dunham's Bluff. There they crossed over the Pee Dee to Snow's Island. They crossed the island to the plantation of William Goddard.

Goddard was an ardent, warmhearted Whig, who was willing to turn over his cabin, barn, and bins to the defenders of his country. Marion found Snow's Island fit for the headquarters of a partisan chief. Along its eastern shore ran the wide Pee Dee. Lynches River lay on the north. Along the western and southern borders ran Clark's Creek, one of the tributaries of Lynches. To the west lay Snow's Lake and the swamps of Muddy Creek and Sockee.

William Goddard's house was on the high ground toward the middle of the island, safe above the flood waters of the Pee Dee. On the ridges around his fields were a virgin growth of gum, oak, and pine. In the woods were undergrowth of thick bushes. Dogwood, haw, and hornbeam branches entangled with wild muscadine vines. On the side of the island along Clark's Creek the undergrowth gave way to a green, almost impenetrable cane brake.

The Swamp Foxes set up camp in the woods near Goddard's cabin. They built crude, lean-to style huts to shield and protect them from the wind and rain. For their puny stores of food and military supplies, they built storage bins. And for their prisoners, they shored up Goddard's barn. Joseph called the new improved prison the "Bull Pen," and pretty soon it became commonly known by that name. It was Joseph's job to destroy all bridges to the island. A fortified redoubt was set up and manned with a guard.

When the camp was finished, Marion called in those former militiamen who could be trusted with a knowledge of his new hideaway. As his regiment swelled, he began sending out foragers and scouts. Soon his camp was like a beehive. His patrols ranged far and wide, their way lighted only by the moon and stars. Before long, the Swamp Foxes numbered seven hundred men.

On December 30, 1780, a courier from the Continental Army headquarters in Hillsboro found his way to Snow's Island with a letter from General George Washington and General Nathaniel Greene. Washington had appointed Greene, his friend and confidant, to be the commander of the Southern forces, to replace Horatio Gates. Marion had been appointed a Brigadier and put in charge of all regiments east of Santee, Wateree, and Catawba Rivers. His men cheered wildly when told the news of his promotion.

General Greene also requested that Marion's men serve as his intelligence-gathering arm. The Swamp Foxes immediately honored the General's request and set up a steady stream of communication, advising of British movements and troop strength in Kingstree, Georgetown, and Charles Town.

As soon as the brigade was properly organized, General Marion turned to routine duties. His failure to obtain powder, flints, or cartridge paper from Harrington or Greene, or to capture any from the British supply boats, had disarmed half of his men. Because of this constant shortage of ammunition, he decided to convert part of his infantry to cavalry. Commandeering every horse in Williamsburg owned by sympathetic supporters, he mounted his new cavalry division. All he needed now were proper weapons with which to arm them.

Joseph was put in charge of the blacksmith shop on Snow's Island. He picked young William James to help him. Colonel

Horry supplied five men to travel throughout the area and visit every Whig plantation, soliciting saw blades, pewter plates and bowls, and any form of lead, which could be forged into weapons and ball. While Joseph and William worked diligently on shoeing the new horses, these men scoured the countryside for the needed items. Within two days, they returned with dozens of cross-cut saw blades, bags full of pewter plates, saucers, bowls and pitchers, as well as several boxes of lead weights.

Joseph and William James set their hammers to ringing and the fires to burning. As he swang the hammer, Joseph began chanting and singing a song:

> "De sun is ridin' high today,
>   An' parches de earth below.
> Grass is brown for lack a' rain,
>   Oh! I long ta feel de snow.
> Summer's been hot, an' long it seems.
>   It makes de tongue so dry.
> I pour cool water on me head,
>   An' curse at all de flies.
> Workin in dis field all day,
>   De sun beats on me brow.
> I till de soil wit' my rusty hoe,
>   Boss yells, 'Get ta work, right now!'
> Sittin' in his house, so fine,
>   I guess he wouldn't know
> What it's like da work all day
>   Behind dis rusty hoe.
> Old man winter, you'se got it made.
>   An' I need ya' clouds so gray.
> Jes once, I'd like a little shade.
>   'Foe I die in dis fiel' some day."

"Where did you learn that, Joe?" Will James asked with a chuckle. "That sounds real good. I like it."

"Isaiah used to sing it to me when I was a little boy," he answered with a reminiscent smile. "He was one of our slaves; a wonderful and wise man."

Joseph stopped, reached into his pocket and said, "See this little fish charm? My papa made it for me in his blacksmith shop. It saved my life in the battle at Savannah. I wonder if my papa is all right. Somehow I feel I should go home and check on him." He placed the little charm back in his pocket, hesitated a while as if he wanted to say something else, and started back with his hammering.

From the saw blades Joseph and Will hammered out broad swords for the cavalry. Soon each man was armed with a long, keen, deadly weapon. They also melted down the pewter housewares as well as the lead that had been brought, and made musket balls and bullets for the sharpshooters.

Toward the end of the raw material supply Joseph observed to young William, "It's still not enough. We need at least twice this amount of ammunition for one good skirmish."

He looked over the large piles of musket balls and cartridge heads and continued, "I'd say we don't have more than five rounds per man. What do you say, Will?"

"You're probably right, Joe," he said with an air of hope, "maybe we should request another scouting party search for more materials."

About that time the old Swamp Fox himself walked in and looked over the new supply of ammunition. With a sincere air of appreciation in his voice, he addressed them in a very informal way, "Joe, William, I'll always remember how both of you have stuck with me like glue. And now, you've done a fine job in the blacksmith shop. You've probably done as much as any one in the country toward defeating the enemy. This supply of ammunition and the swords just might make the difference between victory and defeat, not only for my troops, but for the entire struggle."

He paused, as if pondering some deep question, and continued, "I've already sent another search party to look for more pewter and lead, but don't count on much more. The British had already taken most of it before we had a chance to ask. Listen, we'll just have to raid one of their depots and take it back."

With a twinkle in his eye, he continued, "It looks like help is on the way. Things are looking up. I'm going to promote you boys for your good work, when order is restored."

Joseph interrupted cautiously, and said, "Sir, I'm happy with my rank. I have no ambitions for a career in the army. Just as soon as I can leave with a good conscience, I must return home. My papa is getting old and needs me on the plantation. I've got several sisters who're saddled with the responsibility of running the farm. Thank you very much for this consideration, but it's reward enough just serving with you and the Swamp Foxes and helping in the cause."

"The same applies for me too, sir!" William hesitantly added. "I'm proud to be a small part of your group."

"Thank you, men," the grateful general said with confidence in his voice. "I believe it's time to start recruiting again." He smiled, looked at the homemade ammunition again, and left.

General Marion reminded Joseph of David in the Bible. He was a small man—he probably did not weigh over a hundred and fifty pounds—yet he was effectively slaying Goliath, and the British knew it.

The General began recruiting, and his numbers increased. Many of the Tories laid down their arms, and lukewarm or neutral patriots and Whigs reaffirmed their allegiance. He also began collecting supplies for his troops. While Marion was preparing his men, General Greene received notification that Lieutenant Colonel Henry Lee and his legion were on their way to join the southern strategy.

"Light Horse Harry" Lee and his legion arrived at Camp Hicks on January 9, 1781. His group of about two hundred sixty men was considered the finest combat team in the American army. They were fresh and ready for action. Greene sent him on to join Marion's men.

On January 17, 1781, news was brought into the camp that the American army under General Daniel Morgan, Colonel Andrew Pickens, with his South Carolina militia, and the Continentals commanded by Colonel John Eager Howard, had defeated the British General Banastre Tarleton. The British general had saved only his horse from the debacle. The men shouted and cheered the news. The Swamp Foxes had a burning dislike for Tarleton because of his ruthless treatment of civilians.

One January 24th, Marion and "Light Horse Harry" Lee, with their combined forces, attacked Georgetown successfully and took all but the British fort. During this campaign, these two great men with highly contrasting backgrounds learned a never-ending respect for each other. Lee allowed Marion to command the combined forces without argument and was pleased with what he saw.

Just when Marion began to have large dreams of the things he and Colonel Lee could do together, General Greene changed his strategy and recalled his officers in the field. This recall included Lee, and the Swamp Fox was again left alone with his homespun militia. Undaunted, the Swamp Foxes continued carrying out Marion's orders to attack and destroy the stores and depots of the British. They burned a large quantity of military stores from Manigault's Ferry to Monck's Corner.

One such incident occurred when Captain Zach Cantey spotted an encampment of British troops under Colonel Watson's command. He reconnoitered it and galloped away to warn Marion. The Swamp Foxes were on their way to meet General Thomas Sumter when they received this information. Marion realized this was the supreme attempt of the British to drive them from the low country. He knew also that his militia would now have the bloodiest kind of fighting— man to man, gun to gun, sword to sword. They would be entirely on their own, for there was no chance of any reinforcements. General Sumter was on his way back to the Waxhaws. Colonel Lee was with Greene, far to the north.

The next morning, Marion set up an ambush at Wadboo Swamp, a difficult pass on the Santee Road about midway between Murray's and Nelson's Ferries. There they ambushed Watson's troops and, after a bloody battle, retreated. During the battle, Joseph's horse was shot from under him. He hit the ground and, just as soon as his senses returned to him, ran for the underbrush along the edge of the woods. He lay quietly and watched the British regain their composure. They had captured three of Joseph's friends.

Colonel Watson rode over to where the prisoners were and heatedly talked with his men for a few minutes. He then led them toward the spot in the edge of the woods where Joseph was hiding. They were within fifty feet. Joseph was afraid they could hear his breathing, but he lay as still as he could. He could see the scared faces of the young militiamen.

Upon the signal by Colonel Watson, one of his men brought three well-worn ropes from his saddle bags. Quickly they made nooses and placed them around the necks of the prisoners. The redcoats pushed all three onto horses and threw the ropes over large limbs of the great live oak tree.

"I'm going to ask you one more time!" Watson growled. "Where is that dirty Swamp Fox's hideout?"

One of the men pleaded for mercy, "I have a wife and a six-month-old daughter. Please have mercy on us!" The other two sat like frozen statues. From the underbrush where he was hiding, Joseph felt that Watson was only bluffing. The colonel, however, waved his arm, and his men hit the horses with the flat side of their swords. The horses ran out from under the three victims, leaving them swinging in the air. Joseph could see the expressions of panic and horror on their faces. He closed his eyes but could still see the bulging eyes and the blue horror-ridden faces. Watson then gave another signal and motioned for his men to mount up and move out. The bodies of the three Swamp Foxes were left swinging as the British galloped down the road toward the retreating Marion and his men.

After waiting about five minutes, and scanning over the area to make sure there were no laggers, Joseph struggled to his feet, cut the ropes loose with his hunting knife, and checked to see if any of the bodies had any life left in them. They were all dead. He pulled the ropes from around their necks and since he had nothing with which to cover them, turned them over face down. After doing what he could for his dead comrades, Joseph started walking along the edge of the woods, following the road toward his company. He saw an idle horse, fully saddled, grazing on the long grass in the clearing, about fifty feet off the road. Pausing for a moment, looking in every direction for an owner, he finally decided it must have belonged to one of his dead comrades. He quickly leaped onto it and headed off with a gallop. His only safety was with the Swamp Fox.

Joseph finally made it back to Snow's Island and reported the tragedy to General Marion. He was enraged, wrote a hot letter, and sent it to Colonel Watson under a white flag, for delivery to Lord Rawdon. Watson ignored it and continued his march after the Swamp Foxes. Marion retaliated by ordering his nightly patrols to shoot Watson's sentinels and cut off his pickets, before disappearing into the swamp.

After resting and reorganizing his corps, Watson continued his pursuit, but the Swamp Fox was waiting, his horsemen already regrouping on the Santee Road. At Mount Hope Swamp, Marion broke down the bridge and left Hugh Horry and McCottrey's riflemen to prevent any crossing. Watson penetrated the swamp and crossed over. The Swamp Foxes then continued their retreat and headed toward Georgetown. Initially, Watson took up the pursuit in the direction of Georgetown, but then he changed his mind and turned his column back to attack Kingstree. Major John James and McCottrey's sharpshooters were dispatched by Marion to protect the bridge. Watson sent his troops in column toward the ford, being led by a sword-waving captain. Captain McCottrey's men took position, and with careful aim, fired. The wildly advancing British Captain and four of his men were killed. Colonel Watson then retreated to John Witherspoon's plantation about a mile above the bridge. The Swamp Foxes stayed to prevent his taking the bridge. Simple countrymen in blue denims, armed with squirrel rifles, fowling pieces, and homemade swords had thrown back one of the finest regiments of the British Army.

Before daybreak the following morning, Marion was up, rousing and deploying his men. He pushed Captains McCottrey and Conyers across the Black River with orders to pick off Watson's pickets and sentinels. All day they skirmished and picked off the British troops.

By nightfall Watson moved about a half mile farther up the river and camped in a large open field on the Blakely plantation. To further avenge the hangings of their friends, the McCottrey sharpshooters followed him there and continued picking off his men, which kept the British regulars in a panic. Colonel Watson swallowed his pride and wrote to Marion, asking that he be allowed to leave with his wounded. Marion wrote a pass for him to send only the wounded.

Watson started retreating to Georgetown, but Marion's men followed him, attacking his rear flanks from behind trees and from behind every thicket and swamp. Marion sent Colonel Horry's horsemen dashing ahead to destroy the planks of the bridge over the

Sampit River. He then charged upon the rear guard with a fury when Watson's men reached the destroyed bridge.

The ensuing skirmish was brief but bloody. Colonel Watson sought to rally his men, but a sharpshooter killed his horse. Quickly mounting another, Watson ordered his artillery to open fire with grapeshot. When Marion's horsemen wheeled back from the cannon fire, Watson loaded his wounded into two wagons, leaving twenty dead upon the field. He plunged across the ford with the blood on the wagon floors turning the waters of the Sampit a dark red.

Before Marion's men could rest, a messenger came to the camp and brought distressing news. The British Colonel Walbore Doyle and the Tory New York Volunteers had crossed Lynches River at Witherspoon's and were already marching through the swamps toward Snow's Island. It was a full day's march to the threatened action, and Marion's men were exhausted from riding and fighting. They would have to wait until morning before starting their return march.

Colonel Doyle captured Snow's Island without losing a man. His exploit was brilliant, climaxing a frenzied march from McCallum's Ferry to the Pee Dee Road. He had forever destroyed the usefulness of the favorite lair of the Swamp Foxes.

Marion returned swiftly from the Sampit River. In his march through Williamsburg, it was necessary to pass near the homes of many of his followers. One by one they dropped out of his band until he was down to seventy men when he arrived at Indiantown.

At daybreak the following day, he sent Colonel Horry's men to drive away Doyle's troops who had been seen ransacking and foraging a Whig plantation south of the Lynches River. His men killed nine and captured sixteen of the fleeing marauders. After the skirmish, Captain McCottrey and his riflemen pursued the enemy to Witherspoon's. There they caught the frantic rear guard scuttling the ferry boat.

After frightening the British away from the sinking craft, the sharpshooters fanned out along the river's edge and began intermittently firing into Doyle's camp. The balls from their long rifles carried well, and although Lynches River was flooded and wide, they toppled a private and an officer of the volunteers. Doyle returned the fire vigorously, but being outflanked and outgunned, broke camp and retreated toward the Pee Dee.

In early April, Colonel Light Horse Harry Lee was allowed to return to the low country with his Continental army. Without quibble about rank, Henry Lee placed himself and his legion under the command of General Marion. They decided to attack Fort Watson.

After laying siege to the fort for several days, Marion realized it could not be taken by force. He did not have a cannon. An ingenious Continental officer from St. Stephens, Major Maham, who had recently joined, suggested a way to overcome the fort without a cannon. Horsemen were sent out to scour the neighborhood plantations for axes. Marion then put the woodsmen to cutting down pine trees. Others were ordered to carry the slender poles and dump them in a pile just out of range of the British muskets.

During the evening Joseph and a squad of volunteers began chopping, lifting, and settling the logs into an oblong tower. At a point higher than the enemy's rampart, a floor was laid. The front was reinforced with a shield of timber.

Before morning the crack shots from McCottrey's men climbed into the tower. By daylight on April 23rd, the British commander found himself staring up to a tower filled with sharpshooters. The buckshot from his muskets could not penetrate the logs, but the bullets from the long rifles whistled into the fort. Safe from enemy fire, Joseph and two of the patriots started pulling down a section of the stockade. After a while, Lieutenant McKay raised the white flag.

Marion and Lee offered generous terms to the men who had defended themselves bravely for eight days. For the first time since the invasion of South Carolina, American troops had toppled a British stronghold.

In early May the Swamp Fox and Light Horse Harry Lee were on their way to Fort Motte when an escaped American prisoner met them on the road and brought good and bad news. General Greene, the man reported, had engaged Lord Rawdon at Hobkirk's Hill, and after a bloody battle, was forced to retreat about five miles north of Camden. Rawdon had headed back to

Logtown, leaving Captain Coffin to hold the field. Colonel Washington had been waiting for such an opportunity, however; concealing his dragoons behind a thicket, the American patriot had sent a weak detachment to lure Coffin's horsemen into ambush. After cutting them to pieces, Washington took undisputed possession of Hobkirk's Hill.

Within the next few days, Lord Rawdon evacuated Camden, burning and destroying much of the town, releasing the prisoners, and burning the jail. He burned the mills and many private dwellings as well. Then, after setting fire to all remaining supplies, he collected his sick, except thirty, too ill to travel, and set his army retreating down the road toward Charles Town.

After occupying Camden, General Greene met with Marion and Lee and expressed his great appreciation and affection for each. He ordered Lee to join General Andrew Pickens in his siege of Augusta. Marion was to remain in the area around Camden.

Joseph had not heard from his family for almost two years. He had thought many times about going home but could not bring himself to leave General Marion while things had been difficult.

When he heard the news that Colonel Lee was going to Augusta, he became excited. Maybe he could go along with Colonel Lee's legion.

He waited until meal time to approach Colonel Lee with his request. Lee had finished eating, had drawn a sheet of paper, and was about to begin writing when Joseph interrupted, "Colonel Lee, sir, I'm Private Joseph Dicks. I'm from the New Windsor Township in Granville County, which is only about five miles from Augusta. I understand you are headed in that direction, and I'd like to go along with you. I can be helpful in the Augusta area. I know all the roads, creeks, rivers, and trails in that part of the country."

Colonel Lee paused for a moment and asked, "What do you have in mind, Private Dicks?"

"I'd just like to travel along with you, sir," Joseph answered. "I'll return to the Swamp Fox when my business is finished at home."

"Very well, Dicks," Colonel Lee responded as he made a salute.

"You get me a letter from Marion, giving permission, and I'll be more than happy to let you ride along."

The excitement began to mount for Joseph. He hurried to General Marion's tent and nervously fingered his little fish charm as he waited.

"All right, Joe. You've been one of my most faithful men for almost two years," the general answered with a note of sincerity. "I'll have the quartermaster write a letter of permission for you. If you'll wait a minute, I'll write my own personal recommendation to Colonel Lee."

Long before daybreak the following morning, Joseph was up and following the Continental Legion, led by Colonel Light Horse Harry Lee, on his way to the Augusta area and home.

Will James had followed him to his horse and wished him well. They had shaken hands and promised to see each other again. Now Joseph waved to him as the body of men and horses moved away from the group of men he had learned to love and respect. He had been proud to serve with the Swamp Foxes and hoped he could return within a few months.

The bright May sun was hot overhead, and the smell of a hundred horses and sweaty men, mixed with the dust from the horses' hooves, was enough to stifle any healthy man. But Joseph noticed only the beautiful light and the colorful beginnings of summer all around him. He was on his way home.

5

Trouble at Home

1780-1781

"Hey, you can't take everything we've got!" John yelled with fury in his voice, as he ran out the door of the little log house with his long barrel musket. "What do you think we'll live on?"

Catherine and Sarah had been down at the cattle lot, begging and pleading with the ten British soldiers not to take all their livestock. Isaiah, Phoebe, and all the other slaves had been told to stay in their house, but they peeped out the windows and watched with fear the confiscation of almost all of John Dicks' livestock except for two horses, two hogs, two cows, and two sheep. As the soldiers herded away the rest of the livestock, the girls followed, running behind their horses until they reached the corner of the house.

After yelling in desperation, John took aim at the British soldier who was bringing up the rear of the herd. Before he could pull the trigger, the redcoat wheeled around and, followed by two more, galloped close to the house, drew his sidearm, and shot him through the thigh of his right leg. The jolt from the shot and the loud ringing blast stunned John, and he blacked out.

Seeing the brazenly raw violence, Catherine lost all control. She ran over, took the unfired musket from the ground where it had fallen, and aimed it at the guilty soldier. Before she could fire it, one of the other returning redcoats shot her through the heart.

Thinking her father and sister were dead, Sarah took the gun and started running after the retreating soldiers. She fired the musket. It apparently wounded one of the men, who wheeled around and shot her in the head. Mary, who had been guarding the three younger girls in the house, dashed out the door, screamed in terror and fell upon John. Elizabeth bolted from the door and came out to help her drag him into the house. The British troops herded the livestock on down the lane as if it were all in a day's work.

After the British soldiers had left, Isaiah and Sam came running around the corner of the house and helped to carry the girls inside. After laying them on the bed, Phoebe and Augustine, who had slipped in the back door, rushed over to help take care of them. Mary was lying on John, in the middle of the floor. She cried out in anguish, "John, John, you can't die. We all need you. Oh, God! Please don't let him die!"

Phoebe came over, took Mary by the shoulders, and managed, among sobs, to cry out, "Dey's both gone, Miss Mary! Dey's both gone! God help us! Dey's gone!"

Wilma and Martha huddled in the corner of the kitchen in a state of shock, while Elizabeth tried to comfort them. They were frozen at the sight of all the blood on the floor and the beds and by the hysterical screams of their mother and the old slave woman. Augustine, not knowing what else to do, hurredly ran her small children, who had also slipped in the back door, out of the house and began busily wiping up the blood from the floor. Princess, Lunnon, Sylvia, Sarah, and Rose, seeing their mother through the door busily cleaning the floor, took the straw brooms which lay by the door, and began sweeping the bloody sand from in front of the steps.

When Mary jumped up and threw herself on the bed over her bloody, lifeless, daughters, Isaiah kneeled over John, felt his neck, and ran his hand over his mouth and nose. He sprang up and shouted, "Praise de lawd! Praise de lawd! Missy Mary, he's 'live! He's 'live!"

He kneeled again, shook John's head, and cried out through his tears, "Wake up, Massa John! Wake up! Lawd, make him wake up!"

John groaned, looked up at Isaiah, and said, "Isaiah, what happened? Where are those redcoats?" He started to get up but let out another groan of anguish. He could not move his right leg.

"Now, jes be still, Massa John. You been shot. De redcoats done gone and took all de animals wit dem." Isaiah cried excitedly. "Let 'em go. Dey done shot Missy Cat'rin and Missy Sarah. Let 'em go. Ya in no shape ta do nothin'!"

Phoebe had helped Mary lie down on the other bed and had covered the bodies of Sarah and Catherine. When Mary heard John, she began crying uncontrollably and cried out with an anguish only known by a mother who had lost her two daughters in such a tragic and brutal way.

It was a cold January morning as the family, the slaves, and several friends gathered around the family cemetery on the banks of Town Creek. The drizzling rain and the chilling wind made the occasion even more unbearable. The aged chief of the Cofitachequi Indians, with a delegation consisting of his daughter, son-in-law, and several of the young council members, stood solemnly by the hedgerow at the far end of the cemetery. Several of George Galphin's children joined the family near the double graves. Several other planters and livestock farmers, whom John had befriended, stood in silence as the aged Reverend John Tobler, with gray hair and beard waving in the cold wind, offered final words over the graves.

John lay in the wagon on a thick cushion of quilts, near the graves. Mary was so grief-stricken she could stand only with the help of William and John, Jr. Martha and Elizabeth held on to the arms of Thomas. Wilma, who had been sickly most of her life, sat on the wagon beside her father. Isaiah, Phoebe, and all their children and grandchildren stood by the wagon, wiping away tears.

"Dust thou art, to dust returneth, was not spoken of the Soul," the white-haired minister said in slow and measured tones. "We have these promises to sustain us in times like these," he continued as he lifted his hands toward the family. "Now may the peace that passeth understanding be yours, and may you all put your complete dependence in the God of Peace, now and forevermore, in the name of the Father, the Son, and the Holy Ghost. Amen."

Reverend Tobler turned, hugged Mary and the girls, shook the hands of the Dicks' sons, and walked over to the wagon to speak to

John and Wilma. "If I can be of further service, John, just send for me," he said in a sincere and fatherly tone.

"Thank you, Reverend," John finally whispered from a swelled throat. "Thank you for coming."

"I'm sorry it's circumstances like these that have brought us together," Tobler replied. "God bless you and your bereaved family."

He bent over the wagon so he could whisper to John. "Be careful, John. You know there are more Loyalist Tories here in this township than Whigs. I can't help but believe that some Loyalist Tory is causing the British to harass you. Keep that in mind, John, and be careful."

"Thank you again, Reverend, I'll keep it in mind," he replied feebly as he tried to pull more quilts over his legs.

"The boys helped Mary into the wagon, and the sad little party slowly dispersed. Isaiah and Sam began shoveling the newly dug dirt over the wooden coffins of the two beautiful Dicks girls whose lives had been cut short in their prime.

Before William could rein the horses toward home, John Parkinson rushed over toward the wagon. He was George Galphin's nephew, and had been operating the trading post since Galphin's death. "Wait up, John," he called as he rushed over. When he was near enough to speak in low tones, he said, "John, keep your eye out for Daniel Dues. He and his boys have been the most blatant Tories in the area. They've caused the redcoats to take almost everything Mr. George owned. They're a violent bunch, too. Watch out for them.

"John, I've tried to be neutral in this conflict. I resigned my position as judge only because I couldn't, in good conscience, administer the new laws the Crown has imposed over the past few years."

"Yes, but they know you have a son fighting against the Crown. They think you're actively working as a patriot," Parkinson replied quickly. "So keep up your guard, and watch out for the Tories, especially the Dues clan. I'm sorry about your great tragedy. If you need me, you know where I am," he continued as he moved back away from the wagon.

John nodded as the wagon slowly began moving toward home.

The fire was blazing hot and bright that evening in the little log house, but it seemed cold and empty when William, John, Jr. and Thomas, with their wives and children, stopped in to sit a while with the family. John lay on the bed nearest the fire and appeared to be in a daze. As the boys left one by one, with the grandchildren, he remained silent and merely nodded and smiled.

When they had all gone back home, John raised up in his bed and with an air of hope said, "We all must go on living. Liz, I want you to check out the smokehouse and the barn first thing in the morning. We must see how much food we have left."

For several hours, John lay on his bed gazing into the fire and ashes. "Where is Joseph when I need him most?" he thought without blinking an eye. "When will he be coming home? Oh, God, please let him make it back home," he thought as his eyes became hot with tears. He lay there without moving, staring into the fire until the flame died away, leaving only ashes in the darkness.

"Papa, I've been to the smokehouse and the barn. There's nothing left. They didn't have the decency to leave us one piece of meat!" Liz exclaimed as she nudged John's shoulder to awaken him. It was about nine o'clock, and the sun was already high in the winter sky. "The barn is empty except for the indigo. I guess they couldn't eat that," Liz continued with anger in her every word.

"I'll try to kill a deer or a wild boar," John responded as he tried to get up.

"You stay in that bed, Papa," she quickly commanded, like the boss of the work crew. "You're not able to be up. I'll take Isaiah and Sam, and we'll find some meat in the woods. Don't you worry now. What you need is good rest."

She turned to Martha and said, "Martha, take a pail and see if you can get a little milk from the cow. And Wilma, get the fire going again and help Mamma dress Papa's wound. I'm going hunting."

Liz took the long barrel rifle, stopped by to get Isaiah and Sam, and proceeded to the low-lying woods on the bank of Town Creek. She had never shot a gun more than three times, but she had no choice. She must kill something, or the family as well as the slaves would soon face starvation.

They walked for several hours before seeing anything larger than a squirrel. Suddenly, a large deer sprang across the clearing right in front of her. She took fast aim, closed her eyes, and fired, but not being an experienced hunter, she missed it entirely.

After backtracking for about another hour, Liz saw a wild hog moving slowly toward them as it rooted around every tree and amongst the bush. She waited until it was within about thirty feet. With Isaiah and Sam hiding behind a large thicket of underbrush she slowly took aim and pulled the trigger. The lead hit its mark, and the wild boar fell to the ground.

Sam rushed over, stabbed it and slit its throat. When it finally stopped kicking, he and Isaiah tied the feet together, cut a large pole from a sapling, and ran it through the legs. They placed the pole on their shoulders for the long walk home, bearing enough meat for a week.

When they arrived back home, Liz said proudly, "Isaiah, you and Sam take this boar to the smoke house and get it ready for curing. We'll keep out enough for about a couple of days and cure the rest. Now don't waste a thing. We may not be so lucky next time."

"Yessum, Missy 'Lizbeth," Sam eagerly responded. "I'll get Phoebe and Augustine ta hep us. We'se got meat aplenty now."

"Mamma, Papa, we killed a big wild hog," Liz said excitedly as she bolted through the door. "Sam and Isaiah are dressing it now!"

The back door swang open and Phoebe came in struggling with two large bags. "Massa John, Missy Mary, we'se got flour and grits left. Dey missed our house. Here, you take it. We'se got 'bout dis much mo' in de house."

"Thank you, Phoebe," John called from his bed. "We'll share all we have as long as it lasts."

Mary was bending over Wilma who lay in bed. She felt her forehead and said, "I believed you have a little fever, dear. You stay in bed today. We can take care of everything."

She turned to Phoebe and said, "Thank you. Just put it on the table. When I finish things here, I'll come help you with the meat."

John reached under the bed and brought out his little medicine bag. He opened it and flipped through the contents. "All we have is Continental dollars. They aren't worth the paper they're printed on.

We'll need some money to buy the things we can't produce."

He turned to Liz and said, "Maybe you can go down to Galphin's trading post and ask John Parkinson if he'll buy the indigo, or take it in trade on the things we need. I wish George were still alive."

"Papa, I thought I'd better repair the barn and the fences, before the few animals they left us get lost," Liz replied. "Maybe it can wait until I get back."

"I'll go," interrupted Martha. "I'll take Princess with me. She's been there with Sam. We can both ride on the horse."

Martha was a tall slender girl and as shapely as a queen. Her beautiful blond hair was long and smooth from constant brushing. She had always stayed near her mother and the house. A pretty and stately, but delicate girl, she had never done anything that was not very feminine.

Liz, on the other hand, was a tomboy. She was a beautiful one, however, with an outgoing personality. Her long brown hair was naturally curly and had a pleasant appearance even though she spent little time brushing it. Her tanned cheeks had a natural, healthy, pink color which radiated a wholesome glow. She had a very practical manner which caused her to take on the responsibility of caring for the others like a mother hen, while the man of the house was unable to do so.

Liz picked up a hatchet and a hammer from under the bed and started toward the barn and pasture to make the necessary repairs. Martha got Sam to saddle and bridle the mare. Then she left on horseback, with Princess sitting behind her, holding on for dear life.

The cold January wind blew through Martha's long blond hair, and the bright sun did little to warm her freezing face and hands. Little Princess held on tightly with her little black hands, and snuggled against her to hide from the chilling wind.

"I didn't know it was so far," Martha said through the chattering of her teeth.

"It's jes a piece mo', Missy Marda," stammered little Princess through quivering purple lips.

In the road ahead there were two British soldiers and someone who looked like a well-bred planter. As Martha drew near, she recognized the planter. He was Chance Dues, a belligerent Tory spy.

He yelled to her in his usual arrogant voice, "Halt, Miss Dicks. You must come with us.'

"Don't pay dem no mine, Missy Marda. Keep goin' ta Massa Galphin's sto','" Princess whispered as she hugged tighter around Martha's waist and began to cry and whine.

"I can't go with you anywhere, Chance Dues. I'm on an errand for my Papa, and I must hurry back home," she said, trying to be brave.

One of the British soldiers reached over and took the bridle of the horse and said in an authoritative manner, "Miss Dicks, I'm afraid it is necessary. The Indians want to send a message to your father, and they were sending us to fetch one of his children. They wouldn't tell us what they wanted."

Without her permission the soldier held her horse's bridle and pulled them along as they headed toward the Cofitachequi village at Silver Bluff. When the party passed near Galphin's trading post, Chance Dues reached over and put Princess on the ground.

"Now you git," he said in a threatening way. "Them Indians don't allow no nigger children in their village!"

"Hey, you can't do that!" Martha screamed as she tried to pull away from the soldier.

"She'll be alright," he laughed. "Old John Parkinson'll take care of her."

The four of them rode down to the landing and turned toward the village. After trotting leisurely about half a mile through the tall live oak, cypress, and white pine trees, the party came to a clearing, and the soldier snatched her horse off the road. All three dismounted and dragged her from her horse.

"What are you doing?" she cried. "You're not taking me to the Indian village, are you?"

"No, we're not, Miss high and mighty Dicks!" scowled Chance. "We're going to see if you're as pretty as you think you are! Grab her, boys. There's enough for all of us!"

All three grabbed her and began tearing off her clothes. She started screaming in fear and anguish as she clawed, scratched, and kicked. In panic she screamed louder, and louder, as if her life depended on ears that were not likely in hearing range.

Chance Dues hit her across the face and yelled, "Shut your

damned mouth. If you scream again, I'll bust your face!" Martha
screamed even louder, scratching and clawing more than ever. She
suddenly stopped when one of the redcoats pulled his sidearm and
growled with a grin, "I know one way to stop that mouth!"

Martha froze in her tracks, expecting to feel the ball from his gun
at any moment, but suddenly he fell backwards. Chance Dues also
loosed his grip on her and fell on his face. There was a hunting knife
in his back. The other redcoat turned to run but fell with another
knife in his back.

Five young Indian braves came from behind the trees. One had a
blanket which he had pulled from his horse. He placed it around her
and smiled.

"Do not fear," he said comfortingly. "We not harm you. What
your name?"

"I'm Martha Dicks, John Dicks' daughter," she said as she
shivered in the cold wind and cried with a pale face and blue lips.

"I'm Little Eagle," he courteously said as he bowed. "I'm son of
Chief Brown Eagle."

He paused as if in deep reflection, and continued. "This same spot
where your father saved my sister from same grief. We see you home
safely!"

He motioned for two of the others to follow him while the
remaining two checked the slain bodies. They nodded and made a
sign. They were all dead.

Little Eagle motioned for them to dispose of the bodies, helped
Martha on her horse, and said with a half smile, "You safe now."

"What's going on here? What are you boys doing to Miss Dicks?"
John Parkinson yelled.

The Indians had escorted Martha back to Galphin's trading post.
She had remained on the horse, wrapped in the blanket. They had
dismounted so as to enter the trading post to bring Mr. Parkinson to
her. He had been waiting near the doorway, and wheeled around to
look for his musket, when he saw them leap from their horses.

"Wait a minute, Mr. Parkinson," she screamed. "These Indians
have saved my life. They saved me from Chance Dues and the British
soldiers!"

She paused a moment and then continued. "Papa had sent me to ask you if you would be so kind as to buy what indigo we have, or trade it for food and supplies.

"Tell your father I'll be happy to give him top price for it," he said with a smile. "I'm stuck with a box full of Continental dollars too, so tell him it'll be necessary to trade goods for it."

He turned and looked back toward the big fireplace in the rear of the store, motioned for Princess to come forward, and continued. "I believe you've lost something here. She told me what happened, so I let her stay near the fire. She's all right. I had planned to come looking for you if you had not returned within an hour."

Princess bolted from the door, reached up for Martha's hand, and jumped onto the horse behind her. "Is you a'right, Missy Marda? I's feared ta death dem mean men wud hurt you," she said excitedly as she hugged Martha tightly around the waist and began crying and sniffing.

"Thank you, Mr. Parkinson," Martha said as her teeth chattered from the chilling wind and cold fear. "Little Eagle and his friends are going to see me home safely. Papa will be glad to know you'll take the indigo." They turned the snorting horses around and headed toward the Dicks' place, leaving a stream of hot breath vapor in the winter air.

The next day Liz loaded the wagon, took the list of needed supplies from her father, and put the long barrel rifle under the wagon seat. She, Isaiah, and Sam headed to the Galphin trading post with a wagon load of indigo, hoping to be there about noon. The sky continued to turn gray, and there were no sunrays to help warm the three freezing faithfuls from the Dicks' place.

"I sure hope it doesn't snow today," Liz said as she blew on her hands with her warm breath. "That's all we need."

"It might be mo' warm iffen it does snow," Isaiah said as he rubbed his black, calloused hands. "I'ze sho' cold now. Dis wind is sho' nuff knife-cuttin' cold."

About a mile from home, Daniel Dues and three British soldiers sprang out of the woods on their fine horses and blocked the road. "What you got under that quilt in the wagon?" Dues growled. "Is it provisions you're holding back from the Crown?"

Liz reached under the seat for her long barrel rifle. She nervously replied, trying to appear as brave and fearless as possible. "That's nothing but indigo. You can't eat it. You can't drink it. It's just indigo."

"Have you seen my boy, Chance?" old Daniel asked with a tone of suspicion. "He's been missing since yesterday when he left word he was headed to the Dicks' house."

She quickly pulled the rifle from under the seat and aimed it straight at Daniel Dues' head. The end of the long barrel was within six inches of his ugly face, and the hammer was already cocked back, with her nervous finger dancing on the trigger.

"If you don't turn around and head back where you came from, I may lose my patience and pull this trigger," she yelled to him as bravely and as boldly as she could manage. "We've not seen your rotten son, and don't want to see him. Now get out of my way!"

Dues motioned to the redcoats to back off. Liz had suddenly surprised them all and taken away all their options with the long barrel resting in the face of the area's bloodiest Tory. She held the rifle steady, while Isaiah and Sam rested their hands on the butchering knives that lay under the seat. The redcoats, with their Judas goat, backed slowly away. As they wheeled around and galloped on, Liz placed the rifle under the seat once again and breathed a sigh of relief.

"Maybe you better keep de gun in hand, Missy 'Lizbeth. Dem redcoats and spies may be back," Sam suggested, as Isaiah took the reins and started the wagon moving again.

"You're probably right, Sam," she responded as she reached again for the rifle, placing it on her lap. "We've taken about all we're going to take from those thieves," she grunted as she placed her nervous finger on the trigger. "I'm tired of them harassing us all the time. There must be some way to put a stop to it!"

About two weeks later, the Dicks family again was harassed by the Tories and the British soldiers. It was late in the evening after the February sun had almost gone down. John, Mary, Wilma, Martha, and Elizabeth had just begun eating their evening meal when they heard a musket fire just outside their door.

"John Dicks!" came the booming voice. "Come out here. I want to talk to you."

"Be careful, papa," Liz nervously cried. "That's Daniel Dues. I'd never forget his evil voice!"

"Now everyone stay calm. I'll see what he wants," John said in a comforting tone. "Don't any of you do anything foolish." He slowly rose, picked up his walking stick and hobbled out the front door, closing it behind him.

Liz grabbed the rifle and eased out the back door, slipping to the corner of the house to watch. From a good hiding spot behind the well she could see Mr. Daniel Dues, his son Richard, and five redcoats.

John struggled to strand erect, with the help of his stick, and speak in a voice which sounded like a nobleman welcoming guests. "Gentlemen, what can I do for you?"

Daniel Dues straightened himself up in the saddle and growled, "What have you done with my son? He's been missing more than two weeks. The last time I saw him he was on his way to your house."

"Well, he must not have made it," John answered in a calm voice. "I haven't seen him."

Dues lifted his musket and pointed it toward John. He cocked the hammer and scowled, "I'm not going to ask you again. You know something about this, and I'm going to find out what it is. If you don't tell me the truth, you dirty rebel, I'm going to blow your head off."

John had had enough. He dropped his walking stick, pulled open his shirt, showing his bare chest, and screamed, "If you want to kill an innocent man, go ahead. Shoot! Show everyone what a big man you are! Shoot!"

The loud vicious crack of the musket sounded as might have been expected. Daniel Dues reared back in his saddle and shot his gun into the air as he fell from his horse. The sound of a dozen blazing rifles echoed through the house. The evening sky suddenly appeared to be split with lightning, as the shots came ringing from the hedgerow on one side of the house and from the woods on the other. Two of the redcoats fell to the ground, and the others wheeled their horses around and galloped away without looking back.

Captain Patrick O'Neale and his ten men came from the woods, their sharpshooting rifles aimed at Richard Dues and the slain redcoats. "Get your father on his horse and get him away from here!" O'Neale shouted to young Richard. "Joe, Luke, check those redcoats to see if they're alive!"

Joe Carter and Luke Saunders motioned that they were dead.

"Tie them on horses and send them along with Dues!" Captain O'Neale called as he cautiously looked around.

He saw a rifle barrel pointing from behind the well near the house. Pointing his sharpshooting rifle at the well, he cocked the hammer and yelled, "Alright you, come from behind that well with your hands up."

Liz quickly dropped the gun, raised her hands, and meekly stood up.

"My God, girl, that's a good way to get killed!" the Captain bellowed as he lowered his gun. "What on earth were you doing over there? Do you think you can fight a whole brigade of trained soldiers?"

"Someone had to protect us," she cried as she ran to John and frantically hugged him.

"Who are you men?" John asked as he offered his hand to the Captain.

"I'm Captain Patrick O'Neale of the New Windsor militia," he answered as he stood erect. After pausing a moment, he continued. "Well, actually there're only ten of us, and we don't have a commission. As you know, this area is largely made up of Loyalist Tories."

He looked at the horses galloping away with the three slain riders, and Richard Dues leading them. "He's a bloody and ruthless one," he said, as he pointed to Richard. "We overheard him bragging about 'fixing' John Dicks, so we followed them here."

"Won't you boys come in and have something to eat or drink?" John asked in a warm and grateful tone. "We all appreciate what you've done for us today."

"We'd better keep going," O'Neale answered. "It's getting late."

The Captain was the most handsome man Liz had ever seen. His red curly hair was cropped short, as was his neatly trimmed beard.

He had become a hero to her. As he climbed into the saddle, Liz blurted out, "Captain, please stay. We have enough for all of you."

"Well, my men are probably hungry and thirsty from hiding all day and watching those murderers. I guess we can stay a few minutes."

Mary, Wilma, and Martha had remained in the kitchen, looking through the shutters of the window. They rushed to open the door and welcome the brave young men. Martha and Liz pretended they had already eaten so there would be enough ham and beans for the men.

O'Neale was kind, well mannered, and jovial as he sat at the table and talked with his men and the family. He thought he had never seen a more beautiful girl in the world than Martha. Her long blond hair and statuesque frame put him into a daze. It was hard for him not to stare at the quiet, almost regal young girl who had given up her place at the table for such a group of roughnecks.

After about an hour, Captain O'Neale abruptly announced, "Men we must leave. It's getting late, and we'd better go home tonight because we may have other work to do tomorrow."

He turned to John and said reassuringly, "We'll keep our eyes and ears open. And we'll keep checking by to see how you're doing."

He smiled at Martha as he and his men left. She returned the smile, trying to maintain her composure, while a volcano was trying to erupt inside of her.

"Does he feel the same way about me? Oh, I really hope so," she thought as she began clearing the table.

"Isn't he simply the most handsome man you've ever seen?" Liz asked with a thrill in her voice and a sparkle in her eye. "I just love that red curly hair and those deep blue eyes!"

"Who on earth are you talking about?" Martha responded, trying to act unconcerned. "For heaven's sake, Liz, don't act like an overgrown child!"

"That Captain O'Neale," Liz exclaimed without noticing Martha's sharp tongue. "He was simply gorgeous. Or maybe I should have said ravishing. And a braver man I've never seen," she continued as she began to help Martha with the kitchen work.

"Don't go losing your head over a stranger, Liz," Martha

cautioned with an air of indifference. "You may never see him again. And anyway, he probably already has a steady girl."

Over the next three months Captain O'Neale and his small band of patriots kept checking by to see if the Dicks family was all right. Each time he called, it was Martha he wanted to talk to. He was enthralled by her regal beauty, and she was charmed by his brave disposition, muscular frame, and well-bred manners.

On May 21st, 1781, Tory hatred for John Dicks and the personal vengeance of the Dues clan erupted into a climax which would end, once and for all, the harassment. The Dues clan, headed by Richard, led a group of about ten Tories and fifteen British soldiers on a raid of the Dicks home. Liz had been in the field near the stagecoach trail picking spring flowers for the supper table, when she saw the large group of horsemen coming. She rushed home and told the family. John thought for a moment and quickly decided what must be done.

"There's too many of them for us to fight!" he exclaimed in a frantic tone. "Liz, Mary, get all the muskets, rifles, guns, and ammunition. We'll run down to Isaiah's house and wait there."

The band of British troops and Tory supporters, led by Richard Dues, pulled their horses to a stop in front of the Dicks home. Several of the Tories shot into the house as if giving notice of their intentions.

"John Dicks, come out here!" yelled young Richard, as he shot another volley into the house. There was no answer from inside so Richard went on, "We'll bring him out. Put the torch to it."

The redcoats watched from their horses while the enflamed Tories did the dirty work. They shot fire arrows onto the roof of the house and waited.

Suddenly, like lightning, the sharpshooters of Captain Patrick O'Neale started firing from behind the trees. Richard Dues fell to the ground alongside two other Tories and three redcoats. This time, however, the marauders did not run. They leaped from their horses and hid behind anything that would give them cover. For several minutes the shots rang out around the Dicks' farm.

As the flames engulfed their home, John and Liz slipped through the woods to the vicinity of the New Windsor Militia. John dragged his crippled leg as Liz helped him along. They stationed themselves behind large trees and proceeded to help in their own defense. The sound of gunfire gradually slowed on the side of the militia. It seemed that only John and Liz were still firing. Captain O'Neale crawled over to where John and Liz were and gave the bad news. "We're out of ammunition. I don't know what to do."

The Tories and redcoats, sensing the problem, became brave and eased out from behind their barricades. Not a shot was fired from the woods. They slowly walked across the yard with crouched shoulders and raised guns, toward the woods where the brave patriots waited defenselessly.

Suddenly there was a new sound in the air, the thunder of a hundred horses. Colonel "Light Horse Harry" Lee and his troop of the Continental army, hearing the sound of battle and seeing the smoke of the Dicks' home, had reined their horses to a gallop and came blazing down the lane, Joseph in the lead, with muskets and rifles firing. The redcoats and Tories, standing in the yard without protection and seeing the overwhelming numbers of the Continental army, quickly realized it was a formidable foe. They threw down their arms and raised their hands in surrender. Colonel Lee assigned several of his men to take charge of the prisoners, and he greeted the homespun local militia.

When Liz saw Joseph, she sprang up and ran to him as he leaped from his horse to embrace her. John hobbled out of the edge of the woods as they both wheeled around and ran to him. They all shed tears of joy as they embraced each other in the heat, dust, and smoke, made more unbearable by the unusually hot May sun. Martha and Wilma also came running, followed by Isaiah, Sam, and the rest of the slaves. When they saw Joseph, the great loss of their home was pushed to the back of their minds, as they hugged him and mingled their tears of joy. Mary was ecstatic.

"You couldn't have arrived at a better time, sir," Captain O'Neale blurted out as he shook Colonel Lee's hand. "We were completely out of ammunition. And they were coming in for the kill!"

The stately Virginian said he was honored and stated that his men were hungry and thirsty. Since all food had been destroyed in the fire, only water could be offered the guests. Sam and Isaiah were thrilled to draw the water from the well for the men who had become heroes to them. Like a smooth-tongued diplomat, Colonel Lee relayed General Marion's appreciation and commendation of Joseph to his beaming father.

Captain O'Neale, realizing the condition of the men, told Colonel Lee about Fort Galphin which presently had a large store of food and supplies. These goods had been sent by the Crown as the annual gift to the Indians. The fort, which formerly had been the George Galphin home, was a two-story brick house, surrounded by a stockade fence. It was under the control of Colonel William Brown, the British commander in Augusta. Colonel Lee and his troop of Continental soldiers were anxious to take the fort, so Joseph and Captain O'Neale, with his local militia, led them to it.

The sun was unusually hot for May, and the moisture in the air hung heavy as the men and horses became soaked with sweat. When they reached the pine thicket which surrounded the field where Fort Galphin was located, the men paused only for a minute to rest. The British troops were resting quietly within the stockade. The fierce heat had caused them to nap in the middle of the day and casually cook their food over open fires. They had neither seen nor heard the approaching troops.

Colonel Lee sent Captain O'Neale, Joseph, and the local militia to circle around on the opposite side of the fort. They were instructed to start shooting and attracting attention after they had stationed themselves. Colonel Lee then instructed Captain Rudolph to rush the fort from his side when and if the redcoats rushed out of the stockade in pursuit of the militia.

The battle took place pretty much as Colonel Lee had expected. The militia started firing and yelling as they moved toward the fort. The British troops returned the fire, and the militia started retreating. The redcoats, aroused from their resting, and in a state of confusion, rushed out of the stockade after the militia. Captain Rudolph and his infantrymen rushed the fort. Colonel Lee and the other foot soldiers, supported by a troop of dragoons rushed after the British, cutting them off before they could reach the militia. The footsoldiers, dragoons, and the militia quickly closed in on the redcoats. Outnumbered and overpowered, they quickly surrendered.

Colonel Lee lost only one man, and he died from heat exhaustion. Only three or four of the enemy were killed. The remaining men of the two companies were captured and held as prisoners by the Continental army. Lee and his men were overjoyed. They had never seen so much powder, ball, small arms, liquor, salt, blankets, food, and other supplies.

After taking the fort, the Continental soldiers began eating the food that the redcoats had been cooking. The proud Colonel lightheartedly ordered Joseph, Captain O'Neale and his ten men to fill their saddle bags with dried meat, grits, beans, flour, and bacon. He then yelled to his men that they had only ten more minutes to be ready and mounted. He wanted to catch up with General Pickens before he reached Augusta, and did not want to keep the infamous Colonel Brown waiting.

Joseph filled his saddle bags with provisions and started to leave. Captain O'Neale and his men did the same and followed him through the stockade gate. He stopped Joseph and said he and his men had agreed to help rebuild the burned house. "I don't think we'll be having any more trouble from the redcoats or the Tories in this area," he said.

Joseph thanked them graciously and all agreed that they would start work the next day. They were sure their days of fighting were over. At an intersection of the road about a mile outside the fort they parted ways. O'Neale and his men went their way, and Joseph continued on toward Town Creek, and the ashes of what used to be his home.

The sun was still high in the sky when Joseph reached home. The ashes were still smoldering where the house had stood, and he saw a solitary figure standing among them. John Dicks was once again standing among the ashes. He was in the bedroom area and was raking around in the burnt rubble with his walking stick. He called Joseph over and showed him a pile of little iron fish charms. "They're the only thing left in the house. They've been through fire, death and destruction, and always remain unchanged. The strange thing is how they keep coming back to me. Don't you think that's strange?" he said as he scratched his head with a far away look in his eyes.

"Yes, I do, Papa," Joseph replied with amazement. "But I'm not surprised in the least. The charm you gave me saved my life in battle." He took the charm from his left shirt pocket and showed it to John.

"See this dent, Papa," he said as he handed it to him. "It was made by a musket shot. I thought I was dead for sure, but when I recovered my senses, I realized I hadn't been hurt at all, except for a bruise on my chest, over my heart. I was so shaken and thankful I couldn't get it off my mind. All the way from Savannah to Charleston I thought about what had happened. When we stopped long enough to rest, I walked alone into the edge of the woods, sat down on a hollow log, and tried to write down my thoughts about this little charm."

He took a wrinkled piece of paper with brown and frayed edges from his pocket and carefully unfolded it. "I've carried this little piece of paper since the battle at Savannah, over two years ago." He cleared his throat and began to read:

THE RUSTY CHARM

One man's trash is another man's treasure
    It depends on how he sees his part.
The widow's mite is abundant measure,
    For him who understands the heart.

The poor is rich and the rich is poor
    And only wise men understand.
The skillful man must be a doer,
    Knowledge alone can't heal the land.

The strong is weak and the weak is strong.
    And who can ever really know
Who is right and who is wrong?
    Since value from the heart must grow.

Moth and rust cannot erase
    Treasure that was meant to last.
Golden charms cannot replace
    Greater wealth from treasured past.

Little is much when God is in it.
And wealth is safe from spoiler's harm.
Worthless, as a term, may fit.
But priceless is the rusty charm.

"Well, thank the Lord!" John shouted with a glow. "God works in mysterious ways, his wonders to perform!" He turned back to the ashes and began picking up the charms, one by one, and placing them in a cloth he had taken from his pocket.

After a while John and Joseph walked toward the barn, leading the horse, with the loaded saddle bags. The animal was unsaddled, fed, and watered. After that, both men started toward the slave quarters. The Dicks family would have to spend the night with Isaiah and Phoebe, in their neat little two room house, which sat about a hundred yards behind the smouldering ashes.

Phoebe was a frail, dark-skinned Negro woman who had been Isaiah's common law wife for almost fifty years. From the first day on the Dicks' place, she had served as a house servant. Her hair was, for some strange reason, almost straight, and was sprinkled sparingly with strands of gray. Not surprisingly, only two big teeth remained in her mouth. When she smiled, they looked like two big white grains of corn. Her dark eyes twinkled out from behind a thin wrinkled face. She was the "mammy" to all the other slaves, and had been for a long time. She had learned to deal with disappointment and pain with little outward show of emotion, but quite frequently she openly displayed her joy or happiness.

Joseph brought in the saddle bags and emptied them on the table. "This ought to last for several days, until we can make other arrangements," he said with a smile. "Colonel Lee took Fort Galphin without much resistance, and he took the stores of food and supplies. He allowed me and O'Neale's men to take part of it." At the sound of that name, Liz and Martha both sat up and took a special interest in what was being said.

"By the way, O'Neale and all his men are coming in the morning to help us rebuild the house," he continued excitedly. "That Patrick O'Neale is a mighty fine man. In fact I like all his men, especially Joe Carter and Luke Saunders."

"Dey sho' did hep us, Massa Joe, when you wuz gone," Isaiah said energetically. "Iffen dey didn't show up, dat ole Dan'l Dues and dem redcoats wuz sho' to kilt us all."

At the thought of Captain O'Neale coming again, Liz and Martha found it hard to hide their excitement. It was difficult for them to fall asleep on their pallets that night.

Liz was up before the sun the next morning, getting ready to go hunting. She slipped over to the pallet where Joseph was asleep and nudged his shoulder. "Joe, wake up. Let's go down by the creek and get us a deer for dinner," she whispered. "I'll go to Sam's house and wake him. I'll need two good men to bring home the one I'm going to kill today."

Joseph rolled over, wiped his eyes and yawned. "How can anyone be so bright and cheerful this early in the morning?" he said with a groan as he pulled on his boots.

Liz ignored her brother's remark, bounded out the door and headed toward Sam's cabin. There she met the middle-aged black man just as he was coming out the cabin door. Liz explained her plans to go hunting as they both sat down on the porch.

Sam and Liz were still waiting on the porch of Sam's little four room log house at the edge of the woods, when Joseph reached them. She had the long barrel rifle, and he brought the musket. Together, the three of them headed down the trail toward Town Creek and the spot where the deer and other animals usually came for water. Liz had become a skilled hunter over the past few months, and had kept the family and the slaves supplied with fresh meat from the woods.

Before the sleepy hunting party reached the creek bank, a large buck sprang from the underbrush, right in front of the unprepared hunters. Joseph quickly fired his rifle, missing it completely. Liz saw another magnificent deer standing in the edge of the creek. She motioned for complete stillness, and eased to within about thirty feet of the beautiful animal. Slowly she raised her long barrel rifle, took aim, eased back the hammer, and gently squeezed the trigger. As soon as the crack of the shot sounded, the large beautiful buck fell back into the water, and began kicking. Sam rushed down to it and slit its throat.

" 'Mon', Massa Joe!" Sam called from the creek. "I needs hep wit dis fine animal." He took some cord from his pocket and tied all the feet together, and continued. "Cut a saplin', Massa Joe. We needs a pole for ta carry him on."

Joseph cut a small tree and trimmed a good pole with the hatchet Sam had brought. Then he slid down the bank to where Sam was waiting.

"Liz, you surprise me," Joseph said, as he laughed while climbing up the creek bank with the deer hanging between him and Sam on the pole. "If General Marion had you in his army, the British would already be sailing on the ocean toward home."

They laid the deer on the porch of Sam's house, as the bright rays of the sun streamed through the leaves of the big black walnut tree and sparkled on the dew-covered grass. "Missy 'Lizbeth, I get 'Gustine and Phoebe ta dress dis deer, and I fix a fire to cook it," Sam said as he went in to wake his family.

Joseph and Liz slowly walked back to Isaiah's house, where Isaiah and John were sitting on the porch pulling on their boots. Isaiah spoke first. "Massa Joe, what you and Missy 'Lizbeth been up to so early dis mornin'?" he asked with a smile.

"Liz has already killed a deer this morning. She wants to feed Captain O'Neale and his men like kings, today," Joseph replied with a wink of the eye and a smile.

"Isaiah, I want you to collect up all the axes, hammers, planing hooks, and saws you can find," John said in a businesslike way. "While Mary and the girls help prepare and cook the meat and the meals, I want you and Sam to help Joseph and the young men Captain O'Neale is bringing to work on the house. I can't do much with my wounded leg, but I'll do what I can."

Just as surely as he had promised, Captain O'Neale and his men came riding in, ready to work, before the sun could dry the dew from the ground. Martha and Liz anxiously leaned against the frame of the open door of Isaiah's house and waved to the men. They smiled at all of the young men, but they had eyes only for Captain O'Neale.

Liz decided she would help work on the house. She joined Joe Carter in raking and clearing away all the debris and ashes, while Joseph, Sam and Isaiah, as well as O'Neale and the rest of his men cut trees and trimmed them for use in building the house. Joseph hooked and chained each log as it was readied and, using a team of horses, pulled them from the woods. John gladly joined Liz and Joe Carter in the task of clearing away all the debris from the house site. The busy crew worked like a colony of ants all morning.

Martha left the women and the kitchen several times to bring around water for the thirsty workers. Captain O'Neale didn't have a chance all day to become thirsty. By noon the industrious woodsmen had piled up enough logs to begin work on the house. The crew divided, and about half began working on the house while the remaining half continued to cut trees and prepare logs.

Martha came a little after noon to let everyone know that dinner was ready. The whole deer had been cooked over hot coals in front of Sam's house. Mary and Phoebe had cooked several large pots of dried beans. Martha had made several pans of large fluffy biscuits. A large iron washpot hung over the fire, filled with boiled fresh corn from the garden. Augustine also had cooked a large pot of hominy, of which she was very proud.

It was indeed a meal fit for a king, especially during the trying times of 1781 when it seemed that everything had been ravished by the warring factions: British against Americans, Tories against Whigs, patriots against loyalists. Now for a little while all this could be put behind these industrious New Windsor settlers. They all dug into the food as though they had not seen any for many days.

Captain O'Neale took his plate and headed for Martha. They both walked to the edge of the woods and sat down on the grass in the shade. As they picnicked together, Liz fumed within herself. She walked over to Joe Carter and started a conversation with him. To her amazement, he was a most intelligent and interesting person who had ambitions to resume his studies as a doctor when the war ended. She liked him very much and felt very comfortable talking with him.

Joe was indeed a rather handsome as well as intelligent man. His hair was dark brown and had several small natural waves near the front. It was not parted at all, but combed straight back. He was clean shaven, showing a uniform, well-tanned, ruddy skin on his squared jaws and face. His smile was quick, his brown eyes were piercing, and his tongue was fast and intelligent. His frame was no less impressive, at six feet tall. His muscular appearance gave the impression that he was well acquainted with hard work. Yet his keen mind indicated he had spent much time in school.

Liz had forgotten everyone else and was engrossed in conversation with Carter when John called out, "It's time to get back to work. Has everyone had enough to eat? If you haven't, now's the time to get it before everything is put away."

"Don't fret 'bout bustin' you gut, now," Isaiah said with a hearty laugh. "Dis deer'll still be here fa supper, 'less Phoebe don't keep de flies and skeeters from totin' it off."

"Hush up, old man," she answered with her two teeth showing in a big grin. "I'se not too old ta do my job. I can work yo' breeches off any day or night."

"Yea, yea, ya done dat many times. . .thank de Lawd. I'll 'member dat tonight, when de light's out."

"Hush up, old man, and get back ta work," she said as she hit him over the head with the fan. He acted like he was dodging a rolling pin, held his stomach with both arms, and shook with a spontaneous laugh. The whole crowd joined in and ended their meal on a lighthearted note.

The crew neatly cleaned their plates, turned them in to Mary, and slowly marched back to work. Once on the job, they again moved around like a colony of ants, and by sundown, a lot had been accomplished.

In the evening, with much hard work behind them, everyone gathered again around the fire in front of Sam's house, to finish off the deer and the other leftovers.

There was ample food to be had by everyone, and a number of stories and jokes passed around the fire as the men relaxed after a long day's work. Finally Captain O'Neale indicated that it was time to head for home. As he and his men started to mount up, Martha walked him to his horse and stood talking with him for several minutes, while Liz chatted with Joe Carter. After promising to be back the next day, all the men rode off for home.

Work on the Dicks' new house progressed rapidly. By the end of the week the new two story log structure was almost complete. It had four rooms downstairs and four rooms upstairs. It was the only two story log house in the New Windsor Township. By the end of the same week, Martha and Captain O'Neale had gotten to know each other quite well. Liz and Joe Carter were more than good friends, and Wilma had developed a keen liking for Luke Saunders, the friendly giant. With all these developments, it was little surprise to Joseph when the men promised to return the following Monday to help finish the house.

When the house was complete, Captain O'Neale and several of his friends continued working for several days, making tables, chairs, and other items of furniture for the Dicks family. Thus it was that on June 5th, John and Mary could stand in front of their new home and admire the craftsmanship of the industrious young men and the beauty of the two story structure. It was on that day they moved into their new home, the best one they had ever had.

"It's ironic, isn't it, Mary?" John thoughtfully said as he held her hand. "Every time we lose what we have, we end up with something better. Isn't that wonderful?"

"Well, you always said, dear, it's better to have friends than money, and honor instead of riches," she replied with a warm smile. "This is an example of just how right those principles are. Let's go into our new home and start enjoying it."

"A mighty fine idea, Mrs. Dicks," he said lightheartedly. "Let's leave all the scars of the past outside when we walk through that door. It's the biggest house we've ever had, but it's still too small for hate and grudges."

"Well said, Mr. Dicks!" she added as they walked through the door.

Captain O'Neale came that night to call on Martha. He brought exciting news. The notorious British officer, Colonel William Brown, had surrendered to Lee and Pickens. Augusta had fallen. There were no British troops nearer than Charles Town. Any uncaptured Tories would forget the King and disappear upon the farms and plantations of the area. For the New Windsor Township, the war was over.

For the next few weeks, John and Joseph sat up late at night, talking about the war and how it was going in other parts of the state. They became closer than ever—John realizing what a fine young man his son had become, and Joseph becoming more aware of his father's strong character.

John's leg had almost healed. He had no need for the walking stick any longer. Mary was well, and Wilma seemed to be in better health since she had become so interested in Luke Saunders. Martha and Liz could always take care of themselves. Their future looked bright. Joseph was torn between staying home and returning to the Swamp Fox.

Finally, one night after one of their long and heartwarming talks, John said with a sad heart, "Joe, I know you want to go back to Marion and help end this struggle. You go ahead. We'll be all right until you get back."

Early the next morning Joseph left in search of Captain O'Neale. He had developed a warm friendship for the man and had just realized he did not even know where he lived. With a feeling of excitement, he galloped all the way to Galphin's trading post in the early morning sun and fresh air. The early summer crops were green and beautiful, making him realize how truly beautiful his homeland was.

John Parkinson saw him coming and smiled a big welcome. He looked much younger than Joseph had remembered. "Come on in out of the sun, Joe," he called with lightness in every word. "It's over for us. I don't have much left, but at least I don't have to worry about the redcoats or the Tories anymore!"

"I can't stop, Mr. Parkinson," he replied. "I'm looking for Patrick O'Neale. Could you tell me how to find him?"

"I sure can, Joe. Just follow this road and take a left on the next trail. His family lives in the big brick house near the river."

"Thank you, Mr. Parkinson," Joseph called as he galloped away.

Patrick was on his way to the barn when Joseph rode into the yard. He turned around and walked swiftly out to meet him. "Is there anything wrong, Joe?" he asked with concern in his voice. "No, Pat. I just came to tell you I'm returning to General Marion today. I wanted to ask you to keep an eye on my family until I get back."

"Joe, you know I'll be more than glad to do that," he responded with a grin. "I'll visit several times each week. If they need anything, I'll take care of it."

Patrick and Joseph shook hands and started to part when Beth

O'Neale appeared, standing in the doorway of their beautiful plantation house. "Wait a minute, Joe," Pat suddenly blurted out. "I want you to meet my family before you go."

They walked into the house, and Pat introduced him to his mother and father, who smiled warmly. He then turned and said impishly, "This is my sister, Beth. I must admit she sometimes thinks she's the boss around here, since she's the only girl in the family."

She stood by the stairway with her eyes looking at the floor. When she looked up and smiled at Joseph, his dignified stance melted. He completely forgot where he was. She was the most beautiful girl he had ever seen. Her long blazing auburn hair and bright hazel eyes made an especially beautiful combination. Her tall, thin, statuesque body gave a regal appearance under a brightly colored dress. Her face was smooth and fair, and dimples graced her cheeks when she smiled. Just looking at her made him weak. He must have been staring at her because Patrick had to call him twice. "Joe. . .Joe, would you like something to eat or drink?"

Joseph was jolted back to reality and quickly stammered, "No. . .No. . .I must hurry back so I can leave for the low country." Departing a bit clumsily, he mounted his horse, waved to them all, and galloped away, with the beautiful and enchanting face of Beth O'Neale frozen in his mind. He was almost sorry he was leaving home again.

Joseph returned to the farm where he packed his saddlebags with needed clothing and supplies. It was nearly midday by the time he was ready to go. After assuring himself that all the family was taken care of, and would be safe, Joseph embraced them all, and waved as he galloped toward the end of the lane, and the low country.

6

The Foxes Finish the Chase

1781-1783

"Halt! Who goes there?" yelled a voice in the dark, as the sound of footsteps and heavy breathing became audible.

"Is that you, Will?" Joseph whispered as he cautiously paused. "Is that you, William James?"

"Is that you, Joe?" he answered in hushed tones. "How did you find us?"

Joseph led his horse to the edge of the new camp of the Swamp Foxes to where young William James was standing watch. "It sure wasn't easy. I guess I've traveled a hundred miles out of the way," he said as he reached out and embraced his good friend. "What's been happening since I've been gone?"

Will motioned for some of the Jenkins boys, who had just finished eating by the campfire, to come and relieve him of guard duty. As he walked with Joseph and led his horse toward the campfire, he excitedly answered, "We've got 'em on the run, Joe! We chased Lord Rawdon to St. Stephen. There were so many people there who were friendly to us, it was hard to believe. Some of the General's Huguenot friends allowed us to set up this new camp here at Peyre Plantation. We marched into Georgetown back in May and found the British had left. We burned the abandoned fort."

"What about General Greene and General Sumter?" Joseph asked, anxious to know what the overall picture looked like.

"Well, General Greene was defeated at Ninety-Six and retreated across the Bush River. From all I hear, General Sumter has been plundering and stealing from the Tories to support his troops. It'll probably get him in trouble with General Greene."

"By the way, Will," Joseph interrupted. "Where's the General?"

William pointed toward one of the larger log cabins which had been built as part of the new hideaway and said, "He's in that building. Come on, I'll take you to him."

Joseph knocked on the makeshift door and entered after Captain John James opened it for him. He stood to attention and saluted, as the Swamp Fox rose from his chair. "Private Dicks, reporting for duty, sir!"

General Marion smiled and extended his hand toward Joseph. "How were things at home, Joe?" he asked as he motioned for him to be at ease.

"Not too good, sir," he quickly answered. "But since Colonel Lee and Pickens captured Augusta and Fort Galphin, I'm sure everything will be fine."

"That's good. Real good, Joe," Marion replied, and then turned to more sobering news. "You'd better get plenty of rest tonight. We need to leave early in the morning. I just received word that Major Thomas Fraser captured Colonel Isaac Hayne while he was in command of American troops, held a court martial, and hanged him. By God, he'll pay dearly for that!"

Before sunrise the general was picking two hundred men from his brigade to go after Fraser. Joseph was chosen to ride with the cavalry. They rode all day and then continued moving by night, making sure their movements were skillfully concealed from spying eyes. They crossed the Edisto River after traveling about a hundred miles.

On August 13th, Marion's men joined Colonel Harden, who informed them that Fraser and his dragoons were on their way back to the Edisto. The Swamp Foxes concealed themselves at Parker's Ferry, in the swamp, and lay in ambush, while a detachment of the swiftest horses was sent to lure them into the trap. Joseph rode with the detachment, led by Captain John James.

When they saw Fraser's dragoons coming down the sandy road the Americans waited until they were about a thousand yards away. They then began firing. Major Fraser spurred his horse, and his men followed at top speed, while Joseph and the detachment wheeled around and retreated from the sound of thundering dragoons. Joseph did not stop spurring his horse until after he had passed the location of the ambush. He then followed the other men off the road and into the woods to watch the action.

When the signal was given, Marion's men opened fire. The entire line of dragoons reeled. Horses screamed and reared as men fell to the ground. Fraser tried to rally his horsemen by a charge into the swamp, but the confusion and delay allowed the Swamp Foxes time to reload and fire. He then turned back from the ferry and retreated again. As he did so he came parallel to the ambush again. After his third attempt at rallying his troops failed, he fled, leaving the causeway choked with dead and dying men and horses. Following the battle, Marion and his men withdrew through the swamp.

The next morning Joseph and Captain Melton, with several others, slipped back to the battleground and found at least a hundred of Fraser's dragoons and several Tories had been killed—a partial payment on the score for Isaac Hayne. The scene was too horrible to imagine. The blood from the swollen dead men and horses, lying in the shallow marshy water, had colored it a bright pink as far as Joseph could see. He paused a moment to reflect on the somber scene. His thoughts were interrupted by a groan.

"Captain Melton, did you hear that?" he asked as the goose bumps rose over his whole body and it felt like his hair must be standing on end.

"Hear what, Dicks?" Captain Melton answered from his horse about thirty feet away. He was deep in thought, taking a count of the dead bodies.

"I thought I heard a groan, sir," Joseph answered timidly, almost feeling ashamed for thinking he had heard one of the dead bodies groan.

Shortly he heard the groan again and saw the hand of a young Tory move. The groaning boy was partially covered by the dead body of a redcoat which had fallen upon him and had rested there all night. Joseph rushed over and pulled the dead body from off him. Captain Melton leaped from his horse and ran over to take a look.

It appeared the boy's skull had been penetrated by a sharpshooter's bullet. The wound was above the left eye. Joseph tore off the pants leg from one of the dead British soldiers and made a bandage from it. He tied it around the wounded boy's head to stop the slow bleeding. "What's your name, soldier?"

The young Tory mustered enough strength to whisper, "Cassels, sir."

"Are you Colonel James Cassels' son?" Joseph asked, remembering the infamous Tory Colonel of Georgetown. He could feel nothing now, however, except sympathy. This wounded Tory was little more than a boy and had been surrounded by over a hundred dead bodies all night.

"Yes, sir," the young man said with a struggle as he tried to stand.

"Just take it easy now," Joseph whispered. "We'll try to help you. Maybe we can send you home."

After giving young Wallace Cassels water and food, Joseph and the detachment gathered as many of the dragoon's field pieces as they could pull behind their horses. They started back for camp, with the wounded prisoner riding double with Joseph.

When a report of the day's events was given to Marion, he appeared pleased. Being the compassionate man that he was, he sent Joseph and William James to escort young Cassels to his home. Cassels appeared to be strong and hardy. He had lost little blood, but the bullet had to be somewhere in his head. Joseph was puzzled at how he could still be alive.

As William and Wallace, who appeared to be about the same age, chatted to the rhythm of the horse hoofs, Joseph let his mind wander back to the beautiful girl at Silver Bluff. The beautiful and tender face of sweet Beth O'Neale was still frozen in his mind. Suddenly he felt a strong yearning to return home.

In September, General Greene camped on Henry Lauren's plantation near Eutaw. Organizing his troops for a strike against Colonel Stewart, he put General Jethro Sumner in charge of the Continental soldiers and General Francis Marion in charge of the militia troops.

At four o'clock on the morning of September 8th the American army marched toward Eutaw in four columns. Colonel Henderson led the advance with his South Carolina state troops and Lee's legion. Marion came next with the combined militia of North and South Carolina. Sumner followed with the Continentals, and Colonel Washington last with his cavalry. They all marched and rode as quickly and quietly as a body that large could. Apparently their efforts at stealth paid off.

Colonel Stewart's army was taken by complete surprise, but Major Coffin and his detachment of horse and foot soldiers met the advancing army and were repulsed by the first column of Henderson. They fled in panic. Colonel Stewart then sent his infantry to meet the American army. Marion's militia began advancing and pushed them back through the woods and into the British line. When his ammunition was exhausted, he retreated, leaving the fighting to Sumner's Continentals.

The Continentals moved with spirit and vigor, pushing the British line back in disorder. Colonel Lee then pushed his infantry upon them, increasing their confusion. In the center the British line held, meeting Continentals in hand-to-hand fighting, swords clashing and bayonets slashing. The center finally fell back when the Marylanders fired mercilessly.

As the British line retreated beyond their camp, however, the hungry and thirsty Continentals stopped to pilfer. As they fought for food, their line fell into confusion. Fearing greater disorder, General Greene ordered a retreat. In response, the British marksmen sprayed the surging mob with fury and death.

Faced with the British sniper fire and a cavalry charge, the Continental troops fell like flies and were soon overrun. Only the vicious fighting of the soldiers under Colonel Wade Hampton's command could hold back the British, and eventually Hampton, too, was driven back. The Americans were forced to retreat from the field of battle. The British commander, Stewart, thus was able to claim victory, though his army was shattered. Fearing a second attack, he burnt his supplies and retreated toward Monck's Corner.

Soon after the battle of Eutaw Springs, General Marion dismissed his men. The British had been driven from all of South Carolina except a small district around Charles Town. Marion, therefore, felt that there was little need to keep his men any longer from their homes and families.

Before leaving for New Windsor Township, Joseph stopped by the Canty Plantation to say a final goodbye to the Swamp Fox. Marion was sitting behind a large desk in the drawing room of the plantation house. It was quite different from the makeshift table he had used at his camps. He was wearing the blue uniform coat and white breeches of the Continental army. They were clean and smoothly pressed. His reddish sandy hair was neatly combed and his green eyes sparkled with satisfaction. His thin, neatly shaven face and squared chin somehow appeared more confident than ever. He was much shorter than Joseph, but he had always been a big man in the latter's eyes.

The general rose from his chair and extended his strong hand toward Joseph, with a smile. "I guess I'll be tied to this desk for the remainder of the conflict," he said with a half smile and half frown. "Looks like I'm going to be a messenger boy for Governor Rutledge and General Greene."

"I just wanted to say goodbye," Joseph said with sadness in his voice. "I'm happy the conflict is almost over and victory assured, but I've been honored to serve with you, sir, and I'm going to miss you and all my friends."

Marion gave Joseph a penetrating look and responded, "Son, you've done a good job, but it's time to go home and start rebuilding that dream of liberty and peace. You can return knowing you've served your country with honor during the time of its greatest need."

"Thank you, sir," Joseph replied, trying hard to keep a tear from view. "I'll always treasure my days with the Swamp Fox." General Marion turned his head to the side as if he were also trying to hide a tear, and motioned a farewell to him.

Most of the released farmer-soldiers were milling around in front of the Canty plantation house. Apparently each one wanted to say a personal farewell to their admired leader. As he left, Joseph shook hands and embraced young William James, John James, the Jenkins brothers, Colonel Horry, and several of the other Swamp Foxes with whom he had become very close during the years of desperate struggle. He mounted his horse, and without looking back, headed for home.

Sam had sent Princess to chase one of the little goats back into the goat lot. The playful little kid had led her almost to the main road, tricking her farther and farther away from the house. Finally she dived on top of it and grabbed it by the hind legs. Every tooth in her mouth looked like great white pearls as she smiled with satisfaction at her victory over the mischievous pest.

Just as she was taking great pride and youthful pleasure in the capture, she saw a horseman coming down the main road. She squinted her eyes and gazed for several seconds as she held onto the little varmint. In a moment she forgot about the goat and yelled and screamed in excitement as she ran fast as she could toward the house.

"It's Massa Joe! Lord 'ave mercy! It's Massa Joe! Mamma, Papa, Massa Joe done come home." She jumped up and down while Isaiah, Phoebe, Sam, Augustine, and all the little slave children came running from their houses.

Isaiah knocked on the door and called, "Missy Mary! Come quick! Massa Joe done come home!"

Martha, Wilma, and Liz ran from the door beaming with excitement. An aging Mary followed, with her mouth wide open. "Liz, run down to the blacksmith shop and get your papa!" she exclaimed. "He'll want to be the first to greet Joe!"

John ran all the way to the house, almost keeping up with the pretty tomboy, Liz—quite an accomplishment for a sixty-one year old man who had been burned, beaten, and shot during his lifetime. Joseph leaped from his horse before it came to a complete stop. He grabbed John and Mary and embraced both at the same time. Liz, Martha, and Wilma swarmed over him like bees after honey, and excitedly hugged his neck and kissed him on the cheeks.

John blurted out with excitement, "It's sure good to have you home, son!"

Isaiah and all his family just could not be still. They were filled with excitement, and Isaiah shouted loudly, "Thank de Lawd! Thank de Lawd! Ya made it back, Massa Joe! I hopes ya is home ta stay! I sho' do!"

"I am home to stay!" Joseph answered with a thrilling shout. "The war is over. We won the victory. And I'm home to stay."

It was early in the afternoon when the jubilant party followed Joseph into the house. Sam took care of the horse and rushed back to join the celebration. It would have been difficult to decide which family was the more excited, John's or Isaiah's, as they sat together on the chilly October evening. The only light in the house was supplied by the warm, glowing fireplace. Those gathered round it, however, just could not hear enough of Joseph's battle stories, and he could not hear enough about what had been happening in the New Windsor Township since he had been gone.

"Patrick O'Neale has become a regular caller aroiund here," Wilma teased as she winked at Joseph.

Martha smiled with satisfaction and retorted, "Beth O'Neale thinks you're a knight in shining armor, Joe. She thinks you're the most handsome man she's ever seen."

"How'd you know that, Martha?" Joseph quickly asked, as if this new subject suddenly overshadowed everything they had talked about.

"Oh, I've visited Pat's house several times. She's always asking if we've heard anything from you," Martha replied in a teasing manner.

Isaiah smiled, while the little Negro girls giggled with glee. Mary lit a lantern and John smiled broadly as he shook the ashes from his pipe into the fireplace. Liz and Wilma sat on the floor by Joseph's chair, as if grasping for his every word.

Isaiah took this change of subject as his cue to start for home. "Come on, Phoebe; it's gettin' late. Time fa us ta hit de hay," he said as he yawned and stretched back in his chair. "Sam, 'Gustine, it's time ta get dem chilrun ta bed. We's sho'nuff glad ta haff ya home, Massa Joe!"

All Isaiah's family went to their little houses, while Mary and the girls went upstairs to bed. John and Joseph stayed up late and talked until their minds began to wander in and out of consciousness. It was such a heartwarming time together neither of them wanted to be the first to surrender to physical exhaustion. Begrudgingly they pulled off their boots and stumbled toward their beds.

The times had changed for the better since the British had been driven from the area. A strangely precarious peace had prevailed, even with the former Tories. On the surface, at least, the planters, stock farmers, and woodsmen of the New Windsor Township had put the terror of the war behind them. Patriots and Tories treated each other with a distant politeness and went about their business of working their land and raising their children.

The Galphin trading post, which had been the center of commerce for so many years, had lost its glory. Galphin had died in 1780 before knowing which way the war would end. His nephews, John Parkinson and David Holmes had continued to operate it under the name of Galphin, Holmes and Company. There were no more imported items from London, and the variety of available items had become limited. Consequently, even though there was peace, times were difficult, and there were many things to which the new Americans had to adjust. Since the apron strings of England had been cut, the settlers had to learn to improvise and produce everything necessary for survival in the new frontier.

The next morning, Joseph was the first one in the house out of bed. While the family slept, he took great pains and much time washing and grooming himself. He combed and brushed his black wavy hair vigorously.

After about an hour, Mary was up and getting ready to cook breakfast. "What are you doing up so early, Joseph?" she asked as he surprised her with a kiss on the back of her neck.

"I'm going over to see Patrick O'Neale this morning. I want to get an early start because I know Papa will want me to help him around the place today," he answered as he brushed through his hair again.

Mary smiled and looked out of the corner of her eyes at Joseph, as she said casually, "Tell Beth hello for me if you see her." She paused for a moment and continued, "Invite her and Pat to Sunday dinner. That ham in the smokehouse ought to be cured by now."

"I'll try to remember it, Mama," he replied as he went out the back door and peeped in with an impish smile. "Do you want me to tell Mr. and Mrs. O'Neale anything for you?"

Joseph hardly noticed the cutting October wind as he galloped toward the O'Neale house in Silver Bluff. He still had the lovely and delicate face of Beth O'Neale frozen in his memory. This morning he could think of nothing else but her. As he approached the O'Neale house, it struck him for the first time how large and imposing it was. Somehow that day it appeared threatening and intimidating. He was not sure if all his shaking was due to the cold wind or his "cold feet," as he knocked on the big, beautifully carved door.

The door swung open, and Patrick bolted from it with a warm

embrace. "Joe Dicks, you swamp fox, when did you get home?"

"I reached home yesterday," Joseph answered with a smile. "The British have left every area of the state except Charles Town, and there was talk about a surrender there too before I left. The war is over. We won't have to worry about the redcoats any more."

"Come on in, Joe," Patrick exclaimed. "Come say hello to the family!"

Joseph was surprised at the magnificence of the O'Neale home. The spacious rooms and high ceilings were painted and decorated like the finer homes of Charles Town. The fine imported furniture gave the appearance of great wealth, and it made him even more nervous. Standing among all their splendor made him feel insignificant and undeserving of their friendship, especially the attention of beautiful Beth.

As his eyes moved around the exquisite home, he saw Beth standing at the top of the spacious stairway. Her long auburn hair curled below her shoulders, accentuating her fair complexion. It appeared that she had dressed for some special occasion in her long colorful dress.

"Come on down, Beth," Patrick called. "I want you to meet Joe Dicks!"

Joseph lost touch with everything else as he watched her gracefully descend the stairs. No royal queen could have been more graceful, nor exquisitely formed.

"Well, I'm pleased to meet you, Joseph," she said as she offered him her hand. "I've heard so much about you from Pat and Martha."

The words would not come out of Joseph's throat. He had seen the horrors of death and war without losing his control and confidence, but now he could not even speak. He took her hand, smiled, and nervously kissed it.

"You must tell me about your exciting experiences with General Marion," she continued. "Pat has told us many of them already. I really would like to hear more."

Mr. and Mrs. O'Neale came from the kitchen and appeared surprised to see Joseph. They were both in their sixties and were distinguished looking with their neatly groomed gray hair and fine clothes. Mrs. O'Neale was about medium height and had a pleasing round figure. Mr. O'Neale was tall and lean and appeared hardy. His gray beard was neatly trimmed, and he wore little round spectacles on his nose. He extended his hand to Joseph and said, "It's good to see you're back, Dicks. Many of our brave young men won't be coming back home. I understand the war is over."

"Yes, sir," Joseph managed to say by sheer nervous energy. "I think you're right. It's not officially over, but I'm satisfied it's finished as far as the British are concerned."

"Won't you have something to eat or drink?" Mrs. O'Neale asked as she motioned toward the kitchen.

"I'm much obliged, Mrs. O'Neale, but I can't stay very long," he answered courteously. "Papa will want me to help him around the farm on my first day back home."

They sat around in the finely appointed drawing room and talked about the experiences of the war, the death of George Galphin, the money crops of the future, and almost every other subject under the sun. The whole morning passed so fast Joseph almost forgot he was needed at home. He was brought back to reality by the slaves ringing the dinner bell.

"I must get back home," he said as he stood and started for the door. "By the way, Pat, Mamma asked me to invite you and Beth over for Sunday dinner. Can I tell her you'll come?"

"Sure thing, Joe," Patrick answered as he caught Beth's eye and an anxious nod of her head. "We'll be there around noon."

Mr. and Mrs. O'Neale said goodbye and left the room. Patrick and Beth followed Joseph to the door. Pat shook his hand, and Beth handed him the back of her hand again. He politely kissed it and smiled, trying to hide his nervousness. As he floated back home on his snorting, galloping horse, Joseph felt as light as a feather.

During the next month Joseph and Sam repaired the fences, cut up some firewood, repaired the barns, and filled the smokehouse with everything from rabbits and squirrels to wild hogs and deer. John and Isaiah did little work. They sat around together on the porch most of the time, like two old feeble friends. Isaiah industriously carved on a little cedar chest. He cut and rubbed the cedar wood like he was making a rare gift for a king, while John talked about the old days.

Toward the middle of November, when the wind became too cold for the porch, the two men moved into John's house to sit near the open fire. John had become weak and thin. His full head of hair was now mostly gray, with a few black strands holding on in remembrance of earlier times. His straight shoulders had now begun to slump, and his ruddy face was more pink and pale. His beard and mustache was completely gray, and fine wrinkles were etched across his forehead. His short leg had been more noticeable since being shot by the British, and he always used a walking stick. Isaiah was unchanged except for the white hair and beard. He looked much like he did on the day John saved him and his family from the auction block, except for a slight slump in his shoulders and several new graceful wrinkles on his black face.

"What ya think 'bout dis cedar box, Massa John?" he said one morning when it appeared he had finished it.

"Isaiah, it's as fine a carving job as I've ever seen," he answered sincerely as he took it in his hands and examined it carefully. "I didn't know you were such a good carver."

"It's yo's, Massa John," Isaiah said proudly. "I's been makin' it all along fa da fishes. I knows de medicine bag done burned, an' I knows how much ya loves dem fishes, so I made dis fa ya."

"Thank you, Isaiah," John said as he grabbed his hand and shook it warmly. "I can think of no better container for my prized fish charms."

John lifted the mattress on his bed and took the charms, which he had wrapped in cloth on the day of the house fire. He sat back down and began putting them in the chest.

Of the original and the twelve he had made, there were still ten in the collection. He looked at the one his father had made for him and slowly put it into the chest as memories of the past flooded his mind. He picked up the one which he had given to Dr. Daniel Smith, fingered it for a moment and remembered the day he found him brutally beaten in the woods. He could see old George LeGrow's scowling face as he raised his whip to start his fatal fight. After putting it in the chest he picked up Wilma's rusty charm, and the traumatic scene in the little frame country church flashed before his mind's eye. Morgan Sweitzer's tormented face also flashed into his mind. Then there was the one he had given to Catherine Smith, the only mother he had ever really known. He rubbed it like he was rubbing her cheek, and gently laid it in the chest. He counted the others and there were six left. He slowly dropped them in the cedar chest and paused a moment in deep thought.

"You know, Isaiah, maybe these last six charms should not be given away. It seems that bad things have happened to every person who had one."

"But, Massa John, I'se got one, an' it sho brung me good luck," Isaiah quickly responded with a bright gleam in his eye. "An look at Massa Joe. It done save his life in de war. An' whut 'bout de Injun Chief? He done save us all. Only de Lawd knows why dem bad thangs happen."

"I guess you're right, Isaiah. All I ever meant for them to represent was something good, a special bond of honor or friendship."

"Dey sho' means dat, Massa John!"

"Thank you, Isaiah; I'll treasure this beautiful cedar chest all my life. I hope it'll remain in my family for many years to come," he said, as he looked around for a safe place to put it. He placed it under the bed and continued, "I guess our time is short, my friend. I just can't get my strength back. Ever since I was shot, I haven't been worth very much. I don't believe I've got much longer to live."

"Don't say dat, Massa John. Yo' sho' ta be 'round ta see dem great-gran' chilrun. Yo may be hobblin', but yo be here."

Later that evening, after Isaiah had gone back to his house, Joseph, John, Mary, and the girls were about to sit down to the supper table when there came a knock on the door. Joseph opened it and quickly exclaimed, "Joe Carter. It's good to see you. Come on in!"

Liz rushed over to Joe and said, "You're just in time for supper, Joe. Come in and let me fix you a plate."

"Thank you very much, Liz. I'll have to make it some other time. I just stopped by to tell Joseph I was at the trading post when the stagecoach driver brought word that Cornwallis had surrendered to General Lincoln, at Charles Town. He said it happened on October 19."

"Thank you for stopping by, Joe," Joseph said. "That sure is good news. The war is really over now."

"I thought you'd want to know about it," Carter responded as he started toward the door, followed by an excited Liz. "By the way, the Thanksgiving day Festival is on Saturday at the community meeting house. You all be sure to come. I've already signed up for the shooting match and the wrestling contest. Joe, you ought to sign up for the competition. You should do real good in the shooting match."

"I might just do that," Joseph replied as he sat down at the table. "In fact, maybe we all can come."

The next day Joseph visited Patrick and Beth O'Neale, and they made plans for both families to ride together in their hay wagons, to the community house at Beech Island. Both families were excited and looked forward to a day of fun and enjoyment.

At the crack of dawn on Saturday morning, the Dicks home was buzzing like a bee hive. Wilma had made plans to meet Luke Saunders at the festival, and Liz had agreed with Joe Carter that she would ride with the family and meet him there. Joseph and Martha were excited about riding along with the O'Neales. Even John seemed to perk up a little. Maybe a little recreation would help him recover from his weakness. Mary was as excited as anyone as she packed a basket of food, while the ham and grits for breakfast were cooking over the fire.

"Joe, how about going to Isaiah's and Sam's after breakfast and telling them we'll be gone all day," John said as he took his place at the head of the table.

After breakfast, Joseph went to tell Isaiah and Sam about their trip, and to hitch the hay wagon. He placed a good thick layer of hay in the bed of the wagon to make a comfortable cushion on which to ride. Pulling the wagon to the front door, he went back in to see if everyone was ready. The girls were still brushing their hair, working on their dresses, and generally over-grooming themselves. Mary and John were ready and began carrying out the basket of food and several quilts for the wagon.

"Let's go, girls!" Joseph impatiently called. "If we don't leave now we'll be late. I surely don't want to keep the O'Neales waiting." After a lot of pushing and pulling, the family was loaded onto the soft cushion of hay in the wagon, and was on its merry way.

The O'Neales were waiting in their wagon at the end of the lane to their house. After greeting each other, Martha traded places with Beth, and the two happy families rolled on to the community meeting house at Beech Island.

"I didn't know this many people lived in the whole township of New Windsor," Joseph exclaimed excitedly as the wagons pulled into the edge of the large field where the meeting house was located. "There must be five hundred people here!"

There were dozens of wagons tied up to the hitching rail. Dozens of saddled horses stood motionless by the watering trough, tied to another rail. There were three or four little tables set outside on the meeting house porch. They were the registration tables for each of the contests.

Joseph signed up for the shooting match, the wrestling match, and the running contest. Liz wanted to sign up for the shooting match, but was told it was for men only. She insisted, so the girl at the table went to ask the promoter. In a few minutes they both came back to the table and after much discussion allowed Liz to register.

"I don't guess it'll matter anyway. Maybe it'll give the boys a good laugh!" the promoter said as he walked away, leaving Liz fuming.

The weather was perfect. The cool late November wind was warmed by the bright sun which blazed hot through the cloudless blue sky. The weather was almost like spring.

The shooting contest was just starting at one end of the field when the Dicks and O'Neale families arrived. There were fifteen contestants which included Joseph, Patrick, Joe Carter, and Luke Saunders, as well as Liz. The order was assigned, and Liz had to wait until last. She fumed at the thought of such discrimination. The target was placed a hundred feet away, and the sharpshooters began. Each contestant had two chances, with five shots each time.

After about an hour of shooting the first round was over, and Joe Carter was the leader with four bullseyes out of the five. Liz was second with three bullseyes and two just barely outside the line. Joseph was third with three bullseyes and two in the outer ring.

As word spread that a woman was in on the shooting, the crowd around the shooting match end of the field increased in size. The second round started as the tension mounted. All the men took their time and slowly aimed each time they squeezed the trigger. When the turn finally came to Liz, Joe Carter was in the lead with four bullseyes and the other shot barely outside the bullseye line.

Liz propped her long barrel rifle on the shooting stand and carefully and deliberately took aim each time she cocked the hammer. One, two, three, four bullseyes. She looked out the corner of her eye at Joe Carter. Large beads of sweat popped out on his forehead in the cool November air. He had really counted on winning.

Every girl and woman in the crowd screamed and yelled with excitement. "Come on, Liz, you can win! You can win!" Liz slowly sighted the center of the bullseye, then moved the sight to the lower bottom of the target. She squeezed the trigger as a loud cheer arose from all the female spectators. When the judge inspected the target he proudly announced that Joe Carter was the winner of the contest and the proud owner of the turkey.

Joe rushed over to Liz and tightly hugged her as her heart almost melted. He then shook the hands of all the other contestants as they gathered around to congratulate him. He was about the happiest person at the festival, except for Liz. She had won the prize she had wanted all along.

The large dinner bell sounded which meant that another contest was about to begin. It was the running event. There were about thirty runners, which included Joseph, Patrick, Luke, Pat McElmurray, and Payton Dues, the last surviving son of Daniel Dues. The contestants were all lined up across the field and instructed to run to the end of the open field, rip a piece of ribbon off the rope which was strung across the trees, and return it to the starting point.

The gun sounded, and the runners bolted from the starting line like a bolt of lightning. Joseph took the lead, with Payton Dues at his heels. As he reached the end of the field and tore off a ribbon from the rope, he wheeled around and started rushing back toward the final goal. As he wheeled around, Payton Dues purposely rammed him and reached for his ribbon. Joseph hit the ground, rolled with a big flip, and did not even slow down. He barreled across the finish line and handed the judge the ribbon, with Patrick O'Neale coming in second.

As the judge made the announcement of the winner, Payton Dues ran over to Joseph and screamed, "You dirty swamp fox, you pushed me! I oughta knock your block off!"

He hit Joseph solidly on the chin and sent him reeling to the ground. Before Joseph could get back up, Patrick O'Neale had grabbed Dues and held him as Mrs. Dues and the Dues girls rushed over to the scene. Joseph got up, shook himself off, and trying to control his temper, said, "The war's over Dues. Go on and cool off!"

The large dinner bell rang again. It was noon and time for a lunch break. The Dicks and O'Neale families gathered around their wagons, spread the quilts, and set out their food for a splendid winter picnic. Martha and Pat sat on the back of the O'Neale wagon as they ate and enjoyed their time together. Joseph and Beth O'Neale sat on the quilts with John and Mary, and picnicked with great delight. Liz and Wilma met Joe and Luke and ate with their families. It was a wonderful occasion, too nice to be marred by old resentments.

"I'm proud of you, son, for using restraint," John said in a pleasant but serious tone. "It'll take a long time for some of the hate to die."

Beth rubbed the big bump on Joseph's chin, and softly whispered, "I'm proud of you too, Joe. I know it would have been easier to fight."

Joseph felt high as the sky. Beth's comforting and warm sentiments made him feel much better than he could have ever felt if he had beaten Payton Dues to a pulp. Her soft warm hands, dark auburn hair, and smiling hazel eyes were reward enough.

At one o'clock the big bell sounded again, indicating that the festival contests would resume shortly. The quilting contest would be held in the building, and the wrestling match would be held on the outside. All the women of the Dicks and O'Neale families sacrificed the quilting contest because they wanted to see how Joseph and Patrick would do at wrestling.

There were six contestants, which included Pat and Joseph, and Luke Saunders. Luke was a strong bull of a man. He was about six feet, two inches tall with not an ounce of fat on him, and weighed about two hundred and thirty pounds. Patrick was also about six feet tall and very muscular, but weighed only a little over two hundred pounds. Joseph was five feet eleven inches tall and weighed in at only a hundred and eighty pounds.

The first match was between Luke Saunders and Pat McElmurray. They were about the same size, but Luke was too much for Pat. The second match was between Joseph and Malcolm Davies. It was a long struggle between two evenly matched wrestlers. Joseph tripped Malcolm and threw him to the ground but could not pin him. Davies twisted Joseph's arm and forced him to the ground but could not pin him.

As the spectators yelled and screamed encouragement to them, Payton Dues again began harassing Joseph. "Hey, you chicken-livered swamp fox, you can't beat a real man! You better go hide again in the swamp!"

Joseph tried to ignore Dues and continued his struggle with Davies. Finally he pinned Malcolm and became the winner of the second match. The third match was between Patrick O'Neale and James Wilson. James was no match for the lightning fast and strong O'Neale. It was an easy win.

The elimination matches began with Joseph against Luke, the giant of a man who outweighed him by fifty pounds. They both fought hard and valiantly, but Joseph was no match for his big friend.

After a five minute rest, the final elimination match between Pat O'Neale and Luke Saunders began. Both big men struggled, hit the ground many times, and scampered around and around, but neither could pin the shoulders of the other. After about thirty minutes of exhausting struggle, the friendly giant tired. Patrick pinned him and was the winner.

Martha wiped the sweat from Pat's face with her handkerchief and whispered, "You were wonderful, Pat. I knew you could do it."

The big dinner bell sounded once again as the sun hung low in the heavens. It was time for the boxing match. The sponsor of the festival announced that the only person who had signed up for this match was Payton Dues. He asked for volunteers to fight Dues.

Payton Dues stood in the middle of the fighting circle all alone and yelled out into the crowd. "Hey, Dicks, you yellow-bellied swamp fox. Why don't you fight a real man. Quit hidin' behind those skirt tails and stand up like a man!" He pointed toward Joseph and continued his harangue. "Come on, war hero. Let's see how big you are without a gun."

Beth O'Neale cried, "Don't pay him any attention, Joe! Let's leave!"

"I can't do that, Beth. If I do, he'll never stop harassing me." Joseph calmly and quietly began unbuttoning his shirt as he headed toward the ring.

The promoter announced loudly. "Joseph Dicks has volunteered to fight Payton Dues. Let's give him a big hand folks as he comes to the ring."

The promoter explained the rules. "No kicking, no biting, and no scratching. If you hit below the belt you can be disqualified. All right, at the sound of the bell, begin!"

Joseph and Payton stood in the circle, bare chested, and bare knuckled. The anger in Payton's eyes was very visible to all the spectators. Joseph was successful in hiding his fear. John and the rest of the family were not as successful. Fear showed on all their faces as someone rang the bell.

Payton charged at Joseph, swinging his right fist. Joseph ducked and came up with a powerful right, under his rib cage, and hit him on the nose with his left. The blood gushed from Payton's nose as he swang again and hit Joseph squarely on the left eye. He fell back but recoiled immediately to land another crushing blow to the mouth of Dues. Dues fell to the ground while Joseph stood back and waited for him to get up. Dues got up, shook himself, and charged again, with a sweeping right which caught Joseph on the temple.

Joseph fell to the ground, and before he could get up, Payton kicked him in the stomach. He rolled over and sprang to his feet. With all the strength he could muster, Joseph swang a powerful right which landed on Payton's right eye, opening a cut under it. Dues cursed and swang wildly at Joseph's head. Joseph jumped back and dodged the wild blows.

Dues' face was covered with his own blood. Joseph's knuckles and hands, as well as his bare chest, were also covered with blood. Payton screamed again and lunged at Joseph. His bloody face met with Joseph's bare and bloody knuckles one more time, and he fell to the ground. He tried to get up, but slumped back down and was counted out.

The promoter announced that Joseph was the winner. As the announcement was being made, one of Payton's friends, James Randell, charged into the ring catching Joseph by surprise, and planted a solid right on his chin. Patrick O'Neale jumped into the fight and floored Randell with one swinging blow. He jumped back up and rushed Pat again, landing a heavy blow to his midsection. Another of Dues' friends caught Patrick from the rear with a hard blow on his back. Luke Saunders ran into the melee and flattened the third Tory while Patrick and Joseph continued to make a bloody mess of the other agitators.

Members of the different families tried to stop the fight but without success. Another former Tory ran toward Luke Saunders with a large club. Joe Carter caught him by surprise with a knee to his midsection. Joe then grabbed the club, flung it out of his reach, and planted another blow squarely on his nose. Nothing could stop the fight but the fighters themselves. It lasted about thirty minutes and gave the spectators more than they had asked for.

As Joseph and his friends walked away from the fighting ring, Payton Dues and his three friends were still lying on the ground, covered with their own blood. John let out a big sigh of relief and said, "It's time for us to get back home. Mary, get the girls together. Let's go!"

Mr. and Mrs. O'Neale agreed that this melee had ended all the enjoyment of the festival, and they too should head for home. The two families rode together as far as the O'Neale house, with Martha in the O'Neale wagon nursing Pat's wounds, and Beth O'Neale in the Dicks' wagon nursing Joseph's bruises.

At the junction of the road where the O'Neale's lived, Mr. O'Neale pulled along side of the Dicks wagon and invited John and Mary to stop in for a short visit. "I've got some of my own tobacco I want to give you," he called to John as he reined the horse. "I still sell most of it to the British and French sea captains. But I always like to cure some of it for my own use."

John nodded that they would stay for a while, and both wagons turned in at the beautiful brick house of Thomas O'Neale. After they pulled up in front of the house, Beth and Martha took Joseph and

Patrick back to the kitchen to finish washing away the dried blood. Mary was awestruck at the beauty of the O'Neale home, and John was curious about Thomas O'Neale's special tobacco.

While the young people were in the kitchen, Mr. O'Neale took John into his study. There he picked up a large glass jar from the shelf of a bookcase and invited John to sample the contents. John took some of the tobacco out of the jar, smelled it, and tried some of it in his pipe. He offered to send Mr. O'Neale some of his homemade berry wine. Mr. O'Neale reciprocated by offering to visit the Dicks farm and teach them how to plant tobacco. All things considered, it was a satisfying and successful day for both families.

Joseph was awakened the following morning by the loud laughter of Isaiah and Phoebe. John and Mary had been telling them about the events of the festival, and how Joseph had finally decided to fight Payton Dues after being harassed all day, and being called a "yellow-bellied swamp fox."

"I sho' nuff wish I'd seen dem fist flyin', Massa John. Dat Dues boy didn't learn his lesson durin' da war. Maybe he be mo' smart now," Isaiah said proudly as he chuckled.

"Well, it was bad, but it was also good, Isaiah," John said in a cautiously proud manner. "I think sometimes I would have been better off, if I had fought back when certain people tried to cause me trouble."

"Massa John, I 'most forgot why I's here," Isaiah quickly interrupted as he remembered the happenings of the day before. "Dem Injun boys came here yestiday and left dis fish fo' ya. Dey say de Chief done died."

Isaiah pulled the fish charm from his pocket. It still had the same leather chord attached that John had tied to it over twenty years before.

John's smile turned sober as he took the charm and thought about Chief Brown Eagle. "I must visit the Cofitachequi village today and pay my respects to the family of the Chief," he said sadly. "He was truly a good friend. Good friends are scarce, aren't they, Isaiah?"

"Dey sho is, Massa John," Isaiah answered brightly. "Dey sho' nuff is!"

Joseph had been lying in bed, listening to the conversation. Every bone in his body was sore. He struggled to sit up and groaned like a man who had been kicked by a horse. "I'll go with you, Papa, if I can get out of this bed," he moaned as he sat up and searched around for his boots.

"It's time for breakfast," Mary announced. "Martha, call your sisters. Isaiah, Phoebe, come join us. There's plenty."

As all six of the Dicks family and the two slaves gathered around the table, Joseph's thoughts turned to the meaning of real friendship. As he saw his father and Isaiah sitting at the same table, his mind went back to his wartime friends and of how General Marion had eaten and slept under the same conditions as his men. He remembered William James and his father, John James. Those were days when a friend meant life or death. Now he thought about Patrick O'Neale. He had been as good a friend as any person could ever expect. His thoughts were interrupted when a cheerful Mary said, "What's wrong Joseph? Are you not hungry this morning?"

"Yes, Mamma," he answered with a broad smile. "I was just thinking about some of my friends."

John and Joseph left after breakfast for a visit to the Indian village. As they came near, they noticed the young braves guarding the entrance, and John held up the fish charm which had been returned the day before. The Indians were dressed in colorful costumes, and their faces were covered with paint, like there was a celebration going on. They waved him forward as did every other young brave they encountered on the way to the Chief's home.

The Chief's daughter, whom John had rescued about twenty years earlier, was still as beautiful as she was on that day. She was dressed in the usual Indian animal skin dress, but it had colorful symbols painted all over it. She also wore a crown of brightly colored feathers on her head and her face had several colorful symbols painted on it. She graciously bowed and welcomed them into her home where several other family members sat on the floor in their celebration costumes.

The chief was fully dressed with his headgear and jewelry, lying on a long table covered with a very colorful quilt. John and Joseph walked around the table, bowed in respect, and wished the Princess and her family well.

"The Chief was one of my special friends," John said to her with a sad voice. "He felt same way 'bout you," she replied as she led him out. "You still good friend to us all. Now we celebrate Chief's move to happy home in sky." John and Joseph waved goodbye to them as they left the mourning Indians of the Cofitachequi village.

Christmas came and went, with the Dicks family and the O'Neale family visiting each other and sharing gifts and warm friendship. They all attended the little Huguenot church near the Dicks home on Town Creek and sat up late afterward talking about the special joys of the season. Throughout the winter months, the young people of both families continued to see each other, despite the inconveniences of the weather.

In April, when the ground became warm enough to start planting crops, Thomas O'Neale came over to the Dicks place and showed John and Joseph how he planted and cared for his tobacco. He demonstrated how to plant the tobacco and cover up the slips. Before he left, he offered to help sell the crop to the ship captains, if they had a good harvest. Joseph and John taught Isaiah and Sam what they had learned, and they set out two large fields of tobacco slips. They also planted the usual corn, indigo, field peas, potatoes, squash, and several varieties of beans.

The summer weather was ideal during 1782. The rainfall was adequate and the heat was not as overbearing as it had been some of the years during which John had been trying to become a successful planter. With the industrious help of Isaiah, Sam, and the other slaves, both farms were planted and worked. John and Joseph labored side by side with them to ensure a good crop.

Liz helped with much of the work while Wilma and Martha helped with the meals, and cared for the animals. Martha detested trying to milk goats. The cows would stay still for the milking, but she had to chase the goats most of the time with the pail in one hand and the rope in the other.

By harvesting season, it was apparent this would be one of the most successful years the Dicks family had ever known. Patrick O'Neale, Joe Carter, and Luke Saunders came over near the end of the harvesting season, bringing many of their family slaves, and helped build two tobacco barns and two corn cribs. When the harvest was finished, all of the Dicks barns were bursting at the seams with good produce. Mr. O'Neale helped them get a premium price for the tobacco from a French sea captain, who sent his men, in their pole boats, up the river from Savannah to pick it up.

When the harvest had passed, Beth O'Neale wanted to start a school for the children of the New Windsor Township. She asked Joseph to set up a meeting with as many families as were interested, at the O'Neale house. Joseph called upon Malcolm Davies, Pat McElmurray, and John Parkinson. David Holmes was away in Georgia, operating one of the Galphin trading posts, but sent word that he would support the effort. Several other local planters were invited and indicated an interest in the worthwhile project.

The house was full on the evening of the meeting, and Patrick announced that Beth would offer her proposal. Beth took the floor and in her usual graceful manner said, "I've tried to take a count of the children in this community, and to the best of my knowledge there are over fifty children who need to be in school. Now, I will donate my time and efforts free of charge if we can agree upon a location, and can build a suitable building."

The group argued for several minutes over where the most central location would be. Finally John Parkinson, operator of the Galphin, Holmes and Company trading post at Silver Bluff, rose to address the group.

"I have a piece of property about a mile above the trading post. It seems to me it would be near the center of where most of the children live. Now, if you want to use that location, I'll be glad to donate two acres."

After several minutes of hushed discussion, Beth said, "If there are no objection or better offers, we'll accept this generous contribution." She graciously thanked him and asked. "How many can help on the building?"

There was a show of hands, and it appeared that everyone would help. After setting a date for the school raising she thanked them all and encouraged the ladies to bring lunch buckets on that day.

On the morning of September 25, 1782, the wagons began

streaming in at the site for the school. Each family brought as many slaves as they could spare to help with the project. Joseph helped Beth oversee the work, while Patrick and Luke served as leaders of the crew that cut the trees and prepared the logs. Joe Carter and Liz, with the help of Isaiah and Sam, and several of the Carter slaves, cleared the spot and dug the foundation for the building. The work moved amazingly fast. There was enough help to build two schools.

By lunch time the walls were halfway up, and there were almost enough logs piled next to the building to complete it. John Parkinson had sent a large bell from the trading post, which could be used for the school bell. Joseph installed it on a pole about head high. He promptly rang it to sound the break for lunch.

The lunch was carried out in a festival atmosphere. The weather was crisp, clear, and beautiful—an ideal day for a picnic. As each couple or each family spread their lunch on the ground under the giant virgin pines, oaks, and sweet gum trees, it appeared that everyone in the New Windsor Township was present. Joseph shared Beth's excitement over the school. Patrick laughed and teased Martha as they sat on their picnic cloth in the edge of the woods. Wilma and the friendly giant, Luke Saunders, ate heartily of the ham and bread she had brought.

Liz and Joe Carter were oblivious to everyone else as they sat on a quilt near the edge of the woods and ate together, smiling and enjoying the fresh air of the open country. When they had finished eating, Joe Carter took his guitar from the wagon and began playing and singing a song he had written for Liz:

> "The sun is bright,
>   the grass is green,
> You're the prettiest
>   girl I've seen.
> I'll love you 'til death,
>   My sweet Elizabeth.
>
> The mosquitoes quit biting.
>   The squirrels are dancing.
> The dogs aren't fighting,

> and the deer are prancing.
> I'll love you 'til death,
>   My sweet Elizabeth.
>
> 'Til the July snow falls,
>   'Til the mountains fall down.
> 'Til the Good Lord calls,
>   To hand me a crown,
> I'll love you 'til death,
>   My sweet Elizabeth.

As he finished, Patrick took his banjo from the wagon, and Luke grabbed his fiddle. Pat McElmurray took his mouth organ from his pocket, and Malcolm Davies dragged out his bass fiddle. They all adjusted the strings and tuned their instruments in harmony with each other, and in a few minutes, happy music filled the woods and echoed across the fields. The girls clapped their hands and danced around to the rhythm of the music. Isaiah and Sam, and all the other slaves clapped their hands and patted their feet wildly like little children.

After a while Joseph called out, "Hey Isaiah, sing about the rusty hoe!"

"No suh, Massa Joe! You knows I can't sing!" he answered bashfully.

The whole crowd began clapping and chanting, "We want Isaiah to sing! We want Isaiah to sing! We want Isaiah to sing!"

"Awright, awright, I sing." he shouted as he spryly walked to the center of the group. He began singing, and shortly after he started, the musicians caught on to the tune and followed along.

THE RUSTY HOE

> De sun is ridin' high today,
>   An' parches de earth below.
> Grass is brown fa lack a' rain,
>   I long ta feel de snow.
> Summer's been hot, an' long it seems,

> It makes de tongue so dry.
> I pour cool water on me head,
> > An' cuss at all de flies.
> Workin' in dis field all day,
> > De sun beats on me brow.
> I till de soil wit' my rusty hoe,
> > Boss yells, "Get ta work, rat now!"
> Sittin' in his house, so fine
> > I guess he wouldn't know
> What it's like ta work all day
> > Behind dis rusty hoe.
> Old man winter, you'se got it made.
> > An' I needs ya clouds so gray,
> Jes once, I'd like a little shade.
> > 'Foe I die in dis field some day.

The music swelled, the hands clapped, and Isaiah danced as he sang. He sang it over and over again appearing to enjoy it more each time he sang it. Finally Isaiah's breath gave out, and he slumped to the ground and continued laughing and clapping his hands. The musicians swung out on a good lively dancing tune, and all the young men and women grabbed a partner and raised a cloud of dust in the dry yard of the half-finished school. They danced under the bright September sun until their clothes were wet with sweat.

Patrick laughed as he played the banjo, and yelled to the dancers, "If ya'll sweat as much working on the school as you do dancing, we'll finish early."

Beth and Joseph were standing next to the bell, leaning against its post. "Isn't it wonderful to have such fun again, free from fear and harassment," she said to Joseph as she took his hand in both of hers.

"Yes it is, sweetheart," he answered as he squeezed her hand. "It's also wonderful to have such a nice group of friends and neighbors."

Everyone was having such a good time, Joseph hated to see the lunch time come to an end. He and Beth agreed, however, that it was time for the work on the school to continue. The day's pleasure passed too fast. After about an hour he rang the bell with a guilty smile. He knew everyone had probably lost track of time and didn't want to be reminded.

"Back to work," he announced. "Lunch hour is over! We want to have this school ready to occupy by nightfall!"

All the men resumed their task, while the ladies slowly folded the table cloths and quilts and put away the food. Isaiah and Sam were helping Pat McElmurray dig a well. Isaiah laughed and slapped his knees when Sam was drawn up from the bottom, covered with a light colored mud. "Yo looks like a ghost, Sam. Iffen yo don't wash up, 'Gustine'll think she done got a white man tryin' ta git in de house."

After a few more minutes Pat McElmurray yelled from the well, "We've struck water! We've struck water! And a mighty fine spring it is. Get me out of here, Isaiah, before I drown!"

Before the sun set, the two-room school was complete with bench seats, writing tables, school bell, and well. As the crowd stood back admiring the fruits of their labor, Beth announced that school would begin on Monday morning at eight. Everyone shook hands proudly, said their goodbyes, and left for home. Joseph asked Luke and Joe to see Liz and Wilma home, so he and Martha could stop by the O'Neale's house for a while.

Beth was beaming with pride when they arrived at home and she had a chance to tell her mother and father how successful the day had been. Mr. O'Neale smiled with satisfaction and quipped. "I guess all that money I spent sending you to school in Savannah is worthwhile after all." He continued teasing her, as he winked at Joseph, "What do you think, Joe?"

"Yes, sir. I'd say it was very worthwhile. Money well spent."

For the next two months, Beth taught the new Silver Bluff grammar school without pay and enjoyed every minute of it. The children were so eager to learn they reminded her of thirsty piglets in the watering trough.

In late November, John called Joseph to his bedside. He had been in bed for several weeks with weak spells and something like consumption. "Joe, I don't believe I'll be around much longer," he said, trying to be brave. "I just can't get back my strength, and now it's hard to breathe."

"Don't worry, Papa, you'll be good as new in a few weeks,"

Joseph interrupted before he had finished. "You'll be around here a long time yet."

"No, Joe, listen to me," he continued in a serious manner. "You've been the man of the house for several months now, and I'm proud of the way you take care of things. I want to give you this."

He took the little cedar chest, which Isaiah had made for him, from under the cover of the bed. Apparently he had been holding it for a long time. He handed the warm box to Joseph as he continued. "You know how precious these fish charms have been to me all my life. I give them to you in hopes that you'll feel the same way about them. Let them always be a symbol of honor and respect, Joe. I know you will."

"Papa, there's plenty of time for this. You'll be here to see your great-grandchildren," Joseph interrupted again to reassure him before he had time to say anything more pessimistic.

"Now Joseph, I know how I feel. Just listen. There are five charms which I gave away and which have been returned, and there are six more which have never been given away. Only yours and Isaiah's are missing from the collection. Now Joseph, I'm giving this collection of little rusty charms to you. You can do with them what you will, but please try to preserve the meaning which I have cherished all my life. I know they wouldn't be worth keeping for anyone else, but I hope they'll be as precious to you as they have been to me."

"They are, Papa, and you've been a wonderful father. You've taught us more than you know. Your children and grandchildren, and many generations to come will remember you," he said as he took his hand and rubbed it gently. John closed his eyes and dozed off again into a peaceful sleep.

For the next few weeks, John stayed in bed, sleeping most of the time and waking only to call for Mary or Isaiah, or one of the children. Isaiah sat by his bed most of the time during the first week of December, holding his hand and talking to him as if he were awake. He knew the end was near for the best friend he had ever known. Mary also stayed near the bed, ready to feed him when he awoke. She bathed and cared for him as if he were a newborn baby.

One morning John awoke, opened his eyes, and appeared to be fully conscious. He slowly rolled his eyes around until he saw Isaiah, his long-time friend and servant. He was faithfully sitting by his bed. His statuesque appearance had been unchanged by all the years except for his slumped shoulders and his distinguished white hair and beard. His sculptured face had been etched with fine lines which only honor and dignity could have produced.

"Isaiah, it's good to see you. How long have you been sitting here?" John asked in a weak voice as he struggled to touch him with his feeble hand.

"I don't know, Massa John. I'ze been here 'bout two days," he answered with a twinkle in his eye. "I'ze sho' glad ta see yo' wake up. I knows yo's gonna be fine now!"

"I hope I've not been too hard on you, Isaiah."

"Too hard? No suh. Yo's been too good ta me. Everybody's got ta be someplace all de time, and I'ze sho'glad ta be wit you, Massa John," he replied with admiration as he reached for John's weak hand.

"I hope I've been as good a friend as you've been to me," John said, as he struggled to look Isaiah in the face.

"Good friend? Why, yes suh, Massa John. Yo's been da best friend I'ze ever had. Why, I 'member da first day I seed you. You wuz a skinny little boy 'bout my same age. I knowed dat day you wuz a fine man. An' when yo kicked dat hay on Massa George LaGrow ta keep him from usin' dat whip on me, I knowed you wuz de best friend I'd ever had. Why, I'll never forget da day you gave me dat fish. Iffen de Lawd hisself had come down from de sky and give it ta me, I wouldn't have prized it mo'. I'ze still got it, Massa John, and I'll keep it 'til I pass. See here," he said excitedly, as he pulled it from his pocket and showed how worn it had become. "I ain't drawed a breath wit out it since dat day.

"A good friend? Lawd bless ya soul. I ain't forgot dat day when we 'as 'bout da be busted up, Phoebe and me and de chilrun. We'd cried and prayed all night dat de Lawd would undertake. We wuz gittin' ready ta go on de auction block when I looked over and seed ya sittin' under dat big old tree. I runs over ta ya and shows ya de fish, an' I knowed de Lawd done answered my prayers. I ain't forgot what ya did fa us all.

"When I climbed in dat wagon with all my chilrun, I knowed we would never be busted up again. It 'as all I could do ta keep from cryin' and shoutin' at de same time. Good friend? Why, yo been de best friend in dis world. I ain't never doubted dat. Lawd bless ya kind soul, Massa John. I loves you. You been mo' dan a friend!''

John smiled, closed his eyes, and drifted off into a peaceful sleep. Isaiah leaned back in his chair and continued his patient and loyal vigil. On the morning of December 10th, 1782, with Mary, Joseph, Isaiah, and the girls standing around his bed, John opened his eyes, smiled at them all, and fell into an eternal sleep with a smile on his face. He had been through a lot of valleys, had known a lot of disappointments, but he had always remained a man of peace. He died in his own bed, surrounded by friends, at peace with himself and the world.

On December 14th, 1782, the British left Charles Town forever. Ironically it was the day John Dicks was laid to rest in the family cemetery on the bank of Town Creek. A large crowd of planters, stock farmers, slaves, and Indians were present to pay their final respects. A light snow was falling as they wept softly, and the young Huguenot minister said the final prayer over the open grave.

"Lord, we know John Dicks is not here in this old house of clay. His troubles are over. He'll never know pain or sorrow again. He has finished his race while we're still running.''

A large black spider slowly descended from one of the low-lying limbs of an old live oak tree, and dangled just above the minister's bare head. It started to land on his fluffy brown hair but then pulled itself up again as if it had decided against a nest which might not be very permanent. It did this several times as Isaiah and Phoebe watched the strange action, and their eyes became big. Suddenly the dynamic minister raised his hands to make his prayer more fervent.

"Oh Lord, help us that are living and remain, to run the race as well as he did. Help us to keep our heads and our honor during trying times as he did.''

The ugly spider had come upon the scene as if nature itself had made one last try at pestering and harassing what was left of the man of peace. The minister's waving hands caught the web and slung the fluttering insect somewhere into the shadows of the cold green ivy which covered the ground. Isaiah slumped back against a tree, and

Phoebe turned her mind back to the prayer.

"Now comfort the family, and let them know that he is at peace. Now may the Father, Son, and Holy Ghost be with you and in each of you, now and forever more. In Jesus' name we pray. Amen."

As Joseph and the family walked back to the house he said in a wistful voice, "It's a shame Papa didn't live to see the British leave Charles Town. He always thought of Charles Town as the place of his roots."

For the next several months Joseph spent much time reading and re-reading the will of his father, and the inventory list which had been made. His will was dated April 20, 1776. It had been made when John was fifty-five years old:

In the name of God, Amen. The Twenty Day of April, One Thousand, Seven Hundred, and Seventy Six. I John Dicks of Granville County, in South Carolina, being of perfect mind and memory, thanks be to God, therefore, calling unto mind the mortallety of the Body and knowing that it is appointed for all men once to die, do make and ordain this my last will and testament, that is to say, principally and first of all, I give and recommend Soul into the hands of God that Gave it, and for my body, I recommend it to the earth to be buried in a Christian like manner at the discretion of my Executors, nothing doubting but at the General Resurrection, I shall receive the same again by the mighty power of God; and as touching such worldly possessions wherewith it hath pleased almighty God to bless me with in this life, I give and devise and dispose of the same in the following manner and form. . .impremis it is. . .My will and I do order principally in the first, all my just debts be paid and satisfied. Item. It is my will that all my estate shall remain in the hands and possession of my well beloved Mary, my wife, as long as it shall please Almighty God, she shall live, for the support of her and her small children. I leave with her, and after her death it is my will that my land whereon I dwell and a Negro fellow named Sam, shall be my son Joseph's. My other lands to be occupied for the support of my young children until they are grown up and married, and then to be divided, my three sons, William, John, and Thomas, my other

333

Negroes to labour in the aforesaid land for the support of the aforesaid children. I leave in the hands of my son Joseph, after death of his mother, if it shall please God to spare him and he shall support his sisters until they are grown up to provide for themselves, as for my stock of each kind being but small. It is my will they be divided between my four youngest children. My Negroes all but Sam after the girls are married shall be divided among all my children. . .and it is my will and I do order that no part of my estate be sold to defraud any of my children, by any person whatsoever, and it is my will that whatsoever part or portion of this my estate that falleth to either of my children, the same shall devolve back to the living at their death, leaving no lawful issue to be equally divided among all my children living, and it is my will that what cash I leave behind me to be laid out upon slaves for my children, and I do hereby constitute, make and ordain my well beloved Mary, my wife, with Joseph my son to be my lawful executors of this my last will and testament. In witness whereof I have hereunto set my hand and seal this Twenty first day of April, one thousand, seven hundred, and seventy six. Signed, Sealed, Published and declared by the said John Dicks as his last will and testament.

Witnesses	Ann Newman	John Dicks
	John Newman	
	Alexander Newman	

Probated by Alexander Newman, one of the above subscribing witnesses, before John Ewing Calhoun, Esquire: Ordinary of 96th District, the 8th day of April, 1783.*

John had not referred to Isaiah as a slave. He had considered him a friend and a member of the family. He just could not bring himself to think of him as a slave. Joseph had promised John that he would personally see that Isaiah was taken care of the rest of his life. He decided that Phoebe would never be separated from Isaiah, except by death. For the time being, it was apparent that Sam and Augustine and their girls would remain together for many years.

---

*Taken from records of Ninety Sixth District.

"Mamma, do you think this appraisal is fair?" he asked one morning, while sitting at the table studying the inventory list of the property of his father's estate.

"I don't know, Joe," she answered as she prepared breakfast. "You'd know more about those things than me."

"Well, I guess it doesn't matter," he responded thoughtfully. "Looks to me like the values are a little low. I just want to make sure all the children are treated fairly when you pass on."

"I know you'll see that's done, Joe," she replied with confidence. "You handle things as you see best."

Joseph took the inventory list and began reading it again:

An inventory & Appraisement of the estate of John Dicks of Beech Island, in the District of Ninety Six, Testator, made the 10th day of December, 1782, by Michael Myer, John Sturzenegger & Natl. Howell, Sworn appraiser, Mary Dicks acting Executrix—as followeth, in old currency:

	lbs.	S.	P
1 Negro named Sam	560	-	-
1 Negro named Augustine	500	-	-
1 Do Princess.....1 do Lunnon	490	-	-
1 Negro Wench, Phebee	400	-	-
1 Negro girl, Sylvia	340	-	-
1 Do Sarah	450	-	-
1 Do Rose	280	-	-
42 head of cattle .. 8-10 lbs	357	-	-
26 head sheep .. 3-10 lbs	91	-	-
19 head of Hogs .. 50	47	10	-
1 iron bound cart	50	-	-
2 old carts	25	-	-
1 Mare & colt, 1 young horse	65	-	-
1 old and 1 small do	90	-	-
141 sides of tanned leather	493	10	-
2 wire sives .. 7	14	-	-
14 reaping hooks & 5 grubbing hoes	12	5	-
2 shears & cotters, 8 weeding hoes	30	-	-

3 falling axes	6	-	-
1 old spade & fro	3	-	-
1 hand mill, 1 bed & furneture	184	-	-
1 small bed, 1 silver hetted sword	52	10	-
1 Mohogany bedsted	14	-	-
1 small tea table	5	-	-
4 pine tables	14	-	-
6 large pewter basin	42	-	-
5 pewter dishes, & 11 plates	42	-	-
3 parcel old Pewter	8	-	-
1 small spice morter	7	-	-
Old seals & weights	3	10	-
11 Queens ware plates	5	-	-
1 Bufat	35	-	-
3 pr. of fire dogs	16	-	-
2 pair of Tongs & 2 shovels	7	-	-
5 iron wedges	10	-	-
1 Gin case & Bottles	3	10	-
2 coths-press	100	-	-
2 pair of Stillards	3	10	-
4 iron pots & brass kettle	28	-	-
1 Tea Kettle	7	-	-
1 Cut saw, 1 Tenent saw	14	-	-
4 Flax Brake	2	10	-
1 Loom .. 14, 1 frying pan .. 2	16	-	-
29 lbs of iron	10	3	-
19 lb of Steel	13	6	-
554 lbs of Indigo	969	10	-
Amount of Appraisement	5946	4	0

No sale Returned.
Examined & Certified, by Pat Calhoun Surrogate for
John E. Calhoun, Esqr. Ordinary*

---

*Taken from the records of Ninety Sixth District.

"I've just got to get away from here for a while, Mamma," Joseph said as he laid the will and inventory list aside. "I think I'll hurry and finish all my chores so I can go to the cock fight at Luke Saunders' house tonight."

"Pat and I are going," Martha said with a boast. "Are you taking Beth?"

"I hadn't thought about it," he answered as he scratched his head in amazement. "Isn't a cock fight a little bloody for you ladies to enjoy?"

"Well, I'll find out tonight," she replied with a smile. "I've already told Pat I'd go with him."

"Where's Liz? Is she planning on going?" he asked, looking around.

"She and Wilma have plans to ride over there with Joe Carter," Martha answered. "They're upstairs making the beds."

"I guess I'll leave early enough tonight to stop by the O'Neale's and ask Beth to go with me," he said as he hesitated thoughtfully. "Maybe she'll enjoy it."

Luke Saunders' house sat on a little knoll in the Beech Island section of the New Windsor Township. His house was constructed of finished weather boarding and was surrounded by several slave houses and several large barns. Joseph could tell where the action was by the number of horses and wagons tied to the hitching post. They waited patiently in front of the largest barn at the end of the little lane which ran down behind the house. He, Beth, Patrick, and Martha had ridden together from the O'Neale house.

"I must confess," Joseph said as he laughed out loud, "I've never been to a cock fight."

"Neither have I," Beth and Martha said at the same time with a big laugh.

"Well it's a little gory," Patrick said with a laugh. "But not as bloody as the Thanksgiving Festival. I think you'll enjoy it."

The barn was filled with excited, laughing people who had either come to see a good fight, or were betting on their own favorite gamecock. All this was new to Joseph, and he was not sure he would like it. The heat of the May sun had left plenty of warmth in the big barn, and the odor of sweat mixed with the smell of several milk cows, and weeks of their droppings, almost stifled him. The big crowd sat around on logs and log benches, on the hay, and on the stall rails. Some stood against the walls. Over in one corner there were about a dozen little cages which had been brought by the gamecock owners, who had been given the order in which their gamecock would fight.

The excitement mounted when Luke announced that the fight would begin with Pat McElmurray's and James Swan's gamecocks. They quickly rushed to the cages and took out their finest cock. They met in the center of the floor and, before turning them loose, rubbed the birds' heads together and rammed them against each other to get them in a fighting mood. When they turned them loose, the cocks were ready to fight. They paused only a moment, with the feathers on the back of their necks standing straight up, and then dived at each other, pecking and scratching. Flapping their wings, they went around and around, pouncing on each other, and drawing blood, while the crowd cheered and yelled.

"What makes them continue to fight?" Martha asked Patrick as she held tightly to his arm.

"I don't know. Don't they remind you of some people? I saw a few like them at the festival a few months ago, didn't you?"

Martha smiled and nodded. She still could not understand how anyone could enjoy this kind of thing.

Pat McElmurray's gamecock ran out of steam and fell, bleeding and dying, to the floor. The other gamecock continued pecking and attacking until it was stopped by James Swan, and put back in its cage to await the second round of fighting.

Luke then announced that he would put his gamecock up against the pride of Thomas Wilson. They took the birds from their cages and went through the same ceremony. The cocks attacked each other with vicious vigor, repeatedly, as they flapped their wings, scratched, and clawed. Around and around they jumped, attacking spitefully again and again until blood and feathers covered the floor. Finally, Thomas Wilson's gamecock fell to the floor, fluttering its wings while its opponent continued to peck and attack its dying carcass.

Beth looked at Joseph and said, "Let's get out of here. I need fresh air!"

Taking her by the arm he led her toward the barn door. He was surprised to see Wilma leaning against the outside wall, pale as a ghost. It was obvious she had been vomiting.

"I was afraid this kind of thing would be too much for you girls," he teased as he and Beth walked toward the wagon.

"We'll go back in after a while," Beth whispered as she held on to his arm. "I just needed a breath of fresh air."

Joseph picked her up and sat her on the back of the wagon. The moonlight danced on her auburn hair, and her beautiful white teeth glittered as she smiled broadly.

"You know, school will be over this week, Joe," she said as she held his warm hand. "Wouldn't you like to come visit the school on the last day and watch the activities?"

"Sure," he quickly responded. "I'll bring a present for the prettiest teacher in the state."

"I've told all the children to invite their parents," she continued. "I'd like for them to see what we're doing. I'm afraid most of them don't appreciate the value of a good education. Several took their children out of school early to help with the farming. She paused for a moment and continued with excitement in her voice. "Those are the most wonderful children in the world. I feel like they're all mine."

"Speaking of children," Joseph nervously interrupted. "Don't you think we need to start talking about getting married?" There was a long silence. They had been seeing each other steadily over the past two years, and this was the first time marriage had been mentioned.

"Oh, that's a sweet thought, Joe. And I do love you very much," she whispered as she embraced him tightly. "But let me think about it. I've become so involved with the school, and I love it so much. You know the parents expect a teacher to remain single as long as she teaches."

"We'll talk about it again. Let's go back in and see the rest of the fights," he said with disappointment clearly showing on his face and in his voice. They walked back to the barn in silence, to be assaulted by the noise, odor, and excitement once again.

The wild frenzy of the cock fight ended about eleven o'clock, with

Luke's big gamecock being declared the winner. He was scratched, cut, almost featherless, and covered with blood, but he was the winner. When Joseph saw the pitiful gamecock he was reminded of how he felt, and must have looked, after his fight with Payton Dues at the festival.

Joseph and Beth were silent, deep in their thoughts, as they rode home with Patrick and Martha that night. Martha would not stop chattering about the fights, and Patrick only got a word in edgewise every now and then. Beth held Joseph's arm tightly and snuggled up to him as they sat on the hay in the back of the wagon. She had a lot to think about, and so did he.

While Patrick and Martha laughed and chatted by the wagon, Joseph kissed Beth goodbye without a word and called for Martha to get into the wagon. They both waved goodbye as he headed the old bay horse toward home.

As he had promised, Joseph arrived at school on Wednesday morning just as the bell was ringing. The parents followed their children inside the building to witness the last day's activities. The children sat at their usual places, and the parents stood by the wall.

"Now, I would like to explain to you parents how we usually conduct the school," Beth announced as she called the classes to order. "Obviously we will not have a usual school day today. It's the last day; we must hand out certificates; and the children have prepared a program for you. So I'll just tell you how we usually conduct both classes."

She paused for a moment and continued, "Each morning when the bell rings, each student finds his usual place. The younger students are in this room, and the older ones are over there." She pointed to the next room as she continued. "I greet the students and give assignments in one room while the other room waits. While the first class carries out their assignments, I give assignments to the other class. So you see, I work back and forth between the two rooms, and usually everything works out fine."

In one room Beth set the children in motion with their program. Each recited by memory certain children's stories, poems, and other things which had been planned. She then moved to the second room and did the same thing there. The passing out of certificates was handled the same way. After about three hours she had Joseph go outside and ring the bell, indicating that the short final day was over.

As the parents stood around talking to each other and thanking Beth for her fine work, the children played their usual little games in the school yard. Some of them played tag, others played marbles, leapfrog, or blind man's bluff. Some of the girls played hopscotch, while others played ring-around-the-rosey or London bridge. After everyone had left, Joseph and Beth walked back into the school building to gather all her books and papers.

"Have you thought any more about my proposal?" he asked as he helped her gather the books and papers.

"What proposal?" she said as she smiled in a teasing way.

"You know perfectly well what I'm talking about, Beth O'Neale," he answered in frustration.

"You just said we ought to talk about marriage," she quickly responded. "You didn't make a proposal to me."

Joseph got down on one knee and looked up at her pitifully as he said in a deliberate manner, "Alright, Miss Beth O'Neale, will you please marry me?"

He placed his hand over his heart in jest, and wiped an imaginary tear from his eye, as he continued. "Please say yes. I can't live without you. If you say no, I'll kill myself."

"Now be serious, Joe," she said as she smiled and looked around again.

Joseph stood up, took her by the shoulders and looked into her eyes. "I am serious, Beth. You've known for a long time. I want to get married."

"I do too, Joe," she said with an agreeable but wistful voice. "But I must consider what will happen to the school."

"Well, I'm not getting any younger, and I can't wait forever," he blurted out in frustration. "You'll just have to decide whether you're going to marry me or the school." He thought for a minute and said in a very serious voice, "It's easy to love the whole world, Beth. That doesn't take a commitment. But it takes a commitment to love just one person. I'm willing to make that commitment. I know what I want out of life. I love you, and I want you to share my life. I was hoping you felt the same way. You'll have to decide what you really want from life, whether you want fifty children who will never be yours, or whether you want to have children of your own flesh and blood."

Joseph turned and started toward his horse. He paused, turned around and called back to her. "I'll be waiting for an answer, Beth!" He slipped into the saddle and left without looking back.

Beth stood in the school yard, watching him until he was out of sight. She then loaded her books into the wagon and headed for home with a sad heart.

For the next few days, Joseph made himself busy around the farm. In fact he had more to do than he could get done. Both farms needed to be planted and cared for. He worked from sunup until after sundown, planting the crops and working side by side with the slaves, making another large planting of tobacco, corn, indigo, hay and peas. He tried a little cotton and flax, just as an experiment, and planted a garden with beans, peas, squash, okra, corn, and several other vegetables for use by the family.

About a week later, while Patrick was visiting Martha, he asked her to marry him. She agreed without hesitation, and they excitedly came to ask for Mary's permission. Joseph was sitting by the fire, trying to read his father's will again. When he overheard the conversation in the kitchen, he jumped up and ran to embrace them both.

"I'm very pleased and happy for you both," he exclaimed with a broad grin. "I know you'll be happy."

"Thank you, Joe," Patrick said proudly. "I hope you and Beth start thinking about the same thing."

"I've already asked her several times, Pat," he replied with a serious face. "But she feels she will have to give up the school. I guess it's just a matter of which she loves the most—me or the school."

Wilma and Liz heard the conversation downstairs and came running with their congratulations. "I'm so happy for you," Wilma cried as she wiped a tear from her eye and hugged them both.

Liz embraced them both as well and said in a lighthearted and jovial manner, "I'm really happy for you both. I envy your joy, and I hope my time will come before I'm considered an old maid."

She laughed, turned to Joseph, and said, "Is there any of Papa's berry wine left? This calls for a celebration!"

Late one evening several weeks later when Patrick came calling on Martha, he had Beth with him. Joseph was down at the barn feeding the animals when she slipped in the door and surprised him. Before he could remember he was still waiting on an answer, he grabbed her and embraced her warm body, which he had missed over the past few weeks.

"Oh, Joseph!" she cried with tears streaming down her face. "I love you more than I had thought!" She kissed him passionately, and tearfully said, "Yes. Yes. I will marry you. There's no happiness in my life without you. I couldn't live without you."

Joseph lifted her from the floor and swung her around and around like a rag doll as they eagerly embraced. They ran from the barn and into the house to tell the news. The whole family tried to talk at one time with great excitement. Mary, Wilma, Martha, and Liz, all laughed and cried alternately, while Patrick shook Joseph's hand and then embraced them both.

Isaiah and Phoebe had been in the garden hoeing the beans and squash. They came in the back door when they heard the commotion. When he heard the news, Isaiah laughed and shouted, "I knowed it! I knowed it! I knowed two lovebirds purty as Massa Joe and Missy Beth wouldn't bust up. I knowed they jes had ta get hitched sooner or later. I'se happy fa yo all. May de Lawd bless yo, and may yo haff lots of chilrun as good as yo be now!"

Joseph and Beth left immediately for the O'Neale home so that he could ask for the permission and blessings of her parents. When the marriage proposal was presented to them, neither Beth's father nor her mother showed any real surprise. They had been watching the growing closeness between their daughter and Joseph for a number of months. Both felt that he would make a fine husband for their daughter. They therefore gave their assent and warmest blessings to Joseph's request.

As the days passed, Martha and Beth decided they would like to have a double wedding. Since the two couples had always been so close, Patrick and Joseph quickly agreed. So plans were made for a big double wedding, to be held at the O'Neale home, on September

3, 1783.

The next two months were the longest two months Joseph could remember. If he had not been so busy managing both farms, he could not have made it. During this exciting time the rest of the world outside of the New Windsor Township was of little interest to the two happy couples. Even the news that Charles Town had changed its name to Charleston seemed unimportant. The weather was good for the crops, and it appeared that the Dicks farms would do well again this year. The O'Neale plantation appeared to be highly successful too; a good beginning for the coming marriages.

The whole world appeared rosy and bright for the two young men who had just lived through several dark years of danger and heartache. The war was over; the danger was past; and the future looked promising indeed. They were both happy and contented. Everything was fine. There was nothing for Joseph or Patrick to do except wait, and waiting was something that neither could get used to.

September 3rd, 1783, finally came, as had all the other millions of days which had preceded it, but somehow the sun seemed a little brighter to the two couples as they anticipated the six o'clock wedding. The wedding and reception ball was one of the biggest and most colorful affairs the New Windsor Township had ever experienced. Many friends of the brides, the grooms, and both sets of parents came dressed in their Sunday best. The young Huguenot minister, Peter Durouzeaux, stood at the bottom of the elegant staircase, with Bible in hand, waiting for both brides to descend. Joseph stood on one side of him, with Mary and the family. Patrick stood on the other side of Rev. Durouzeaux with Mr. and Mrs. O'Neale.

At six o'clock the large dinner bell began ringing outside. Both brides appeared at the top of the stairs. They had never appeared lovelier. Both white linen dresses were long and dragged behind them as they descended the stairs together. Martha's long golden hair, with hat and veil, looked like sunshine with a little cloud sitting on top, while Beth's blazing auburn hair appeared as a flame behind a misty vapor. Both looked like angels to the waiting grooms.

As they took their places beside the grooms, the bell stopped ringing, and Rev. Durouzeaux began the ceremony. "Beloved, we gather here today to unite these two fine young couples in holy matrimony: Joseph Dicks and Elizabeth O'Neale, Patrick O'Neale and Martha Dicks."

The ceremony lasted for forty-five minutes. The French minister apparently believed in a long and meaningful rite. He finally said, "I now pronounce you man and wife!"

The crowd was surprised and embarrassed when both men grabbed their brides and kissed them passionately. . .in public. Mr. O'Neale interrupted the oohs and aahs of the crowd, when he yelled, "The music is ready,so let's all dance."

Joseph and Patrick and their new brides led the throng into the large drawing room where Joe Carter, Luke Saunders, Pat McElmurray, Malcolm Davies, and the rest of the small band had already started the music. They danced for hours without stopping.

"I don't think my feet have touched the floor all night," Beth whispered to Joseph when they finally did stop for rest and refreshment.

"I feel pretty light, too," he admitted as he nibbled on the food at the table.

Friends converged upon them when they paused for a rest, congratulating them and wishing them well. Mrs. O'Neale, Mary, Wilma, and Liz Dicks had worked for several days decorating the house, making the punch and preparing the food. They had done a splendid job, and the guests appeared to appreciate it. The celebration continued late into the night until the guests gradually began to tire and leave for home. They wished the newlyweds well again and left.

John Parkinson came over to Joseph and Beth late in the evening and said with a glow, "I've got some news you should be interested in, Joe. He shook Joseph's hand, kissed the back of Beth's hand and continued. "The stagecoach driver told me this afternoon that a notice was posted on the door of the stagecoach inn in Charles Town. . .I mean Charleston, which said the war is officially over. It seems that the declaration had been drawn up in England and ratified in Philadelphia, and postdated September 3rd, 1783."

"That's wonderful news, John," Joseph exclaimed excitedly. "It looks like today ends the old fox chase in more ways than one!"

7

Building a Dream
1783-1800

Like two roses cut from separate vines simultaneously, the two brides of the double wedding were plucked from their childhood bush. Beth O'Neale moved to the Dicks home, and Martha Dicks moved to the O'Neale plantation.

Joseph continued to manage both Dicks farms for his mother and made preparations for the next farming year. Liz married Joe Carter and moved away. Wilma, who had been sickly all her life, continued to be thin and pale most of the time, but her eyes glowed when she heard the name of Luke Saunders. She always called her two-hundred-thirty-pound, six-foot two-inch sweetheart the "friendly giant."

Saunders had become a regular visitor at the Dicks home, and in January of 1784 he asked Wilma to marry him. They had been seeing each other steadily for four years, and it was no surprise to Joseph or Mary. They happily gave their permission, and Wilma's health appeared to improve with the excitement and anticipation of a June wedding.

Beth's pregnancy was showing clearly in May when Wilma had another weak spell and had to stay in bed. Beth and Mary took care of her night and day for several weeks, while she remained in bed. Big

Luke came to see her regularly, and sat by her bed or gently picked her up and set her on the porch, when she wanted to see the bright May sunshine or green grass and trees. His big blue eyes were filled with sadness when he looked at her and realized that the only girl he had ever loved was slowly dying.

"Darling Wilma," the big man said one day in late May as he sat her on the front porch in the sun, "do you think we should postpone the wedding until your health improves?"

"No, no!" she cried as tears ran down her pale cheeks. "I'll be better in a few days."

Luke brushed the shiny black hair back from her forehead with his big broad hand and whispered, "I love you, Wilma. We'll do whatever you want. I'll wait, or I'm ready. It depends on you." She looked up at the big lovable giant and smiled as she kissed his hand.

As June approached, Wilma became worse instead of better. She had to struggle every minute of her life for breath. Her weight continued to drop until she weighed less than ninety pounds. Joseph did all he could do for her. He visited Augusta and brought a doctor to treat her. He met the doctor at the Sandbar Ferry one time and Luke met him the next. Nothing the doctor prescribed helped her at all. Joseph even had a "root doctor" visit Wilma and treat her with his mixture of boiled roots and herbs, but still she became worse.

On the evening of June 4th, 1784, just two days before her wedding, Wilma gave up the gallant fight for breath. With Luke Saunders, Joseph, Mary, Beth, and the rest of the Dicks family gathered around the bed, she opened her eyes, smiled, and relaxed. Then she dropped off into a sleep from which she never awoke.

She was buried on the day which had been set aside for her wedding. She was wearing her white linen dress, made by Mary for the eagerly anticipated wedding which would never come. Luke was crushed, and felt he could not leave her alone in the family cemetery. Joseph and Patrick finally had to almost wrestle him away from the grave so Isaiah and Sam could cover it with the cold, white, lifeless sand.

Mary never did quite get over the untimely death of Wilma. She never was the same again as long as she lived. There were times when she thought she saw Wilma and heard her delicate voice.

Joseph became increasingly concerned about his mother. One night when he and Beth were sitting alone at the table, he put his arm around her gently and said, "Beth, I want you to keep an eye on Mamma. I'm afraid her mind is failing." He paused as he placed his hand gently on her abdomen, and continued, "I know you're the one who needs someone to be taking care of you right now, but maybe she'll get better with a little time."

"I'm doing fine, dear," Beth responded as she snuggled against his chest and put down her needle and thread. "She's a sweet person who's been through more than most women. I'll be patient with her."

"By the way, Beth," he said as he hugged her gently. "I saw Patrick today at the trading post. He said Martha is expecting to deliver sometime in August. Isn't that about the time you expect to get down?"

"I'm not sure, Joe," she answered with a sly grin. "The way I feel and look, I don't believe I'll make it until August."

Joseph kissed her on the lips and replied with a big smile. "You may feel bad, but you're still the prettiest girl in the world."

They sat together talking for several hours as Beth sewed by the light of the lantern, and he reviewed the seed bills and harvesting plans.

The following day Martha and Patrick came for a visit in the early afternoon. She, too, had been concerned about her mother and wanted to spend some time with her. While she chatted with Beth and Mary, Patrick went down to the blacksmith shop where Joseph was making door hinges.

"Come on in, Pat," Joseph called as he looked up from his anvil. "How's Martha? Is anything wrong?"

"No. No. Everything's fine. Just came for a friendly visit."

"I've been wanting to see you. I've got something for you," Joseph said as he put down his hammer and picked up a little fish charm from his work table. He had already cut Pat's initials on the back of it.

"Pat, I want to give you this fish charm," he said as he handed it to him. "It doesn't look like much but it's become a tradition in our family. . .almost a legend. Grandpa Josephus made one for Papa, and Papa made twelve. . .He gave me one before I went away to fight in the war with General Marion. It saved my life. I've never told anyone the story except the family. I guess it's because it's such a personal thing. The strange thing is that the fish charms keep coming back to the family. Of the six Papa gave away for one reason or another, all have come back except mine and Isaiah's. We're the only two people with the charms still living. We'll carry them as long as we live. Someday I'll tell you all about the stories behind them when we have more time. But the main thing is. . .this fish charm represents a special bond between the giver and the receiver. . .sort of a symbol of honor."

Joseph paused for a moment, as if embarrassed, and continued. "Well, it's always been a special symbol for our family, and since you're part of the family, and we've always been so close, I want you to have one."

Patrick looked at the fish; the three crosses on one side, and his initials on the other, and said in a very sincere voice, "I really appreciate this, Joe. It's about the nicest thing that's ever happened to me. I've heard Martha talk about the fishes, but I never expected to have one. Somehow I feel this represents a special relationship to you and the family." He put the charm in his pocket and added in a serious tone. "This is where it'll stay until I die."

"Here, let's shake on it," Joseph said in a pleased tone when he saw Patrick's enthusiastic acceptance. "I suppose we're about as close as any two friends could be." They shook hands again and laughed together as they left the shop.

Rocking together, they sat on the porch all evening, talking about their crops and how successful they appeared to be, while Martha, Beth, and Mary talked of the expected babies. Joseph related his dream of building a big plantation house, being a successful planter, and raising a fine breed of race horses. Pat talked about his tobacco crop and the needed repairs on the O'Neale plantation house.

"By the way, Joe, why don't you petition the new government for some land?" he suggested as they swatted the flies, gnats, and mosquitoes. "I heard one of the stagecoach passengers from Charleston telling Mr. Parkinson that the government is giving land to many of the men who fought in the Continental Army. Didn't you serve part of the time in the Continental Army when you were with

Marion?"

"Yes, two different times." Joseph replied with an aroused curiosity. "Do you suppose I could get a free grant of some land?"

"I'm sure if you can find a vacant tract, the government will give it to you. . .that is, if they're giving it to anyone, like the man said," he answered as he patted Joseph on the back. "If anyone deserves it, you do."

"I might just check into it," Joseph replied as his brain started churning.

Several weeks later, Joseph and all the slaves were in a field of corn near the house, pulling the ears and stripping the fodder, when Mary sent Phoebe to bring him home. Beth was in labor. Joseph rushed home to see what he could do. Beth was in bed when he arrived, looking scared and in pain. He bent over the bed and kissed her as she grasped him around the neck and squeezed him with all her might.

"Is there anything I can do?" he asked as Mary and Phoebe busied themselves making preparations.

"Massa Joe, you knows we can take care of Missy Beth," Phoebe said in her grandmotherly way. "You jes sit down and rest ya po' bones. We'se got thangs under control."

Liz and Joe Carter came by late that evening. They thought it was about time for Beth to deliver, but were surprised to find her in labor. She had been in labor for four hours by then.

"Joseph, why don't you and Joe go down to the barn, or find something else to do? I'll go in and help Mamma and Phoebe. If she delivers before you get back, I'll come for you," Liz said as she pushed them toward the barn, and went into the house.

The date was August 8, 1784, and the heat was almost stifling. Joseph and Joe were sweating, doing nothing except fighting gnats, mosquitoes and flies. Joseph refused to leave, so he and Joe sat on the steps of the porch. Every now and then, through the swelter of the heat, Beth's loud screams could be heard. They rose in intensity and then died down for a while. As the minutes went by, the screams grew louder and closer together. Joseph began to sweat even more.

After a while, Liz came to the door and said, "You can come in now."

Joseph detected a sadness in her voice and quickly asked, "What's wrong, Liz? Is Beth all right?"

Phoebe was standing in the doorway to the bedroom, holding a fine big boy. "Jes look at dis fine boy, Massa Joe. He de spittin' image of you!" she said as she showed both of her teeth in a big smile.

Joseph quickly looked at the baby and asked again, almost in panic, "Is Beth all right? Can I see her?"

Mary stepped from the bedroom and said, "Now be patient, Joe. She's doing fine. The reason we all look so sad. . ." She paused and wiped a tear from her eye and said, "She had twins. The other little boy didn't make it."

Joseph rushed into the room and embraced Beth as he kissed her on the face. "I'm sorry you had such a hard time, sweetheart. I could almost feel the pain. How do you feel?" he asked as he brushed her red hair back from her forehead and wiped away the perspiration with his hand.

"I'm a lot better now," she whispered. "Have you seen our boys?"

"Yes, they're the most beautiful babies I've ever seen," he answered as he jumped up to take another look and to avoid further questions.

"Beth, the second one didn't make it," Mary said as she stood by the bed and took Beth's hand. "I'm sorry."

Joseph had turned his back to hide a tear. He turned around, bent over her once more, and kissed her as he managed to say with a tight throat, "The main thing is you, Beth. We have a fine baby boy, and you're doing fine. That's all that matters. I'm a happy and a thankful man today. My wonderful wife and fine baby boy is all I need. You make my life complete."

"Thank you my darling. I needed that," Beth said with a broad smile. "Now you can have the honor of naming him. What will it be?"

Joseph thought for a moment and said, "I'd like to name him after Papa. How does 'Johnathan' sound?"

Beth smiled and answered as Phoebe handed her the newborn baby. "I think that's a perfectly wonderful name for a perfectly handsome little boy."

Joe Carter and Liz smiled at each other as they witnessed the new life and the naming of the new baby. "We must go," Liz said as she placed her hand on Beth's arm. "I'm so happy for you, but we really must be home before too late. We'll come back in a few days and help you take care of him."

Several days later Joseph was pondering over his new role as father, when he decided to petition the government for a grant of land. He searched around until he found some vacant public land. It was less than two miles away, in a high, dry area near Beech Island. As best he could tell, there were at least five hundred acres in the parcel, and he could find no owner of record.

A few days before Christmas, in December of 1784, Joseph was out near the main stagecoach road, hunting for squirrels, when he noticed the stagecoach had stopped and the driver had started walking down the lane toward his house. Joseph came out of the woods and greeted him.

"Good morning, Mr. Walker." He stopped and leaned his rifle against a tree. "What brings you here this morning?"

"Morning, Mr. Dicks," he replied. "I have an important looking letter for you, so I thought I'd stop to see if you were at home."

"Much obliged, Mr. Walker." Joseph smiled broadly as he reached for the letter. "I've been looking for a deed to some property, and I believe this is it."

"Well, have a good day now, Captain Dicks." He walked quickly back down the lane and climbed onto the seat of the stagecoach.

Joseph was thrilled beyond measure when he opened the letter and saw a grant to the land and a cover letter from the Governor.

". . .We have concluded that you are one of the most worthy persons in the state to become owner of the property, because of your courageous service in winning our freedom.

We are aware that you not only served in the Continental army, but served as one of the most faithful followers of our General Francis Marion, when your state and country needed you most.

It therefore gives me great pleasure as Governor of the new state government, to grant your petition, and enclosed is a deed, free and clear, to the five hundred acres for which you petitioned.

Gratefully yours, John Rutledge
Governor of S. Carolina"

He ran all the way to the house, calling as he went, "Beth, oh Beth, look what I've got! It's the deed to the five hundred acres of land!"

Beth opened the door and exclaimed with excitement, "What in the name of common sense are you yelling about, Joseph Dicks? You scared me half to death." She held her abdomen and breathed a sigh of relief. "I thought something was wrong. You'll make me lose this baby if you scare me again."

"Look, Beth, I have the deed from the Governor for the five hundred acres of land. We now have enough land to provide for a good sized family, and it's all ours!" he continued ecstatically. "We're rich!"

Mary was sitting near the fire with little Johnathan and heard all the excitement. She laughed and said jokingly, "What happened, Joe? Did they make you governor?"

"Better than that, Mamma. I got a clear deed to the five hundred acres I asked the Governor for! It's all ours, free and clear!"

"That's wonderful dear," she replied without the same excitement. "But don't wake little Johnathan. He's been ill-tempered all morning."

Joseph and Beth sat up late that night by the warm fire and talked about all the dreams they had for a fine home and several beautiful children. "Isn't it a wonderful Christmas present?" he asked with a sparkle in his eyes. "I can't wait to tell Pat and Martha."

"Why don't we ride over there tomorrow?" Beth interrupted as she moved her feet closer to the fire. "I've been wanting to see them, and little Joe."

Early the next morning they both bundled up warmly and set out in the buggy to visit Patrick and Martha. Snow began falling lightly, and Joseph was not sure they should continue the trip. "Are you sure you want to continue the trip, Beth?" he asked with concern showing in his eyes. "Are you sure you're up to it?"

"I'm fine," she responded with an air of complete confidence. "I want to see Little Joe, and your mother is taking perfectly good care of little Johnathan. If we don't go now, I probably won't get to see them until after the new baby comes."

As they rode along, Joseph was careful to miss every bump in the road. He knew she could not feel as well as she pretended. About half way there, they saw a horse and wagon speeding toward them recklessly. It was in the middle of the road and gave no indication of moving over. As the wagon speedily moved nearer, it looked like it would hit them head-on. Joseph pulled on the reins of his horse and ran into the ditch to avoid the collision. The buggy bounced around like a toy and almost turned over.

"Are you all right, Beth?" Joseph asked as he brought the buggy to a stop in the ditch.

She held her abdomen with both hands, stretched her neck, and replied cautiously, "I think so, dear," she stretched her back and said, "My back hurts a little, but I think everything's all right."

"That was Payton Dues," he growled as he gritted his teeth. "Some people never grow up. That boy hunts for trouble. Someday he's going to find it."

As the spring planting season approached, Joseph started making plans to farm the new land as well as his mother's two smaller farms. In February he rushed to Charleston to buy slaves. Sam was taken along to help decide which to buy. He was honored to have such an important job. At the slave market, among the hollering and hand waving, Sam looked over the young, strong slaves as they were put on the block. Every time one came up that Sam liked, he nodded his head wildly, and Joseph bid until everyone else stopped.

Joseph had never seen Sam so intense. It looked like he was picking husbands for his girls. After buying ten big, strapping young men, he waved for Sam to leave the auction block. "I believe we've bought all we can afford at this time, Sam," he said as he motioned for all of them to follow him to the wagon. "You did a good job. It looked like you were picking husbands for your daughters."

"Never can tell, Massa Joe," he replied with a broad grin. "Iffen dey do get hitched ta my chilrun, I wants dem ta be strong and able ta work hard. Iffen dey don't, I still wants dem ta be strong and able ta work hard. It'll save me own back." He laughed and patted them on their backs as they climbed into the wagon.

During the last weeks of February, Joseph, Sam, and the new

slaves set out to clear and prepare the new land for farming. Joseph called all of them together and explained what he wanted them to do. He put Sam in charge of them as the foreman. He also announced that he had a plan to reward the slaves if they worked hard and made a successful crop.

"My father never believed in owning slaves," he said, as he looked each one squarely in the eye. "He was a good man who always thought of his slaves as part of the family. He was never overbearing. I intend to be the same way, but I must warn you, we must get this land cleared in time for planting. Now, Sam and I will be working by your side. We'll not tell you to do anything we wouldn't do. And if we make a success, I'll have a special reward for all of you." He pulled the bill of sale out of his pocket and continued, "Now I want to know each of you by name. When I read your name, I want you to raise your hand."

He began reading the names on the list: Bo, Noah, Bill, Jesse, Roy, Ezekiel, Jonah, Willie, Hezekiah, and Daniel. Each raised his hand as his name was called. Sam smiled with satisfaction. Any one or all of them would make good prospects for sons-in-law.

Everyone worked hard for the next two months, clearing the trees, pulling up the stumps, storing the good timber for future use, and plowing the land. By planting time the job was finished. Joseph was happy, and Sam was proud.

As a reward Joseph planned a little festival for all the slaves. Two days were set aside for nothing but food and fun. He helped Isaiah cook two hogs over the large outside pit. Augustine and Phoebe helped Mary and Beth cook the turnup greens, collards, potatoes, corn, and grits. Princess and Lunnon had the responsibility for getting plenty of cornbread and biscuits made and ready to eat. Joseph invited Patrick, Martha, Little Joe, and the O'Neales to come and bring all their slaves for the training days festival on the Dicks farm. Luke Saunders, Pat McElmurray, Malcolm Davies, and several other neighbors were also invited. It was an exciting time for the slaves. They had never been treated this way. In fact, they had never even been able to watch their masters enjoy a festival. Joseph was the manager of the festival events. Almost every event he had seen at the community center in Beech Island was planned, except the boxing match. He did not want violence of any nature to be a part of the festival.

Beth and Martha were excited about the festival atmosphere. They were both expecting their second child and were not able to help very much with the preparations. They were both pleased to find that Liz was also expecting her first child in a few months. Somehow the feeling of new life all around them and the happy smiles on the faces of the family and slaves made them feel that the future was going to be wonderful and peaceful.

Patrick had helped Joseph set up the day's activities. They were designed to include all slaves from both farms. A wrestling match, running match, arm wrestling contest, pole climbing, and horseshoe throwing contest were planned. They also added a log lifting and a rock throwing match.

The first day started with a big breakfast of ham and grits. Lunnon and Princess served the plates from the large pots over the fire, where everyone lined up and marched by with plate in hand. There were about fifty-five plates served; a good crowd for a little homemade fun.

Sam and Isaiah moved among the young boys and picked the contestants for each event. As Joseph rang the dinner bell, each contest began. The weather was perfect; not too hot and not too cold.

The first contest was the wrestling match. Bo and Daniel grappled with each other, and finally Daniel pinned Bo to the ground. Bo was the biggest of the slaves. His big body looked like one of the big black bears that roamed the swamp. His mind was as weak as his body was strong. He was slow to think and slow to speak. He viewed everything through the eyes of a ten year old. But he never complained and always gladly did his share of the work. All the other slaves liked Bo.

Daniel had broad shoulders and large muscles. His skin was so black it was almost blue-black. He was strong and quick, and quick to smile. Several of the slave girls had been eyeballing him for a long time. He took on two more contestants but they were no match for him. When he was announced the winner, Princess came over and led him out of the crowd. She had decided, on her own, that she should be the prize.

Princess was a pleasant light-skinned Negro with big white teeth and shiny fuzzy black hair. Her small frame was thin and petite. She was full of energy, and even though one of her legs was shorter than the other, she was an attractive girl—clearly Daniel thought so.

"We're ready for the running contest," Joseph announced as he rang the old dinner bell. Isaiah and Sam lined up Noah, Bill, Willie, and Hezekiah. Patrick put three of his young slaves in the lineup. Joseph explained the rules and fired the gun. They all leaped from the starting line like bobcats, and ran like they were expecting another of the girls for a reward. It was a fast contest which took only a few minutes. Hezekiah crossed the finish line with the strip of cloth he had pulled from the trees at the other end of the yard.

Hezekiah was only about five and a half feet tall, but he was as tough as a hickory nut and was fast as lightning. When he was announced as winner, Lunnon, who was a small black girl with bright gray eyes, came over and in a bashful manner, took his hand, as if it had been planned, and led him toward the barn. The older slaves laughed, slapped their knees, and pointed toward the couple who were quickly moving out of the crowd.

Since Beth and Martha were expecting new babies within a few weeks, they watched the activities from their chairs on the porch. Mr. O'Neale was also having the time of his life and said to Patrick, "Son, this is the kind of thing we should have on our plantation. It's a brilliant idea."

Joseph rang the bell loudly and announced the beginning of the arm wrestling match. Sam had picked two of the strongest-looking men he had. He first put Jesse up against Roy. They sat at the pine table with wrists locked together, grunted, groaned, and struggled until Jesse forced Roy's hand down.

Patrick then put up Samson, one of his strongest-looking slaves, against Jesse. Samson was about the size of Bo and had big strong hands to match his strong arms. He had a slow deliberate walk, and a confident smile. Jesse was no match for him. After a valiant try, with many grunts and groans, he surrendered and Samson was the champion.

Just as if it had been planned, one of Patrick's slave girls, called

Lillie Mae, who had been watching Samson for a long time, took the opportunity, came over with a broad grin, and led him away toward the woods. She was a chubby dark-skinned girl with a red bandanna about her short fuzzy hair. She smiled, showing a string of pearly white teeth. They both grinned sheepishly as they rushed from the crowd. Joseph and all the white planters, as well as all the slaves, noticed the spontaneous matchmaking which each contest had produced, but acquiesced with a smile and continued the festivities.

Joseph announced that there was time for one more contest before the lunch break. It would be the pole climbing contest. The rules of the contest were explained. The one climbing to the top of the twenty-foot tree trunk, which had all its limbs cut off smoothly, in the least amount of time, would be the winner. Sam lined up Ezekiel, Jonah, and Bo, while Patrick put up two of his young men.

As the crowd cheered, yelled, clapped their hands, and laughed wildly, the contestants shinnied up the slick tree trunk like monkeys in flight for their lives. One by one they struggled while Joseph kept the time. When the last one had taken his chance, Joseph announced the winner. Bo, surprisingly, had climbed the pole the fastest, even though he was usually slow because of his big size. He was the champion.

As the bell rang again for the lunch break, Sylvia, a tall, light-skinned, straight-haired young girl, slipped over to Bo. "I'ze been saving maself fa ya, Bo, honey. I'ze been wantin' ya ta be ma man fa a long time," she whispered in his ear as she took his hand.

"Lawd God a'mighty, girl, why didn't ya say so. I'ze been dreamin' 'bout 'ya eva since I first seed ya," he said with a proud grin as he lifted her off the ground. "I'ze yo's, honey!"

"Now, there's plenty to eat, so everyone eat hardy," Joseph announced, as everyone rushed to the roast pigs, which had been cooking over the hot coals for the last several hours.

Joseph had invited Pat McElmurray, Luke Saunders, and Malcolm Davies to come join Patrick O'Neale in playing music for the festival. They brought out their banjo, guitar, mouth organ, fiddle and bass fiddle. In just a few minutes they were swinging out on one of their favorite songs, while greasy hands clapped and greasy mouths laughed behind big bites of roasted pork, boiled potatoes, collard greens, rice, and biscuits. Their music echoed through the woods and across the freshly plowed fields.

As they finished lunch, one by one, the participants began to dance in the dusty yard. Isaiah was called upon to sing his "rusty hoe" song, which he did with great delight, and Joe Carter sang the song he had written for Liz. The fun and dancing continued as all the slaves got in on the act. Even Isaiah and Phoebe tried to kick up their heels.

Beth and Martha could not stand it any longer. They left their seats on the porch and moved into the crowd to be nearer the music and musicians. After a while, Beth went over to her brother, Patrick, who was playing the guitar and serving as leader of the band. She whispered something in his ear and stood back, clapping, as they finished the song they were playing.

When they finished the song, Patrick motioned for the crowd to be quiet. "Beth is going to sing her song for us," he announced with delight. "I don't know any that could be more appropriate."

Beth's big abdomen clearly showed she was carrying new life inside, as she stood to sing her song entitled, "There's a New Life Coming."

1   There's a new life coming to these green hills.
             When we trade our frocks for satin and frills.
      We'll all be healthy and happy at play.
             Every child can go to school each day.
      We'll live in houses so big and bright,
             Each room will glow with love's pure light.

2   There's a new life coming that will be so grand.
             When every neighbor lends a helping hand.
      A life that's rid of its bitterness and hate.
             And every new day starts with a clean slate.
      We'll love, respect, and honor each other,
             We'll learn that every man is a brother.

3   There's a new life coming. There'll be no pain.
             We'll all have sun and just enough rain.
      We'll keep the good, and throw away the bad,

And remember all the wonderful friends we've had.
There's a new day coming, we'll have no fear,
   A time of joy, and peace so dear.

4.   There's a new life coming, the womb is tight.
         Let life begin and end with right.
      Let all the little children flourish and live.
         And the family be judged by the love they give.
      Let love come alive and never die.
         'Til the children have children in the by and by.

Beth sang every verse with great intensity and emotion, and after every verse she sang the chorus with great feeling. The crowd did not quite know how to react to the song, so they stood in silence and watched her face as she sang the chorus for the last time:

There's a new life coming to these green hills.
   A time of celebration, with fun and thrills.
There's a new day coming to this good land,
   When everyone says, "Let me take your hand."
A brand new day of honor and love,
   A day that pleases our God above.
There's a new life coming and it won't be long.
   When all God's children can sing this song.

When she finished, the audience wildly clapped their hands and squealed in delight. Somehow the song seemed to be especially appropriate for her to sing since she would probably be the next person in the crowd to give birth to new life.

"That was beautiful!" Joseph exclaimed as he came over and kissed her on the cheek. "We're ready to start the afternoon games, Beth, so maybe you should sit back down on the porch."

He rushed over to the bell and began ringing it. The music stopped, and he announced that it was time to start the horseshoe throwing contest. The one ringing the stake the most times within the allotted number of throws would be the winner.

Sam put up Noah, Bill, Jesse, and Roy. Patrick put up two of his men. They threw the horseshoes, in turn, toward a stake about twenty feet away. Jesse eliminated Noah in the first match, and then was eliminated by Bill in the second. Bill was defeated by one of Patrick's slaves, Alonzo, who also won over the other slave.

The final match pitted Alonzo against Roy. They both concentrated on the game as though they did not want to miss the reward or prize. Finally Roy was declared the winner. Before the announcement was finished, Sarah, Sam's fourth daughter, slipped over, took Roy by the hand and led him away.

The bell was rung again and Joseph announced it was time for the log lifting contest. He explained the rules as he pointed to the logs nearby. Sam lined up Ezekiel, Jonah, and Bill for this contest because they had the broadest shoulders and largest arms. Patrick put up two of his strongest men, Alex and Bob. The contestants could pick up the log any way they chose, so long as it was completely off the ground. They could start with one end and move in to the middle to balance it so the other end would come off the ground.

After struggling, grunting, and puffing, Bill was eventually declared the winner and looked around for Rose, the last of Sam's daughters. "I'ze here, Billy boy," she said with a sparkle in her eyes as she peeped around the pile of logs. "I'ze ready if you is."

"What ya doin', gal? Is ya hidin' from me?" he squealed as he ran toward the log pile. "Run all ya wants, gal, but I'ze gonna git ya now!" Rose ran toward the woods, looking back to make sure Bill was gaining on her.

The crowd appeared to be tireless as Joseph rang the bell for the last contest. It would be the rock throwing contest, the final one of the evening and one which would allow every man in the crowd to participate. Every contestant would have a chance to see how far he could throw the large rock which had been selected for its size and weight. It weighed about ten pounds.

For over an hour every strong male slave tried his hand at throwing the big stone. Some threw it straight out while others turned around and around and let it go like a sling shot. After all the huffing and puffing, Patrick's man named Alonzo was declared the winner. He looked around for his reward. His eyes searched as if he knew who he was looking for. He did. Betty Jean was standing bashfully by the well. He walked over to her and whispered in her ear. They joined hands and headed away from the crowd in a trot.

The bell was rung again to signal an end to the contests, and the beginning of the supper meal. Joseph raised his hands and announced, "There's still plenty of meat, potatoes, and other vegetables left, so help yourself." The music began again and echoed through the green hills and plowed fields as the shades of evening fell on the exciting homemade festival. The next day nothing was planned except rest and recuperation from the activities of the first day. It would be a much-needed day of rest.

The crops were successful during 1785. The fields were bursting forth with indigo, corn, flax, tobacco, and cotton. The cows, goats, sheep, and horses increased and received plenty of food from the fertile pastures. Joseph began experimenting with breeding race horses, but it would take several years to determine how successful he was at animal husbandry.

The crops were almost harvested when William Dicks was born September 11, 1785. Emily was born in 1786, Adolphus in 1787, Louisa in 1788, and Mary Beth in 1789. Most of these years were highly successful ones because of the ingenuity and industriousness of Joseph and the loyalty of his slaves. He continued to operate a blacksmith shop with the help of Bo, who did most of the work. Planters throughout the area also continued to call upon Joseph when they needed someone to treat the ills of their animals. He became well known as the "animal doctor" throughout Beech Island and surrounding areas.

He continued to operate his mother's two farms, which were prosperous; however, he was becoming a wealthy man in his own right. His new and larger farm had been so successful it was a major job to build enough barns and storage bins to preserve the produce until it could be sold or until it was used by his cattle, sheep, goats, and fine horses.

In May of 1791, Joseph was still industriously managing the farms and tending his growing crops. He worked from sunup to sundown alongside his slaves for many days, weeding and caring for his young emerging crops. He was almost ready to drop.

As the sun's rays peeped over the roof of the barn one morning, he was up and making plans for the day. Before he could leave the house, Pat and Little Joe came riding up with excitement in their eyes.

"Is anything wrong?" Joseph asked as he greeted them at the door. "It's mighty early for you to be rambling all the way over here."

"No, Joe," he answered with enthusiasm. "I just came to see if you wanted to go with Little Joe and me to see President Washington."

"President Washington?" he asked with a surprised grin. "You must be working too hard. What are you talking about?"

"I heard late last night that President Washington has been in Augusta conferring with the Governor and that he'll be leaving by noon today. We'd better get a move on if you want to see him. He'll be crossing the bridge above Savannah Town on his way to Columbia. He has Colonel Hampton and Colonel Taylor with him. A whole delegation from Columbia is supposed to meet him as he crosses into South Carolina. I'd like to see him. Since you fought for him in the Continental Army, I thought you'd want to see him too."

"Are you sure, Pat?" Joseph asked with growing interest. "I've never heard of him visiting places so far south before."

"Mr. Parkinson told me one of his customers from Augusta said he was there visiting the Governor. He had personally seen him and heard him make a speech on Broad Street." Patrick answered with an air of certainty. "He said President Washington mentioned in his talk that he was leaving today."

"I sure do want to see him!" Joseph answered with enthusiasm. "General Greene was the highest official of the Continental Army I ever personally saw. I'm not sure General Marion ever saw General George Washington during the war. He might have seen him after he became President."

"We'd better hurry," Patrick said impatiently. "He's supposed to cross the bridge around noon."

"Let me wake Johnathan. I want him to see the President. He may never have another chance," Joseph exclaimed as he hurriedly jumped up from his chair. "I'll be ready in five minutes!"

Joseph roused his son and saddled their horses. Shortly, he, Patrick, and their seven year old sons were on the road toward

Savannah Town. They pushed their horses through Beech Island and on toward the wooden bridge which was about fifteen miles away, hoping that their information concerning President Washington's visit was correct.

When they came near the landing to the bridge, they were not surprised to see a large crowd gathered on both sides of the river. It was almost noon, and apparently President Washington was making a farewell speech to the crowd on the Georgia side. As the President and his entourage crossed the wooden bridge in their buggies, the crowd on the South Carolina side began clapping their hands, cheering and chanting, "God bless the President! God bless the President!"

Joseph noticed Payton Dues in the crowd. He was with several of his bullish relatives who had been ruthless Tories during the war. He stared at Joseph and Patrick as though he was trying to think up a way to cause trouble.

"Let's move nearer the front if we can," Joseph whispered to Patrick. "I see Payton Dues, and I want to avoid him today if I can. I'd hate for him to ruin this historic occasion for us and our children."

They moved through the crowd and ended up near the front of the large and enthusiastic group. They were close enough to reach out and touch the President when he passed.

When the President's party reached the landing of the bridge he stopped and made a short speech. He welcomed and greeted all present and said, "We have a great, free, and independent country. It's to the credit of some of you in this very group that we gained our independence. For your bravery and your courageous service I am truly thankful. We have the liberty for which we have long fought. It's ours if we can keep it. And whether or not we can keep it depends on you and millions of other good people just like you in the towns, villages, hamlets and farms all over this great land."

Joseph felt goose bumps rise up all over his body as President Washington eloquently expressed his appreciation to those who had served in the war for independence. He saluted the President as his party started moving again up the dusty trail toward Edgefield and Columbia.

"Seeing and hearing the President today makes all my struggles in the army seem worthwhile," Joseph said as they turned to leave. "This is just what I needed. Johnathan, you may never do anything in your life so important again. Many people who made great sacrifices for this country may never see their President."

"And this is a privilege we probably will never have again," Patrick interrupted. "Hey, Little Joe, have you or Johnathan ever heard the story about how he confessed to his father about chopping down the cherry tree because he couldn't tell a lie?"

"The teacher told us about it in school," Little Joe answered excitedly.

"Well, we don't know if it's the truth, but one thing is for sure, he's a great man," Patrick said as they climbed into the saddles.

"I heard General Marion talking about how Washington and his men suffered at Valley Forge in the early days of the war," Joseph said in a reflective mood. "He said they almost starved to death and almost froze for lack of support and supplies."

"I'm sure proud of you, Papa," Johnathan said as his face beamed. "I'm proud you fought for the President."

"Don't forget, Uncle Patrick was fighting to protect our homes here when I was away," Joseph said with a wink and a quick turn of the head. "We have every reason to be proud of him too."

"I'm proud of Papa," Little Joe called out from his horse on the other side. "I want to grow up to be just like him."

On September 1st, 1793, Mary died without any warning. She had been doing well right up until the last. Since the grandchildren had come into the home, she had lived a fulfilled and happy life. The home place became the property of Joseph in accordance with the will of his father. Joseph purchased the slaves which had been willed to Thomas, William, and the others, and kept them all together.

Joseph had been talking a long time about building a fine home on his large acreage. Now that Mary was gone he felt at liberty to proceed with his plans. He did not want to take labor away from the farm because it was very important to keep it producing at full capacity. The fields were bursting forth with the spring crops when he finalized the drawings and plans. Every hand would be needed to tend the crops and see that they were properly allowed to grow to fullest potential.

One night when Joseph was studying over the plans for the house, Beth was excitedly looking over his shoulder. "Why don't you get the carpenter crew that's working on the Jones house to build ours, dear," she said as she placed her hands on his shoulders. "Patrick told me several days ago they were almost through with it. He had noticed it when he rode through Beech Island last week."

"I'll take a ride over there tomorrow," he responded with a smile. "I'd rather pay someone to build it instead of doing it with unskilled labor. I want this house to be the most beautiful one in the whole state."

The next day he rode over to Beech Island where the carpenters were finishing the new house for Mr. and Mrs. Jones. He was led to the boss of the crew who appeared very anxious to obtain another job.

After talking with him and looking over the fine house he had almost completed, Joseph made a firm decision, on the spot. Instead of building his dream house himself, he hired these carpenters and craftsmen, who had been working in the area so successfully. He was convinced of their ability and stability since they had stayed in the area for several years, and had built houses for several prominent Beech Island families.

The construction took almost a year and the excitement mounted for Joseph and Beth each time they inspected the new magnificent plantation house. Almost everything necessary for construction was readily available on one or more of the three farms. The heart pine and cypress lumber were in abundance along Town Creek. The live oak lumber for the floors came from the highland plantation. Mud for the bricks came from the swampy area around the creek. As the house neared completion, Joseph realized he had made the right decision by letting skilled craftsmen do the work.

The finished house had large elevated porches in the front and rear, with wide, majestic stairs leading straight to the large inviting double doors. The large rooms, well ventilated and lighted by ten foot windows, would make a comfortable and pleasant home for their large family.

"Let's call our new home Granville Plantation," Joseph said with an enthusiastic smile one morning in 1798, as he and Beth were admiring the beautifully proportioned exterior of the house. "I always did like that name. I don't know why the new government had to change the name of the county. Granville was a perfectly good name. I've seen much of this state, and there is no grander place than these green hills and fertile fields."

"Oh, Joe," Beth responded with excitement in her voice, "That's a superb name. It sounds so rich and grand. And it'll always remind us of the days when our children were small and filled our home with joy."

The crops continued to be good during these years, and the growing Dicks family prospered beyond their wildest dreams. Joseph had been preoccupied for several years with breeding a fine strain of horses. He had purchased several horses from Arabia through a broker in Charleston, and bred them with some of the finest horses he could find among the Creek Indians. He had three second generation colts which he was sure would be the fastest horses in the state. He cared for them like children and fed them hay, grain, and a finely ground mixture of corn, oats, and barley, blended with sorghum. They were beautifully proportioned, strong, and fast. He took great pride in brushing their shiny coats and grooming them continuously. On the new plantation, just behind where the new house was being built, he and his team of slaves cleared a wide circular trail around the wooded field. They leveled the dirt and smoothed it with great care.

"What in tarnation is we doin', massa Joe?" Sam asked one day when he and all the young men had stopped for a lunch break. "Iffen we'se buildin' a road, it don't go nowhere."

"We're building a race track for my horses," Joseph answered with glee. "I'm going to start training my special breed of horses to run."

"Heavens ta Betsy," Sam replied as he scratched his head. "Why can't dey run on de wagon trail?"

"Because I intend for them to race against other horses, and I want to have a safe place for it. You know, Sam, I've got a lot invested in my horses."

Ephraim Ramsey and Charlie Goodwin owned all the land surrounding the old Dicks place, which had been originally granted to John Dicks from King George II. They had offered to buy the old home place several times, but Joseph had refused. Finally in 1798, with his main interest and his future tied to the new Granville Plantation, he sold it to them for five hundred dollars.

Joseph, Beth, and all the children moved into the new magnificent grand house on Granville Plantation, and celebrated the occasion by inviting all their family and friends to an all-day housewarming. During the day Joseph promoted horse races with his friends. Those who were not interested in the horses were allowed to hunt deer.

The wives had a quilting party during the day and also helped Beth and Phoebe with the bounteous cooking for all the guests.

It was a long and exciting day for the husbands. Most of them excitedly raced their horses against Joseph's prized race horses. He had named one of them "Swamp Fox," another "Ginger," and the third one "Lightning." They were the fastest horses in the area and won every race by several lengths.

After the first race, no one was willing to bet against either of Joseph's slick race horses. He knew he had a great financial potential in them, but was not sure how best to develop it.

Mr. Fitzsimmons, William's father-in-law, was a wealthy landowner and planter. He had come for the festivities as a guest of William. He was standing with William and Joseph, getting ready to observe a race between Lightning and two of Mr. O'Neale's horses, which was about to begin. Little Joe was riding one of the O'Neale horses and Patrick was riding the other. Johnathan was riding Lightning.

Lightning bolted from the starting area when the gun was fired. Joseph yelled to him to bear down. Mr. O'Neale bellowed to Little Joe to keep spurring.

The excited yells, whistles, and hand clapping sounded like a crowd twice the size of the approximately fifty men and boys.

Like a lightning bolt streaking across the sky, Lightning led all the way around the track. By the time he crossed the finish line he was at least several lengths ahead of the others.

Mr. Fitzsimmons was highly excited and impressed with the race and blurted out spontaneously, "Mr. Dicks, that is the finest race horse I've ever seen. How much will it take for you to part with him?"

"Well, I've never thought about selling any of my race horses. They've become like members of the family."

"Dicks, there are only two ways to make money on race horses," Mr. Fitzsimmons said authoritatively. "You'll either have to race them and win bets, or you'll have to breed and raise them to sell. Either way, if you use your head, you can make a lot of money."

"I'll give it some thought," Joseph responded as another race was about to begin between Swamp Fox, Ginger, and two of Mr. Fitzsimmons' horses.

Joseph fired the gun and all the horses leaped from the starting line. Swamp Fox took the lead, among yells, screams, hand waving, and whistles. He never relinquished that lead, and when he crossed the finish line, he was about a head in front of Ginger. They were both more than five lengths ahead of the next fastest horse.

Mr. Fitzsimmons scratched his head excitedly and exclaimed again, "I still say I've never seen such a fine group of race horses. Listen, Dicks, I'll give you five hundred dollars for Lightning." Joseph was startled by the large offer. He had just sold the old Dicks Homeplace which contained two hundred acres of prime land, the two story home, several barns, stables, and slave houses, for five hundred dollars. He tried not to sound too anxious as he answered, "Mr. Fitzsimmons, I might just take you up on that offer, but I'll have to talk with my son Johnathan. He's been very close to the horses, especially Lightning."

After the races had ended, Joseph found Johnathan in the stables rubbing down Lightning. He was only about fourteen years old but had become quite an accomplished horseman.

"That was a mighty fine piece of riding, son," he said with a smile as he walked up to Lightning and rubbed his neck. "What do you think about selling Lightning, John?"

"No, Papa!" he answered in panic. "Please don't sell Lightning! I wouldn't mind your selling Swamp Fox or Ginger, but not Lightning, please!"

"All right, son," Joseph answered with pride. "I've received a mighty good offer for Lightning, but since you care so much for him, I'll offer to sell one of the others for the same price. If he wants it, well and good; if he doesn't, it'll still be all right. Don't forget to give them all some mixed feed with sorghum before you leave them for the night."

As the evening sun began to hang low in the bright blue April sky, the musicians started arriving for the evening ball. Most of the visitors had remained at Granville all day and had changed their clothes in one of the many rooms of the plantation house. Others who could not come for the entire day started arriving for the ball, and Isaiah met them out front. After wildly motioning for them to enter the ball through the upstairs door, he parked the buggies and tied the horses.

Sam had lighted torches all along the walkway to the front door and Augustine had helped Beth decorate the drawing room. Lunnon, Princess, and Sylvia had worked all day in the kitchen, helping to cook the food for the expected crowd. Rose and Sarah helped Beth make the punch.

Joseph and Beth stood at the door to the drawing room and welcomed all the guests as they arrived and chatted around the punch bowl and food table. At six o'clock the music started. Joseph was relieved when he heard the first few bars of music. He had engaged the large string ensemble entirely on the recommendation of Joe Carter. Joe had heard them at another gala ball and was impressed with their talent. The band was composed of five violinists, three guitarists, four mouth organists, three viola players and three cellists. They had come all the way from Edgefield, and it was apparent they were artists of a high calibre.

The new plantation house echoed and vibrated with the beautiful drawing room music. The floor was filled with beautiful young ladies in their long, flowing dresses and handsome young men dressed in their Sunday best. They danced with grace and gusto. The dancing went on and on while everyone delighted in the elegance of the new Granville plantation house. Joseph and Beth stopped for a while to rest and drink some of the delicious punch.

"You're as pretty as you were on our wedding day," Joseph whispered to her as they sipped on the punch.

"And you're as handsome," she replied with a bright smile.

Patrick and Martha greeted them at the punch bowl, and Patrick exclaimed as he shook Joseph's hand, "You two have really outdone yourselves. This ball makes our wedding reception at the O'Neale house look like a school picnic. It's the finest and most elegant event I've ever seen!"

"And what's wrong with a school picnic?" Beth asked with a sly grin.

"We're just glad you two could be here," Joseph said with a sincere look. "You both look as distinguished and proud as the successful planters that you are. I'm proud of you both and happy we're all family."

Mr. Fitzsimmons interrupted the conversation when he and his lovely wife came huffing and puffing to the punch bowl.

"I'm not as young as I used to be," he said laughingly as he shook Joseph's hand. He paused for a moment and moved closer to Joseph. "Have you decided about the horse? My offer is still good."

"Yes, Mr. Fitzsimmons, I've talked to Johnathan about it. I can't sell Lightning. I'll sell either of the other two horses at the same price."

Mr. Fitzsimmons rubbed his chin for a moment and finally said, "All right, all right, I'll take Ginger. I believe she can become as good as Lightning. I'll give you the cash before we leave the ball, and will take her as we go."

"By the way," he continued, "this is a mighty fine event. Thank you for inviting us."

Liz and Joe Carter stopped dancing and joined the crowd at the punch bowl. Tomboy Liz did not look much like a tomboy now. Her shapely figure and dark brown hair were accentuated by her long flowing dress.

"It's a mighty fine ball," she exclaimed as she reached for a ham biscuit. "I'm proud of you, big brother! And the house is gorgeous!"

"Thank you, sis," he replied with a grin. "Your husband is responsible for the music." He turned to Joe Carter and continued, "You didn't let me down. They're really good, and well worth their fee."

"I'm sure glad you like them," he responded with satisfaction. Jokingly, he continued, "They can't be beat for a high class affair like this."

David Meyers, one of Joseph's neighbors who had land joining Granville Plantation joined the conversation. "It's been a pleasure having you and Beth and your beautiful family as neighbors this year." He shook Joseph's hand and continued, "Looks like you have a winner with those race horses!" Picking up a cup of punch and a ham biscuit, he thoughtfully continued. "I've been thinking, Joe. I've got a hundred and thirty acres of land joining you on the south side. I had to buy out my brothers after the death of my father. If you're interested in it I might be willing to sell at a fair price."

"I'll give it some thought, David," he replied. "It might be good land for raising tobacco. I'll take a look at it when I get a chance."

"By the way, Joe," Patrick interrupted, "I hope we can continue selling our tobacco to the British sea captains. According to what I hear, the British have been harassing American ships on the high seas recently. I sure hope it doesn't lead to further problems."

"So do I," Joseph responded with a grim face. "I've had enough fighting. I hope they have too."

"Let's not ruin the fun. This is our night of joy and pleasure," Beth interrupted with a jovial smile. "Let's all dance!"

The little crowd joined the others on the dance floor and forgot about the serious and mundane events of world affairs. The ball lasted until midnight, and the crowd was having so much fun and pleasure, not a single couple left early. When the band played the last song, gathered up their instruments and headed for home, the happy throng finally begrudgingly left, after expressing enthusiastic enjoyment and appreciation to Joseph and Beth once again.

In September of 1799, Joseph purchased the land from David Meyers and made plans to have it ready for the next planting season.

Another hundred or so acres of tobacco would make him one of the largest tobacco farmers in the area.

Isaiah and Phoebe were moved into the bottom floor of the plantation house. They had a room all their own, with fireplace and exterior door. They could come and go any time they pleased without disturbing anyone. Sam and Augustine lived across the hall in another smaller room, with their own privacy. The slave girls had all married the strong young men who had been brought from Charleston in 1785. They had houses of their own behind the main house on Granville Plantation.

One day Isaiah sent Phoebe to bring Joseph to his bedside. He had been sick for several days and felt very weak. "Massa Joe, I'se not gonna be here long," he said in a weak voice as Joseph took his hand.

"Now Isaiah, don't you talk like that. You'll be up and around soon."

"No suh, Massa Joe," he interrupted as he feebly waved his other hand. "I feels it in ma bones. I knows de time is short. Dat's why I sent fa ya. I wants ta give ya dis."

He reached for his pants which hung on the back of a chair next to the bed, and fished around in the pockets for a while. Finally a big smile crossed his face as he pulled the fish charm out and clutched it in his hand. "I'ze been carryin' dis fish nigh unto sixty years. It's 'most worn out. I told Massa John I'd keep it on me as long as I live. He was de finest man ever draw a breath. I sho' wish he could see ya now, in dis fine rich man's house. I knows he'd be powerful proud."

"Why don't you keep the fish?" Joseph said quickly as he wiped his eye with the back of his hand. "I'm sure you'll be good as new in a few days."

"Well, suh, I'se gonna keep it fa now, but I wants ya ta know dat when I do pass, I wants de fish back among de others. Massa John would want me to do dat, I'm sho'."

"All right, Isaiah," Joseph responded with a sincere smile. "When you pass, I'll see that your fish goes into the little cedar chest."

Isaiah smiled with satisfaction and fell asleep. Joseph nodded to Phoebe and left the room. She followed him out and whispered, "Massa Joe, I 'lieve dis is de time fa him. I feels it in ma bones."

"Let's hope not, Phoebe," he replied as he patted her on the back. "I know he's seventy-eight years old, but he's been in very good health. Maybe he'll be well in a few days."

That evening Little Joe came riding to Granville as fast as his horse could carry him. Johnathan was in the stable grooming Lightning and Swamp Fox when he heard the fast hoofbeats. He ran out and saw Little Joe dismounting from his lathered and blowing horse.

"What in the world do you mean, pushing that horse like that, Little Joe?" he asked with disgust and concern for the hard-breathing animal.

"Where's Uncle Joe?" he asked excitedly. "Mamma sent me to fetch him."

"I just saw him go by here. He must be in the house." Johnathan recognized that something must be wrong. "Wait a minute, I'll go with you."

Joseph greeted his nephew with a smile and asked, "What's wrong, Little Joe? Is your mother all right?"

"Uncle Joe," he said in a desperate tone, almost in tears. "Mamma sent me to tell you that Papa hasn't come home for two days. She's afraid something has happened to him."

"Where was he the last time he was seen?"

"He left home two days ago saying he was going to the trading post, and we haven't heard a word from him since. I rode to the trading post yesterday to ask if anyone had seen him. Mr. Holmes and Mr. Parkinson said they hadn't seen him in over a week."

Beth overheard the intense conversation from the kitchen and came to see what was wrong.

"Beth, let's get ready and ride over to see Martha. She's worried about Pat. He hasn't come home in two days."

"I'll be ready in two minutes," she quickly responded. "Just let me slip on a more decent dress."

"Johnathan, take care of everything while we're gone, and check on Isaiah. He's been mighty sick for the past few days," Joseph called as he rushed out toward the stables. He came back in the door and continued. "Will, Adolph, and the girls don't have a ride to school, so if we don't get back tonight, see that they get to school on time.

Miss Simmons doesn't like for her children to be late." He left once more to get the buggy ready, with a million questions rolling over in his mind.

When he and Beth reached the O'Neale house, Martha was in tears. "Something has happened to Pat," she cried as she greeted them with a hug. "We've been married for more than sixteen years, and he's never stayed away from home one night. It's just not like him to do this!"

Joseph looked around the room at the children. Patrick and Martha had six children. Their family was close to being identical to his and Beth's, as close as a family could be. Little Joe was the oldest and same age as Johnathan. Mary was fourteen; about the same as William. Lillie was thirteen; same as Emily. Patrick, Jr. was twelve; the same as Adolphus. Elizabeth was eleven; the same as Louisa. And Rachel was ten; about the same as Mary Beth. They were a beautiful group of well-mannered children, and Patrick had always taken special pride in them.

"Something must be wrong," Joseph thought to himself as he attempted to reassure Martha.

"I'm sure there's a good explanation," he said in a confident tone. "Pat is a smart man and he can take care of himself." He paused a moment with a serious look, and continued. "When did you last see him, Martha? Did he seem troubled or different in any way?"

"No," she quickly answered. "He was in a happy mood when he kissed me goodbye. He said he was going to the trading post to pick up a few things. He was expecting to meet one of Captain McCartney's men at Silver Bluff. He wanted to see if the captain would be taking his tobacco this year. Maybe he went to the boat landing first."

"It's too late to do much tonight," Joseph said as he scratched his head in consternation. "We'll spend the night, and I'll start looking for him early in the morning."

"I'll help you put the children to bed," Beth said as she put her arm around Martha's shoulders. "Then we can sit and talk for a while."

Fear began to slip into Joseph's mind. Patrick was the best friend he had. He was a lot closer to him than his own brothers. He knew Patrick was a man of genuine unblemished character. This meant that something dreadful must have happened to him to keep him away from his home and family. He tried to hide the fear and concern as they sat up and talked until the lantern became dim.

Early the next morning, Joseph took Martha's children by the Silver Bluff grammar school and headed toward the boat landing. There was no one at the landing, and after searching around in the clearing and in the nearby woods without a clue, he decided to visit the Indian village. He was welcomed at the Cofitachequi village, but none of the Indians reported seeing anyone fitting Patrick's description. Just as Joseph was riding down the lane, away from the village, however, a young brave came running up behind him, waving and yelling. "Cap'n Dicks, I saw him. I saw him on way to boat landing with squaw. I think it was squaw. Hair was long. Coat was long. Squaw had arm around him. They got into boat."

"Are you sure it was him?" Joseph insisted. "Are you sure it was a woman with him?"

"Brown Eagle my grandfather," the Indian responded as if to state the basis for his truthfulness. "I see Cap'n O'Neale at trading post many times. I sure it was him, I not sure it was squaw. Hair was long. Coat was long. Looked like squaw."

Joseph thanked him and proceeded to visit every farm and plantation in the area for a clue to his whereabouts. After searching all day he wearily returned to the O'Neale home without one shred of hope.

Early the next morning, Joseph and Beth prepared to return home. Martha was in tears at their departure and asked them to stay another day or two. Beth told her that they had to go home to look after the children and to manage things on the plantation. Joseph assured her, however, that they would never stop searching for Patrick until he was either found or at home once again.

For several weeks, Joseph worked with his slaves to prepare for the winter crops. About every other day he saddled up his horse and headed out in the cold winter air to visit other homes and plantations, looking for any person who could shed some light on the mysterious disappearance or any clue that might lead him to the truth. All his efforts were in vain.

On January 26, 1800, sleet was falling and the cold winter wind whipped the trees around like broom straw at Granville. Joseph and Beth gathered all the children around the breakfast table and told them they would have to stay home from school because of the weather. They were about to begin breakfast when a light knock came at the kitchen door.

Phoebe stuck her head in with tears running down her face. She reached out her hand toward Joseph and opened it, revealing the well-worn iron fish in her palm. "Isaiah says give dis ta ya, Massa Joe. He done passed."

Beth jumped up from the table and hugged her tightly as she said, "I'm so sorry. Come sit down for a while."

"No, ma'am, Missy Beth, I'se gonna go back ta Isaiah. I be waitin' wit 'em, Massa Joe. You take care of 'rangements please."

Joseph looked at the worn fish charm in his hand. The crosses were almost worn off, and the initial which John had cut into the other side was barely visible. Isaiah had carried it, as one of the most important things in his life, for at least sixty of his seventy-nine years.

Joseph's heart was heavy and his eyes were moist as he answered Phoebe, "I'm sorry, Phoebe. We'll surely miss Isaiah. Don't worry, I'll take care of everything."

He followed Phoebe to her room and stood staring at Isaiah's lifeless body. Somehow the relaxed look and the peaceful expression on his face reminded Joseph of his father's last day. Slowly and respectfully, he pulled the covers over his head, turned and said, "I know you'll miss him, Phoebe, but he was a good man. He's at peace now. I want him buried in the family cemetery beside Papa, if you don't mind."

"I thanks ya, Massa Joe," she said as she wiped away the tears. "Dat's good. I knows Massa John would be proud of such a good son."

Isaiah's funeral was on the last day of January in 1800. Joseph and Beth with their six children, Joe Carter and Liz with their three, Martha and her six, William, Thomas, John, Jr., and all their children were present. Isaiah had always been a beloved father figure to them. Sam, Augustine, Lunnon, Princess, Rose, Sylvia, and Sarah, with their husbands and children were also present. All the O'Neale slaves had come with Martha and the children. The little family cemetery was filled with family and friends as Isaiah was laid to rest beside John and Mary.

Rev. Durouzeaux, the kind Huguenot minister, performed the rites. He read from the Bible the story of the good Samaritan, and likened Isaiah to the Samaritan who was considered to be less than acceptable to the Jews. He waved his hand and said in a compassionate voice, "It's not the color of the skin that makes the man. It's the attitude of the heart. All God's children, regardless of their color, have the opportunity to be good and live honorably. They also have the opportunity to follow evil and live mean, ungodly lives. Isaiah chose to live a good and honorable life, the life of a good man. Today we bury the body of that good man, but he's not here. He has left the body and is shaking hands up there with his beloved friends John Dicks and Mary Dicks. He's in the presence of his Lord. His troubles are over. His pain and sorrow are gone. He has a new body that will not bend with age; new eyes that will never become dim, and new ears that will never become deaf. So let us not mourn, but rejoice for our brother Isaiah is now at peace forever. And let us live honorably, choosing the narrow path of right, for we must soon follow him on this long journey."

The Negroes clapped their hands with delight. Some said, "Amen," while others said, "Praise de Lawd." It was difficult to remember that a funeral was being conducted. It was more like a celebration. Phoebe had dried her eyes and began smiling as she realized the truth of what the minister was saying. All the children and grandchildren dried their eyes and stood erect as if Isaiah were looking down on them with pride.

After the funeral, Phoebe came over to Joseph and Beth and said in her sad voice, "Massa Joe, I be movin' out de big house jes soon as I git ma things together. I knows ya need de room fa able-bodied slaves."

"You stop talking foolish, Phoebe," he replied quickly. "That's your room as long as you live."

He looked around and saw Martha and her six children leaving the cemetery. His heart almost burst, and his mind was torn apart when he caught himself looking for Patrick. He hugged her and the children and asked, "Have you heard anything from Pat?"

"I don't expect to hear anything from him, Joe. I've finally decided I won't. I must face the facts. He's dead. I just know he is," she said as she wiped a tear from her eye. "I've run out of tears. I can't even cry anymore. Just because he's not in this cemetery doesn't mean he's not dead."

All Joseph's brothers and sisters stopped by Granville on their way home. They had all their children with them. Joseph was shocked to realize that he had lost track of many of the nieces and nephews. He said to William as the crowd gathered in the drawing room, "I'm ashamed to admit it, but I don't know all the members of our family. Let's start having a family reunion each year so we can keep up with each other."

"That's a good idea," William responded. "At least we can have everyone together once a year."

Joseph knocked on the wall to quiet the loud mob of the family. Everyone stopped talking at the same time and waited for him to speak.

"I've been thinking," he began with a sober tone. "None of us have a promise of tomorrow, and it's a shame for us to become so busy we lose contact with each other. I'm proposing that we start an annual family reunion. I'll be glad to have it here at Granville, or I'll be happy to cooperate if you want to move it around each year."

"Why don't we set a time now so we won't have to contact everyone again," Martha interrupted, as if she were afraid the suggestion would not become reality.

"I suggest that we have it on the first Sunday in June of each year, and that we have it here at Granville Plantation," Liz said as she stepped from behind the chair where Joe Carter was seated, trying to lace his boot.

"If there's no objection then, we'll expect to see all of you and all the children here on the first Sunday in June," Joseph announced. The crowd resumed with the enthusiastic noise, everyone talking at the same time.

Spring planting time came, and Joseph stayed busy almost night and day. He and Johnathan supervised the planting of all the crops at

Granville and also helped Little Joe and Martha supervise their planting. Still he found time every now and then to ride over the county trying to find someone who might have information about the missing Patrick.

One day in late May Joseph was riding one of his prized race horses, Swamp Fox, through a narrow trail near Beech Island. There were large oak, beech, and pine trees on both sides of the trail. The crack of a rifle broke the rhythm of the horse's hoofbeats. Joseph felt a pain in his shoulder and the bright May sun turned black. He fell from Swamp Fox and rolled in the silver sand.

In just a few seconds, he regained consciousness to see Payton Dues leading Swamp Fox off, behind his own horse. He panicked. Drawing his small pistol from his boot, he shot Payton in the leg. Dues fell from his horse and turned Swamp Fox loose.

Joseph whistled for Swamp Fox as he struggled to stand on his feet, and the horse came running back, shaking his head and neighing. Joseph had been hit in the arm near the shoulder. With blood running down his left arm, he struggled into the saddle and spurred Swamp Fox toward home, bouncing in the saddle with his arm swinging loosely by his side.

When the family reunion was held on the first Sunday in June, Joseph's arm was still in a sling. He tried to play down the incident because Beth and the children were worrying enough for everyone. Also, he didn't want Martha to have something else over which to worry. Joseph had built a roasting pit and had started roasting two pigs over it on Saturday night. The fragrance of roast pork filled the air around Granville Plantation as the family started gathering.

Martha and her six children arrived early. She still looked like a widow in mourning. William, his wife and eight children came next. They brought several pies and cakes. Thomas and his family of ten brought large bowls of potato salad. John, Jr., his wife and nine children came loaded in their wagon with several pots of vegetables. Liz and Joe Carter, with their three children, had spent the night at Granville so Joe could help roast the pigs. All together there were over fifty excited and happy members of the Dicks family present at the reunion.

During the morning while the old folks sat around and talked about old times, the children played hop scotch, ring-around-the-rosey, blind man's bluff, hide and seek, and marbles. The older children threw horseshoes, investigated the adventurous things around the farm and in the woods, wrestled, and ran foot races. Pat O'Neale was missing from the large group. His absence was obvious and stood out like a sore thumb. Everyone was careful not to mention his name because Martha's grief was still apparent, and also there had been rumors that Patrick had left home with another woman.

Joseph's joy was incomplete on the day of this first family reunion because Patrick was his closest friend. Regardless of the rumor and regardless what anyone might have said, he believed that something horrible had happened to him. Maybe he had been killed and buried someplace in a shallow grave, right here in the area. Joseph vowed to himself that he would keep searching for his lost friend.

As surely as all good things must come to an end, the Sunday of the first family reunion drew to a close. All the brothers and sisters departed their own ways after embracing each other and renewing the flame of family love and loyalty. Even the younger generation felt satisfied about getting to know their cousins a little better and meeting some of them for the first time.

"It's a worthwhile event," Joseph declared to Beth as the last wagon rolled slowly down the lane. "It's worth all the time and money we spent just to see all the family together at one time. I just wish Pat had been here."

"I know, dear," Beth responded in a quiet and serious tone. "It's been over nine months since he disappeared. I wish I knew if he were dead or alive. I think I would be satisfied just to know the truth."

"Well, I'll not stop searching," he said in frustration. "I know Pat well enough to know he's either dead, or was taken away against his will. I'll never believe he left with another woman, and I'll spend the rest of my life trying to prove it if necessary!"

For the next four months Joseph searched for Patrick with renewed vigor and determination. He had to supervise the harvest, which was better than expected, and help Martha and Little Joe with theirs. The sale of the tobacco from both plantations once again became his responsibility. The burden for the successful operation of both farms was squarely on his shoulders.

In late September he visited Charleston and took Johnathan with him. Wanting to make a contact for the sale of the tobacco, he visited the docks first. He also wanted to find a good school for Johnathan, since he had successfully completed all the formal study offered at home.

The first day he found the ship of Captain McCartney. McCartney made him a good offer for his crop of tobacco, but had not heard from Pat. "I wondered what happened to him," the old "salty dog" captain said as he walked Joseph toward his ship. "I never did hear from him last year. I just assumed he sold his crop to someone else."

Joseph visited several other ships, received offers for his tobacco, and asked questions about Patrick. Late in the evening when Joseph was about to leave the docks, Johnathan said, "Papa, we've covered all the ships except that French vessel tied up at the end of the dock. We might as well ask if they know anything about Uncle Patrick."

"I guess you're right, son," he responded as he headed the buggy toward the end of the dock.

A crewman was standing by the ship and when asked if he could speak English, said he could speak a little. Joseph aproached him and inquired, "I'm looking for a man who disappeared about a year ago. He was six feet tall, red hair and beard, green eyes, and would have been wearing clothes about like ours. He had a long scar on his right hand and part of his smallest finger was missing. He was a farmer in the upper country along the Savannah River."

"Last year, I see man like that on this ship. He could be same. He was prisoner of some sort," the crewman replied in broken English. "I recall 'cause he tried to sell me a little iron fish for ridiculous sum when I carried food to him. I say, 'You crazy.' "

"Was it like this one?" Joseph asked as he pulled his charm out.

"Oui, oui!" exclaimed the seaman. "The very same. He tried to sell it to every man on ship for large crazy sum. He always say he not deserter, he O'Neale. . .somebody."

"Could he have said Patrick O'Neale?" Joseph quickly asked.

"Oui, oui, that's it," he replied with certainty. "Patrick O'Neale. That the name for sure."

"Is your captain on the ship?" Joseph asked as he put his fish charm back into his pocket and smiled his satisfaction to Johnathan.

"Oui, oui, follow me," the crewman answered as he led them on the ship.

The captain was anxious to be cooperative and told Joseph he remembered a man that fit that description. "He was a prisoner of two British men. They had long hair and wore long red coats. One of them almost looked like a woman. I believe they said he was a deserter from the British army, and they were returning him to stand trial. They booked a passage to England. I believe it was about this same time last year."

"Did he show you something like this?" Joseph asked as he pulled the fish charm from his pocket.

"Oui, he surely did." The captain grinned slyly. "I went down to check on the prisoners in the hold and he tried to sell me one like that for some ridiculous amount. When I got near him he said he was not a deserter. He was O'Peale Parson or some name like that. But you know, they all say the same thing. I didn't pay any attention to him. I laughed at the price he wanted for the little worthless piece of iron. I thought he must be crazy."

"Could he have said his name was Patrick O'Neale?"

"Oui, oui," answered the captain. "That could well have been the name."

"Do you have any idea where he may be now?" Joseph asked impatiently.

"No, the last time I saw him he was leaving the ship at the dock in London, with the two British men."

"Much obliged, Captain," Joseph said as he shook his hand and turned to leave. "You've been a lot of help."

When Joseph's excitement died down, he began to wonder if Patrick were still alive or if he had been mistakenly hung in England as a deserter from the British army. Then his excitement turned to frustration and fear. He had found that Patrick was possibly alive. Apparently he had tried to leave a trail by showing his charm to everyone, under the pretext of trying to sell it for a price he knew was ridiculously high. What could he do next?

The next morning Joseph visited the office of the new governor and asked him what he could do to help. The governor was friendly and encouraging. "The Continental Government handles all matters of foreign affairs," he said as he stood up behind his ornate desk. "But I'll keep the name and check into the matter for you. Thank you for coming by, Mr. Dicks." Joseph shook his hand and thanked him for any assistance he could give.

"I'm afraid he'll do nothing," Joseph said to Johnathan as they left the governor's office. "Somehow I've got to do something to help Pat. There must be a way. This is all like a dream."

They spent the rest of the day checking into schools for Johnathan and put all the information in an envelope to carry to Beth. She was the school expert in the family, and would have to help make the decision on which school he should attend.

On the way home, as the hooves of the horse beat out a steady rhythm and the rolling wheels of the buggy let out an occasional squeak, Joseph and Johnathan had plenty of time to talk. They had a father and son talk which covered every subject Johnathan was brave enough to bring up.

After a while Joseph looked at Johnathan and said spontaneously, "Son, I'm very proud of you. I couldn't expect a finer son. I want you to have everything I own, when your mother and I, and the younger girls have no further need for it. I know you'll manage the plantation with integrity after I'm gone. But just as a reminder, I want to give you this fish charm. I took it from the cedar chest and cut your initials on it. I've been carrying it for weeks, waiting for the right time to give it to you. I wanted to explain what it has always meant to this family." He took the charm from his pocket and handed it to Johnathan. Johnathan was only sixteen years old, but somehow he felt he had come of age. Receiving the charm made him feel like a man.

"The first one of these charms was made by my Grandpa, Josephus Dicks in 1732. He gave it to Papa before he was killed in a house fire. Papa became a good blacksmith, among other things, like his father. He made twelve of the fishes, and gave me one of them. He gave Isaiah one, and he gave one to several other friends and family members. Over the years, all of the charms have returned to the family collection. I'm now in charge of the collection. If anything ever happens to me, I want you to take charge of it. When we built the new house, I made a hollow place in the chimney of the drawing room and put loose bricks over it. I'll show it to you when we get home. That's where I keep the cedar chest and the collection of fishes."

"I'm proud to have this, Papa," Johnathan said in as mature a way as he knew how. He felt like, and wanted to be like an adult. "I'll always keep it."

"Now, Johnathan, I want you to always remember," Joseph continued, "these little fish charms are worthless to anyone but us. To our family they have been priceless because of what they represent. Mine actually stopped a musket ball and saved my life during the war. In the beginning, Papa had in mind that the fish charm would be a symbol of honor. It would represent a special bond of honor between the giver and the receiver. So far as I know, this has always been the case. The honor of the fish charm has never been breached. I hope you realize the importance of my giving you this little iron fish."

"I do, Papa," he responded proudly. "I won't ever let you down."

"There have been nine fishes given away, including the original one," Joseph said as he continued like a school teacher who was afraid he would lose his moment to teach. "Now all have been returned to the chest, except mine, Uncle Patrick's, and yours. That makes the three of us share something special, a common bond of honor. Always let it mean that to you, son. To me it has a unique and priceless meaning. To Papa it represented a link to his heritage and the good teaching of his Mamma and Papa. We've come to learn it's actually a Christian symbol. Grandpa probably got the idea from his Quaker upbringing, but the family has always looked upon it in very simple terms. It's a symbol of honor. I want you to always remember that."

"I will, Papa," Johnathan responded with pride and sincerity. "I'll always carry this fish, and I'll always try to make you proud."

For several hours they sat in silence with the rhythm of the hoof-beats being the only sound to interrupt the singing of the insects. It was a lovely fall day, and the woods and fields were still lush and green. Both father and son enjoyed the beauty of nature as the buggy rolled through the low-lying trails and the marshy areas in the cool of the evening. It was past eight o'clock when they finally turned into the lane of Granville Plantation.

The next day Joseph and Beth drove over to the O'Neale home. Joseph wanted to inform Martha of what he had heard while in Charleston. When he told her the news, Martha burst into tears. "He's alive! I know he's alive," she cried as she hugged her smaller children. "There must be some way we can bring him back home!"

"I'll never give up," Joseph responded with determination. "I hope and pray we can find him before it's too late."

Martha and the children celebrated the wonderful news. It had not dawned upon them what great difficulties still had to be overcome before they could see Patrick again. Beth was overjoyed also. She had given up all hope that her brother was still alive. Now she had renewed faith in his eventual return.

The following Sunday, November 1, 1800, Beth and the children got ready for church. The family had been regular members of the little Huguenot church down by Town Creek since the funeral of Joseph's father.

"I don't feel like going to church today," Joseph said to Beth as he stood up from the breakfast table. "I'm a little tired and weak this morning. I think I'll go back to bed."

Phoebe, Sam, Augustine, and all the slaves loaded into the wagon and followed the buggy. Johnathan drove the buggy, and Beth sat beside him with Emily on her lap. The other children sat in the back. Joseph looked from the window as they slowly rolled down the lane toward church. He sat back down in his easy chair and contemplated how fortunate he was, and whether or not he would go back to bed.

As he sat in his chair, Joseph dozed lightly. After a bit, he was awakened by what he thought was a sound. Sitting up and shaking himself, he was sure he had heard something, but did not know what kind of sound it was. He walked over to the window and saw Payton Dues going into the horse stable.

"What is that scoundrel up to?" he said out loud as he pulled on his boots and took his pistol from the dresser. "I guess he figured we'd all be in church."

Easing out the back door, Joseph ran quietly to the stable where Lightning and Swamp Fox were kept. He surprised Payton as he was attempting to put a bridle on Lightning.

"What are you doing here, Payton Dues?" Joseph yelled as he entered.

Before he could say or do anything else, Payton had pulled his pistol and shot him in the head. Joseph looked at Payton with questioning eyes which immediately went blank as he fell on the hay.

"I've been waiting to do this for a long time, you dirty swamp fox," he growled as he kicked Joseph's limp body again and again. "Now let's see how big and powerful you are, mister rich man. I'll show you and your family how big and rich you really are."

Payton dropped the bridle which he had been trying to put on Lightning and ran from the stable. He ran up to the plantation house and in the back door. Looking around as if he had robbery in mind, he moved over to the hot fireplace and pulled several burning logs out onto the floor. He pulled the curtains off the wall and threw them in a pile on top of the burning logs. In just a few seconds the room was filled with smoke. Payton started to run out but as he passed the foot of the stairs leading to the second floor, he noticed Joseph's prized rifle which he had used in the war. It was hanging on the wall at the top of the stairs.

"I'll take that dirty swamp fox's rifle," he scowled as he bolted up the stairs.

Grabbing the rifle from the wall, he wheeled around to run back down the stairs. The smoke and heat had already filled the stairwell. The smoke hit his eyes, and the heat filled his lungs. He tripped and tumbled down the stairs. During the tumble he somehow became entangled with the Revolutionary War rifle and fell on the bayonet. He struggled to crawl away from the heat and smoke, but was overcome. He made it to the threshhold of the back door and died with his hand outstretched toward fresh air.

The beautiful plantation house, which had long been a dream for Joseph and his family, was reduced to ashes within less than an hour. The majestic columns and the ornate dentil work which trimmed the elegant mansion disintegrated before the fury of the flame. A dream that had taken many years of hard work to build had turned into a flaming nightmare, and had heaped vengeance upon its chief tormentor and destroyer in the process.

8
End of the Dream
1800

"That Rev. Durouzeaux is a mighty fine preacher," Beth said to Johnathan as the buggy rolled slowly along the trail toward Granville, followed by the wagon load of slaves. "He delivers a powerful message."

"Look, Mamma, that's a bad cloud of smoke across the woods," he interrupted. "I hope there's not a house on fire in our community. Maybe someone's burning off a field."

"Who would be burning a field on the Sabbath?" Beth asked with a hint of concern in her voice. "It looks like it's coming from near our house."

Sam wildly snapped the wagon reins and came rushing alongside the buggy. "Massa John, we'se gonna rush 'long. Dat smoke jes might be comin' from one of de houses at Granville."

"I hope he's not right," William said as he stood up in the back and leaned over the front seat. "I'm glad Papa's at home. I'm sure everything's all right there."

"Mamma, that smoke is coming from the direction of our house," Johnathan said as he stiffly hit the horse with the reins. "Maybe we'd better hurry!"

Sam and the wagon with the slaves had already turned the bend in the trail and were out of sight. Johnathan's eyes watched the heavy cloud of black smoke as it circled into the air. The closer the buggy came to home the more it looked like the fire might be somewhere on Granville Plantation.

As the horse turned the final curve in the road and started down the lane to the plantation house, fear fell on all the Dicks family. In the distance a bright blaze was leaping from the partially destroyed plantation house which had been the fulfillment of their dreams. It was crumbling like a sandcastle being swept away by the incoming ocean tide.

Sam and all the other slaves had jumped from the wagon and were standing as near as they dared to the flaming inferno. There were several other persons standing by their buggies and wagons. They had seen the smoke and had come to help fight the fire, but it was too late. Any effort to stop or even slow the flames would be futile.

"Where's Joseph?" Beth screamed as panic struck with the realization that he had stayed home from church. "He said he might go back to bed!" She turned pale and fell to the ground in shock.

"Sam, help me with Mamma!" Johnathan yelled as he caught her by the arms and tried to move her to a more comfortable place.

"Let 'Gustine hep, Massa John," Sam exclaimed as he came running.

"All right, Sam, have all the boys scour the place and look for Papa! He's either in the house, or in the stable where we keep Lightning and Swamp Fox! I'll run to the stable!"

Augustine pulled a quilt from the buggy and placed it under Beth's head and began fanning, while William and Adolphus tried to calm Louisa, Emily, and Mary Beth.

"Lawd, God, hep us!" Augustine cried as she fanned faster and prayed harder. "Now don't you pass out Missy Beth! Thangs gonna be awright!"

Daniel and Princess came running, waving their hands wildly and frantically, trying to talk at the same time. They stopped Johnathan before he could move very far toward the stables.

"Calm down. Just calm down and talk so I can understand you!" Johnathan excitedly yelled at them. "Now what is it?"

"Massa John!" Princess screamed in panic. "We seed a black body

in de doorway ob de house. It's burn black! I jes know it be Massa Joe!
I jes know it!"

Johnathan and Daniel ran toward the front door of the house. Only
a shell was standing. The flames were so hot the hairs on their heads
and hands singed as they came to within about twenty feet of the wall
which had been the front of the house.

"My God! That is a body in there!" Johnathan screamed as he
looked at Daniel with horror in his eyes. "It must be Papa. Oh God,
no! Please don't let it be Papa!"

"Now, Massa John, don't do nothin' foolish. Ya knows ya can't get
ta it now!" Daniel begged as he held Johnathan by the shoulders. "Ya
Mamma don't need ta lose no mo' family! Don't go an' kill yaself
tryin' ta git dat body out. Da breath's done long gone anyway!"

Johnathan was in a state of panic. He ran in a crazed dash toward
the body, but fell on the ground and rolled away from the scorching
heat, as his eyebrows, hair, and beard singed into little tight balls and
curls.

"Massa John! Massa John! We'se done found Massa Joe down at de
stable!" Sam yelled as he came running toward Johnathan and
Daniel.

Johnathan forgot about the blackened body in the doorway and
yelled back over the noise of the crackling fire and the excited
chatter of the crowd that had continued to gather. "Is he all right,
Sam?"

"No suh, Massa John," he answered as he wildly shook his head.
"He done been shot!"

Johnathan ran toward the stable in a state of shock while Daniel,
Sam, and several of the other slaves followed like dogs chasing a
deer.

When he swang open the door to the stable, he stopped dead in his
tracks. Ezekiel was hovering over Joseph, holding his head in his
arms and crying in anguish, "Ma-ma-ma-Massa Joe! Ma-ma-Massa
Joe! Wha-wha-what we ga-ga-gonna do now? Who'd b-b-be so me-
me-mean ta do so-so-somethin' li-li-like dis ta su-su-such a ga-ga-
good man?"

Johnathan regained his senses and took Sam by the shoulders.
"Sam, let's get a blanket and wrap him in it. Will you take him to

Ezekiel's house until I can decide what to do next?"

"Yes suh, Massa John," Sam responded in a pitiful voice. "Ezekiel, fetch a blanket and hep me wit Massa Joe!"

Johnathan turned and ran from the stable. His mind turned once again to his mother whom he had left lying on the ground in Augustine's care. She was sitting on a blanket and still looked pale and shocked. He knelt on the ground and took her hand as he blurted out between sobs, "Papa's dead! There's a body in the fire but it's not him! He's in the stable! Someone shot him!"

They hugged each other frantically as they sobbed and shed tears together. William and Adolphus heard his report and sobbed pitifully as they tried to comfort the smaller children. William was barely a teenager at thirteen, and he looked even younger. His freckles and sandy-colored hair were traits he had received from Beth. Adolphus was only eleven, tall, thin, and had black hair, with a clear complexion, like his father. Emily was nine, large for her age, and had black curly hair and a pleasant smile. Her blue eyes flowed with tears as she seemingly understood what was happening. Louisa's big eyes were almost as red as her hair. She held to William's hand and cried pitifully. Mary Beth was a chubby little girl, not much more than a baby. She stood alone near the others, holding her little rag doll with one hand, and sucking her thumb on the other. She had no idea how tragic all this excitement really was.

Johnathan saw the two tall chimneys standing among the flames, smoke, and ashes, and was reminded of his conversation with his father about the fish charms. He turned from his mother and ran back down to Sam's house. Sam and Ezekiel were placing Joseph's body on a bed as he entered. It was wrapped in a blanket as he had instructed.

"Sam, did you search Papa's pockets?" Johnathan asked as he started toward the bed.

"No suh, Massa John!" he quickly responded. "You knows I wouldn't do such a thang!"

"Well I just wanted to know if someone might have robbed him." Johnathan replied with a tone of bitterness in his voice. "I also wanted to know if his fish charm was still on him."

"Wal, Massa John, ya jes haff ta do it yaself," Sam said in a fearful tone as he backed away from the bed. "I jes can't do that ta Massa

Joe!"

Johnathan unwrapped the body and searched through all the pockets on his clothing. All pockets were empty.

"I don't know what he might have had in his pockets." Johnathan said as he started wrapping the body again with the blanket. "One thing's for sure. He always carried his fish charm. It should have been on him. Maybe it fell out of his pocket in the stable."

He pulled his own fish charm from his pocket and continued, "Ezekiel, Bo, Willie, how about going back to the stable and searching everywhere for a charm like this."

"Ye-ye-yes suh," Ezekiel replied quickly. "Isaiah had wo-wo-one dem. I knows wha--wha-wha-what ya ta-ta-talkin' 'bout."

"Now be sure and search good. I'm going back to check on Mamma, but it's very important to me to find that charm!" he said firmly as he left the little slave house.

He returned to what used to be the front yard of the plantation house and joined his mother and family who had calmed down and sat motionless, watching the flames die away as their dream home gradually disintegrated into nothing more than a huge pile of dreary gray ashes.

Just a soon as the ashes became cool enough to get near it, Pat McElmurray and several other neighbors who had come to investigate the smoke took the charred body and wrapped it in a blanket taken from one of the buggies, and laid it over in the edge of the yard.

Johnathan, his mother Beth, and the family slowly rose from the ground and started toward the old log house which had been Isaiah's and Phoebe's home before Granville was built.

"Is there anything we can do?" Pat McElmurray asked in a sympathetic voice as he and several neighbors approached the dejected family.

"Thank you, Pat," Beth answered in an humble and pitiful voice. "I guess we'll clean up the old house and move into it until we can do better."

"Well if you need us for anything, just let us know," he continued. "We're all very sorry about this great tragedy. We'll be glad to help you with the plantation or with anything else, so be sure to call on us."

"Pat, I would appreciate a favor," Johnathan said as he stepped aside to talk a little more privately to him. "Would you please ride over to the undertaker's house in Beech Island and have him come pick up the bodies?"

"Sure, John," he replied immediately. "I'll take care of that right now."

Johnathan, Beth, William, Adolphus, Louisa, Emily, and Mary Beth moved into the old house which Joseph had built for Isaiah and Phoebe. It had remained partially furnished since Phoebe and Isaiah had moved into their quarters on the first floor of the grand new plantation house. Sam and Augustine moved in with Bo and Sylvia, and Phoebe moved in with Daniel and Princess.

After a sleepless night the family was up early, trying to organize the house in a liveable order. Hezekiah and Lunnon brought breakfast to the family before the dew was dry on the scorched ground.

After breakfast, Rev. Durouzeaux came, followed by the undertaker. Beth took care of the funeral arrangements while Johnathan walked over to the ash heap which had been, only the day before, the most magnificent home in the district. The large, strong columns, the beautifully carved ornate trim, the elegant polished floors over which many light feet had danced, and the expensive colorful furnishings, now lay on the ground, reduced to pitifully humble and ugly ashes. Here and there a small wisp of smoke still arose from some stubborn piece of wood which had refused to give up easily to the force of the flame.

Johnathan walked through the ashes, kicking and poking as he went, until he reached the chimney which had been the fireplace to the drawing room. He remembered the words his father had spoken in the buggy, on the trip back from Charleston, as if it had been yesterday. He looked up at the big opening which had been the fireplace on the second floor, where the formal drawing room had been, and remembered the chest with the collection of fishes.

He quickly ran to the barn and came back dragging a ladder. After climbing to the spot where the secret hiding place was supposed to be, he took his knife and started scratching and hunting for the loose bricks. After prying and scratching for a few moments, he felt a brick move. When he dug out the loose bricks, there it was, securely hid in the cleft, protected from the ravage of the infernal heat and tragic destruction. It was barely scorched, but still warm from the intense heat which had surrounded it.

He slid down the ladder with the chest in hand and quickly opened it as he knelt on the ground among the ashes. All the fish charms were undisturbed and in their places. Johnathan closed the chest and ran toward the house with a feeling he had found the one thing which had a value so great it overshadowed the loss of the elegant house.

As he neared the old house, Bo came running and waving his arms wildly. "Massa John! Massa John! I's done found de fish!" he called as he continued running. "It 'as amongst de hay in de stable!"

"Thank you, Bo," Johnathan replied quickly. "I've found the collection of fishes. I'll put it in its place."

Joseph Dicks' funeral was held on Thursday of the following week. Despite the cold and the misting rain, nearly two hundred people were present. Joseph's brothers and sisters and their families as well as many of the large planters and farmers of the community attended. Beth, the children, and the family slaves stood silently at the graveside. Rev. Durouzeaux was eloquent in his praise of Joseph, calling to mind his service during the revolutionary war against England, his devotion to his wife and family, and his service to the community. Few could help shedding a tear as Joseph's coffin was lowered into its grave.

Soon after Joseph's funeral, Beth began to grow restless. She was only forty-five years old, a widow well before anyone reasonably might have expected. She felt she would lose her mind unless she did something to keep it busy. So it was welcomed news when the school board asked her to take over the Silver Bluff Grammer School again as the teacher. Miss Simmons had decided to give up teaching for marriage. In December, 1800, therefore, Elizabeth O'Neale Dicks once again became a school teacher.

On the Sunday before she was scheduled to begin classes, she made a trip to the little school house. She stood in the well-used yard, facing the building, for a long time. While the cold winter wind chilled her face her mind moved back over the twenty years that had elapsed. She could almost see the steady stream of neighbors who had come in their wagons to help build the school.

Handsome Joseph Dicks was there by her side, and her brother, Patrick, took charge of the work crew. Joe Carter and Liz, with the help of Isaiah and Sam had cleared the spot and dug the foundation. John Parkinson had donated the school bell. She could almost see Joseph as he installed it on a pole and proudly rang it for the lunch break.

Reminiscing further, she also remembered Joe Carter as he sang his song for Liz. Her heart almost burst as she recalled her brother, Patrick, grabbing his Banjo from the wagon, while Luke Saunders took his fiddle and Pat McElmurray brought out his mouth organ. She could see Malcolm Davies as he drug his big bass fiddle from the wagon, and as the group swang out on a foot-tapping, hand-clapping, lively dancing song, which echoed through the woods and green fields.

She could almost see and hear Isaiah as he danced and sang his "Rusty Hoe" song. In her mind she saw the dancing feet of the happy crowd as they stirred up the dust to the rhythm of the happy music. And she could see young and handsome Joseph, leaning against the bell pole, and hear him say, "It's so wonderful to have such a nice group of friends and neighbors."

She remembered the twinkle in his eye as he rang the bell to end the lunch break and announced with his strong voice, "Back to work. Lunch hour is over. We want to have this school ready to occupy by nightfall!"

She recalled Isaiah laughing and slapping his knees when Sam came up out of the well with white mud all over him. And she could hear Pat McElmurray yell, "We've struck water! And a mighty fine spring it is! Get me out of here, Isaiah, before I drown!" She could remember how they all stood back and looked at the finished school before the sun set. It had been completed with bench seats, writing tables, school bell, and well in just one day.

Other memories flowed back to her as well, as she entered the classroom. As she looked at the worn benches and writing desks, her mind went back to the graduation exercises of the first class. She could see Joseph as he slipped in the back door and looked around, and could remember how her heart almost burst in her breast when she first saw him. She remembered what a relief it had been when the activities were finally over, and she and Joseph were left alone in the little building.

It seemed almost like yesterday when Joseph, in answer to her accusation that he had not made a proposal, got down on his knees, looked up at her, and said in a lighthearted manner, "Alright, Miss Beth O'Neale, will you marry me?" and continued as he placed his hand over his heart in jest, and wiped an imaginary tear from his eye. "Please say yes. I can't live without you. If you say no, I'll kill myself!" She remembered too how he had turned serious and blurted out in frustration, "Well, I'm not getting any younger, and I can't wait forever. You'll just have to decide whether you're going to marry me or the school. It's easy to love the whole world, Beth. That doesn't take a commitment. But it takes a commitment to love just one person. I'm willing to make that commitment. You'll have to decide what you really want from life; whether you want fifty children who will never be yours, or whether you want to have children of your own flesh and blood."

"Oh, if I could just hold his warm, live, and loving body one more time," she thought aloud as she stood with her hand on the door knob. "I love you, my darling. I'll always love you."

In a state of melancholy, she began to sing another song she had written. "The Light of My Life is Gone":

CHORUS:

The light of my life has gone out,
    How quickly our fortunes we lose.
The hope of new life is in doubt,
    Whatever the pathway we choose.

VERSES:

Why must the Eagle fall from the sky?
    Why must the darkness conquer the night?
Why must something so beautiful die?
    While it's light is burning so bright?

The light of my life was quickly blown out.
    The warm flame of love was stolen so fast.
Once so young with never a doubt,
    Left only with memories and dreams of the past.

The joy of my life is brought to an end,
    Robbed of its meaning, purpose, and worth,
A life without love is mine now to spend,
    'Til I also go the way of the earth.

The hope of new life has now been cut down
    By a world of jealousy, evil, and hate.
How can a new world ever be found,
    When the power of evil remains so great.

A tear trickled down her cheek as she walked out the door. "I don't know if I can work here again. There are so many memories here," she thought as she slowly shook her head. "But I'll try. I must live in the present. Life must go on. But oh, Joe, I miss you so much!"

She stood outside the little school building, turned and looked at the rusty school bell, and sang the chorus again from a broken and lonely heart:

The light of my life has gone out,
    How quickly our fortunes we lose.
The hope of new life is in doubt,
    Whatever the pathway we choose.

Johnathan had a warm feeling every time he looked at the little scorched cedar chest. Somehow, finding his father's little rusty fish charm allowed him to put it in its place, and at the same time, to put his father properly to rest.

Though he was only sixteen years old, Johnathan realized the responsibility of heading the family and managing the plantation had fallen, like a heavy mantle upon his shoulders. As he placed the rusty little fish, with a dent in its side, in the little scorched cedar chest he thought back on the trip from Charleston with his father and on the evening he had been given one of the fishes. He could almost see the twinkle in his father's eye when he said, "The first one of these charms was made by my grandfather, Josephus Dicks, in 1732."

He could almost hear the rhythm of the horse's hooves and the singing of the insects as his father had said, "I'm now in charge of the collection of charms. If anything ever happens to me, I want you to take charge of it." He could remember how important he felt as his father took him into his confidence and said, "These little fish charms are worthless to anyone but us. To our family they have been priceless because of what they represent. My life was saved during the war when the musket ball hit the fish in my left pocket. . .The honor of the fish charm has never been breeched. I hope you realize the importance of my giving you this little iron fish."

A heavy burden of responsibility also overpowered Johnathan's thoughts, however, as he heard his Papa say once more, "Now all have been returned to the collections except mine, your Uncle Patrick's, and yours. That makes the three of us share something special; a common bond of honor. Always let it mean that to you, son."

Now his Papa was dead. His Uncle Patrick was missing, probably dead. He was the only one of the three left to keep alive the tradition of the fish charm. Yet, maybe Uncle Patrick was still alive. He must know for sure. The search must continue and he was bound by the little rusty charm. It was his responsibility.

If Patrick were alive, there was a special bond of honor between them. At the same time, he had a responsibility to his mother, brothers, sisters, and family slaves, all of whom would be depending upon him. The weight of these responsibilities would be great.

As Johnathan's mind returned to the present, he put his hand into his pocket and tightly gripped his own little fish charm. To the whole world it was nothing more than a worthless little piece of iron. But to him it meant a direct link to his heritage, and the strength of his father and grandfather. Somehow, because of the little rusty charm, he felt more able to take on the overwhelming responsibility which had fallen so suddenly upon him.

THE END

About the Author

Businessman, historian and speaker, James H. Goodman came from a poor family in a cotton mill town, the middle child of seven.

By the age of 21, he became president of a bank. He has been active in politics, having served two terms on the city council of Jackson, South Carolina. In addition, he has served as president of an insurance and real estate agency, president of a consumer finance corporation, and president of an industrial development board. Mr. Goodman is also a member of civic, fraternal and historical organizations, and is co-owner with his brother of Goodman Chevrolet.

He attended Augusta College in Augusta, Georgia, and the University of South Carolina in Aiken. He is a well known churchman and civic leader in South Carolina.

GRANVILLE

Under majestic live oak trees, too beautiful for words,
　　I'm fanned by nature's gentle breeze and entertained by birds.
For nearly a century and a half I've known the fragrance of flowers
　　　　sweet,
　　Wild roses, honey suckle, and others have grown, freely around
　　my feet,

Hanging moss and whippoorwill combine when sun is set,
　　The evening air with pleasures fill as darkness falls, and yet,
When morning sun comes streaming down to chase away the dew,
　　Every old and glorious sound of nature becomes new.

My name is Granville and it's grand to be a strong exciting place.
　　You'll agree and believe in me, if my history you will trace.
I've known women and war as well, and men of determination.
　　I've seen bounteous tables swell, and I've seen near starvation.

In 1840 skillful men made me strong and grand.
　　A better time more simple when craftsmen had a caring hand.
Those unknown days in distant past, when Granville was its name,
　　This land had treasures meant to last, and fields too wild to
　　tame.

When men were blindly earning fame and victory drove them mad,
　　They threw away the county's name, discarding good with
　　bad.
I took the name and proudly wear it. To spoil it I refuse.
　　Refined by time, I still can share it . . . a name too good
　　to lose.

Many live feet my floors have walked, in times of joy and sorrow.
   Old black slaves and masters talked of fears they'd face
      tomorrow.
Seven generations or more have dwelled within my massive walls,
   Sometimes the rooms with laughter swelled and echoed
      through the halls.

When the clouds of war and pain passed over where I stood,
   I saw a ray of hope again and felt that times were good.
The Blue and Gray I treated the same. I aided neither side.
   But reconstruction brought more pain, when all the fighting
      died.

I've seen white abusing black men, and black abusing white,
   Brothers fighting brothers when none were clearly in the right.
They all appeared the same to me, when dying on their bed.
   The only blood I could see was sadly flowing red.

Angry men with hoods of white to hide their face and name,
   Threatened me by dark of night, with fury of their flame.
And black men came with just as much mischief on their mind.
   Black and white were never such ignoble members of their
      kind.

The Union Leagues and the Ku Klux Klan were all the same to me.
   Pretending to have a glorious plan to set their brothers free,
They burned the cross and later when the lead they did release,
   They almost turned the heads of men who otherwise loved
peace.

Since we become what we recall, I'll think upon the best,
    To minimize the bad in all, and amplify the rest.
For I've known joy and ecstacy from every generation.
    The grand delight for all to see in times of celebration.

I've loved your wives and children small, who smiled as if they knew,
    When their dancing filled my hall, I felt like dancing too.
When music echoed from my grounds and floated through the air,
    Neighbors heard the happy sounds and came, the fun to share.

I've seen new life being born, I've seen it fade away.
    And when I feel old and worn, I think of a better day.
When I recall the good I've known, the bad days seem but few,
    Life's morning sun begins to dawn, making me brand new.

Granville, Granville, I cherish the thought, and yet I understand,
    The meaning of the word is nought without the master's hand.
I'm just a house and so much land, unless his grace imparts,
    Through me the hope and love so grand, which only springs
        from human hearts.

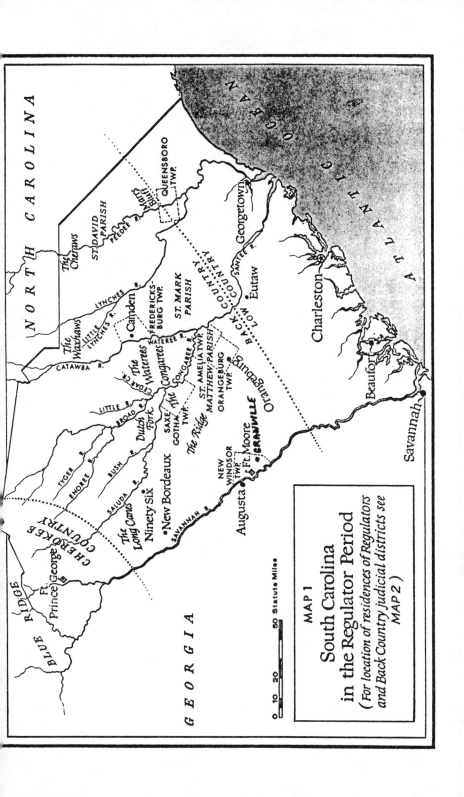

MAP 1
South Carolina
in the Regulator Period
(For location of residences of Regulators
and Back Country judicial districts see
MAP 2)

0 10 20   50 Statute Miles